SLEEPERS BOOK SERIES

AWAKENING

BOOK II

BY

TED CUMMINGS

AWAKENING is a work of fiction. Names, characters, places, and incidents are the products of the author's imagination or are used fictitiously. Any resemblance to actual events, locales, or persons, living or dead, is entirely coincidental.

Published in the United States by Sleepers Books, LLC.

Library of Congress Cataloging-in-Publication Data
Names: Cummings, Ted, author.

Title: **AWAKENING**
Description: First edition.
Identifiers: ISBN 9798483799504 (soft cover: acid-dree paper)
Subjects: Science Fiction – America – Post-Apocalyptic – Viral Outbreak. | BISAC: FICTION / Science Fiction / Apocalyptic & Post-Apocalyptic / African American /FICTION / Science Fiction / General | GSAFD: Science Fiction

Printed in the United States of America on acid-free paper

Sleepersbooks.com

Book design by Maria Thrasher and Theodore P. Cummings

Dedication:

For my Ancestors on whose shoulders I stand.
For my Descendants for whom I till
the ground.

PROLOGUE

Stanley feels something cold and wet against his face and then feels something warm on his cheek. *A tongue*, he thinks, *Somethings licking me*. Opening his eyes, he sees a large deer, aten-point buck, staring down at him with what looks like concern. Stanley is startled, but he does not move because his head hurts too much to get his body to do anything quickly. He also admires how beautiful the deer is up close and remembers that he had been hunting it and hoping to bag it before hunting season was concluded.

Where there had just been concern, the buck's eyes now reveal wariness followed closely by fear. It raises its head from Stanley's face but does not otherwise move. Stanley knows that he ought not to move either as one well-positioned strike from the buck would skewer and probably kill him. After several long seconds, the buck snorts and backs up a few short steps. Slightly relieved, Stanley believes that this massive animal has decided not to kill him though it could easily do so.

The buck turns its massive head away from Stanley, who follows the deer's line of sight. He sees a family of four to five more deer standing a few feet away from them. He realizes that this is the buck's family and that he is the patriarch. The buck looks back at him and now seemingly gives him one more look of compassionate regard, but also of warning before backing entirelyaway from him and trotting in the direction of his deer family. In seconds, the entire herd retreats, and he is alone.

Stanley remains still while he ponders his condition and what had brought him here. He had been out on his four-wheeler hunting along a well-worn path in the woods just a few miles from his house. Instead of using his rifle, he'd brought his crossbow, his favorite weapon with which to hunt. He remembers being about to stop when he decided to set up a blind to catch his quarry,the ten-point buck. His last memory is of him dismounting and then grabbing his crossbow. His very next memory is of the buck sniffing and licking him and of his massive headache, which he still has.

Forcing himself onto his elbows, Stanley sits up and looks around. *All is as it should be*, he thinks. *Let me get on up and make my way home*, he says to himself. There will be no hunting today, he concludes. As he rises, his joints and muscles protest in searing pain and crack their annoyance at him. His lower back, too, is afire with soreness and stiffness. He hurts so much that it makes him wonder whether he'd been in an accident and been thrown from his four-wheeler, not that he remembers. With great effort, he picks up his crossbow, which lays next to him, stores it away, and then mounts his four-wheeler. He starts it and then turns it in the direction of his home. *Yep*, he thinks, *I'm definitely going to need some medicine for this headache when I get home*. Stanley drives for several miles before he notices that his hands are now dark brown.

* * *

Sabrina awakens in a panic. She is in tremendous pain and is disoriented. Her last memory is of Solomon's ridiculous Jeep, hitting something in the road, her brother losing control, and his Jeep rolling over and over again until it stops. By the time it had stopped rolling, Sabrina and her brothers, Solomon–Solo--and Xavier, were unconscious.

Now, Sabrina finds herself in a crouch upon her knees, her arms raised above her while tied at her wrists, her eyes blindfolded, and her mouth gagged. A distinct pain in her right shoulder tells her that it might be dislocated, and her back aches. She wiggles her toes to check whether her legs work. They do. She has the distinct taste of copper in her mouth and knows that the trickle extending from the top of her forehead to her mouth is her own blood.

Sabrina can't see through her blindfold, but she can tell she's in a darkened room. She remembers that they had been rolling along pretty well on their fourth or fifth day of travel from L.A. to New York City when the accident happened. They had chosen to get off the highway somewhere in Tennessee because it had become too cluttered with accidents caused by the Sleepers virus. Their thinking had been that fewer people on the roads would mean fewer problems. Sabrina now sees that they had been mistaken. Fewer people had also meant less help for an accident like theirs. *Whatever this is, it ain't help*, she thinks ruefully.

As she struggles to gain her bearings, Sabrina feels that the cloth binding her mouth is a bit slack. It's loose enough for her to begin working it out of her mouth. She struggles for what feels like many minutes to move it until finally, the front of it drops below her chin. Her mouth feels awful. Whoever gagged her had not cared at all what the cloth had been used for previously. This thing is disgusting, she assesses. Her mouth tastes like some godawful mixture of gas, lawn mower oil, and turpentine. *I hope I haven't been poisoned,* she muses.

In addition to the horrible taste in her mouth, Sabrina also recognizes that she is thirsty, supremely thirsty. I'm dehydrated, she surmises. She has no idea how long she's been in her current physical condition, bound and gagged, but she thinks that it's been for at least six hours and quite possibly more. Her blindfold, unlike the cloth in her mouth, is tight about her eyes. She won't be able to move it unless and until she can get one of her arms free which may mean only one of her arms since she's worried that her left shoulder is dislocated.

By the faint smell of mildew and the dampness in the air, Sabrina senses that she's in a basement, an old one, probably one of those with the stone foundation instead of poured concrete. She remembers that of the few houses that they'd seen while traveling on their new country road away from the main highway, none had been modern, and all had looked to be one-hundred years old or older.

Suddenly, Sabrina hears a stirring to her left. It startles her so much that she jumps and pays a heavy price since her already sore knees take the brunt of it. She can't tell whether what she hears stirring is man or animal, and her heart races. With great effort, she tries to be as quiet as possible. Her inability to see anything causes her to panic even more as her now anxiety-induced imagination presents her with the worst of all possibilities to her mind's eye. *Being eaten by a wild animal right now would genuinely suck,* she thinks. *I hope it's not an animal!*

As Sabrina considers her Friday the 13th worst, she hears a low groan from whatever or whomever it is to her left. She still can't see anything, but the groaning sounds familiar, not the groaning itself, but the voice of the groaner. *Xavier,* she thinks. She believes she hears her brother. He's obviously hurt like she is or maybe worse than she is. As her mind races, Sabrina believes that if Xavier is here, Solomon could be too. At least, she hopes so.

"Xavier," she whispers. There is no answer. "Xavier!" she whispers more urgently. "Are you okay?" Again, she receives no response, and she's afraid to speak more loudly. She still doesn't know where they are. She still doesn't know why she's tied up, and she has no idea who brought them here. Sabrina is afraid, but her fear becomes overwhelmed by her concern for her brothers and herself. *Whatever this is,* she thinks, *we must survive and get away from here!*

Gathering all of her courage, Sabrina says audibly, "XAVIER!" She waits a few long seconds until she hears, "Sis?" It's faint but unmistakable. It's Xavier, her brother, and he's in bad shape, she can tell.

"What happened, Sis?" Xavier says in a raspy voice, no louder than a whisper.

"A crash, and then I don't know what after that," Sabrina begins. "We're not in the Jeep anymore. We're someplace else. I've been awake for the last few minutes. Body hurts all over. But I think that I can walk. I am tied up, though."

"Tied up? Yeah, me too", Xavier responds. "Arms are tied behind me. Feet are tied. Feels like zip ties, not rope. Entire body hurts, but I don't think anything's broken. I'm blindfolded and laid out on my stomach. Can't really move at all. Head hurts likehell. Feels like a pretty bad concussion. I'm glad that I can't see anything."

"X!" Sabrina says, hearing her brother get louder with each word spoken, "Please whisper. I don't know where we are or how we got here", she pleads in hushed tones.

"Got you, Sis," Xavier responds, fully whispering again.

Right as Xavier finishes speaking, they hear a door creak open. Neither Sabrina nor Xavier can see, but they feel the presence of someone step into the room. Instinctively, they each become very still. Sabrina goes limp as if she hasn't been moving at all. Xavier, laid out on his front, even closes his eyes again, attempting to feign the sleep from which he had recently awakened.

"Coulda swore I heard something," Sabrina and Xavier hear a voice say. The voice is decidedly accented. It sounds southern and what their parents would say is "country as hell." Sabrina remembers that they had been traveling the back roads of western Tennessee when they had their accident. *This had not been the best of ideas*, she thinks, chastising herself.

"Ya'll darkies awake?" The voice asks. "I think y'all might be awake." Sabrina hears the speaker walk further into the room. It sounds like he's coming towards her. In her flaccid state, she girds for the worst, one-thousand horrible ideas racing through her brain at once. Moments later, she hears a dull thud that sounds like a kick and then hears another in rapid succession. Sabrina knows the sound well from her many hours of martial arts training, which her father had insisted upon. This person, whoever he is, is kicking Xavier, who remains still uttering nary a sound.

Sabrina hears the speaker take two steps toward her, away from her brother. *He's now right in front of me!* She thinks in a panic. She can smell the unwashed stench coming from his body and feels his disgusting breath on her face.

"You're a pretty one, ain'tcha," the voice says. She is so disgusted that she wants to retch but instead uses all of her will to hold the sensation in, never moving an inch.

"Well, alright. I guess ya'll still out. That's no fun anyway. I don't know why y'all are here, or why I look like this", Sabrina hears the speaker say, "but I know one dang thing, 'ol Stanley is gonna get some answers from you darkies one way or the other."

Sabrina feels Stanley rise away from her and senses him back out of the room, his eyes still on her and Xavier. When they hear the door close, neither makes a move for several long minutes as they wait to ensure that he is truly gone. At some point, Sabrina hears Xavier make a low groan.

"I think he broke some of my ribs, Sis," Xavier says in a hushed, labored breath.

Sabrina's joints are all on fire and in great pain, but she knows what she must now do. "X, we've got to get the hell out of here. That man, whoever he is, is a psychopath. We can't stay here."

"I know, Sis, I know, but what's your plan? I'm sure now that my leg and ribs are broken. And where is Solo? I don't think that he's in here with us," he says, whispering.

Sabrina considers what her brother has just said and silently agrees with him about Solomon's whereabouts. "Hold on, X, I've got a plan. It's gonna hurt like hell, and we still have to be quiet, but I think that I can get us out of here."

"Okay, Sabrina, I'll follow your lead. You're in charge."

Sabrina takes a moment to appreciate that. Never had she been given charge of anything from her big brothers. She had always been their little Sis. Now, she recognizes she is in charge, at least, of getting them out of this place. "Hold on, Big Bro," Sabrina says more confidently than she feels. "Lil Sis is coming."

* * *

Dr. Alexandria Taylor stares at the ceiling. *Yet another sleepless night since the Sleepers virus was released,* she muses. In the week since Dr. Taylor released the virus all over the continental United States, she has observed the worst of all possible outcomes. Millions had been put to sleep by the virus, it seems, irreversibly. Thousands of accidents by car, plane and train have occurred, injuring and killing many. Dr. Taylor knows that every single injury and death is on her.

What had started as almost a prank to cause harm to her company, Pharmatech, had ended in significant loss of life, property damage, and a country that no longer exists. She wonders again, for the millionth time, if white people are no longer awake, what is America? As a Black woman in America, she'd esoterically pondered that possibility and even debated it many evenings at her all-Black residence hall during her time at Harvard. Now, it is real, and she had been the cause of it. Instead of triumph, she feels the bitterness of inconsolable grief.

Dr. Taylor looks to her left at a clock sitting on her nightstand. It reads "3:04 a.m." *Great,* she thinks. On top of her almost overwhelming guilt and now self-loathing, she can't sleep despite her best efforts. By now, Dr. Taylor had tried alcohol, allergy medicine, herbal tea, and other remedies to put her to sleep and keep her there. Nothing worked. Every day is becoming more laborious than the day before it. It is taking its toll on her. Suicide is never far from her thoughts.

After releasing the virus, Dr. Taylor had driven home to

her apartment in Chicago, where she decided to remain. As the first news reports began filtering in, she sequestered herself insideher bedroom, fearing that the slightest movement would expose her. *You'll get life for this*, she thinks. *They'll call you a mass murderer. They'll find new ways to torture you and then kill you. God will never forgive you,* she says to herself as the torment envelopes her. By day three of the crisis, Dr. Taylor opens the vialof sleeping pills and counts out twenty. I'm ready, she concludes. After taking the first two pills, Dr. Taylor is wracked with another wave of guilt, not for what she's already done, but now for choosing to leave the entirety of this mess to others to fix and cleanup. *I'm a coward*, she thinks. Looking at the still opened vial, she walks to her bedroom's toilet, dumps the vial out, and flushes all of the remaining pills away.

Every day since that fateful day, Dr. Taylor musters the courage to get off her bed, wash, put on fresh clothes and go out into the open air. She has no idea where she should go most days but at least wants to take the temperature of her city and see for herself what's happening. She knows that she must begin to fix what she has created. At 3:20 a.m., exactly one week after the Sleeper virus is released, Dr. Taylor cracks her toes, bends her knees, and gets out of bed, ready to face the day unsure of anything but that she'll face it.

* * *

Dr. Krauss looks up to see his laboratory engulfed in flames as the first of two loud explosions boom across the expansive yard of his research facility. It is early, and he's usually in the lab at this time; however, today, he had returned to his apartment for a quick shower and some nourishment before facing what was sure to be another long day.

Before the explosions, he had been excited about what lay before him. He and his niece, Dr. Jessica Lundgren, had made fantastic strides in finding a vaccine for the Sleepers virus. He had been excited to share the news with President Douglas. Just the day before, he'd shared it with Dr. Alexandria Taylor, the North American director of Pharmatech.

In his first few interactions with Dr. Taylor, he had been a little chilly towards her. He believed that she was an intellectual lightweight and most likely a diversity hire. Several of her previous supervisors and managers had described her work as mediocre at best and had given her low marks. However, Dr. Krauss had also seen how her research had advanced several projects and brought and made a few of their products highly profitable. Perhaps her managers, all white men, had gotten it wrong, he wonders, we'll see. In his work with her over the last several months, he found her to be bright, highly capable, and intellectually curious. In fact,he had begun to wonder whether she might be more intelligent than his own niece, whom he considered to be amongst the most intelligent people that he had ever met.

Now, looking at the bright fireball spilling out of the fourth floor of his research building, he is horrified. All of his work and research are in that building and on that floor. There may have evenbeen three or four researchers there too. He is not sure about that. *Hopefully, Jessica hadn't arrived yet,* he thinks.

Fortunately, Dr. Krauss's apartment is only one hundred yards away from his office. He begins to trot toward the lab, hoping that he can help if anyone is injured. It's so early that it's still dark outside, and the bright orange plume is a stark contrast to the dark sky. As Dr. Krauss jogs toward the fire, he suddenly feels the searing pain of electricity course through his body.

"We've got him. He's right here", he hears.

Dr. Krauss never sees the speaker. He feels someone put an opaque bag over his head. He next feels two sets of hands roughly pick him up and begin to carry him. Dr. Krauss can't walk or move at all.

"Careful. We must not injure him. He's just an old guy," the speaker says.

"Stop your crying, grandma," a second speaker says. "He's fine. We'll get him there in one piece."

Dr. Krauss next feels himself being loaded into a vehicle of some sort. He hears a door slide open and then slams close. He can't see at all. He then feels a pinprick in his neck. His next thoughts are of how tired he is and how he can't wait to go to sleep.

CHAPTER I

Six Months After Sleep Day

President Douglas is perturbed. He has been on a video chat with the off-land members of Congress for well over an hour and is now starting to repeat himself. About thirty of them are huddled together around a large conference table in the U.S. Embassy in Switzerland. Before today, many had been spread out around the world outside of the country when the Sleeper virus struck. Today, six months after the virus had put about two-thirdsof the population to sleep, they are all in one place. Members of the President's staff had taken to calling them the IM Cons, shorthand for the IM members of Congress who had been fortunateenough not to have been in America on Sleep Day. Even though they haven't fallen victim to the virus, they really have become a bit infuriating, President Douglass admits to himself. He now has to speak with this group multiple times per week to address their concerns and anger at the many changes occurring. Today, they are not at all happy.

"President Douglas," their leader, Congresswoman Jane Stowe, says, "we are more than a little concerned about changes that we know about, officially, as well as those that we hear about through the grapevine. As you know, most of us here vehemently disagreed with you regarding the re-allocation of property from, to use your term, the IMs", she says with pointed irritation in her voice. "However, we relented when you promised that certain safeguards would be put in place for the return of any and all property should our loved ones wake up soon. Since then, it seems like it's been full steam ahead with the transfer of property, businesses, and other entities that we never agreed to. How do you explain that?"

President Douglas measures his words carefully before speaking. The group before him is small but influential.There are SM members of the new Congress to whom they frequently speak, some very conservative SMs who gladly carry Congresswoman Stowe's concerns and her allies. He alsoknows that Congresswoman Stowe has been talking to foreign governments to attempt to freeze U.S. assets abroad. So far, she's been unsuccessful, but it's still a concern. President Douglas is also well aware that once most of Europe kicked out their resident SM populations, many of those same countries wanted to remove any and all U.S. military presence from their borders as well. He and his team had thus far been able to stop that, but their presence hangs on by a mere thread. Though tempting, pressing the 'end' button to this transmission is not an option for the President. He resolves to answer her absurd questions, but he doesn't like it.

"Congresswoman Stowe, there has been no change in the status of the property transfer program that we discussed several months ago. We are keeping a fastidious account of any and all property that has been transferred. We know the original owners of each house, building, gold bar, business, etc., that has been moved to a new owner. If the original owner should awaken, he or she will retrieve the property or be duly compensated for it. We have also put all of your property into a trust. It still belongs to each of you. In fact, we've taken the liberty of installing cameras in and around each of your homes and businesses so that you can check in on them at any time. Other than placing armed guards around them, we have done all that we can do to secure your property."

President Douglas stops speaking for a moment to measure the participants' faces around the conference table before continuing. He sees that maybe half of them look at him with both belief and understanding. The other half, however, look on coldly, even disdainfully. This is the half that he knows he will never convince. President Douglas recognizes among them some of the Congresspersons who had argued during the viral pandemic of the previous Presidential administration that it was no big deal and that America's businesses should remain open. For their ignorance and the ignorance of the previous President, nearly one million Americans had needlessly perished. Such poor decision-making had cost the last President dearly, making him a one-termer and relegating him to the dustbin of history.

"But Mr. President," Congresswoman Stowe says, "since you illicitly and ill-advisedly allowed so many new immigrants into the country, it seems that our property is being scooped up and doled out at an alarming rate. We never gave you permission to let in millions of immigrants! How will we ever get them out when our people wake up?!" Congresswoman Stowe says, her voice rising into a near shout. "And on top of everything else," she continues, "Krauss' lab and all of his research have been destroyed and he's either dead or missing! What exactly are you doing about that?!" Stowe bellows.

"Our property?" President Douglas asks. "You know, and I just told you, again, that your property is still yours and is being protected. Who is this 'our' of whom you speak?" he asks. "And you know good and doggone well that we're moving heaven and earth to uncover what's happened with Krauss. You've been a part of every single one of those meetings and conversations."

Infuriated, Congresswoman Stowe starts to speak again but feels a gentle tap at her elbow, which is her signal not to speak. It is a reminder that this and all video conferences are recorded, of which several had been leaked to the press.

"I think what Congresswoman Stowe is trying to say and what we're all concerned about, Mr. President," Congressman Victor Anthony chimes in to say, "is that you seem, among other things, to have taken on too much authority and done some things too quickly. We were on a downward trend on immigration before this latest viral outbreak, but now it seems that we're on an irreversible curve upward with no end in sight. You haven't just let in the SMs from Europe, but also many others from Africa, the Caribbean, South America, and elsewhere. Is America now to be a land of open borders, Mr. President?" Congressman Anthony asks.

Slick, President Douglas thinks. *This guy is slick, or at least he believes that he is.* The President now sees that this had been theirplan all along: raise the property transfer issue in a huff, which is what Congresswoman Stowe had done, but launch into the actual attack once the preliminaries had been concluded. They're upset about immigration. They know that if too many Black and Brown immigrants are here when the IMs wake up, it could permanently skew overall population numbers and diminish their power. Property is an issue, but the real issue is losing their ethnic majority, the President realizes.

President Douglas clears his throat. "Congresspersons, allow me to lay out again the challenge that is before us. Europe kicked out its SM population. We welcomed them in with open arms, and we did so because of our depleted numbers and because the Sleepers virus doesn't immobilize persons with a sufficient amount of melanin. Almost every person allowed in from Europe, except for the very young children, has either some skill or education to offer in securing and maintaining the country.

But even with those additions, we lacked the proper number of people to do the work to maintain and advance our most vital industries and resources. Given that, we requested help from ourfellow SMs in Africa, the Caribbean, and South America. Brazilhas been particularly helpful in this regard. Remember folks that before Sleep Day, we were a nation of almost four-hundred million people. Today, even with all of the new folks, we're barely scraping the bottom of one-hundred-fifty million awake persons. It's still not enough, and we need more. We need every able-bodied person of color to come to the States and help out. We have a massive infrastructure project underway, and we need help. This infrastructure, of course, includes the housing and safety of our sleeping IMs, your people", President Douglas says sarcastically, looking directly at Congresswoman Stowe, whose face flushes red with rage, taking his comment for the offense intended.

"All of what I've just said to you is not new. It's been public for a while now. Why all of a sudden are our largely successful immigration efforts a problem? This seems to be coming out of left field," President Douglas says. In truth, he is well aware of whence and why these questions arise. Most of the assembled Congresspersons do not like that People of Color from the Diaspora are a) coming to the country, b) gaining immediate U.S. citizenship, and c) being enriched from the property, homes, businesses, and land previously belonging to the IMs. The IM Cons also fear that time is running out on the possibility of the IMs regaining consciousness before the one-year due date runs out. Once the year is up, all of the property transfers are permanent, and even if the IMs wake up sometime after that, there will be no transfer reversal.

"Congresspersons, I think that we should table further discussion on these matters until we speak again in the next seventy-two hours. I appreciate your time today and look forward to our next meeting," President Douglas says, clearly lying. One of his aides presses the end transmission button on the monitor, and the President allows himself a moment to relax and sink into his large chair. Asking no one in particular, he says, "That was kind of rough, wasn't it?"

"Yes, it certainly was," says Trevor Campbell, his head of the National Security Agency and one of his top advisors. "Mr. President, I think that we need to step up our surveillance efforts of Congresswoman Stowe and everyone in her circle, including Congressman Anthony. They're clearly plotting something." Trevor pauses before continuing, "I'd hate for us to be caught slipping if something bad happens."

President Douglas sighs his acknowledgement to Trevor and all others in the Oval Office with him. They were his closest advisors, Valerie King, his Chief of Staff, his wife Helen who had been officially placed onto his staff as a top advisor months ago, and Arnetta Davis, the President's new head of Health & Human Services. Arnetta leads the agency that had taken responsibility for most of the significant shift in resources to the SM and new immigrant populations.

"Congresswoman Stowe is correct about one thing, Mr. President," Arnetta Davis says. "If the IMs wake up before the one-year property transfer agreement is completed, it will be beyond complicated to uproot the millions of families that have taken possession of their homes, businesses, and material items. At this point, many of the bank accounts belonging to the IMs have either been claimed by individual persons or claimed outright by the government. As you know, Sir, millions of IMs perished either from natural causes, starvation, abandonment, or even abuse."

"Understood, Arnetta. Where are we on immigration?" President Douglas asks.

"We're exactly where you just articulated to the IM Cons, Sir. I would add that we've been working to assign every able-bodied SM immigrant to a job either in government or in industry. Many have come here with advanced degrees. We're using those who speak English to be teachers. Per your orders, we're paying our teachers more, much more since they're in high demand right now.

At present, we're very close to full capacity in manufacturing. However, we lack in scientific research, which has to become the key point of focus to move us forward. We think that we should get there with some of our key immigrants from Africa, India, and Pakistan. Infrastructure needs more bodies, but we're making hires on that every day. There's more than enough work for our present population. Unemployment is in the single digits. All of the big cities are bustling, and our projections tell us that atthis rate, we'll be filling out the medium and small-sized cities as well. Small towns within the country are another matter. Without the IMs, some of them may never come back. This could become a major issue concerning our farming infrastructure and its supply chain. There are some thoughts that automation could help with that. We're looking at all possible options, including incentivizing a percentage of all new immigrants to take up residence in our more rural farming communities."

"This is all excellent work. Thank you, Arnetta. Where are we on a cure?" President Douglas asks.

She glances furtively at Trevor before answering. President Douglas doesn't see her look, but Helen, his wife who misses nothing, does. "Well, Sir, I think that we're further away than we've led the public or the world to believe in. Dr. Krauss thought that he was on the right track, according to his most recent communication. However, after his laboratory and offices in Europe were blown up and he and his top researcher disappeared, we're back to square one. All of Dr. Krauss' research was in that lab on those computers. He kept his research cordoned off from the internet. There are no other known copies."

"Excuse me, Mr. President," Trevor interrupts, "but we're looking into the Krauss matter and placing our best resources on it. It's a bit more challenging in light of the Sleepers virus, as you might imagine. But we've got IM and SM agents from CIA, FBI, and NSA pursuing every possibility. It could be terrorism, but we're not one hundred percent sure yet. My gut tells me terrorism, but I'd like to connect the dots a bit more before formalizing a hypothesis," he says.

"So, what's our plan B, Trevor?" the President asks, the irritation in his voice evident and unmistakable.

"Plan B, Sir?" Trevor asks.

"Yes, plan B!" President Douglas shouts, his voice booming. "What precisely is our plan B for how we wake up, I don't know, one hundred fifty million or more of our fellow American citizens from the Sleepers virus?! What's our plan B?!"

President Douglas' voice shakes the room. Rarely had he ever lost his temper, and never had he lost it in the Oval Office. He is well known for his poise under tremendous stress and has often practiced restraint in the face of many problems and many obstacles. Today, the reminder of Krauss' probable demise and the loss of his research encroaches upon his hopes of reviving his fellow citizens and getting the country back on track. He is bewildered and feels himself starting to come unglued at that prospect.

Looking at the attendees in the room, he notices them all focused pointedly on their shoes. He draws breath to begin speaking again but stops when Helen touches his hand. The look on her face is of utter concern, compassion but also caution. He elects to keep his next words to himself, and instead clears the room. He needs a moment to think, recuperate and plan.

"Very well, all. As you were," the President says. "Please clear the room. I need a moment to think and rest. That was a long call, and its implications are a bit overwhelming at the moment. We need to start thinking about what a Europe devoid of a U.S. military and diplomatic presence might look like. If that happens, it will certainly impact us here and around the world. Helen, can you stay for a moment after everyone else leaves?"

After everyone else has filed out of the Oval Office, she says, "I have concerns about Trevor. I don't believe that he's telling you everything, and I think that you have given him too much power too quickly. He's now got responsibility for domestic and international security issues. That is a job that used to be shared between about four to six people. It's too much for one person."

"Helen, I hear your concerns, but I've known Trevor for a very long time. I've practically groomed him for this job, my job," President Douglas says.

"Honey, he doesn't want your job. He wants more of what he has. Why be the President when you can be more powerful than the President?" she queries.

Helen's question, which is more statement than question, cuts directly into the President and his insecurities. He is not a haughty man, but he has an ego. "Ouch," he says to his wife to let her know that he had been pricked.

"Did that hurt, Baron?" she asks almost playfully. "Good. Then perhaps the reality of the situation will cause you to be a bit more circumspect where Trevor Campbell is concerned."

"Noted," he retorts. "Now can a brotha' get a hug or a kiss from his wife or what?" President Douglas asks mischievously.

"Of course you can, Mr. President, but do not squeeze my booty in the Oval Office. It would be unseemly," she says playfully.

As the President and the First Lady embrace, he, fortunately for them both, fails to honor her command.

* * *

"Don't forget what we talked about, Arnetta, and don't forget who got you here," Trevor Campbell says. "We have an amazing opportunity to advance our agenda and to right some wrongs. We're close, but the next six months are crucial. I need to see every vital communiqué from your office to the White House before it's sent, understand?"

"Of course, Tre-, er Mr. Campbell. But I'm concerned about what might happen if a cure is developed or worse, IMs start waking up on their own. All of the information that we're sharing with the President says the opposite."

"Let me worry about that. For now, just get me the information that I request and do what I tell you. Also, don't look at me in our meetings from now on. I think that Helen saw you do that. I don't trust that woman. I don't think that she likes me."

Arnetta exits Trevor's office in the White House and heads back to the Hubert H. Humphrey Building, which houses the Health and Human Services headquarters. Trevor's following thoughts are of Dr. Krauss and his top scientist, Jessica Lundgren and what to do about them.

* * *

Jerome feels a warm, wet lick on his left hand. He cracks

his left eye open to peer at the clock sitting on his nightstand. It reads "6:00 a.m." *Great,* he thinks ruefully. For the last month, since they'd adopted Max, their rescue collie, he had been coming into their room, to his side of the bed and waking him up for his morning walk. Max had been the dog for an IM family in Hyde Park, Cincinnati. His family had obviously been one of the running/walking families for which the Hyde Park neighborhood had been famous. Clearly, Max had been included in those walks and runs. Jerome, therefore, has no choice but to continue in the tradition, much to his dismay since no one else in the house seems capable of helping out.

"Okay, Max, I'm coming," he says while rubbing his head. "And oh great, the leash is already in your mouth. Who taught you that little trick?" he asks while shuffling out of bed. While hastily dressing for their walk, Jerome thinks about the last six months and all that has happened. Six months after Sleep Day, the country and his own life look very different. He no longer collects trash. Now, he is a full-fledged police officer, a lieutenant, and on his way to being captain for the Cincinnati Federalized Police Department. The neighborhood in which he and his family now live looks different too. What was previously a well-to-do, mostly IM neighborhood and community is now a well-to-do SM neighborhood and community.

From Jerome's perspective, it looks more like one of the affluent Black communities of Atlanta or the DC metro areas before the Sleeper virus struck. Now, most of the country's affluent communities look like this one, whether Black or Brown, since millions had moved from less affluent and often impoverished situations to homes like his and Elena's.

He and his family moved into this new house and claimed it as their own a few months ago. It had been the home of an IM family just a little while ago. It had in fact been one of the homes that he searched when he was assigned to the Hyde Park neighborhood by what was formerly the Cincinnati police department. He and Darryl had gone through this house personally.Jerome remembers who the occupants had been: a father, mother, and three children. The Dad and mom were a little older than he and Elena. Their kids are about the same age as the children of the IM couple. He and Darryl had been very careful with this family, packing them securely away for transport and ultimate care and "storage." Jerome hates that word, storage, as if he were putting meat on ice, but there didn't seem to be a better word for what had happened to more than half of their population. Storage, he says again to himself. The word hangs in his mind like some unclean thing.

Putting his shoes on, Jerome again feels the twinge of guilt that had pricked him ever since he and Elena chose this house as their own. Certainly, they had been happy to move here and to begin their new lives. They know and understand that if not for the Sleepers virus, they never would have been able to afford it or one like it anywhere in Cincinnati. *We would never have earned or saved enough money for a home like this*, he thinks. Jerome is sure that even if they had saved enough for the down payment, a bank would not have loaned them the money to purchase it. He often wonders whether reaping the benefits of the work and money of others makes him a bad person. Conversely, Elena's thoughts and opinions on this subject are far more pragmatic than his own.

Jerome and Elena's home has been previously owned by the Crawleys, an upper-middle-class family by Hyde Park standards. By most others' standards, they had been rich. Months ago, when Elena and Jerome entered the home, they found it immaculate and well furnished. Both Mr. and Mrs. Crawley had been professionals. Mr. Crawley, as determined by his many degrees hanging on the wall in his study, is a Harvard-educated doctor. Dr. Crawley is a surgeon, one of the best in Cincinnati, given the many awards found in his office. Mrs. Crawley is some sort of corporate executive at Procter & Gamble. Judging by her degrees, she and her husband had met in college at Georgetown University in Washington, D.C. Before Sleep Day, all three of their children had attended Hyde Park Country Day School, the same school as Jerome and Elena's kids. From here, it is only a stone's throw from their front door.

Before they'd taken possession, the Crawley's home had been completely furnished and had not been broken into during the entire period that the IM search and rescue period occurred or even months afterward. In his new capacity as Lieutenant in the

Federalized Cincinnati Police Department, Jerome had personally seen to that. He is now responsible for the Hyde Park neighborhood and several others. Months ago, he'd assembled a group of the city's sharpest and most honest police officers, including Oakley and Indian Hill. He and Darryl had worked hard to keep would-be looters away. They had also worked to uphold the highest moral standards amongst themselves so that theft of IM property would be kept to a minimum.

In addition to their furnished home, Jerome and Elena gained ownership of the vehicles in their three-car garage—an SUV, a BMW sedan, and a vintage two-door sports car. All three had belonged to the Crawley's, so the vehicles had become Jerome and Elena's property. *It hardly seems fair*, Jerome thinks again for the fiftieth time, but this is the way of things now in their country. There is a massive multi-trillion dollar real estate, personal property, and business transfer happening, and they, along with millions of other SMs, are benefitting from it.

When Jerome had first shared his concerns with his wife, she responded directly and succinctly to her husband's misgivings. "Jerome, this entire country, as you well know, is built upon theft and the transfer of property from entire groups of people to one group, white men. And that theft happened violently and systematically to the point that, hundreds of years later, white peoples' advantages over all others are staggering. We didn't steal. We didn't rob. We didn't murder. This happened, and we're blessed to be able to assume ownership of this beautiful house and its things, at least for a little while. At least until this home's family wakes up."

Having lived in their new home for the last four months, Jerome silently hopes that its original family never wakes up, or at least prior to the one-year time limit to reclaim the house. Perhaps this is the real source of my guilt, he wonders. Jerome admits to himself that he loves the house and their new lives and doesn't want to give them up. Where Jerome has kept his hopes silent, others loudly proclaim their wishes in the press and on social media every day.

Many like Elena, Jerome, and their family, have found themselves in entirely new circumstances both in property ownership and in possession of wealth. SM families were able to claim unoccupied homes and businesses, bank accounts, and whatever tangible property they found. Many millionaires had been made overnight, including Jerome and Elena Middleton.

The depth and breadth of IM wealth had long been known. However, when Black and Brown SMs got to see it up close and possess it, the results had been relatively predictable. Consumer spending skyrocketed. Car dealerships didn't seem capable of keeping luxury vehicles in stock. Even without IM help, the car industry in America was booming. Once realizing the wide wealth disparity that was in existence prior to Sleep Day, many SMs had become even angrier at what America had been given. They vowed never to let it return to that state again, whether the IMs ever wake up or not.

When they took possession of their house and all its property, Elena and Jerome followed all of the government's rules for making a proper claim. There were no IMs in it on theday that they made their claim. They had filled out the requisite paperwork. They had confirmed that the property had actually been that of former IM residents by reviewing records at the county real estate title office, and there had been no IM family members living abroad that made or could make a claim for ownership of the residence.

According to the new property transfer law passed by the new Congress, they are also entitled to any and all personal property they found in the residence. Because they already owned a home in Westwood, Cincinnati, they did not have to take the mandatory classes for property ownership and upkeep which is a government requirement for all new homeowners. Going forward, they would only owe the property taxes on the home but otherwise owned it outright; unless and until the original IM owners wake up in the next six months.

Despite his guilty feelings, Jerome acknowledges that much had changed for the better in the lives of many SMs. He realizes that his family's lives and the lives of many other SMs had dramatically improved over the last six months. It seems that everyone is either working, in school, or both. Many, like his family, now reside in homes that they never dreamed would become available to them. His kids, who had already been attending a topflight school, are now being educated in the new education system, which had also changed and continues to evolve.

As dictated by the President, educators are now better paid and rival most other top-paying professionals in the nation. In fact, education had become so lucrative that only the best of the best were allowed to become teachers. This is a far cry from the public school education that Jerome himself had received. He wonders to himself as he puts Max on his leash and exits their home, that if all of these changes had happened in just six months, what might it look like a year from now? Three years from now? He knows that President Douglas will soon announce his first budget and a major infrastructure program, the biggest since the end of World War II. The rumors are that he's improving or changing every single thing possible: roads, electrical grids, the internet, bridges, railroads and so much more.

Wealthy neighborhoods like Hyde Park are almost full in and around Cincinnati. In contrast, the suburbs had been all but abandoned when the property transfer program was first initiated. Since the addition of so many new immigrants to the States, the suburbs had begun to re-populate, but they are nowhere near as full as they had been.

Prior to Sleep Day, the suburbs were predominantly occupied by IMs, with a tiny SM population. The SMs living there had all moved into the city as requested by the President and New Congress. Now, most of Cincinnati's neighborhoods are full of folks from all walks of life. Many SMs no longer have the jobs they once had except for the corporate types who'd had white-collar jobs. Most of them had remained in their jobs but also greatly elevated to executive levels in their companies. A great many of the corporate SMs had also jumped ship from their companies to take on leadership positions in other companies or to work directly for the federal government in leadership positions there. A few of these SMs had also run for office and were some of the Congresspersons and Senators of the New Congress. It had often seemed to Elena and Jerome that everyone was working andthat nearly everyone had been promoted in one form or another.

Jerome looks at his own life as a testament to this new

reality. He and Elena hadn't just gained a new home and property, they had new lives. He is on his way to being a captain in the police force, and he and Elena now own several businesses together as well. When they had taken inventory of the property and cash of the Crawleys, they decided to put those resources to good use. They'd claimed several businesses in and around Hyde Park that met the needs of the new residents. Elena had wisely chosen high cash flow businesses. Her rationale was that as long as the ventures continually showed positive flow, capital for other investments would always be available. Jerome rejoices in his choice of such a good partner in Elena. Of course, she had been right. Capital flows freely in the new economy in a way that neither Jerome nor Elena had ever experienced.

As Jerome walks Max along their usual route, he continues to muse about all of the changes happening of which he's been a significant part. He thinks about Stacey Iverson, a Black woman from Cincinnati and one of Elena's best friends from their childhood. Before Sleep Day, she had worked at Procter & Gamble as a brand manager. She often expressed her dismay regarding her long workdays and organizational politics. On Sleep Day, Procter & Gamble, headquartered in Cincinnati, experienced major losses. Most of its IM corporate population had fallen asleep except for its few ex-pats and international travelers.

Procter & Gamble's CEO and entire leadership had been in the country on Sleep Day and had therefore been immobilized by the Sleepers virus. At the time, Procter did not have any SMs in senior leadership in its U.S. offices, and the company's international division had been ill-equipped to run its U.S. operations from overseas. The remaining leadership decided that something needed to be done to maintain daily operations given how manufacturing heavy the company is. Overnight, the highest-ranking SM in the States, Stacey Iverson, had been named CEO of the company, a role that no African American had ever come close to having there. Jerome marvels at the fact that P&G's newest CEO is a Black woman, an SM, which is something that might never have happened before Sleep Day.

Over the next six months, she deftly righted the ship and got Procter's U.S. operations back to fifty percent of what they had been. Today, P&G runs smoothly and is flush with new investor money and confidence. Its U.S. operations are 100% SM and work to meet the nation's consumer goods needs.

As they walk down the street, Jerome feels Max trying to pull him into a run. "Okay, boy, give me a minute to pull it together," he says. Soon after, Jerome keeps pace with Max as they jog. Before Sleep Day, Hyde Park had been a jogger's neighborhood. He is glad to see that that legacy has endured. When Hyde Park was on his trash route, he'd often enjoyed seeing its denizens get out of their homes and hit the pavement. He is glad tosee it again this morning.

Turning left at the end of his street, Jerome decides to jog into Hyde Park Square with Max. Most of its shops are alive and active again. In addition to their home, Jerome and Elena claimed a coffee shop that sits right on the Square, a dry cleaners, and a UPS store. Since Jerome's promotion to lieutenant, he had been awarded three businesses instead of just one. He could have claimed much larger businesses, but he and Elena had decided to be practical and to keep their interests local. Jerome believes that he has found his calling. He wants to remain a police officer. That plus these businesses Elena runs are enough for them. By anyone's standards, they're rich. By their own standards, they're happy.

Elena spends her days operating the dry cleaners and also managing the coffee house. She hired a full-time manager for the UPS store since attempting to run a third business would have stretched her too thinly. What is especially gratifying to Elena and Jerome is that they have several employees, other SMs, who, prior to Sleep Day, would not have had these kinds of work opportunities. Almost all of their employees are in a school of some sort, whether finishing high school, college, or graduate school. Some of them had been recently freed from prison. Not only had education become more accessible to all, but it had also become financially possible.

Crime is down significantly, and gun violence has become all but non-existent. Since the President had increased the penalty on using a gun to commit a crime, most criminals decided that it just wasn't worth it, especially in this new era of work and education. Many had rightly decided to give up a life of crime and gotten jobs. With the re-arrival of so many non-violent offenders newly released from prison, their influence had convinced many to participate in the new economy rather than continue criminal endeavors. The few that had not made the transition were quickly rounded up and carted away to long prison terms.

As he continues his jog with Max, Jerome silently notes to himself another new pervasive sight in and around Cincinnati and elsewhere around the country as reported by the news. He chuckles to himself as he notices all of the newly pregnant ladies he sees walking around. Something about newfound prosperity and the need to replenish the citizenry was influencing the creation of new relationships and new marriages, especially amongst the new immigrant population. At times, it seems like every other woman that Jerome sees is pregnant.

He considers all of this as he stops in front of their dry cleaners. Elena would be getting up soon but today, Saturday, is her day off. Their part-time manager will handle the open and close for today and tomorrow. Seeing that all is well with the dry cleaners, Jerome walks with Max for another block around the corner to their coffee shop. At about 7:45 a.m. on a summer Saturday, it is beginning to bustle with early morning patrons like himself. He decides to go in and order a latte.

“Hi, Jerome,” a young woman named Lydia says to him cheerfully.

“Hey, Liddy, how are you?” he asks.

“Busy. We’ve been swamped since opening. Do you want your regular? The latte?” Lydia queries.

“Absolutely. But can you be sure to make it?” Jerome asks. “Michael doesn’t put the foam on it as you do,” he whispers conspiratorially, hoping that Michael doesn’t hear him.

“Gotchu, Boss,” she whispers back with a knowing wink and nod.

As he waits for his latte, Jerome peers across the street into the Square. Six months ago, it had been a wreck. There had been multiple accidents and carnage everywhere. Bodies of the injured, dead and dying had been strewn about it. Dozens of IMs, now asleep, had lined the sidewalks and cafes as if they had been stricken, which they had, right where they lay. Cars and trucks of all types had crashed, and some had even overturned.

It had been a mess for which he and Darryl had been principally responsible for cleaning up. The work had been gruesome. Strangely enough, he and Darryl's expertise in trash clean-up had come in handy for their IM recovery work. They were both far less squeamish in the work than other IM recovery persons that they'd come across for whom finding IMs in various states of unconsciousness, injury, or death had been too much to bear. It wasn't that either Jerome or Darryl had escaped their IM recovery duties emotionally or even physically unscathed, but they had fared better than most. Still, it helps that Jerome has had therapy and still has it. Elena insists upon it.

Looking back into the coffee shop, Jerome sees something that he loves. He sees people of all hues inside. Black people, Brown people, Asians, and many others of various melanated hues and ethnicities are coming together in his coffee shop. There is an industriousness and energy about them. Everyone he sees seems to have a look of strength, renewal, and joy on their faces. It's as if a spirit of making the impossible possible is shared by them all.The last few months had sorely tested the mettle of the country's remaining inhabitants and continue to test it. So far, as one nation, they had risen to the challenge, and President Douglas' leadership and steadfastness had been critical for that.

Once again, it seems that they have the world's begrudging respect. The United States was and is the United States. After North Korea's miscalculated debacle, no nation would now directly test the country's might or resolve. Internal security issues seemed to be under control. *Probably the most important thing that the President did was to federalize all gun manufacturing, sales, and ammunition creation and sales,* Jerome muses. That, along with the stiff penalties for being caught with a gun and the incredible opportunities to work and become educated, have all worked to stifle gang-related activity, organized crime, and all other criminal behavior. In fact, it seems that the old gangs are doing a lot of the work to get guns off the streets since the President's new community policing initiative had been put into effect.

He considers how old gang allegiances had simply melted away in Cincinnati as families moved out of the ghettos and bad neighborhoods and into very lovely homes in very nice neighborhoods all across the city and suburbs. Families that had not previously owned homes had to sit through a six-week course on homeownership and upkeep. However, they had a new home at the end of the course, fully paid for with only the property taxes owing. Since all of the banks and mortgage companies had been owned, primarily, by IMs, there was no one to complain or file suit for the property transfers. When a property is transferred, any existing lien would be removed, and the property is owned free and clear. With ninety-nine percent of the SM population working, no one is fearful about the ability to pay their taxes.

"Jerome! Latte up!" he hears Lydia say.

"Thank you, Lydia," he says. Lifting his cup, Jerome sees the foam on top that he cherishes. Looking at his watch, he realizes that Elena will be awake and up soon. He wants to get back home to her before she gets moving. They have some making up to do from an argument about his slipping on his trash and dish duties. *Women,* he thinks to himself, *I almost single handedly saved about five neighborhoods, and she can't give a brotha' no slack.* He smiles to himself as he walks outside to retrieve Max. "Come on, boy, we need to get home to Momma." Max barks impatiently. He wants to run. Jerome compromises with him and gives Max a brisk walk instead. Max leads the way.

CHAPTER II

Raheem arrives at the headquarters of the Secret Service about a half-hour earlier than requested. The Secret Service headquarters building takes up half a city block on H Street, N.W. in downtown DC. Other than that, it is nondescript and seems to blend into the landscape that is drab DC.

He steps up to the visitors' desk where a pleasant-looking woman sits and speaks: "Raheem Gates here for Agent Gerald Atkins, please," he says.

"I'll notify him of your arrival, Mr. Gates. Please have a seat over there if you would," the receptionist tells him. Raheem readily recognizes that the receptionist is far more than she appears to be. She is tall, athletic, and very pretty. She appraises him with a ready knowing that only highly trained operators like Raheem are able to do. *She's probably thinking the same thing about me*, Raheem muses, and he notices a faint wry smile cross her lips. *Game recognize game*, he thinks to himself and sits down.

Raheem is sure that she is armed to the teeth as well. He wonders what caliber of gun that she has hidden under her desk. It's probably a .45, he guesses. That's what he would use since it's his favorite. Indeed, a .45 caliber semi-automatic handgun is strapped beneath her desk and is within easy reach should she need it. Though pretty and courteous, she is also sure to be an expert marksman.

Raheem is dressed in his best navy two-button suit. His shirt is a starched white, and he wears a simple blue and white striped tie. His face shines in the reflection of his well-polished black tie-up shoes. That is a talent that he hadn't lost since his days in the military.

On the outside, Raheem is the picture of a handsome, calm reserve. Inside, he feels the butterflies of anticipation for a new opportunity into highly unchartered territory. Six months ago, he had expected to still be in prison with 12 months left on his sentence. Not only had his circumstances dramatically changed, but the country had also too. Raheem hopes that it's for the better. As a former soldier, he has his doubts.

When he and Candace moved from her small house in

Lorton, Virginia to an immaculate three-story row house in Washington, DC, just off of Dupont Circle, neither of them could believe their good fortune. Like most such homes being transferred to SM families, it had come fully furnished. He and Candace only needed to fill out a short application to claim the home and all its property, which they painstakingly listed in their application. The previous owners, a gay married couple named Robert and Felix, hadn't had any children. However, a perusal of their personal effects before they were boxed up indicated that they had been in the midst of an adoption when the Sleepers virus struck. They hadn't had a car, but cars in DC are not as much a necessity as they are a convenience.

When Raheem was freed from prison, he had been initially assigned to a job in the Pentagon, not as a soldier, but to work logistics foreach of the armed services. When his boss' boss read his file, he called Raheem into his office to verify his status as a former special forces member of the military. Confirming his status, he told Raheem that he'd be better suited for a job in the Secret Service since that branch had been left severely depleted by the Sleepers virus; and that it needed the most qualified, military-trained civilian personnel that the country has to offer. Raheem fit that bill in spades, his boss's boss tells him, and it will come with a significant pay increase.

Raheem had been happy to hear about the increase but also hesitant to put himself in potential harm's way without first conferring with Candace. After work that night, he told Candace about the offer. She was immediately against the move. Raheem thinks back to that conversation.

"We just got you back!" Candace exclaims. "Why would you want to put yourself in harm's way again, at least so quickly?"

"I'm honestly not sure that I do. I have the same concerns, Baby," Raheem says. "It would be a lot more money, but money isn't everything," he shrugs. "We just got this new house. We're only responsible for the property tax. The kids are in school and daycare. Your job is good. My job is good. We're straight as near as I can tell. I'm okay to let this pass."

Candace replied, "Maybe in a few months, Rah. Let me get my bearings first. Sheesh, I just want to love on you and the kids for a minute before any more major change happens."

"Understood, Baby," he says. "Now come here and lemme squeeze them cakes," he says playfully. Candace feigns resistance but soon melts into her husband's arms and chest.

Raheem smiles to himself at the memory. Four months later, here he sits at Secret Service headquarters, waiting to be interviewed for a job as a Secret Service agent. The intervening months had brought much prosperity and opportunity to his family and him, but it had also brought boredom. Raheem liked his job at the Pentagon, but it's one that he can almost do with his eyes closed, and it kept him tied to a desk sitting. Raheem hates to sit too much. He is athletic and a man of action, and he'd served in the military because it had given him a higher purpose. His job in military logistics has purpose, but not the kind that Raheem likes or is used to.

Surprisingly, Candace had shifted her stance a bit. She'd noticed Raheem's restlessness a few months ago. She had even commented upon it, suggesting to him that perhaps he needed to work out a bit more, especially since he sits all day. He listened to his wife, joined a gym, and became busy with his martial arts training. Raheem had always enjoyed Krav Maga. Unfortunately, this new activity had the opposite effect. It had only served to make him more restless until one day recently, he came home and told Candace that he wanted to apply for the Secret Service position. She reluctantly relented but not as reluctantly as Raheem had thought she might.

Waiting for Agent Atkins, Raheem wonders what his first assignment might be. He hopes and prays that it will be one that keeps him and his family close to DC. He is concerned enough about the possibility of moving that he visited with his Imam to request a blessing and spiritual covering. He hadn't practiced his faith in years, not even in prison, but he reasoned that seeking Allah's protection while he seeks to protect others is an excellent time to pray.

Raheem had heard rumblings about trouble in Texas and California along their respective Mexican borders. He knows that the army, FBI, and CIA are active there. Like the North Koreans and Chinese, the Mexican drug cartels had been testing the country's resolve by trying to seize land and resources in the U.S. for their operations. He is sure that if fully provoked, the President will declare war on the cartels if not against Mexico outright.

As Raheem sits in contemplation about the country's geopolitical conflicts, he sees Agent Smith, the young woman interviewing him, approach. "Mr. Brooks, we're ready to see you now," she says. Raheem immediately stands up and follows her through a security checkpoint as she scans her badge for them both.

Agent Smith leads them down a wide hall and into the first open elevator in the first bank of elevators that she sees. Standing next to Ms. Smith, Raheem notices that she is pretty tall for a woman, standing at about 5'8, and has an athletic build. He wonders what kind of athlete she may have been in college since she clearly had recently been there. Agent Smith has medium cocoa skin and is young, very young, and definitely no older than twenty. Raheem wonders whether she is part of the new group of Black, Hispanic, and Asian college students that the President requested leave college and report to various agencies throughout the United States and the military in exchange for receipt of their degrees early. She wears a smart, black skirt-suit that looks tailor-made to her frame. On the left lapel of her suit is the Secret Service crest. On the right lapel is the insignia for her college, Spelman.

"How long were you at Spelman?" he asks.

"Two years," Agent Smith responds curtly.

They exit the elevator on the third floor of the building. The hallway is windowless, with doors on either side marking the entranceway into this floor's offices. The floor is massive but seems relatively empty. Raheem guesses that at one point, the entire floor had been full of agents and support staff. Now, it looks all but empty with few people, all SMs, who work here. *Of course*, he thinks, *this is just one floor of the building*. Raheem wonders how many people now occupy the entire building and how many are protecting the President.

After walking about midway through the floor's offices, Agent Smith stops at a door and once again scans her ID badge. She pushes the door open into an expansive room filled with cubicles at its center and offices on its outside that have clear glass for their walls. Raheem sees an agent sitting in a corner office with a large thermos on his desk accompanied by a porcelain coffee cup. A few moments later, they are at his door, and he beckons them inside.

This agent is obviously far older than either he or Agent Smith. *In fact,* Raheem thinks, *he looks like a retiree.* He's easily older than sixty-five, Raheem determines. He can tell by how he stands, by all of the gray hairs on his head, and by his slightly stooped stance. His bearing and his internal strength are unmistakable to Raheem, however. Both are confirmed in his steel-like handshake with him. Clearly, this man had had significant military training and experience, just like Raheem.

"Mr. Gates," the man says, "my name is Agent Brooks, Wendell Brooks. I will be conducting your interview. Agent Smith here will join us and listen in as part of her training. Are you ready to proceed?" Agent Brooks asks.

"Yes Sir, I am Agent Brooks," Raheem says. As buttoned up as Raheem had been when he entered the building, something about Agent Brooks' presence and steely gaze prompts him to elevate his own bearing and to reach deep into his military preparedness. He knows that every answer that he gives is recorded and every inflection scrutinized.

"Gates, please have a seat, and we shall begin."

Raheem sits down in a chair opposite Agent Brooks as a standard-issue government desk divides the room between them. Agent Smith sits in a chair on the same side of the desk as Raheem and notices that her chair is pulled back a bit from his so that when she sits, she is able to observe him just out of eyeshot of Raheem's peripheral vision. *This must be her body language training,* Raheem thinks. *No bother,* he thinks again to himself, *Agent Brooks is the star of the show. I must keep all of my focus upon him.* Before Agent Brooks clears his throat to begin to speak, the two men regard each other quietly for a moment, two military men nonverbally communicating their respective experiences and carriage.

"As you may have guessed by now, Mr. Gates, I am a career Secret Service man, 40 years. I also served in the military in my younger days in the Navy. I was good and retired and living in

Florida with the Mrs. when Sleep Day occurred. Since two- thirds of our population had been rendered immobile, we have been severely lacking in expertise in several high-level government agencies, the Secret Service being one of them. I was called back from retirement to help run our interviewing and vetting process. I interview each candidate personally and make the final determination for each candidate's fitness for the Service. Agent Smith was in college a few months ago. She agreed to leave early to enter our trainee program and begin her service. She'll still get her degree, but she realizes that she's needed most here to serve her country. In a similar fashion, we are scouring our population of...", Agent Brooks hesitates slightly before continuing, "...SMs for those with the training and comportment to work in the Secret Service." After Agent Brooks finishes speaking, the sound of his bass voice reverberates in the office against its walls and glass front.

"Today, Mr. Gates, as you might imagine, the Secret Service is a bit of a shadow, pardon the pun, of its former self. Sleep Day greatly depleted our numbers and left the President and his family minimally unprotected, which is unacceptable. In those early days, no one went home, and no one slept. The remaining SM agents lived in the White House around the clock to keep the Presidential family safe. We're in a bit better situation now, but we're still hurting for expertise and experience, especially MILITARY experience like yours," Agent Brooks emphasizes. "Our core responsibility is to keep the President, his family, and staff safe. We will eventually build back out to all of the other services we provide in the next six months. If you are selected, your first assignment will be on the White House detail. Is that understood?"

"Yes, Sir, it is," Raheem replies.

"Very good then," Agent Brooks says. "First question: why are you sitting here today instead of sitting in your cell at the Lorton correctional facility?"

Agent Brooks' question hits Raheem in his chest like a heavy, unexpected fist. Raheem hadn't expected that particular question, and he realizes, immediately, that he had been a fool not to. He knew that he got released from prison earlier than expected because his old correctional officer, Roscoe, had hidden the truth of his conviction from the officials seeking to release all nonviolent offenders. Raheem is not a nonviolent offender. His conviction had been for aggravated assault which is literally violence. He was due to be released within about five months, but Raheem received and took a get out of jail free card. He understands that what is most at issue now is his honesty to the question posed.

"Agent Brooks," he begins, "my conviction was for aggravated assault. I was sent to prison for too long. I believe this was based upon the biases of the judge on my case. I was a model prisoner and a trustee for the warden. I did my time with no issues. My prison record is clean. When Sleep Day occurred, I was one of the prisoners entrusted with the care of the other inmates, and I helped to squelch at least one break- out attempt. When the call came for the release of non-violent offenders, my CO hid my assault conviction from the government officials making the query. I knew what he had done and accepted the opportunity to be released earlier. I felt that I had earned it. I'm not sorry. My family needed me, and I had more than paid for my crime."

At this moment, Raheem is sure that he's just lost this opportunity. He gave the straightest answer possible. It is not in him to deflect. That trait had certainly caused him difficulty before. He hopes that his answer doesn't land him back at Lorton to serve out the rest of his sentence. *Candace would be so pissed,* he knows.

"Mr. Gates," Agent Brooks says, "we know all of this, of course. What did you think that we at the Secret Service would not do our due diligence for every potential hire? No, of course, we know all the details and more about your crime and your release. The goal of my question was to see how honest and transparent that you would be. And I'd say that you more than answered that question. Agent Smith, what do you think?" Agent Smith gives Agent Brooks a nonverbal affirmation that Raheem never sees except on Agent Brooks' face.

The interview continues for about an hour more. By the end, Raheem is sure that he's answered every possible question about his training, time in prison, family, current job, and more. By the arc of Agent Brooks' questions, he can tell that his background had been thoroughly vetted and that his closest friends, family, and associates had all been interviewed. Raheem thinks that they still spared no expense in their personnel evaluation as thin as the Secret Service is now. He is glad for their thoroughness.

His answers to Agent Brooks' questions may or may not have eliminated him from consideration, but Raheem is glad that he hadbeen honest and transparent in all of his responses.

"Mr. Gates..." Agent Brooks states, "...we know about your extensive military training, but if you're selected, we will also require you to go through our no-frills training course. I have no doubt that you'd be exemplary. Good luck. Agent Smith, please escort Mr. Gates back to the front desk. Good day, Mr. Gates."

"Thank you both for your time today," Raheem says as he acknowledges Agent Brooks and Agent Smith. He and Agent Smith walk out of the office and head back to the elevators on which they had earlier arrived. Agent Smith does not say a word the entire time. At the reception desk on his way out the door, she stops Raheem before he exits.

"You were excellent, Mr. Gates," she says before turning to walk away.

Raheem is surprised that she had spoken at all, let alone given him such positive affirmation. He doesn't have time to thank her as she's already walked back to the elevator and is disappearing behind its doors that are already closing behind her.

* * *

Darryl checks, double checks, and triple checks his rifle again. This might be the last time tonight that he will be able to do so. His sergeant had literally drilled this into him and the other recruits he trained with in North Carolina. Since leaving Ohio, his life had been a whirlwind. Part of him missed the simplicity of his former trash collection days. That work could be challenging, grueling, and most certainly stinky, but it had, in its way, prepared him for this new military life that he had chosen. At thirty-five, he is well past the age of most recruits, but the armed forces need willing bodies, and Darryl had been willing.

His time in Cincinnati as an IM reclamation worker had taught him a lot. He had never become a full-fledged police officer like Jerome had, and he's fine with that. Military life suits him better. It's riskier, but other than being the play uncle to Jerome's kids, he does not have any family to speak of and had felt fine with making this move away from his hometown. Since then, and for a few months now, his life had been non-stop action, training, and activity. Most of the other trainees were far younger than he is, but there had been some 'old heads' seeking a new life in the military just like he was.

Being single and not having kids to look after had freed him to take this kind of risk. *As the country had changed and continues to change, he gets to be a part of it,* he thinks. Opportunities to do new things in new places are everywhere. Darryl hadn't expected for things to become so violent so quickly, but the country's leaders mean business. The President had drawn a line in the sand and declared that we would remain a nation in spite of all obstacles and that we would prevail against all enemies,foreign and domestic. *The President,* Darryl thinks to himself, *had thus far kept his word.* This is why Darryl finds himself in Texas, of all places, right at the border with Mexico leading a squad of about ten marines of his own.

Four months ago, Darryl and his then company rescued a few SMs in a small border town in Texas. There had also beenIMs, but the cartel kidnappers killed some of them and spirited the rest back across the border into Mexico. In response, Darryl and the squad he'd been assigned to had followed the kidnappers across the border, engaged them in a firefight, and took the IMs back. After this first excursion, there had been several more that Marines like Darryl had made to maintain possession of land andproperty along the Texas-Mexico border.

It seemed to Darryl and his military commanders that the cartels escalated their attempts to come into the country. The cartels, apparently, didn't fear the Sleepers virus like the Europeans and Russians did, reasoning that they too possessed sufficient levels of melanin to prevent the Sleeper virus' immobilization.

They've probably tested their theory out, Darryl thinks. Given how ruthless Darryl had seen the cartel soldiers be, he's confident that testing their immunity to the Sleepers virus by forcing unwilling Mexicans to venture into the U.S. is precisely what they had done.

However, Darryl had begun to hear that higher-ups believed

that the Mexican military was behind the incursions. There is no proof yet of that claim, but he thinks his next orders will be to find that proof. Darryl hopes that he and his squad will be selected to be part of the team. He's noticed that whenever he's not on a mission, his training, which his commanders determine, has skewed toward the kind that special forces receive. This is not regular training, he recognizes, and at almost seven months removed from Sleep Day, Darryl is glad for the additional expertise. Also, he is Corporal Darryl Isaacs, U.S. Marine Corp, now, and he likes it. The promotion suits him, and he is glad for it.

"CORPORAL!" he hears his Sergeant say."Yes, Sir!" Darryl replies.

"Get your squad into the Humvees and move out! Your orders will arrive once you reach checkpoint Alpha."

"Sir, yes, Sir!"

Darryl wonders what tonight's mission might be. Usually, they never left the base for a mission without some advance heads up on what the mission is. This is a very different scenario, he realizes. Whatever it is, Darryl knows that it will be dangerous.

As he and his squad load into their Humvees, Darryl looks into the eyes of every single one of his soldiers. They're all ready, he sees. They're lethal too, certified killers every single one of them, men and women.

Previous missions had all been dangerous. They almost always took fire unless they had the element of surprise. On one mission, Darryl recalls, his squad went in super stealthy and silently using nothing but their military-issued bowie knives. It was their use of silence and skill that had won his squad the victory that day, though he'd had nightmares for a week thereafter. There had been a lot of blood.

Since Sleep Day, Mexican drug cartels had begun moving across the border into Texas and California to plant their drugs, cultivate them and sell them in the country. The cartels had also consistently tried to steal sleeping IMs when they could. However, that practice had all but stopped since all of the IMs in and around Texas that could be found had long since been rounded up and housed outside of the state. The President had charged Homeland Security to stop the cartels from coming into the country and setting up shop. This was one of his topmost priorities.

This evening's mission is different, though. Darryl can feel it, and his squad can too. The energy and the urgency of their Sergeant's command is greater. There's electricity in the air that is unmistakable. Darryl's small caravan of Humvees begins to make its way to checkpoint Alpha as it had done many nights before this one. The checkpoint is about three miles from the Mexican border and is the primary rally point of all such missions. At this rate of speed, his squad will arrive at the checkpoint in five minutes or less.

"Private, check your weapons and especially check your munitions. Pass the word to everyone in the squad." The Marine to whom Darryl speaks nods his compliance and immediately does what his squad leader orders. Darryl can hear him speaking into his mic to the other three Humvees that follow them.

After arriving at the checkpoint, Darryl and his squad sitin silence. This close to the border, they know better than to fill the night air with unnecessary conversation. The lights on their Humvees have been extinguished as well. On clear nights, they can be seen from miles away. In civilian life, that's no problem.For military operations, it's a huge liability. Minutes after their arrival, Darryl hears the familiar soft beeps of the notification of their orders arriving on Private Johnson's communication pad. Private Johnson, who is always within arm's reach of Darryl on a mission, is the soldier chiefly responsible for communications within the squad and from the squad out to other squads and their commanders.

"What does it say, Johnson?" Darryl asks, his voice low."It says reconnaissance," Private Johnson replies.

This is it, Darryl now knows. This is the reconnaissance mission that he had been hearing about. The President wants to know whether the Mexican government is behind the cartel's incursions. This is their time to find out.

"What are our orders?" Darryl asks again.

"Sir, they want us to go..." Private Johnson hesitates as he reads the orders "...on foot to Juarez. They want us to infiltrate the Mexican military base there, take pictures and try to penetrate their command center, if not personally, at least with our drones.

They want us to record any and all conversations amongst their commanders. It'll just be us, Sir. We might have air support if things get dicey, but we're the only squad going in. That's all, Sir. They'll track our movements and may provide more orders once we reach Juarez."

"That's it then," Darryl says. "Private, give the word to load out of the Humvees. Everyone needs to grab their packs. We're going on a ten-mile hike," he says. Once Darryl and his squad are outside and assembled, he can see their less than enthusiastic demeanor about having to hike ten miles at night to the locale and then hike the ten miles back.

"Squad, I get it. We didn't expect to have to travel twenty miles on foot tonight or any night. But we've trained for this and worked for this. Our orders are to travel light over the border with our drones, get close enough to hear, take pictures if we can, and then beat it back. Make sure that we have the drones packed and with us and grab your light packs. We shouldn't run into anyone between here and the Mexican base at Juarez if we're smart and lucky. I want suppressors affixed to all of your rifles. Hoorah?"

"Hoorah!" his soldiers respond, but Darryl can still see the looks of trepidation on some of their faces. *They're right to be anxious,* Darryl thinks. He is, too, though he refuses to show it.

He signed up for this, and he's even more anxious to complete the mission. As a thinking man, which is what Jerome used to call him after one of their many philosophical debates on the trash truck, Darryl has been thinking a lot about how bold Mexico had gotten and how their brazen behavior is about far more than growing drugs or taking property. Mexico, he believes, sees a real play at taking and holding land in the United States. Darryl believes that they think American ranks are too thin to consistently defend their borders and the towns in Texas and Arizona that sit along the border.

Darryl isn't privy to the internal conversations at the White House or even amongst his own commanders, but he has two eyes and can see. What he sees leads him to believe that if a connection between the cartels is established, it may mean war. He knows that they are already working together in some way. However, Darryl is confident in his marines and the military's ability to win a war with Mexico. A protracted conflict, though, could be devastating to their now fledgling population and their resources.

For now, Darryl elects to stay focused on the mission. Get to the base in Juarez, launch the drones, collect information, find a connection between the cartels and the Mexican government, if any. Get home safely. Easy. If it's so easy, Darryl wonders, what is this sinking feeling in his gut? "Black Squad, mount up! On me.

I'll set the pace. We'll be there in no time." They're ready and fit. *Hopefully*, he thinks, *we can all get there and get out of there in one piece.*

* * *

President Douglas sits in the Situation Room with his generals and other support staff. He watches and listens to video and audio of a mission that he authorized in Mexico just today. A squad of marines has been sent to the Mexican base in Juarez. They arrived there just after one a.m. eastern stand time. "Who's leading the squad?" he asks.

"It's Corporal Darryl Isaacs, Sir. He and his squad have been training for this mission for well over a month now. They've had several on the ground experiences fighting against the cartels and liberating captured SMs and IMs," an aide says.

President Douglas looks at the screens in front of him. Four of them are dedicated to the four drones that Darryl's squad has launched. The drones are small, black, nearly silent, and equipped with highly sensitive audio capture equipment that can see in nearly all spectrums. Each cost the military about one million dollars. *That's four million dollars in the air right now*, President Douglas thinks.

"Generals, report. What have we learned thus far?" the President asks.

"Well, Sir, right before you walked into the room, we had established the com links to the drones. We've observed normal military interaction on the ground, but nothing extraordinary yet. We have two of our audio devices trained on their senior commander's office. He's been in there a while with little movement. According to our intelligence sources, tonight is the night to be here," General Rodriguez says. Rodriguez is the lead general on this mission since he is fluent in both English and Spanish and is of Mexican heritage. He was born in America and grew up in El Paso with his family when they immigrated, in the 1940s, to America.

"Thank you, General Rodriguez. When can we expect...." President Douglas' question is cut off because he hears yelling, in Spanish, coming through one of the monitor screens. The audio is loud and crystal clear.

"Why are you just now getting here?!" a Mexican officer on the screen says in Spanish.

"I'm sorry, Captain. We were held up in the city by one of our bosses. He wanted to make sure that we're secure first. There have been rumors of an infiltration. And commandant, keep your voice down. We may have ears," the speaker says, responding in Spanish.

While one of the drones captures the clear audio of the two speakers, another, flying more closely, captures what the two men look like. The Mexican officer, a captain, is dressed in typical Mexican military dress. The other is not dressed as the officer is but instead wears clothes more akin to a paramilitary soldier. It is not clear whether he is a member of the Mexican army.

"Come with me," the captain says. "I'll escort you to Colonel Pérez. He's been in his office most of the day. He asked not to be disturbed unless it's you."

President Douglas and the other attendants in the Situation Room watch as the Mexican captain and his unnamed guest walk, presumably, to Colonel Pérez's office. There is a brief wait outside of his door before they enter and close the door behind them.

President Douglas sees them via their heat signatures on the screen,which two of their four drones capture. The audio coming from them is crystal clear. *It's perfect,* President Douglas thinks. His only struggle is the Spanish, in which he is not fluent. The speakersare native Spanish speakers and speak it too fast for him to follow. General Rodriguez sits very close by him and provides real-time interpretation as the three men speak.

"Sandoval," Colonel Pérez says in Spanish, "I'm getting nervous. The cartel's excursions have become less and less successful, and the Americans don't seem to be nearly as weak or scattered as you and your bosses promised. My commanders have become less and less convinced that the cartels' grand scheme can work." As he speaks, General Rodriguez immediately provides the President the interpretation.

Upon hearing these words, President Douglas' eyes open widely. "Is he saying what I think he's saying, General?" he asks General Rodriguez.

"Maybe, Mr. President," he replies, "let's keep listening." "My point, Sandoval, is that the clock is ticking. El Presidenté nor I will continue to support you in these..." the Colonel hesitates "...missions without some guarantees. First, you have to know that none of your acts can be traced back to us. Second, if you're wrong about America's military capability, you and your cohorts will personally pay the price for that. You will befully disavowed and painted as a rogue military agent. You have exactly thirty days from now to prove your theory. If you fail, you fail alone," Colonel Pérez concludes.

Sandoval looks intently at Colonel Pérez, barely concealing his hatred for the man. *This man is unworthy to serve under the Mexican flag and is nowhere near the soldier that I am,* he thinks. He remembers that Pérez had been an enthusiastic supporter of his plan just three short months ago and had even attempted to take much of the credit when their first few incursions seemed successful. *Now that the Americans have shown some spine and pushed back against the Mexicans, the Colonel, this man,* Sandoval muses bitterly, *wants to cut, run and blame him.*

Sandoval stands rigidly in his spot, coldly considering his options, his hand lightly fingering his German-made .45 caliber pistol. Before he can think his next thought, all three occupants of Colonel Pérez's office hear a loud crash against their building. Sandoval runs to the window to see the source of the commotion. On the ground, about thirty feet beneath them, is a small ball of fire engulfing some kind of propeller-laden machine.

"Drone! Drone! Drone!" they all hear from one of the soldiers shouting outside.

A drone, Sandoval thinks, *we're not alone.* They're still here. "Colonel, it's the Americans. They're probably still here. Permission to pursue?" Sandoval asks.

Colonel Pérez waves his agreement and says, "Sandoval, be careful, Amigo, you better catch them." Sandoval is already halfway down the steps before the Colonel finishes his last words and never sees the look of hatred on Sandoval's face.

* * *

The crap has hit the proverbial fan. Darryl knows it, his squad knows it, they all know it. "What the hell just happened?" Darryl asks from his perch just outside the base's perimeter.

"One of the Mexican soldiers, Sir. He got lucky. Saw the drone and then hit it with something. He must have been standing on top of the building. No way he could have hit it from the ground," Private Johnson says.

"Okay, Squad. It is what it is. But now they know that we're here. Recall all of the remaining drones, grab your gear, and let's go. It's double-time back to the border. They'll be in vehicles. We'll be on foot, but we've got a slight head start. If we can take a transport along the way, we will. Let's go, Marines," Darryl says.

Getting into Juarez under cover of the night had been fairly painless. Aside from the ten-mile hike on foot, they had slipped into the city without being seen. It had helped that the military base sat just outside the city and therefore away from the city center. Now, however, every soldier and every cartel member would know that they're here and who to look for, namely, a group of American SM soldiers. They would most definitely stick out, Darryl realizes.

After considering their most rational and irrational options, Darryl decides that they should do the opposite of what's expected of them. "Listen up. We're going into the city. Since we're on foot, we're going to hide amongst the buildings and the populace. There shouldn't be too many civilians out tonight, this late on a Tuesday. Johnson, call HQ and request pick up in Juarez. We'll give them the rendezvous coordinates once we get there. We still have the element of surprise in our favor. Let's go."

* * *

"General Rodriguez," President Douglas says, "what thehell just happened?"

"We lost one of the drones, Sir. They know that we're there," General Rodriguez responds.

"Where's our squad now?" the President asks.

"Sir, it looks like they're headed into Juarez, which is the opposite of what they should be doing."

"Why would they do that, General?"

"Because it's the opposite of what they should be doing or of what they'd be expected to do. Corporal Isaacs is smart, Sir," General Rodriguez says.

"General Rodriguez!" an aid exclaims, "we've just received a request from Black Squad, Corporal Isaac's squad, for two Black Hawks to rendezvous in the city."

"Do it!" President Douglas says, jumping in before General Rodriguez responds. "Whatever they need to get them out, get them out!" he booms.

The aid looks at General Rodriguez for confirmation. "It's the President. Do what he orders," he says to the aid, who suddenly looks embarrassed.

"General, I'm stepping out back to the Oval. Be sure to give me minute-by-minute updates on what's happening."

President Douglas stands up, and as he does so, all of the attendant military personnel stand to salute them. He waves them off and quickly exits the room. His thoughts are with Corporal Isaacs and his squad. If he gets out, he says to himself, he's getting a promotion. That guy just gave us the information needed to fight a war, and he may not make it out. *Godspeed,* he thinks.

/ Ted Cummings

CHAPTER III

The last six months have seemed like a couple of years to Donnie. Sitting in his office, he wonders what, if anything, he'd previously done that had prepared him for this moment. When the government began its property transfers and brought the country's financial markets back online, Donnie had been uniquely perched to claim the company he had worked for as his own. As an unexpected bonus, he also acquired his CEO's home, having been there for a party or two during his tenure at the company.

Once the new head of the Federal Reserve vetted him and recognized that Donnie had the skills to rebuild the company from the ground up, his requested acquisition was approved. Before Sleep Day, his company, John Richards & Associates Financial Services, had boasted almost five hundred employees. Today, it had nearly one hundred, most of whom he had culled from the various college business schools around the country.

Many of the new employees had just barely graduated from college, and a good thirty percent of them had little more than two years of college under their belts. Given the times and the needs, companies like Donnie's could ill afford to wait for the traditional academic process to work itself out.

To speed up the training and education of these new employees, Donnie created a part-time curriculum that provides practical application to substitute for the theoretical learning they would have received in college. After about five months, Donnie saw almost immediately that his version of on-the-job training worked and was causing his company to prosper.

With so much new wealth being made, Donnie's company, soon to be re-named Hernandez & Associates Financial Services, has more business than associates to attend to it. Since his training program had been so successful, it had also become the standard for other similarly situated companies across the country and the federal government. At a very young 26 years old, Donnie's help and consultancy are much sought after in the financial sector and other industries.

Sitting at his desk, he hears an insistent knock on his open door. "Boss, what are we doing? It's lunchtime." Donnie looks at

Clarence, his big friend, and takes a moment to marvel at how he'd changed too. Clarence is easily ten years Donnie's senior. When he'd met Clarence, he was dressed in a mechanic's jumpsuit that had seen many years' worth of soil, grime, and hardwork. Clarence had clearly been a man used to working with his hands. For the month or so that Donnie had lived with him on the Southside of Chicago, Clarence lived a very humble life with fewpossessions. He had, however, shared everything with Donnie without stipulations and had kept him safe on several occasions on their many forays to retrieve and secure IMs who were at risk from the elements and predators.

"Gimme a sec, BC," Donnie says. BC stands for Big Clarence. It fits. Clarence is 6'6", at least 250 pounds, and looks like he could have played linebacker in the NFL. "Bum knee," he told Donnie when he'd asked about it.

When Donnie knew that he'd be coming back to the company to try and claim it and build it, Clarence had asked him to give him a shot and teach him what he knew. Though Donnie readily agreed, he hadn't believed that Clarence would easily grasp the concepts. As it turned out, Clarence was brighter than most of the young college graduates that Donnie had hired and worked twice as hard. In fact, next to himself, Clarence was the company's top earner.

When Donnie claimed his former CEO's house with his now fiancé, Isabella Fuentes, Clarence and his fiancé's grandmother, Marquita Fuentes, moved into the one right next doorto them. Though not biologically related to the Fuentes, he had served as a son to Marquita and big brother to Isabella for almost as long as Isabella had been alive. Clarence wanted to live with his surrogate grandmother and Isabella, his 'lil sis'.

Donnie hadn't fully appreciated the Fuentes' family dynamic when he and Isabella had gotten together. Like all good big brothers, when Clarence found out about them, he had pulled Donnie to the side, giving him a few choice words to consider before ultimately giving his blessing on their pairing. Donnie had never been afraid of his soon-to-be surrogate brother-in-law, but Donnie is no fool. He understood that his actions and intentions toward Isabella must always be honorable. *Good thing for him that he had fallen head over heels in love with her,* he thinks.

Donnie wraps up a bit of paperwork that he had been pouring over when Clarence walked in. “Okay, let’s go. You choose, or I choose?” Donnie asks. He puts the paperwork back into a large blue folder, stands, and walks toward his office door where Clarence stands.

“I choose,” Clarence says. “I want to show you something.”

Walking out of his office to the main elevators, Donnie quietly observes all of the young faces busy at work and a few of those that acknowledge him and Clarence as they walk by. He is proud of the work that they’re doing and marvels at how different the work environment is. *Most of these kids,* he thinks, *never would have had the opportunity to work here or at a place like this. They certainly never would have the opportunity to dominate in terms of numbers.*

Donnie recalls that he was the only person of color who was an associate in the entire company just six months ago. Though he had been a high performer, he felt that every day could be his last. He had often silently complained to himself about how his white counterparts, in particular the white men, worked and acted as if they did not have a care in the world. Since he is Dominican, Donnie checks the box for both Black and Hispanic. He had often wondered whether his double so-called minority status is what had gotten him in the company in the first place, his high grades notwithstanding.

“Hey, man, I see you over there in heavy thought,” Clarence says when they reach the elevators. “You did all of this, man. You should be proud, no matter what happens in six months.”

By his statement, Clarence touches on one of their shared anxieties. What if the IMs wake up, reclaim everything, and they lose all that they’ve gained? “I appreciate that, Clarence. I am a little worried. World governments are working around the clock trying to find a vaccine for the Sleepers virus. If they find it, and it works, it could be all she wrote. I don’t know how we’d ever recover. As a people, I mean. I don’t know how we would ever get over it. We Blacks and Hispanics are so close to something that we’ve never had here. To take it away would be the ultimate cruelty.

Ultimate."

"Yeah, man, I hear you, but you can't think like that. Even if the IMs wake up, I think that we'll be okay. And if not..." Clarence says, opening up his big arms widely "...then we've got the literal and proverbial keys to the kingdom, my guy," he says with a wide grin. "Oh! Here we are!" Clarence exclaims as he stops suddenly. They had walked for little more than a block down from their offices in downtown Chicago when Clarence stops them.

"BC, where are we?" Donnie asks.

"Why, my new restaurant, of course!" Clarence says excitedly. "We just opened. Today is the first day. I claimed it months ago but needed to make some upgrades and repairs before we could open. Come on in, follow me."

As they enter, Donnie sees Mrs. Fuentes, Isabella's grandmother, greeting some of the seated guests. "Is that?" he says.

"Yep, Momma Fuentes!" Clarence says, calling her his pet name for her. "The entire menu is dedicated to her and is based upon her best dishes. This is homestyle Hispanic cooking, which you know that I love. I'm gonna be rich, Donnie!" he says, laughing as he speaks.

Donnie laughs with him, celebrating in his friend's joy. He thinks again about how far Clarence had come. He almost immediately corrects himself realizing that who Clarence is now is who he'd always been. *But now,* he thinks, *Clarence has no limits, societal or otherwise, to pursue his dreams, express his passions and, most importantly, find capital to fund his projects.* Donnie makes a note to himself to research whether there is a clothing manufacturer business or two that has yet to be claimed. He'd like to see his name on a line of designer suits for men and women. Donnie really likes suits.

"C'mon, D," Clarence says. "We've got the best table in the house, the chef's table." As they go inside and sit down, Donnie takes in the details of the restaurant. It is beautiful and spacious.

Everything is new, including the bar.

"Hey, man, how much did you spend on all of these furnishings?" Donnie asks.

"I spared no expense, really. When I claimed it, I could have opened the very next day, and we'd have been fine. The restaurant had been in fine shape as is. But I really wanted to make it my own, and I wanted it to be a place that Ma, I mean Mrs. Fuentes, could be proud of and feel one-hundred percent comfortable working in. That means a lot to me. Based on how it's turned out, I'd say that it's been worth it," Clarence concludes.

Donnie strongly concurs, looking around the place, watching all of the patrons, and feeling the restaurant's energy. *This had been a good investment,* he thinks. The smells emanating from the kitchen remind him that it's lunchtime and that he's hungry, having skipped breakfast to make an early morning conference call. Now that he knows that his future mother-in-law is the chef, Donnie feels even more hungry. He'd been eating her cooking for the last six months and had the extra poundage to show for it. Isabella, of course, cooks just like her, which is probably not a good thing for his waistline.

"Hey, Donnie, I've been meaning to tell you, you may want to start hitting the gym," Clarence says. "You're starting to look a little," Clarence says as he makes the universal facial expression for a fat face. They both crack up at that.

"Yeah, man, you're right. I need to drop a good fifteen pounds or so. I better hurry up before my Frat brothers see me. They're merciless," Donnie says.

"You got that right, Brother. By the way, I noticed that you were working on your special project today. The blue folder?" Clarence says, questioning.

"Ah, yes, the blue folder. It's the Presidential Commission work that several of us in the financial industry are working on for President Douglas. He calls me at least once per week. The man is very detail-oriented. After all of the crashes, hackings, and attempted hackings of our financial systems and other industries, the President assembled a team of top folks like me to provide policies and infrastructure to protect America's financial structure and re-establish it as the benchmark of the world. It's a tall order, my friend, let me tell you."

"As you know, America's markets went all to crap when the Sleepers virus hit. Because it had been so connected with other world markets, it took the European, Asian, African, and Middle Eastern markets down with it. When the markets started to come back, the Asian and European markets isolated America and attempted a currency coup," Donnie says.

"What? Currency coup?" Clarence says. "Hey man, I'm learning a lot, but I still need you to speak English. What the heck is a currency coup?"

"My bad, man, let me be more clear," Donnie says. "Asia and Europe attempted to replace the American dollar as the world's fiat currency, that is to say, the world's currency. That is something that President Douglas refused to allow to happen both for political reasons and economic ones. So he put about twenty of us together to come up with ways to both protect America's financial systems, ensuring that whether IM or no IM, we remain the world's most powerful country financially and also keep the dollar supreme in the rest of the world."

"Got it," Clarence says. "Now, let's eat."

"Eat?" Donnie asks. "We haven't even ordered yet."

"Yes, you have. It's all of your favorites. Remember, it's my restaurant," Clarence says with gleeful emphasis.

"Outstanding," Donnie retorts, "I'm famished."

About five minutes later, their food arrives. What was meant to be a simple lunch becomes a five-course meal of all of Donnie and Clarence's favorites. Being Dominican, Donnie had grown up eating pretty much like this. Clarence, he knows, doesn't have a drop of Hispanic blood in him, but you couldn't tell him that. He'd been adopted into a Hispanic family, speaks Spanish fluently, eats Puerto Rican and Mexican food predominantly, and had just opened a Hispanic restaurant that serves cuisine from several different Hispanic cultures. The fact that Clarence is a large Black man clearly provided no hesitation in his adoption of a culture not his own.

About an hour later, after both Donnie and Clarence have had their fill, he says to Clarence: "I don't know how we're going to get any work done this afternoon. Bro, I'm full as a tick."

"Yeah, not me," Clarence says. "I've got about ten more clients to call today. I need to help them put their newfound wealth to good use. You know how I do." Clarence says with a wink.

"Why yes, I do, Mr. Junior VP," Donnie says proudly in recognition of his friend's most recent promotion. Donnie remembers what his plan had been when Clarence joined the company. He would walk shoulder to shoulder with his friend to help ensure his success. At the time, Donnie had been worried that Clarence was biting off more than he could chew when he joined Donnie's company. Donnie needn't have worried. Big C understands people have a huge heart and had been gifted with the innate ability to identify and speak to peoples' real needs, especially people like him who found themselves newly wealthyand newly propertied.

When the President's property transfer program began, and so many people had both new property, wealth, and access to the capital markets like never before, the predictable over-spending on depreciating assets like cars, boats, and other items had occurred. Even Donnie had added his favorite Porsche to his garage and had given his BMW to Isabella. Now that the initial spending splurge had subsided a bit, millions of SMs refocused on building and protecting their new wealth. This appears to be a reaction to the very real possibility of the IMs waking up before the one-year date and taking the wealth back. Clarence's best marketing tactic had been to tell prospective clients to 'build upon the wealth that you gained just in case you have to return the principal.' Donnie swears that Clarence is signing up ten new clients per day with that line.

Donnie knows and is acutely sensitive to the fact that IM reemergence could spell the financial doom of millions of folks like him. He wonders how newly wealthy SMs will voluntarily return their acquired property to the IMs. *It's difficult to unring a bell,* he thinks. Donnie recounts the news stories that he'd seen in which many SMs had begun suffering a sort of new wealth PTSD. For the first time in the history of the United States, millions of SMs are now able to see, up close and personal, just how wealthy America really is. When the reality of that wealth became widely known, anger or rage, even at just how much SMs had been missing out on for many centuries, followed. Donnie remembers when Chris Rock had said that if poor people knew just how rich "rich" people are, there would be riots. Given that all of America's IMs within the country are either asleep, missing, or dead, there had not been any riots, but there had been anger, lots of it.

Donnie had known and understood that wealth since he

began his studies in college and certainly through each one of his college internships at places like Goldman Sachs and Morgan Stanley. Even he, though, had had to adjust to his own newfound wealth when he assumed command of his company and his CEO's property. The estate on which his CEO had lived was massive.

Other than the removal of the CEO's personal effects, he and Isabella had not changed much. His CEO's wife was a woman ofimpeccable taste, and Isabella had approved. Some of the art had been replaced, but that was about it. When the IM recovery team searched the estate, they found the couple resting comfortably in their beds. All of their children are adults, and none had been found at home with them. Other than their dogs, which Donnie and Isabella now owned and cared for, the CEO and his wife had been the only people there.

Though extravagantly wealthy, Donnie's CEO lived a relatively modest life. The home contained a six-car garage, but only three cars filled it. Donnie and Isabella had elected to keep the cars, an SUV, a classic silver BMW Z8, and the CEO's college car, an old VW Beetle that he and his wife had had during their college years. Out of respect for the couple, Donnie hadn't sold or otherwise disposed of the cars. He even sometimes drives the VW around the neighborhood, which his CEO had kept in immaculate condition.

Walking back to their offices, Clarence and Donnie can both sense the new energy in their city. "Something's different, D. I can feel it. Hell, I can dang near see it." Donnie knows what he means. Though not a lifelong resident of The Chi, native Chicagoans' nickname for Chicago, Donnie had been here long enough to feel and see the difference.

"Well, yes, Big Bro," Donnie replies, "we can literally see a difference," he says with emphasis. "SMs as far as the eye can see, but I agree, the energy is different too. I feel it every day in our office." Almost as soon as Donnie finishes speaking, his mood turns sullen. "I am concerned, though, about the next six months. What if they wake up? We've done a lot in six months. I'd like for it all not to be for naught."

"For naught," Clarence says mockingly, cracking up at his friend. "You worry too much. I've seen a little more than you. I think that we'll be alright. Let's just grind it out for the next six and see what happens. Plus, you've got a wedding and new bride to think about," Clarence says as he places a firm hand on Donnie's shoulder.

Donnie looks up at Clarence to see that he is in full big brother mode for Isabella. "Easy big fella," he says. "I love her more than she loves me." They both laugh at that together as they enter the big main doors of their office building. *It's going to be a great day*, Donnie thinks. *Let's build until we can't build anymore*, he decides.

* * *

Six months removed from the release of the Sleepers virus, Dr. Alexandria Taylor feels like a new person. Her sleepless nights had largely dissipated, and she feels strengthened with a new purpose. Six months ago, she had been racked with severe depression and guilt over what she had done, the release of the Sleepers virus all over the country. She had not anticipated what its impact would be beyond the ruining of Pharmatech's introduction of its new drug, Zoesterol, to the public. The toll on the American population had been devastating. Many millions of IMs are either asleep, unaccounted for, or dead. Dr. Taylor knows that each one ofthese lives is on her.

The knowledge of her culpability had nearly sent her over the edge. More than once, she had contemplated ending her life. Standing here today, she's not quite sure why she hadn't. Perhaps her mother's words and her strong Christian background had given her the strength that she needed to resist those voices and attempt to move forward. Dr. Taylor has no illusions about what she's done or who she is in light of her actions. She simply decided to keep living.

About a month after she released the Sleepers virus, Dr. Taylor had another decision to make whether she would return to work or flee the city. Taking flight is what guilty people do. She wants to appear to be as non-guilty as possible. She decides, therefore, to return to work, her job at Pharmatech. She reasons that there would be far fewer questions in her return than if she does not.

On her first day back, Dr. Taylor dons her standard work outfit and security badge. Pharmatech's offices comprise one of the larger buildings in downtown Chicago. As she walks through the front doors, she is unprepared for what she sees. Military personnel are stationed throughout the lobby and at each elevator bank. It's clear to her that folks' IDs are being checked and that people are being questioned.

"Who are you?" a soldier dressed completely in black asks as he steps in front of Dr. Taylor.

"I am Dr. Alexandria Taylor," she says. "I work here."

The soldier has a clipboard with what looks like a list of names on it. His finger goes down the page and then stops near the end of it. *T for Taylor,* she thinks.

"I've found your name," the soldier says. "But it says that you haven't been here for the last thirty-five days. Care to explain your absence?" he asks.

"No, I would not," Dr. Taylor says, feeling her temperature rise. She doesn't know who this soldier is or what these other soldiers are doing here, but she determines that she won't be interrogated by him or anyone else in the open out in the lobby.

She can simply turn on her heels and walk out if she wishes. *Perhaps this had been a bad idea,* she thinks.

"Dr. Taylor? Dr. Alexandria Taylor? Would you come with me, please?" a woman says.

Dr. Taylor turns her head to the right to see the identity of the speaker. She is a Black woman sharply dressed in a medium-length black pantsuit, a brilliant white blouse, and black heels.

She is about Dr. Taylor's age and stands a little taller than her. Dr. Taylor does not know who the woman is but is glad for the distraction from the annoying soldier. As the woman approaches, Dr. Taylor sees her interrogator step back several steps and looks as if a much more important matter is demanding his attention. "I've got it from here," the unknown woman says as she approaches Dr. Taylor. The soldier blithely nods his agreement and walks away.

"I'm so sorry about that inconvenience, Dr. Taylor. These lobby interrogations can be so unsettling," she says. "My name is Rebecca Braithwaite. I am the official liaison between the Defense Department and Pharmatech. As you may not know, Pharmatech has been brought under federal jurisdiction since it is now known that the outbreak of the Sleepers virus emanated from here and other Pharmatech facilities. Once we discovered that, the President put Pharmatech on restriction and placed us here to secure its facilities."

At this woman's words, Dr. Taylor has to stifle her overwhelming urge to run as fast as she can for her life. "Released?" she asks haltingly in an attempt to feign genuine curiosity. "What do you mean released?"

"Released," Rebecca says formally and officially with her arms crossed. She then leans in and nearly whispers to Dr. Taylor: "Honestly, we don't know if the so-called release was by accident or on purpose and if on purpose who coordinated it—I'm not really at liberty to say, and frankly, that's not my job to sort through." Regaining her previously stiff posture, she then says, "My job is to secure the Chicago facility and secure the personnel. I'm delighted that you're here. You're one of the last SM Pharmatech employees to show back up, and I think you're one of the highest-ranking ones. If you would follow me upstairs, I can debrief you further and give you your new assignment."

Dr. Taylor is relieved to be walking toward the elevators up to Pharmatech's offices. Two minutes ago, she thought that she might get tackled on her way out the front door, attempting to run away. It had been foolish of her, she now knows, to imagine she would be able to simply walk into Pharmatech's building, go to her officeand just sit at her desk with nary a question or raised eyebrow. *If I make it through today without being arrested, I'll have to be much more careful,* she resolves.

As she and Rebecca exit the elevator onto her office's floor, Dr. Taylor wonders what the rest of her day might look like. She remembers that in her group, she had been the only SM employed there. By the time the Sleepers virus had been released, she had been relegated to a low-level project for Pharmatech. This had been done in retaliation for her several complaints to HR regarding her former manager's constant sexism and racism and his cronies, all of whom had been knocked out by the Sleepers virus.

"In here, Dr. Taylor," Rebecca says as she points to one of the large conference rooms on her floor.

Dr. Taylor joins Rebecca at the conference room table and sits across from her. She's sure that she'll receive more questions from her and perhaps some understanding of a new assignment. There is a monitor at one end of the conference room that hangs from the wall. As Rebecca turns it on, Dr. Taylor sees an unfamiliar face on the monitor.

"Hello, Dr. Taylor," she hears this new person say. "My name is Trevor Campbell. I am the head of the NSA, the National Security Agency. How are you?"

The now familiar feeling of panic sweeps over Dr. Taylor. *Why in the world would the head of the NSA be contacting her?* she wonders in a panic. *This is clearly a set-up. They know! They know!* She says to herself while also eyeing the conference room door. Rebecca sits closer to the door than Dr. Taylor. While considering the odds of her making it to the door while fighting this woman off, Rebecca reaches across the table and touches Dr. Taylor's hand. She looks at Rebecca, who gives her a reassuring, gentle look. This immediately relaxes Dr. Taylor, who ends her thoughts of escape for the time being.

"First, Dr. Taylor, I am very glad to see you. We did not know whether you had left Chicago or if something had happened to you. I am glad that you're okay. And second", he says, "We know what you did. You released the Sleepers virus." Trevor lets his words hang in the air between them as he observes the stark panic on Dr. Taylor's face.

"But frankly, Dr. Taylor, myself and others that know what you've done, consider it a great service to the country," Trevor says.

"What?" Dr. Taylor says, stumbling. "If you know what I've done, then you know what I've DONE." She feels the heavyweight of emotion well up in her. Her fear, her guilt, and her anxiety. She begins to sob and shake. She feels Rebecca's reassuring hands on her shoulders and the passing of tissues to heras she hides her face between her arms and the conference table.

"Dr. Taylor, what you've done is to single-handedly set our people free. In one week, the demographics have shifted in a manner that would have taken one hundred years or more to complete. And even at the end of that one-hundred years, there's no telling whether Black and Brown people would have ever been able to enjoy the shift given the virulent racism of many of the IMs of this country. I assure you that you've done us all a tremendous service. Though this will never be said publicly, and no one will ever know what you've done, I, for one, want to say thank you."

Dr. Taylor looks up at the screen. She cannot believe what she is hearing. On the one hand, the government knows what happened and knows that she caused it. On the other hand, she is being thanked for her actions by the head of the NSA instead of being arrested and hauled into a federal prison. It is both the best and the worst day of her life.

"Where do we go from here?" she asks squeamishly. "Ah, great question, Dr. Taylor. Ms. Braithwaite here will be your handler. She is stationed at this facility and can bring you up to speed on all that is happening. But since you are, for now, the highest-ranking person at the Chicago facility, I am making you its permanent director. No one but me and Ms. Braithwaite knows what you did, and no one else will," Trevor says.

"As the director, you are to manage all of Pharmatech's U.S. operations. Dr. Krauss, who you may or may not know, is back in Switzerland busily working on a cure or vaccine to the Sleepers virus. I want you to align with his lab and keep tabs on his team's progress. It is vital for national security that we know the progress of this supposed cure and its development. Do you agree to do that for us?" Trevor asks.

Dr. Alexandria Taylor is a wise woman, a very wise woman, so she knows when she's being cornered. The NSA director is not making a request. He is making a demand: "Help us, or we'll tell everyone what you did" is Campbell's supposed 'offer'. Everyone will know that she's singly responsible for the immobilization and deaths of millions of people. She'd go down as one of the biggest mass murderers in history, right along with Stalin and Hitler. No one will know or care whether she'd meant to do it or not and if the IMs wake in her lifetime, she's likely to bekilled for her crimes. She weighs her options. It doesn't take her long.

"Yes, Mr. Campbell, I agree. What is it precisely that you want me to do?"

That day had been five months ago. Since then, Dr. Taylor had assumed full control of all of Pharmatech's U.S. operations and acquired multiple government contracts to supply a wide range of pharmaceuticals to armed services and many hospitals. She had even grown some of Pharmatech's more fledgling businesses to the point of profitability.

She checks in with Dr. Krauss frequently and reviews all of his files. She often senses that Krauss sees her as an irritant, but he knows he must comply since President Douglas personally blames him for the creation and the outbreak of the Sleepers virus and is anxious to have the IMs revived. Dr. Taylor wonders what they'd all think if they knew that the NSA Director, Trevor Campbell, may have other ideas.

In the intervening months between Dr. Taylor's first conversation with Trevor and now, some significant event had occurred. Dr. Krauss and his team had inched closer to a cure and were starting to see some real progress. He had even expressed to Dr. Taylor that he hoped to begin trials in the next thirty days and that the cure is imminent. Dr. Taylor, too, is anxious for a cure to be developed. She wants the IMs revived if for no other reason than to have the guilt of her actions removed, even if partially so.

In her last direct conversation with Trevor, she advises him of Dr. Krauss' success and his confidence in imminent IM revival. Trevor thanks her for her report and quickly signs off once she's delivered it.

The next day when Dr. Taylor enters her office, there is a buzz of activity. Rebecca Braithwaite meets her main door to the building. "Please come with me" is all that she says before she ushers Dr. Taylor in.

"Rebecca, what is it? What's wrong?" Dr. Taylor asks.

Rebecca doesn't respond but waits to speak until she and Dr. Taylor enter one of the soundproof rooms that line the floor of one of Pharmatech's primary research and development laboratories.

"Dr. Krauss is missing, presumed dead, and his entire laboratory has been destroyed. Some sort of fire. We're still gathering the details," Rebecca Braithwaite says in rapid-fire succession.

Dr. Taylor is stunned. She had just spoken with Dr. Krauss the previous day. Albeit briefly, he had given her a favorable update on the Sleeper virus vaccine, which she had then shared with Trevor. She stops mid-thought and looks up at Rebecca, eyeing her with a cunning, knowing look. In place of her shock from the news of Dr. Krauss' probable death is terror at what had happened to him and why.

Dr. Taylor is well aware that the NSA Director likes things the way they are, that is, the IMs asleep and the SMs large and in charge. The property transfer agreement has a sunset provision causing all of the property transfers that have occurred to become permanent in six months. Dr. Krauss had expressed an imminent vaccine breakthrough which meant animminent IM reemergence. It is not at all beyond possibility thatTrevor Campbell might want to forestall that reemergence, that awakening.

"What are you thinking, Dr. Taylor?" Rebecca asks. Gone is her usual joviality replaced by a predatory look and demeanor. *Ah,* Dr. Taylor thinks. *This is Rebecca's true face. All else before had been a façade.*

"Well, Rebecca, I'm thinking how sad it is that Dr. Krauss is now dead, and I'm wondering what has become of his research since he famously is the only one who maintained copies of it?" Dr. Taylor asks.

"Yes, that," Rebecca says, a wry smile touching the edges of her mouth. "That is a problem, isn't it?" she asks rhetorically. "If Dr. Krauss is gone and his research is gone, that would seem to reset the clock, wouldn't it? That is indeed a shame."

Dr. Taylor gives Rebecca a blanched look. She is now terrified by the realization that these people killed Dr. Krauss, at the least, destroyed his work, and did so on the information that she had provided Trevor. The crushing guilt that she had felt six months ago comes rushing back as Dr. Taylor understands that the IMs will remain asleep until God knows when, and potentially permanently.

"The good news, though, Dr. Taylor, is that everything shall remain as it has. You'll remain in charge here and may even get bumped to CEO of all of Pharmatech. With Dr. Krauss' absence, you'll be boss of the whole enchilada, as it were, and I'll be right here to help and aid you in whatever you need," Rebecca says lightly as if this is the best news in the world.

Thugs and killers, Dr. Taylor thinks. She's surrounded by thugs and killers. To make matters worse, she is clear that her life is wholly expendable.

"Yes, Rebecca, there is some," she says hesitatingly, "good news out of all of this."

"See!" Rebecca says cheerfully. "I knew that you'd get it. Shoot, let's celebrate. Dinner and drinks on me!"

Dr. Taylor smiles weakly. Rebecca's offer is no offer. This is her way of keeping tabs on Dr. Taylor, who understands very well what is being required of her. Go along or come up missing. This is her choice, and it's no choice at all. "Where would you like to eat, Rebecca?" she asks.

"I just heard about his new spot on Michigan called Isabella's. It's supposed to be high-end authentic Mexican cuisine. I love Mexican food. Let's try there" she says.

"Fine. Let's go tonight after work," Dr. Taylor says. "Great, Dr. Taylor, I'll pick you up," Rebecca says as she exits the soundproof room.

Once gone, Dr. Taylor finds the nearest trash can and relieves herself of that morning's breakfast.

CHAPTER IV

President Douglas stands behind his chair in the large conference room in the West Wing. It's early, and he's alone. There's a meeting scheduled in this room later, but that's not why he's here. He's here to think. Sometimes the Oval, with its history, and all of its implications, is not conducive to the kind of musing and reflecting that he needs to do now.

Yesterday had been a devastating day for his Presidency and for himself personally. His top staff informed him that Dr. Krauss, the leading researcher for a vaccine to the Sleepers virus, had most likely been killed in a pair of explosions to his laboratory in Sweden. Because of how Dr. Krauss worked, there are no known copies of his research, all of which he had with him. So the world's leading expert on the Sleepers virus and his research is now, literally, up in smoke. To make matters worse, his top researcher, Dr. Jessica Lundgren, is missing and presumed dead as well, though that had not yet been verified. Despite the fact that his top staff had not told him directly, President Douglas understands that there is no plan B.

In six months, if the IMs have not awakened from their forced sleep, their country will have irrevocably changed.

President Douglas is not at all certain that that change is for the better, long term for the country. He had been heartened by how hard and how well the remaining one-third of the population had put shoulder to plow to meet some of their significant challenges. *But one-third is still one-third,* President Douglas thinks. The hole left by the sleeping two-thirds is monstrous and seems all but impossible to fill as quickly as it needs to be filled.

The European expulsion of their SMs, most of whom had come to America, helps. However, there is a significant learning curve to their acculturation and blending into the cultural fabric of the new United States. Especially as that fabric is being re-stitched to suit the times. *Eventually, we will be back to full speed,* President Douglas thinks, *but time is what they have the least of.* There are threats within and without and unbelievable international pressure.

To make matters worse, President Douglas is concerned about going to war with Mexico given what they've just learned: the

Mexican government has itself been behind the Mexican drug cartels' incursions into Texas and Arizona. The cartels still hold an unknown number of IMs hostage who may or may not be alive. Soon, the President knows that he will have to confront the Mexican president directly to demand their release or be ready to fight for them or avenge them. As much as he considers war to be the last and worst option, President Douglas cannot rule it out.

Things look and feel differently than just two months ago. Then, they had been four months removed from the Sleepers virus outbreak. President Douglas had just gotten some major new powers and some important legislation passed for the country.

Soon after that, the country held national elections and re-stocked most of Congress and the Supreme Court. The government began to look and act like a fully functioning entity again.

Though not initially a fan of the Property Re-Assignment Act, President Douglas had eventually come to see many of its virtues. He currently still retains major reservations about it. His number one concern is and had been the redistribution back of any and all SM acquired property to the original IM owners should they wake up within the one year. After the one year, the property transfers are to remain permanent, but that doesn't solve the problem either, President Douglas knows. What if the IMs wake up soon after the one year is up? *Technically, the IMs would not be entitled to their property, but so what,* President Douglas thinks. *If the IMs wake up at one year and six months or at twenty-four months, they will still demand the return of all of their property and would surely be willing to fight for it, and who could blame them?*

Of course, President Douglas had heard and hears the rumblings within his own administration and from the public. There is a growing consensus, if one is to believe the CNN and MSNBC polls, that suggests that many SMs would be okay with the IMs not awakening within the one year and perhaps remaining asleep for an extended period. The President's outlook runs counterto this attitude. He wants IMs to be revived as soon as possible. He believes it best for the long-term health of the nation that they return.

President Douglas believes that his administration is aligned to his thinking, but he is a keen student of human nature. President Douglas allows for the possibility that not everyone around him is being fully honest and transparent.

President Douglas acknowledges that much had been accomplished in the last six months despite some of his misgivings. The hackings against all of their major institutions had been all but halted. When international hackers realized that approximately two-thirds of the citizens had been put to sleep, they tried their best to shut down the country's electric grid. They also attempted to destroy several of their oil refineries, steal intellectualproperty from many of the country's businesses or corporations, and even disrupt traffic lights.

To counteract these hacks, the President ordered that internet access in and out of the country be closed and at least severely restricted where possible. Given how the internet was initially constructed, fully closing it is all but impossible, but limiting access points at least slows the attacks. At the time, President Douglas and his top military staff decided to pull the plug from the known version of the Internet and build a new one from the ground up. It would be built alongside the new electric grid, which had long needed a major infrastructure upgrade.

Long term, President Douglas and others had reasoned, they would be better able to stop anyone from connecting to American businesses and government by building an internet with far fewer access points into the United States and more robust in spotting and isolating security threats. The President had also been advised to advance the research and use blockchain technology as part of the new internet infrastructure and use these applications for everything from voting to online shopping. The President's technology team had promised a new working internet with blockchain enhancements by the end of the year. *Good,* he thinks. *Folks have gone a little crazy without their social media and videos.* President Douglas shakes his head in remembrance of a time when the internet had not existed, and call-waiting was the big tech upgrade that he and his peers had dreamed about.

In his musings, the President considers that even if the IMs wake up demanding their property back and a reversal of his new powers, there are some things that they won't be able to undo. The new Congress had approved the ten-trillion-dollar infrastructure package that he wanted. Congresswoman Stowe fought him tooth and nail on the package, but he had prevailed. The day that she realized that she would lose that vote had been a delicious moment for the President. Usually highly reserved, he allowed himself to revel in that victory as the look of pain on her face was evident.

The money for the infrastructure upgrades to their roads, bridges, electric grid, communications systems, internet, renewable energy infrastructure, and more is being spent, and millions are at work on them. The new immigrants provide much needed energy and numbers to all of the new projects. It seems that the entire nation is at work to build and keep the country going. President Douglas feels good about that.

The education system, too, is changing right before their eyes. All of the old Euro-centric, western style educational constraints have been removed. Educational innovation is happening right before their eyes out of necessity and, frankly, a lack of enough teachers to go around. The current education includes standard classroom teaching, mixtures of systems like Montessori with traditional methods of instruction, and use of facilities in a manner that hasn't been attempted before. Many physical schools have been emptied out in place of university and college campuses since teacher resources have been so sparse. The President knows that what the new educational system will become isn't entirely clear. What he is sure about is that the country has an incredible need to educate as many people as quickly as is possible to do the work to keep the country going.

Perhaps in a year, he hopes, they'll know what they are. In the meantime, high school will be shorter for many, college will be shorter for some, and graduate school will be on-the-job training. Donnie Hernandez had taught him that in spades. He's currently running the best on-the-job training graduate studies program in the country at his financial services company. Donnie is proving to them all that school and work can be combined to extract value while also providing a sterling education. His youngest employee, Malik, is sixteen years old and making six figures trading stocks and managing a medium-sized portfolio of about twenty clients. *We need more Maliks*, President Douglas says to himself. And we need them in every vital industry.

As a Harvard-trained lawyer, President Douglas is keenly adept at looking at an issue from multiple angles, weighing the pros and cons of each perspective, and then driving to fact-based decisions. As such, he sees and understands the arguments and the growing voices of those who think that the IMs should stay asleep, at least for a while longer. One of President Douglas' disagreements with that idea is that knowledge, once lost, has to bere-grown slowly over time. It cannot simply be replaced. Scientists and archaeologists still don't know how the Pyramids at Giza were constructed without machines or electricity, yet there they stand.

That knowledge has been lost and has never been replaced. *So too,* he thinks, *will some knowledge and know-how never be replaced in the running of the country.*

Long term, some of these losses may turn out to be a good thing since America had, by its awful political divisions, structural racism and socioeconomic inequities, conducted itself waywardly despite years of warning signs about the environment, police brutality, gang violence, overwhelming drug use and other kinds of violent crime. President Douglas, though, worries about the missing knowledge of which they are completely unaware.

If anything, the immobilization of the IMs provides the major economic, educational and cultural blind spots of the nation in real-time. Not enough of them know, empirically and experientially, what they should do to maintain and protect the country. In fact, the President considers, the nation could have easily gone the otherway. There could have been chaos and much worse death.

If the IMs wake up before the next six months are up, they'll probably blame us for the millions of them who had been lost without realizing that many millions more could have been lost had the SMs, for the most part, not immediately reacted to save many lives. *Given their historical record,* President Douglas muses, *they'll probably blame us, strip us of whatever status and power many SMs are now acquiring and punish him politically as much as is possible.* He is sure that that is exactly what Congresswoman Stowe and many of the now ex-pat Congresspersons want.

"Would it be such a bad thing if the IMs remained asleep

for a little while, Honey?" the President can hear his wife, Helen, say in his mind from one of their recent private conversations.

"Helen," he had said, "it may feel good not to have them around and gain all this new stuff, but we've got to look at what's best for the good of the nation, short term and long term. Plus..." he continues "many of our dearest friends and families are now asleep. That's not good for them or us" he had concluded.

Baron Douglas knows that his wife's statement had been her gentle way of making him look thoroughly at both sides of the issue. *Her Harvard law degree works too*, he knows, and he needs her critical eye now more than ever.

President Douglas is not completely dismissive of the arguments that he hears more and more about the IMs remaining asleep. In the news, more and more discussion about a strange kindof Black and Brown PTSD that had arisen in many as a function of many of the property transfers. It is described as a combination of both anger and high anxiety at what many had discovered abouttheir IM counterparts. Of course, for the most part, it is known that American IMs are wealthy, but the property transfers from them to SMs had brought that wealth into experiential focus. SMs had discovered and continue to discover that many IMs are so wealthy in comparison to what a typical SM has known that it had shocked and offended the conscience.

In addition, the kind of wealth now being transferred to SMs had been wholly unknown for them. In fact, for most SMs in America, there is no personal historical context for the property and attendant that they'd received. The President believes that the property and wealth of the IMs are so much that it literally could not all be transferred to the SMs. There's too much of it, including real estate, businesses, and personal effects. A few months ago, neither the President nor his team had appreciated the extent or amount of the property to be managed. Once its volume came into focus, President Douglas created a separate, albeit temporary, agency to manage the transfers and account for it all called the Property Reclamation Department. He made the first head of the PCD, a Hispanic woman named Marquita Sosa, its first director. So far, she had done an exemplary job.

We've got massive problems in front of us whether the IMs

awaken or not, President Douglas thinks to himself. Mexico is a problem. Their aggression cannot go unanswered. The attacks on their economy from Russia, Europe and China are a problem. They're attempt to wrest control of the fiat currency standard from America is a non-starter. *We will need bright minds to help us keep that from happening,* the President thinks. *It will require innovative thinking and action.* "No one thinks that we'll be successful", he says audibly to himself as he rubs his chin and looks at his watch.

His private time of meditation is almost up, he realizes. He has a meeting starting in fifteen minutes in this very room. There are additional policies that he wants enacted now before the IMs wake up or before the next six months are up, whichever comes first. With his expansive new powers, which are temporary, he knows that he's on the clock to get done what he should have gotten done in the previous seven years of his term: irreversible universal healthcare, universal income for low-income earners--which will be used to aid the millions of new immigrants who have arrived and are coming to the country, further infrastructure upgrades, and the elimination of all existing American debt, to name a few.

President Douglas considers it strategically prudent to lower and rid the nation of its debt in this climate, especially to nations like China. Though their working population had been dramatically reduced, they still have the ability to address and pay off the trillions of dollars owed to foreign debt holders. *This will be done,* he thinks, *through right-sized taxing of the rich and wealthiest among them and other innovative taxing mechanisms that most folks would never see or feel.* Wall Street, however, will see and feel them though, he knows. Folks like Donnie Hernandez and the White House financial advisory board that he had assembled are helping him to think that through. In fact, President Douglas expects to see and meet that team face-to-face later today. He looks forward to the meeting. Now to shave and change into one of the suits that Helen had picked out and his valethad prepared. He can't wait.

* * *

Trevor Campbell is well aware of what his friend President Baron Douglas thinks and believes about the IMs waking up.

He vehemently disagrees with him, however. Trevor is an ardent student of American history. As such, he knows that America had literally been built upon the theft of property and land from the Native Americans and then on the backs of enslaved Africans to cultivate it. For this theft and enslavement, not one penny or reparation had been paid in compensation.

In fact, he thinks, *the mere mention of reparation for, in particular, Black people in America had often been ruled out by previous political powers and American society as a whole.* Now, however, six months after Sleep Day, reparation is exactly what had been occurring so much so that the government had to step into help manage it. *President Douglas can't stop this train,* Trevor thinks, *nor should he. Our time to reclaim what rightfully belongs to us is now.*

Trevor had not himself grown up in Jim Crow America, but he is keenly aware of his great grandparents, grandparents, and parents' trials in Jim Crow. His grandfathers fought in World War II, one in the Pacific theater against the Japanese and one in Europe. Both had been denied access to the GI Bill when they had returned from the war, unlike each and every one of their white counterparts returning.

By the GI Bill, the country had provided a massive wealth transfer to its white male returning soldiers that added generational wealth to them, enabling almost all to buy property, homes, businesses and obtain free education. Such opportunity was denied to the Black, Brown, and Asian soldiers who fought right alongside their white counterparts. This kind of racism is and had been systemic, organized, and intentional.

Once Trevor saw how President Douglas would land on the issue of IM revival, he had decided to keep his thoughts and opinions to himself. *Too much is at stake,* he thinks, *and I now have too much power to risk losing it.* Because of the shrunken numbers in the intelligence community due to the Sleepers virus, President Douglas had consolidated all of the intelligence agencies and federal level law enforcement under the umbrella of the NSA. At the time of his decision, it hadn't made sense to try to maintain the multiple agencies with so few to populate them.

President Douglas considers this a temporary assignment, but Trevor has other plans. With the full view of all American intelligence and full law enforcement authority, he can do almost anything he wants. *At the least,* he thinks, *he can make moves and decisions that can escape close scrutiny. Losing two-thirds of the American population to the Sleepers virus has had and will have its advantages.*

Trevor knows that he must be careful, though. It's clear to him that Helen, the President's wife, does not trust him. She had been cordial and even affectionate toward him for many years, but Trevor had recently observed her observing him and felt a chilly distance forming between them. *She's astute*, he thinks. She knows without knowing. She sees without seeing. If he is to co-op more power and further secure his position, he'll have to move and speak more stealthily than ever before.

As Trevor looks at it, now is the time to take from the country all that it owes the SMs. There will never be a better time than this, he believes, to reposition the social and economic order for the benefit of Black and Brown people. *It never could have been done before because of the IMs overwhelming numbers and penchant for genocidal violence,* he muses. No, he concludes, this is a gift. The Sleepers virus is a gift to us and for us if it is recognized and treated as such. Gifts can be squandered, but Trevor is determined not to let that happen.

Trevor decides that his most obvious first objective isto ensure that the IMs do not wake up. The destruction of Dr. Krauss' lab and his disappearance had been his idea, and it worked perfectly, except for one nagging detail. Krauss and all of his fellow researchers in Sweden, about fifteen of them, had been successfully rounded up and spirited away, all except for Dr. Jessica Lundgren. She had been tracked going into the building housing the lab, but she never made it into the lab itself. Trevor's operatives lost her in all of the commotion, but they're sure that she's alive.

Dr. Krauss' notes and samples had all been destroyed, but containing the knowledge produced for the Sleepers vaccine is also a priority. I must find Lundgren, and we must contain her. She will meet the same fate as Dr. Krauss and his fellow researchers, he decides, all of whom had been dosed with the Sleepers virus and brought back to the United States for storage.

Once we find her, we'll tag and bag her for storage, Trevor thinks coldly. In the meantime, he knows that he will have to hold the company line and appear to President Douglas to be on board with his plan to find a vaccine. Of course, Trevor refuses to let that happen. I'll have to protect my friend from himself, he believes. If he ever finds out, he'll hate me for it, but he and we will be better for it. Trevor resolves not to allow the President to find out.

* * *

Dr. Jessica Lundgren doesn't know how or why she stopped short of going into the laboratory in which she had worked tirelessly with her uncle, Dr. Krauss, for the last several months. Something seemed off, but she couldn't articulate just what.

It is a dark morning, it's early, and all appears too normal. Perhaps it had been the absence of the birds singing, which they normally did at this time in the morning to welcome her at her usual time of entry. Perhaps it had been the outline of several black vans that she hadn't recognized before, and that seemed to be watching her as she strode across the wide yard to the main research building. Maybe it was the electronic chirp that she thought she had heard but couldn't be sure it wasn't one of the birds that normally resided in the trees outlining the yard.

Whatever it was or was not, her teeth had been set on edge, and the hairs on her neck had stood up. Though her logical mind told her that all is well, her hidden senses tell her that all is, in fact, not well. The laboratory sits on the fourth floor of the main research building. Instead of taking the elevator, as she almost always does, she elects to take the stairs. This decision saves her life.

As she makes it to the door from the stairwell that leads into the laboratory, Jessica stops short of pushing it open. Her feelings of unease have only amplified, and suddenly, she thinks it better to leave the main research building altogether. She'll order a sweep of the grounds and the building and sort out who owns those vans and why they're here.

Before she reaches the first floor while still descending the stairwell, she hears the loud boom of the first explosion in the lab. As soon as she hears it, she knows exactly what has happened. *It's been blown up*, she thinks. Her heart now racing and her feet following suit, Jessica decides to follow the stairs all the way to the basement. By the time that she makes it to the basement, she hears the second explosion. It's bigger than the first and sounds like it might cause the building to collapse.

Now, Jessica's mind is racing. There are no explosives or explosive materials in this building or in Dr. Krauss' lab. Given the sensitive nature of his research, he would not allow them anywhere close by. She doesn't believe that there had been gas leaks and knows that there had been no report of one. Sensors throughout the building would have picked up any such leaks long before an explosion could happen. Jessica realizes that these explosions had been intentional, and if someone has targeted Dr. Krauss' research, he and everyone who has worked with him are also targets.

Dr. Krauss personally designed Pharmatech's research center in Switzerland. In his design, he made sure that all of the buildings would be connected by tunnels underground. He designed it in this manner so that employees could take the tunnels on cold days without having to brace for the cold or fight against the snow. Today she knows that those tunnels would be her saving grace. The people who blew up the lab are likely still here, and the vans that she had felt were watching her had humans in them who were doing the watching.

Jessica finds the tunnel in the basement that she needs. It's the one that will take her off the grounds of the research facility and into the woods behind it. She can't go back to her apartment. That is surely being watched, but she can try to make a quick escape off the grounds, through the woods and down into the neighboring town. Pharmatech's research center sits atopa high hill on the outskirts of Martigny, one of Switzerland's smallest towns. Though small and remote, it is modern. Once there, Jessica knows that she'll have access to a cell phone and perhaps transportation. She realizes that she will have to be careful.The people who blew up Dr. Krauss' lab may be capable of far worse. She believes that the lab had been empty at the time of its destruction. Typically, she had been the first person to the lab each morning, even beating Dr. Krauss there. She hopes that her uncle had not been there, but she's not sure. Sometimes, he had liked to surprise her with Swiss coffee and pastries on her arrival. Sheprays that this had not been one of those mornings.

Making her way to the end of the tunnel, Jessica cautiously, slowly opens the exit door. She hears birds cheerfully singing and chirping. *Good,* she thinks, *she's off the grounds of the research facility.* The sounds of the birds comfort her and cause her to believe that she's alone and had not yet been tracked. Martigny is a few kilometers away, but Jessica is in impeccable shape. She is confident that she can get there in just under thirty minutes.

Once there I'll make some calls and get some help, she thinks. She hopes that she's right. If the saboteurs somehow know that she never made it into the lab, they'll be looking for her soon. Shehopes that they believe that she's dead.

* * *

Dr. Krauss is asleep. Strangely, he is aware that he's asleep. He can hear everything around him, including the labored breathing of the two men carrying him and the curses of the one who slipped and nearly fell while holding him. He can also feel everything, including the cold air against the uncovered parts of his skin. He realizes the cold that he feels isn't like what he would feel if he were awake. It's a little less bracing, but he feels it nonetheless.

It then occurs to him that he shouldn't be able to feel, hear or think much of anything in a true sleeping condition. Dr. Krauss is thinking as clearly and lucidly as he would be if he were awake. How is that possible? He asks himself. This is sleep, he concludes, but it's something more. He struggles to remember what had happened to him last. He sees the explosion to his laboratory; he feels rough hands laid upon on; he sees and feels a black cloth bag of some sort lowered and tightened onto his head; he then feels a prick of something in his neck, and then he's out, but also somehow impossibly lucid and aware. *This is not sleep,* he realizes. *This is the Sleepers virus.*

The stunning realization of his current condition informs Dr. Krauss about many things. First, he's been knocked out by the

Sleepers virus, intentionally. Second, it could only have come from one of two places: either America or from his lab in Switzerland, and he doubts the latter. Third, though he cannot see his captors, he can hear them—they're American, and at least one of them is Black. He can tell that by the sound of the captor's voice. In his career, Dr. Krauss has worked with many People of Color throughout the world, including Africans, Afro-Caribbeans, Black Brits, Afro-Brazilians, Black Canadians, Black French men and women and, of course, African Americans. He's not sure, but they both could be Black. Dr. Krauss senses that he had been placed in avan, he'd heard the door slide open, and that its occupants are he, a driver and his two captors.

If, as he believes, the virus that he's been infected with did indeed come from America, Dr. Krauss thinks that the Americans, or someone high in government, doesn't want him to develop a vaccine for the Sleepers virus and that all of the changes ongoing there are meant to be permanent. Until this moment, Dr. Krauss had been weekly speaking with President Douglas, who often pressed him about speeding up his efforts and doing so before property transfers to the SMs had been made permanent. President Douglas sees the permanence of the transfers with the IMs waking up soon thereafter as an existential threat to the country itself. He believes that there would be or could be civil war if the IMs were to awaken any time after the one-year date of the Property Transfer Act within three years of that.

"I'm not going down in American history as the President, the Black President, who forced the country into its second Civil War, Krauss," he had often said to Dr. Krauss. "They won't read that on my epitaph. They might read it on yours, but they won't read it on mine," he had said bitingly to Dr. Krauss on their most recent encrypted Zoom call.

"Mr. President," Dr. Krauss had responded, assuring, "we're doing everything that we can. In fact, I may have some good news for you shortly. I know that you blame me for all of this, and you have a right to, but my team and I are working around the clock to come up with a vaccine. I think that we're closer than ever. Just please give me a little more time."

President Douglas was never satisfied with a request for

more time, knowing that time is in short supply, but he and Dr. Krauss both understood that time could not be forced to either speed up, slow down or replenish itself for some kind of do-over. All of that had been true before Krauss' abduction and the destruction of his laboratory and, presumably, all of his work. In his current state of both sleep and awareness, Dr. Krauss mentally kicks himself for not storing his work anywhere beyond his laboratory in Switzerland. *That had been a mistake,* he thinks, *and one that had made this espionage much easier to execute.*

He'd kept his research in one place because he neither trusted his competitors or the new people running his company in America and elsewhere. Many times, Dr. Alexandria Taylor had tried to gethim to make copies or at least share the results and research with her, but he had refused. He didn't trust her or the Americans. Now the research may be all but lost.

Shortly after being placed into the van, Dr. Krauss feels it stop. Next, he feels his two captors load him out of the van. "Be careful, Dude," he hears captor number one say, "he's an old guy."

"I got it, I got it," captor number two says in protest.

Soon, Dr. Krauss feels that he is laid down horizontally and strapped to something.

"Get him inside. We're wheels up in three minutes," a new voice says.

Inside of three minutes, Dr. Krauss feels the unmistakable sensation of motion within an airplane taxiing down a runway. At the plane's ascension, Dr. Krauss feels his equilibrium displaced as the plane takes a steep angle to climb into the sky, the whine of the plane's engines ringing in his ears.

He can detect that this is a small jet, a Bombardier of some sort, if his ears do not deceive him. His company owns several of these kinds of planes for himself and executive staff. *Dr. Krauss hopes that his captors have at least been good enough to supply their own air travel and not take one of his,* he thinks darkly.

Dr. Krauss does not question where he is going. He knows exactly what his destination is: America. He knows that whoever ordered his capture and his lab's destruction had not ordered his execution, which would have been easy enough to secure. Instead, he had been immobilized with the Sleepers virus, kept away from the possibility of finishing the vaccine for the virus. Whoever had ordered his immobilization and abduction had probably done the same for all of his staff, including his niece, Jessica. Dr. Krauss does not know whether Jessica had been in the laboratory when it exploded. In his lucid state, he tries hard not to consider that as a possibility. Dr. Krauss doesn't want to experience a panic attack in his current state, fearing that it could drive him insane. Resigned to his fate, Dr. Krauss allows the drone of the engines to carry his mind away as he wishes for a sleep and a rest that may forever escape him.

* * *

Jessica peers out from behind a small dumpster that sits in an ally of the town of Martigny. She had made it to the town easily enough and had not been followed. She'd decided to try to hide in plain sight in case her would-be pursuers had tracked her here. Though sparsely populated, the town is dense, and its inhabitants are out on the streets shopping, eating, and enjoying the morning.

Rounding a nearby corner, she stopped short in her tracks when she'd seen one of the two vans that she had seen earlier at Dr. Krauss' research facility. She thought it the better part of valor to use her perch from the alley to observe the van and its occupants, if any. The citizens of Martigny walked and milled about, seemingly, without a care in the world. *Of course they are*, she thinks. The research facility is several kilometers away. There's no way that they could have seen or heard the explosions from her laboratory.For them, this is just another ordinary day. For Jessica, everything had changed.

Jessica sees one of the van's occupants exit the passenger side of the van. He is tall, very pale, and dressed in obvious black military fatigues. He looks warily about but doesn't seem to be looking for anyone. Jessica sees him dip his head back into the van's passenger side window for a moment and thereafter cross the street. A few minutes later, she sees him emerge with a drink container holding three enclosed coffee cups. Is this a coffee run? She asks aloud to no one. Soon, Jessica watches as the van pulls away from his parking spot and drives slowly away. The route that it's taking leads directly out of the town and onto its main road away from it. Exercising an abundance of caution, Jessica waits a few more minutes in the alley until she's convinced that the van and its occupants have fully departed.

She makes a plan in her head: I've got to get to Lionel's flat. I've got a change of clothes there, and I can use his cell phone. Lionel is her on-again, off-again boyfriend for the last two years.

They're mostly just good friends, and dating him had been an easy, safe partnering given her work schedule and penchant for notwanting to be tied down. His place is just three blocks away. She knows that she can make it there in no time. Arriving at his flat, Jessica decides to take the back stairs into it. He lives on the third floor, and she readily makes the climb up. A back door leads to his place that is locked. The hidden key is still in the place in which she had just left it. She needn't have hidden it. There is little to no crime in Martigny, but old habits die hard.

Stepping into the flat, she finds Lionel asleep on his bed. He is alone. She is glad for that. She decides not to wake him. Tiptoeing into his kitchen, she finds his cellphone. This is where he usually keeps it. Jessica sits at his small coffee table in the kitchen. She is unsure who to call first. Her uncle is almost sure to be unavailable for one reason or another. Besides, she reasons, if she has would-be captors, they will have gotten to him already. Jessica then decides that whatever fate Dr. Krauss has met is similar to that of all of her fellow researchers from the laboratory. She is alone, and of course, she cannot involve Lionel in whatever espionage event that this is. She isn't sure of the motivesof the saboteur, whether they intend on taking her life. At present, Jessica needs a plan, and she doesn't have one.

"Good morning, Love. What are you doing here?" Lionel says. "I thought that I wouldn't see you for another week." Lionel stands at the entrance of his kitchen shirtless with just his pajama bottoms on. He is tall, lanky, pale, and his hair is a disheveled, dirty blond mess.

"I'm sorry, Lionel. I didn't mean to wake you," Jessica says. you."

I always felt Jessica wonders again for the 85th time why she hadn't just given Lionel her whole heart. He is patient, kind, and put up with her on-again, off-again shenanigans for the better part of the last two years. He lets her run the show completely. It's unfair, but it is also what she has needed. Her first marriage had been a disaster. She's driven professionally and, frankly, is not all that keen on the idea of having children--a fact that had caused her to be estranged from her mother. After the first one, Jessica doesn't see herself as the marrying type, but she does love Lionel, she admits—after a fashion.

"Lionel, I needed to," she hesitates before continuing, "pop in for a bit. Just some morning coffee and maybe a muffin if you have one," Jessica says.

"Coffee I have in abundance, muffins I do not. But I can go and get you some if you like," he says.

"Sure, Lionel. Please do." Jessica thinks that it will be a good thing for him to step out for a bit. She needs some time to think and could use the twenty minutes that she knows he'll take to hit their favorite pastry shop. Plus, she needs a quick shower. Her run through the woods from the research facility had made her sweat and smelling a bit rank.

While Lionel is gone, Jessica hops into the shower, washes, and then dresses into a dark grey jogging suit that she had left here weeks ago. It is clean and comfortable, its cleanliness due to Lionel's expert washing. *He really is a gem,* she thinks. A few minutes later, she hears Lionel's unmistakable tenor voice calling her. She lays reclined onto his bed and had nearly dozed off.

"Love?" he says. "I have your muffins."

"Coming," she responds.

"Strangest thing, Jess," he says when she reaches the kitchen. "There was a strange black van parked outside of the pastry shop. That's not so strange in and of itself, but all of its windows were completely blacked out, fully opaque, and when I walked by it into the shop, I had the unmistakable feeling that it was watching me. Very strange indeed."

Jessica's face had gone stark white, noticeably so. Lionel sees it. Jessica knows that he sees it because he looks at her with grave concern.

"What's wrong, Love?" Lionel asks.

She doesn't respond verbally. She shakily sits down in the chair closest to her. Lionel sits across from her, leans in, and holds her hands.

"Jessica, what's wrong? What's happened?" he asks earnestly.

"Lionel, there's been an explosion at the research facility.

Everyone may be either dead or..." she hesitates, "taken. They may have been taken. I don't know which. I think that black van is here for me. I think they know who you are and what you are to me. I'm worried that I may have put you in danger."

Lionel, still holding Jessica's hands, leans back from here. Jessica is unsure what he's considering. After a long moment, he says to her, "You need to leave. We need to get you out of here. Give me a moment to pack some things. We'll go in a few minutes."

Jessica is instantly relieved and happy that Lionel is helping her. She is concerned too. Now, he's involved and whatever fate awaits her awaits him too.

No sooner had she finished that thought, they hear a loud crash. Startled, Lionel and Jessica look up to see two large men dressed in black standing at Lionel's door. Jessica stands up and grabs Lionel.

"We leave now!" she says as she pulls him towards his back door. Too late, she sees. Two more men are standing there. *Now it's a problem,* she thinks. Now, they're in trouble.

CHAPTER V

Ever since his transformation, Stanley's dreams have not been good. They'd been nightmares. It had been a little over a week since he'd transformed. He hasn't been able to sleep well since. Once he'd made his way home, he went out into his small town. He wondered what he might find. Everywhere that he went, he found people who would not wake up. Stanley had found some in pretty dire conditions whom he had rescued. Of course, he knows everyone as everyone knows him. His town only has about five hundred people. He'd grown up in this town and probably been in every single house that outlies it.

Stanley doesn't know what's happened to him or the town's inhabitants, but it's clear to him that it's significant. It affected everyone that he'd found, except that he is the only one who woke up with brown skin and dark hair. Looking at himself in the mirror, Stanley sees that his eyes had not changed. They are the same pale blue eyes that he'd always had. His now darkish skin and hair form a stark contrast to his eyes. The image before him in the mirror is foreign and alien. Except for his eyes, he looks like a black man.

What had happened to turn him black? Stanley wonders again for the thousandth time. Stanley is distraught. He is alone, and communication is spotty at best. His favorite television channel is blank. He refuses to watch or listen to any of the liberal, lamestream media. None of his favorite radio stations work. The one and only time that he had passed by one of the cable news stations that he hates, his worst fears were confirmed: everyone he'd seen is Black or Brown. *All of the white people seem to have disappeared,* he thinks. *Did the race war happen and I'd missed it,* he wonders. *Nah, that couldn't be it,* Stanley believes. None of the folk around here are actually dead, he remembers, plus, he's still alive, just black. Everyone else is asleep.

Since the happening, as Stanley had taken to calling it, had occurred, he tasked himself to find and collect as many townspeople as possible and securing them in their respective homes. He is alone in his efforts because all of the town's emergency service people had likewise been affected and are all asleep. Doing the work by himself had been exhausting, as well as heart-wrenching. Stanley knows all of these people, some well, some not so well, but to him, each makes up a piece of the fabric of his life and his town.

Once I find out what happened, he thinks after a long day of collecting and securing about fifty of his fellow townspeople, *somebody is gonna have to give me some answers.* Starting his day, Stanley elects to head out to the edge of town to visit some of the houses out there. It's sparsely populated, but he knows that he'll find some sleep folk. He doesn't know them as well, but he's committed to helping and securing them if they need it. Stanley is frustrated by the lack of help from emergency services. *I believe in small government, but this is ridiculous,* Stanley thinks bitterly. *It's just me out here.*

Stepping out of his small house that he shares with his father, Stanley checks his four-wheel ATV. It's full of gasoline and operating properly. He hitches a small trailer to it that he's used to move people he's found in precarious places. During this crisis, Stanley has both eaten well and been able to get gasoline, both for free, since there's no one to work the cash registers at the stores, restaurant or gas station. He slips on his backpack, which is full of water and snacks to give him fuel for the day. He has a shotgun just in case any bears are about and his favorite gun, a Glock 45, which he won at a shooting competition two years ago. He's ready to work.

He knows all of the trails between his house and the outskirts of town but elects to use the roads in case he comes across any car accidents or folks passed out along the road. It's getting late in the week, but Stanley is hopeful that whoever he finds is still alive and hasn't been eaten by any animals or otherwise died due to hypothermia. Rural Tennessee can be very cold in February, even freezing, he worries.

Stanley guides his ATV onto the main road leaving town, headed west. He travels at a moderate speed, not feeling the urge to rush. He wants to carefully observe his surroundings so that he doesn't miss anyone that could be lying beside the side of the road. That had happened to him a few days ago. At the end of one of his previous days going into the evening, Stanley had begun his return home along a road that he'd traveled upon at the beginning of his day. Now returning, he sees a flash of something on the side of the road, pulls up, and sees someone either asleep or dead laid out near the road. What caught his eye is a bit of reflective fabric reflecting the then dimming sun. Stanley checked and saw that this person, a woman, is still alive, but barely. She'd been out in the elements for the past few days. Stanley thinks that she's been lucky that no wild animal had been around to nibble on her. He gathers her up and takes her home, guiding her securely and safely to the bed in his bedroom. He does not know this person, and she had no identification on her. There's no way for Stanley to tell who she might be. *The least that he can do*, he thinks at the time, *is to get her warm and comfortable*, which he does.

Later that same day, he sees a plume of smoke off to the side of the road on a bend of road on which he traveled. He then notices that several trees leading from the road have been splintered and some broken. *Car crash*, he thinks. Before Stanley sees the car, he thinks it must be a big one, maybe a truck. He can see the tire tracks leading from the road to the point where the vehicle had left it, possibly flipping over. Stanley does not know if the vehicle flipped, but he wouldn't be surprised if it had. He prepares himself for the worst in case there are no survivors.

Stanley wheels his ATV into the woods toward the plume of smoke that he sees still rising from the crash site. The vehicle, a large four-wheel Jeep of some kind, is indeed crashed and turned over. Though he sees it, he cannot yet see its occupants. *Hopefully*, he thinks, *the fool driving this thing had been wearing his seat belt.* If not, Stanley has less than high confidence that he'll be able to retrieve a living body.

Cautiously approaching the Jeep, Stanley parks about ten yards away from it and keeps his engine running. If there's any big animals out here interested in what's in there, Stanley wants to be able to make a quick getaway. The bears in this part of the woods are big and fearless, he knows. *No need losing his life over some fool who can't keep a Jeep straight*, he thinks.

Gingerly walking up to the Jeep, Stanley stops and takes a moment to look and listen. He can now see that there are at least two or three people in the Jeep. He also sees that all three remain enclosed inside of it, all having their seatbelts on. The Jeep is turned over and sits at an angle stopped against a tree. Stanley smells gasoline. He realizes that he may not have much time to get these folks out and away from the vehicle before it catches fire or, worse, explodes.

Abandoning his previous caution, Stanley moves quickly to open one of the doors to begin removing the vehicle's occupants. They all seem to be knocked out as he has found others in similar states. Opening the first door, he peers in and sees Sabrina hung upside down and unconscious. She's brown like he is. Is what happened to her the same as what had happened to him? he wonders. Stanley looks at the driver and the passenger, Solomon and Xavier, and sees that they're brown-skinned like the woman is. Though the woman's hair is straight like Stanley's is, the two other brown men's hair is curly, not straight. *They're Black*, Stanley realizes. *These are genuine American Black people*, he sees.

At this realization, Stanley hesitates. He's not rescuing white people who are asleep. He'd be rescuing Black people who are unconscious and possibly injured from this car crash. He doesn't like Black people. He thinks that they're the scourge of the earth, at least, the scourge of America. Now, he doesn't personallyknow any black people, nor had he ever met any, but he believes what he'd been told, all of his twenty-two-year-old life, about them. But these Black people, he thinks, aren't from here. They may have answers. Stanley needs answers. Making his decision, Stanley begins the process of carefully removing each from their restraints.

The woman is pretty, he sees, very pretty. The two men, who are obviously kinfolk to the woman, are tall and big, bigger than himself. *I'll have to be careful with these two bucks*, he thinks, don't want them to get the better of me. One by one, Stanley loads Sabrina, Solomon, and Xavier onto the trailer of his ATV. The men are heavy, but Stanley manages it well enough.

No sooner had he loaded the Claytons onto his trailer and pulled about fifty away from the Jeep that Stanley hears and sees a loud explosion. The Jeep is engulfed in flames. *Yep*, he thinks, *got these folks out in the nick of time; they should thank me*. Because the trailer is so heavy, Stanley knows that he can't travel quickly back to his house. That is where he has decided to take them. Since they're not unconscious in the way that all of the other townspeople are unconscious, they'll be waking up soon, he reasons. And when they wake up, they'll give me some answers one way or the other.

* * *

With her brother Xavier having a broken leg and now, possibly, broken ribs, Sabrina knows that she's on her own in her bid to find her other brother Solomon. She has no idea what state Solo might be in, but she suspects not a good one either from their crash or from the sounds of the yells that she had heard from him. *But Solo is tough,* she thinks, *football tough.* He played football all of his life and had been a bit of a stand-out in high school and college. He had not wanted to play in the pros, instead choosing to focus on his career in computer science. Unlike her, Solo is techie smart and a bit of a nerd. She and Xavier's nickname for him is "Nerd-Lo", a name that had stuck after he'd won one of his many computer science awards in middle school.

After their captor's recent introduction, Sabrina knows that she has little time to both escape her bonds and get to her brother. She checks the tightness of the duct tape around her wrists. They're tight, really tight. Though sore, she decides to stand up. She does so slowly, gingerly. She hurts like hell, but this is necessary.

Once standing, Sabrina sees that her wrists are suspended upon a makeshift hook connected to a chain that is wrapped around a beam in the ceiling. *First things first,* she thinks. Remove her fastened wrists from the hook. She does so, taking little time. Her captor had probably thought her to be more injured than what sheis, she concludes.

Next, Sabrina tries to wiggle her wrists beneath the duct tape to loosen it. This is particularly difficult since her hands are also substantially covered by the duct tape. The basement is dark, but Sabrina can tell that it's daytime. A little light pierces the darkness here and there from outside through a few of the gray, very old basement windows. Sabrina looks for a sharp object or surface that she can use to cut the tape away. There are no tools down here that she can use. There is, however, an old metal freezer tucked away in one corner of the damp basement.

Sabrina walks over to the freezer as quietly as she can. She's not sure if she had been able to deceive her captor into thinking that she is still asleep. At least, she had not received a hard kick to her ribs like Xavier had. Sabrina looks feverishly for a hard edge that she can use to cut her binds. She finds one and immediately goes to work. Unfortunately, the freezer's edge position that she uses to cut the duct tape forces her to turn her back to the basement door. She is wary about her captor returning and sneaking up on her. As she rubs the tape on her wrists and hands, she looks over her shoulder every few seconds to make surethey are alone. Xavier remains silent, and Sabrina is thankful for that. She knows that he's in a great deal of pain. *That can't be easy*, she thinks.

As Sabrina continues to labor, a small bead of sweat forms onto her forehead. *This is hard work*, she thinks. Suddenly, she hears a creak and stops moving. Her adrenaline begins to flow, but she forces her breath to be quiet and still. *So close! So close!* she thinks anxiously. Five more good rubs and she'll be free. Looking down at her hands, Sabrina decides to tear the remainder of the tape with her teeth. A couple quick tears should do it, she hopes. As she starts to tear the duct tape with her teeth, she looks up and sees Stanley standing at the basement's doorway, looking hungrily at her.

"I knew you were just playing possum, girl," Stanley says as he walks quickly toward her, baseball bat in hand.

* * *

"I wanted to call you personally to welcome you to the Secret Service, Mr. Gates," Agent Brooks says. "I'm not going to lie to you. Several on the committee wanted to exclude you because of your criminal history, but I advocated for you because I believe in you. Don't prove me wrong. See you Monday."

Raheem sits next to Candace during his brief call with Agent Brooks. The look on his face scares Candace because she can't tell whether her husband is happy or sad from disappointment.

"Baby, what is it? What's wrong?" she asks.

"Nothing, absolutely nothing is wrong. I just can't believe it. I got the job. I'm in the Secret Service!" Raheem exclaims.

"What?! You're in?!" Candace shouts. "You're in!!! Jaret, Angel, Pharaoh, come right now!!! Daddy got a new job!!!"

Their children come rushing into the room and jump on their father. He is more than happy to receive them and grabs all three into a wide embrace. He kisses them profusely, something that they pretend to hate, and tells them his good news.

"Kids, your father is in the Secret Service. I'm going to protect the President. At least, I may get the chance to do so," he says.

"Wow, Dad," Jaret, his oldest, says. "What does that mean? Are you going to be in danger?"

Raheem sees the concern in his young son's face. He sometimes forgets that his children and Candace were in a kind of prison when he was in prison. In his absence, they had done their very best to cope, but his absence left sizable holes in them all. He'd given them anxiety that will take years to dissipate. Jaret is usually the court jester of his children, but even he is awash in the kind of anxiety typically voiced by his siblings and his mother.

"My honest answer, Jaret, is that I don't know. But I do know that whatever happens, I'll be trained for it. Also, I won't take any unnecessary chances. None. You guys are way too important to me. I don't plan to go anywhere anytime soon," Raheem says as reassuringly as he can.

"We know that you'll do a great job, Daddy," Angel, his daughter, says. "I believe in you," Angel plants a sloppy wet kiss onto his cheek.

Pharaoh, his youngest, is barely out of diapers, and takes his tiny hands and puts his father's face between them. "Do a good job, Daddy. The President needs you," he says.

There is so much wisdom in this kid, he thinks. *It's crazy that he's just four now. Where had the time gone?* Raheem wonders. Seems like last week he was just three and barely talking. Raheem again questions whether taking this job is the right choice. His children's concern halts, for a moment, the joy that he'd just had at Agent Brooks' phone call.

"Raheem," Candace says, "you're taking that job. We'll be alright. Trust me. You were made for this gig. There's no one braver, stronger or more capable than you. Just keep your temper in check and your head clear. You got this. I believe in you."

Raheem's doubt lifts with his wife's encouraging words.

She's right, he thinks. *I am made for this. Hell, I'm built for this. That job is the right place, right time for me, and us.* Raheem knows that his salary will greatly increase with his Secret Service position. They're offering bonuses because they need qualified bodies since the Sleepers virus immobilized about ninety percent of its staff.

"Okay, kids, we're going for ice cream to celebrate. Don't tell your mother," he says, winking at Candace, who starts to protest but thinks better about it.

"Dinner will be here when ya'll get back," she says. "And Raheem, your dessert will be waiting," Candace says with a mischievous twinkle in her eyes.

* * *

Stanley can't believe his luck. He'd thought that he heard something but wasn't sure. He didn't think that the other big guy in his basement would give him any information since the other one tied up in his room hadn't. The one that he had attempted to interrogate, based on some show he had seen years ago, hadn't cracked at all. He'd yelled but not spoken. *Tough SOB,* Stanley thinks. But with the woman now up and apparently trying to escape, Stanley thinks he'll be able to get some info out of her and maybe a little more.

He quickly closes the distance between the basement door and where she stands. Stanley sees that her wrists and hands are almost free. She is obviously trying to bite through the rest of her binds, he sees. *I'll have to do a better job binding her up next time,* he thinks. He carries a baseball bat with him just in case, mostly for show, but he doesn't think that he'll need it. The woman is shorter than he is and athletic looking, but not skinny. *Shouldn't be a problem at all for this 'ol country boy,* Stanley believes confidently.

He approaches Sabrina and reaches out to grab her hands. He never sees the kick coming but feels its result. Sabrina kicks him so hard in his stomach, Stanley bends over at the waist and drops to one knee. The baseball bat that he'd been holding falls out of his hands as he doubles over, the wind completely knocked out of him. As he lifts his head to draw a breath, he sees that the woman's hands are now completely free and that the fire in her eyes means that he'd made a tragic error. It wasn't the big guys that he needed to fear, but this woman. Stanley doesn't have time to think his next thought. Sabrina swings her left elbow so hard to his temple that he blacks out when she connects with the side of his head. If Stanley had had time to think, his last thought would have been 'night-night, Stanley'.

* * *

Sabrina sees her captor leering at her from across the basement. Her hands are still partially bound. She has seconds to free them before her captor reaches her. He carries a baseball bat inhis right hand. Sabrina prepares for an attack. She is not afraid. Sheis aware, and she's pissed.

Whoever this brown-skinned, blue-eyed man is, he is violent and apparently intends to exact more violence upon her. Forherself and for her brothers, Sabrina is determined not to let that happen. She's almost free. She just needs a couple more seconds, and she'll be all the way there.

Her captor is no more than two steps away from her when she feels the last section of the duct tape tear away from her wrists. They're sore and raw from the tape, but she's free. At one step away from her, Sabrina plants her back foot behind her and closes the distance between her and her captor with a well-placed sliding front kick to his gut. As predicted, her captor folds over like a cheap suit. Xavier had taught her that kick many years ago before she had entered adolescence.

"Trust me, Sis," he'd said. "You'll need this kick in your life someday. I pray that you never have to use it." Sabrina is thankful that she'd listened, learned and trained.

She sees the baseball bat that her captor held fall from his hand and roll away. *He must have thought that he didn't really need it,* Sabrina thinks. Bad choice. She knows that she's not done. Her father had always told her to execute redundant attacks until the threat is completely disarmed. Her attacker, knocked down onto one knee, looks up at her with recognition and fear in his eyes. *He's right to be afraid,* she muses. *He has no idea what he's stumbled upon.*

Sabrina steadies herself and throws the hardest left elbow

directly at her captor's head that she's ever thrown. Her goal is to knock him out, but she also knows this is a potential killing blow. *If he dies, he dies*, she thinks angrily. In truth, Sabrina is no killer. Right at the point of contact, she takes a little force off of the blow, ensuring that her captor does not die. Instead, he drops like a bag of wet potatoes, completely knocked out.

Sabrina watches Stanley fall in a heap and knows that he's out. She finds the bat and picks it up. She considers using it to break one of his legs but thinks better about it. *He should be out for a while*, she thinks. *And if he wakes up, he'll taste this bat*, she decides.

Sabrina turns the man over and checks his pocket. He has a pocket knife stuffed into his jeans. She takes that, walks over to Xavier and frees him from his binds.

"Xavier," she says. "You're free. Are you awake?" Sabrina asks.

"Yeah, I'm up, but I hurt, Sis. I don't know if I can walk," Xavier says.

"Okay, I'm going to sit you up. Slowly."

With great effort, Sabrina sits Xavier up. He groans in pain the entire time. "Yo, this hurts like hell, Sis. Dude really worked me over. Hey, where is he?" he asks.

"He's over there," Sabrina says, looking over her left shoulder pointing to where their captor laid.

"What did you do?" he asks incredulously. "Did you do that, Sis?! Did you knock him the heck out?" Xavier asks excitedly, the distinct sound of pride resident in his tone.

"He's out," Sabrina says flatly. "He's lucky I didn't kill him."

Xavier looks at his sister and marvels at her. Who is this woman, he wonders. Clearly not just my little Sis anymore. I can't wait to tell Solo. "Hey, where's Solo? Have you found him?"

"Not yet," Sabrina replies. "He's next. I don't want to leave you down here with him. You've got to try to stand up, X, and go with me."

Xavier reluctantly agrees with his sister and begins the arduous process of attempting to stand up and walk. After many grunts, groans and curses, Xavier stands gingerly on one leg. He leans heavily onto Sabrina, and she grunts loudly as a result.

"I can't put any weight on my left leg, Sis. It's definitely broken. I can feel it" Xavier says.

"That's fine. Just put all of your weight on me," Sabrina says through gritted teeth and a curse. "Let's go, X. We need to find Solo. I don't know what state he's in."

Xavier agrees and peers over his right shoulder to give Stanley, their captor, one more look. "Sis, are you sure he's not dead?" he asks.

"He'll live," she responds. He'll most definitely have a concussion, she believes, but also knows that their captor is lucky to be alive. His injuries could have been so much worse. "Let's go, X. The time is now."

Sabrina and Xavier shuffle over to the stairs leading out of the basement. Thankfully, they're short. Xavier, the bigger brother, is at least two hundred and fifty pounds, and he's all muscle, having maintained much of his playing shape since college. He tries not to overburden his sister, but it's pretty much impossible for him not to put most of his weight onto her. Any less, and he'd fall, taking her with him.

They reach the door at the top of the stairs, open it, and walk through with great effort. Stanley's house is a small, disheveled mess. Sabrina also sees that it's old, really old. There is a kitchen, a small living room and what appears to be two bedrooms, all of which are one level. There is no second floor. *Great,* Sabrina thinks. *I'm glad that it's small. I don't want to haveto carry this big lug another step while looking for Solo.*

Sabrina finds a large lazy boy recliner and deposits Xavier there. "Sit here, Bro. I'll go find Solo." She sees a hammer sitting nearby and hands it to him. "If that nut comes up here, whack him," she says.

"Oh, no doubt, Sis. I'll finish the job that you started, broken leg or not," Xavier responds.

Sabrina turns to the basement door to see if it can be locked. It appears to have a functioning lock, so she closes and locks it hoping that it holds should their captor re-awaken. Looking at the house's structure, Sabrina reasons that the yelling that she heard coming from Solo earlier probably emanated from one of the bedrooms. There is a short, cluttered hallway leading to the back of the house, and presumably, the bedrooms. Cautiously, Sabrina starts her search for her brother. She maneuvers around the clutter in the hallway until she gets to the closed door of what she thinks is the first bedroom.

With heightened awareness, she slowly opens the door. She is shocked by what she sees. An older man lies still in the queen-sized bed in the room. He looks almost dead. Sabrina takes several tentative steps into the room. There is no one in it except for her and the man. She moves closer to the bed but stops short of his reach and watches him. *There it is*, she thinks. *He's breathing. I can see his chest slowly rising and falling.* Straining, she thinks that she can hear him breathing too. It's very faint, but he is breathing, she concludes.

This is one of them, she thinks. That's a Sleeper, and he's probably some kin to their captor. This further confirms for Sabrina that what happened in California has happened nationwide. In their travels, she and her brothers had witnessed many who had succumbed to the Sleepers virus, especially on the roads and highways upon which they'd traveled. Sabrina decides to leave this Sleeper where he lays and backs slowly out of the room whilekeeping her eyes on him in case she's wrong and he awakens.

Closing the bedroom door behind her, Sabrina re-enters thehallway. She sees the door to the second bedroom which is about six feet away. Solo must be in here, she hopes. Reaching the door, she tries to open it. It's locked. *Never easy*, she thinks. *Things are never easy*, she thinks again ruefully. Sabrina takes a big step back, gathers herself and then, with one kick, kicks the door open, shattering partof the door frame upon which the bedroom door hangs. She had always been a hard kicker. All of her Muay Thai teachers had told her so.

With the door now open, Sabrina walks through it quickly, her concern for her brother causing her to abandon her previous caution. She sees what she thinks is another Sleeper laying on the bed in this room and her brother, Solomon. Solo is tied up and sits stooped over in a chair. He is unconscious and has apparently taken a beating from their captor. His face is bloody and bruised.

His left eye is puffy. Solo is not as big as Xavier is, but he is still a big man. Their captor would normally not have stood a fair chance against him. They must have all really been out of it from the car crash for them to be caught so unaware and helpless.

Sabrina hears a soft groan coming from her brother. She moves quickly to his side and begins the process of releasing his bonds from the exact same duct tape that their captor had used on her. It doesn't take long. Once released, Solo nearly falls to the floor, but she catches him and stops him from falling.

Sabrina works to free him, and she checks for obvious damage. She is most concerned about him having any broken bones. She knows that she'll have to gather her two brothers and somehow transport them from this place. She has no idea where they are but guesses that they're somewhere close to the crash site. *If that's true*, she thinks, *there may be a town of some sort nearby.* Her job then, she decides, is to get Xavier and Solomon up and out of this house all while keeping an ear out for the captor who could, conceivably, wake up at any moment. Sabrina knows that she hadn't killed their captor, and given their dire situation, begins to regret that choice. You're not a killer, Sabrina, she reminds herself. Her best Muay Thai instructor and her father had trained her well beginning with the precept of 'self-defense' vs. 'self-offense'. "You're not a killer", she says softly to herself.

"C'mon, Solo, it's time to go," she says. Sabrina is thankful that Solomon is not as big as Xavier is but soon realizes that she'll get less help from him than she did from X. He's out cold, she sees. She'll have to pretty much carry him out of this room and out of this house, she sees. *Sucks to be me*, she considers bitterly and begins to do the hard work of picking her brother up. Once Sabrinaraises Solo to a near-standing position, she leans him onto the rightside of her body, her strongest side, and begins the slow, arduous shuffle from the bedroom. Once out of the bedroom, they shuffle, awkwardly, down the hall. Sabrina stops two or three times in the hallway to catch her breath and to listen for their captor. She believes that he's secure in his basement, but she trusts nothing at this point.

"Xavier," she calls out breathlessly.

"Yeah, Sis. I'm good. Not a peep from 'ol boy. You have Solo?" Xavier asks.

"Yes," she says, grunting, "I have him, but he's knocked

smooth out. No broken bones that I can tell, but he's out, probably concussed. He took quite a beating."

"Sis, keep walking towards my voice. We need to get out of here. I see something outside," Xavier says.

Sabrina can hear the rage in her brother's voice. Xavier is the biggest and the oldest and had always been highly protective of his siblings. No one who knew them could in any way bully them without threat of violent retribution. Her father had always dissuaded X's heavy-handed actions on their behalf, but in this one area of their family, Xavier had always been willing to bear any punishment available to protect his brother and sister. It wasn't until he had seen Sabrina beat up a grown man in one of her Muay Thai competitions that he stopped being so protective over her.

Xavier had been more than impressed. "You've got a real gift there, Sis. Dang near looks like you could do this professionally. However, no need to talk to Mom and Dad about that. I shan't allow it," he'd said, folding his arms and looking down on her knowing full well that she could probably kick him any which way but loose any time that she'd want to.

"Okay, X," had been her only reply. He'd gone away happy knowing that he needn't worry about her on any of her dates.

"X, what do you see?" Sabrina asks.

"An ATV with a trailer hitched to it. It's right out front. I think that Solo and I can just about fit into it, and you can drive the ATV," he says.

"That would be great if it were true. Let me get Solo loaded up and I'll come back for you," she says.

"Nah, Sis. You've done quite enough. I have the baseball bat. I'll use it as a sort of crutch and waddle my big butt on out there. I've felt worse. Trust me," Xavier says determinedly.

Sabrina knows better than to argue. Once X makes his mind up, that's it. It's usually a wrap, and frankly, she's already too tired and sore to reject the help of his independence. She sees that the front door is about eight feet away from where she stands with Solo slumped over her. She pulls him closer and continues their shuffle walk to the front door. As she reaches it, she hears Xavier begin his work of aligning himself upward as he begins his own, curse-filled stumble to the outside.

Thankfully, the ATV is right outside. *Now,* Sabrina thinks hopefully, *if it has gas and a key, we might be okay.* Opening the front door, Sabrina measures her next steps in her head. *I should be there in about ten steps,* she thinks. *This is harder than when I pushed Roscoe, much harder,* she acknowledges. Longing for a wheelchair but seeing none, Sabrina slowly shuffle walks with her brother until she reaches the trailer. She gently lays him down and makes sure that Solo's head is protected. Remarkably, Xavier soon joins them and lays himself next to his brother, the concern on his face evident.

"I think that he has a head injury, Sabrina. We need to get him to a hospital right away," Xavier says.

Sabrina does not respond. She knows how dire Solo's situation is. She'd listened well enough to Michael, her fiancé, enough to know the most obvious symptoms of a head injury. What she further suspects is that her brother may not just be unconscious. He may be in a coma. If that's true, she fears, time is of the essence. They must leave now and find alternate transportation on their way to finding a hospital. This ATV just won't cut it for as serious a trip as theirs'.

"I'm going to find the center of whatever town exists, X, and then find a vehicle large enough to transport us all safely.

Hopefully, we'll be at a hospital by sundown," she says.

"Sounds right, Sis. I could use some medical attention too," he responds.

Sabrina climbs onto the ATV after making sure that her brothers are secured. She sees the keys for it already attached to the ignition. Of course, he never takes them out. Why would a good 'ol boy like him be worried about somebody stealing his ATV, she wonders silently to herself. Starting the vehicle, Sabrina is glad to see that the gas gauge is on half. That should be enough to do what we need to do, she hopes. Sabrina slowly engages the throttle and starts the bumpy ride down the dirt road leading to their captor's godawful house of torture. She does not look back but decides that should they see their captor again, she'll make him regret it.

*   *   *

Stanley wakes up not knowing where he is. It's dark, and he's cold. His head throbs mercilessly. *This is pain level fifteen on a ten-point scale,* he thinks. Though conscious, cold and in the dark, he allows himself a moment to let his eyes adjust to the lack of light and to listen. His memories about what had happened to him begin to flood back. He'd heard a sound in the basement. He'dcome to check to see what it was. He'd seen the girl standing up and obviously trying to cut herself free. He'd walked over to her believing, erroneously, that she'd be easy to subdue. He had been wrong, and for his drastic miscalculation, had earned at least three broken ribs and a shiny new concussion.

Stanley is hurt, and he curses himself for his arrogance at thinking that he could have had his way with three captives and the girl in particular. *Whoever they are,* he thinks, *they're not weak.* He'd worked one of them over pretty well, to the point of unconsciousness, and he hadn't learned one new thing.

His eyes are now fully adjusted to the dark cellar. Stanley decides to sit up. As he gingerly raises his torso, the pain receptors in his head scream in protest, almost forcing him to lay right back where he'd just laid. By sheer force of will, he sits up and leans back onto his arms. He knows that he cannot stay down in the cellar all night. That would surely make him sick given that there's no protective covering down here, he knows. A few minutes later, he grabs the nearest vertical pole and pulls it to bring himself to a full standing position. *Okay,* he thinks, *so far so good.* It's clear to him that he is alone. Stanley is thankful to be alive. *She could have killed me if she'd wanted to,* he recognizes. *I didn't see either one of those blows.* Stanley faintly remembers that Sabrina had hit him twice.

Stanley is in tremendous pain, but he is determined to escape his own dungeon. Each step he takes brings fresh pain that radiates throughout his body. *I guess I really do need my ribs intact to walk right,* he thinks. He reaches the door and hopes against hope that it's not locked. He curses himself as he tries to turn the resistant doorknob. *Locked,* he thinks. *The damn thing is locked, and the keys are on the other side where he'd left them to keep his captives secure.*

Stanley knows that he has no good options and only one

choice. He must somehow, at an angle, kick the cellar door open. If the steps that I took caused so much pain, he reasons, kicking this door is gonna be far worse. Preparing himself for the worst, Stanley firmly grabs the railing leading to the door with his left hand, plants his left foot on a step and then kicks as hard as he can against the door. The door doesn't move, but he nearly passes out for the effort of the kick. Now, he begins to wonder whether being found in this dark cellar curled up away from the world might not be the worst thing that's ever happened to someone. With great effort, he pushes the seductive thoughts of his own quiet demise forcefully from his head.

After a few long minutes, Stanley decides that he'll try to kick the door open one more time. If it doesn't move or open, he'll resign himself to this quiet resting place. He takes a few more minutes to gather his will and focus. He thinks about the weakest point on the door and determines to aim for it with his right foot.

This time, he thinks, *I'll give it everything*. He has nothing left to lose. Stanley gathers himself, raises his right knee, kicks out, andup with everything he has using his left arm as a brace against falling. By some miracle, the door gives way and opens. Stanley doesn't celebrate. He's in excruciating pain.

That hurt more than the last time. Instead, he leans against the handrail and tries to catch his breath. His ribs are on fire, and his head hurts like hell too. *I've need a doctor*, he thinks. In the fog of his pain, Stanley shuffles out the front doorof his house. His ATV is gone, and he has no other transportation. He's a good three miles from the center of town, but that's his only hope. There will be cars there, he knows, and those folks' keys will be right in them, just like he'd left his key in his ATV. I hate to leave the folks here, but I've got to get some help, he decides. So, walk it is. Stanley is afraid to walk the three miles to town in the dark. Bears and cougars will be out.

Briefly, he considers going in the morning, but knows that he might be too stiff to move at all. If that happens, he's stuck and can't get help for days, or weeks or months. By then, it'd be too late. *Nope*, he decides, *you brought this on yourself. You should've just helped those people, not tried to hurt them.*

Stanley grabs his winter coat, the one that he hunts in, and his big bowie knife. It's not much, but it will provide some protection. Beginning the slow walk down the narrow dirt road that leads to his house, he hopes that he can get help for himself so that he can tell others about all the people in his town who also need help. *He's not sure that he deserves that help, but for their sakes, he has to at least try*, he thinks.

CHAPTER VI

Raheem looks at himself in the mirror one more time. He likes what he sees. He wears his best navy blue suit, starched white shirt and solid burgundy tie. His shoes, a pair of black tie-ups, look like polished glass. Of course, Candace had previously picked out and purchased everything. Raheem is grateful for his wife's good taste. Nothing had needed to be tailored. His athletic form perfectly fits the athletic cut of the suit. Raheem takes a moment to be impressed.

After a weekend of tossing and turning and all day and night discussions with Candace and the kids, he had decided to take the risk, show up on Monday and begin his Secret Service training. By 8:00 p.m. Sunday night, they'd known what their decision would be. Raheem had called Agent Brooks to confirm who, though subdued, registered his satisfaction with Raheem's choice. "Good job, Son. We'll see you in the morning. 8:00 a.m. Sharp." The click of the receiver is the only goodbye that Raheem receives.

Awake at six a.m. this morning, lying next to Candace, Raheem wonders whether he can or should get some couple time before he has to get ready. Candace is asleep. She's beautiful. She's at peace. He decides not to disturb that peace but rather to enjoy her having it. *I guess this is what being a husband is all about versus being just a boyfriend,* he thinks.

At six-thirty, Raheem decides to get out of bed and start his preparation. His now spacious bedroom has a cavernous master bedroom that he never expected to see in his lifetime. The shower had been built for two people and has six showerheads sending blissful rain from multiple directions. There's even a waterfall feature that allows for a literal waterfall to come down. Raheem doesn't elect to turn the waterfall on. He does not have that kind of time.

After showering for about ten minutes, Raheem steps out, dries, and begins his shaving process. He'd always had to be careful about shaving. His father had shown him a technique at how to get close shaves without fear of unsightly razor bumps.

"We can't shave like the white boys do, Son. That's for them. This is for us."

Raheem began shaving at around the age of seventeen and took his father's technique with him into the army and all over the world thereafter until his serving days were over. Crisp, clean and invigorated, Raheem is ready to put on the clothes that Candace had laid out for him just the night before. He can't wait to get dressed and feels his rising excitement.

This is the right choice, he thinks. *I'm going to do something grand with this opportunity.* In no universe would a job like this even be possible given his criminal record and potentially his skin color. It would have been hard enough to get this job even with perfect academics and no criminal record whatsoever, he knows. Finally dressed and ready, Raheem gives himself one final going over. He's ready.

"Raheem," he hears, "it's time, Baby," Candace says."Okay, Love, I'm coming," he says with a whiff of mischief in his voice. He had recently begun to call Candace 'Love' as a nickname. He had many pet names for her. He liked to switch it up. He thinks that she likes it too. It's a game they play. At most, however, Candace only calls her husband 'Baby' or 'Heem, the latter which he does not particularly care for. She's theonly one whom he lets butcher his name.

As Raheem marches to his front door, he sees all three of his children lined up in height order starting with the shortest to the tallest.

"Have a great day, Daddy!" they all say in unison. "We love you and we're proud of you!" they exclaim as one.

He looks at Candace who has a broad, toothy grin on her face. She had obviously arranged this little show for his benefit. *Candace is a trip*, he thinks, *but this is great.* Raheem hugs each of his children and kisses them on their foreheads. He reserves a tight squeeze for his wife and whispers an inappropriate compliment in one of her ears as he also squeezes her booty.

"Later," she replies and then ushers him out of the house. Raheem smiles as he begins his trek to the Secret Service headquarters.

The day is bright and it's already hot. D.C. summers are no joke. The official thermometer reads eighty-two degrees Fahrenheit, but the humidity makes Raheem feel like it's already ninety degrees. He's happy that the suit that he wears is lightweight wool and breathable. He's also happy that he'll be in an air- conditioned building all day, though he's not sure if that's strictly true. He hopes that it is, and wonders what his first day in the Secret Service will be like.

Soon arriving at headquarters, Raheem sees the large front doors leading into the cavernous lobby of the Secret Service. As he approaches the doors, he is surprised when he sees one of them open and Agent Smith standing there, apparently, to greet him.

"Good morning, future Agent Gates. Please take this and follow me." She hands him a small bag and leads him to a small room adjacent to the lobby. "Please step in here, change and come back. There are hangers in the room for your suit. You have three minutes," she says and closes the door behind her.

Raheem looks in the bag and sees a nondescript navy sweatsuit and a pair of Nikes. He quickly takes off his suit, shirt, tie and shoes and hangs them up. Sensing that his time is ending, he speeds to put on the sweat suit and shoes. As soon as he finishes tying up the second shoe, he hears an insistent knock at the door.

"Future Agent Gates," Agent Smith says, "are you ready to come out."

Raheem does not verbally respond but opens the door and steps out as instructed. "I'm ready," he says.

Agent Smith leads Raheem to the bank of elevators that he had taken before. As they step into one that is open, she swipes her badge in front of a pad. At such a swipe, Raheem sees three new floors come up on the digital screen, housing the floor choices. The three new floors read "SF1", "SF2" and "SF3". She selects SF3.

The elevator then descends. Raheem is only slightly surprised at that. When the doors open, he sees a cavernous room that is all concrete floors and pillars. *This must be where my training begins*, he thinks.

"Follow me," Agent Smith says.

They walk to an area near the back of the room. Here, Raheem sees about twenty other people all dressed as he is dressed. They stand in a line, shoulder to shoulder.

"Go and join that line," Agent Smith says. "You're with them," she directs.

Raheem doesn't quite appreciate Agent Smith's dismissive tone, but he jogs over to the line of apparently new recruits and joins them. There is an equal number of men and women. Most look, to Raheem, to be fit and to have been recipients of some former training. Raheem thinks that he can tell who might be ex-military and who might be ex-law enforcement. There seem to be equal numbers of each. *This should be fun,* he thinks. *A bunch of folks like me are ready to do the do. Hurrah.*

"RECRUITS!!" Agent Smith bellows. "ATTENTION!"

On instinct, each recruit, including Raheem, comes to attention and assumes military bearing.

"I am Agent Smith. I am your coordinator. I will facilitate your transition from recruit to agent within the Secret Service. Each of your backgrounds have been checked extensively. Each of you has been chosen, even if you believe that you've chosen us. You will spend the next three weeks learning the curriculum, the code, and the Secret Service culture. I will spend the next three weeks seeing if you are worthy of it."

Raheem can't help but smile inwardly to himself at Agent Smith's words. They hearken back to a time when he was in basic training for first the Marines and then the Special Forces after that.

"RECRUIT GATES!!! AM I BORING YOU!!" Agent Smith yells directly into Raheem's face. Standing at about five-foot seven inches, Agent Smith has to crane her neck to yell up to Raheem's six-foot five face.

"No, Agent Smith, you are not boring me," he says respectfully.

"Well, obviously I am. Why else would you have gotten that dreamy look on your $%#% face when I was just speaking!"she accuses. "RECRUITS, DROP DOWN AND GIVE ME FIFTY!!" she orders. The recruits, begrudgingly, move into push-up position and begin to crank them out.

Raheem is in great shape. He'd already done about two hundred push-ups when he'd awakened this morning as is part of his morning ritual. He finishes first and stands up first. He sees that some of his fellow recruits struggle with them.

"Recruit, Gates," he hears Agent Smith say. "Why are you standing when the rest of your fellow recruits are still down in position?"

Taking her cue, Raheem gets back down into push-up position and holds while he listens to several of his fellow recruits grunt and pant as they struggle to finish.

"Remain in position, Recruits," Agent Smith says as the last recruit finishes his push-ups. "Though I am young, and I am fairly new myself to the Service," she says, "I am also fully committed to our goals, our ideals and our mission. We have existed for well over one hundred and fifty years. We exist to protect this nation's top leadership. We exist to ensure that the President and his staff can do their job. The current crisis cannot dissuade us from that mission. It cannot stop the mission. It cannot make us," she pauses, "weak to the mission. You've never had a job like this, and you never will again. Toughness isn't enough. Skill isn't enough. Strength", she says, squatting down and looking directly into Raheem's eyes, "isn't enough. This job requires that you give the ultimate sacrifice, your life, on command if necessary. The spirit of that sacrifice is what we're looking for today and every day. If you don't have it, there's the door. If you think that you do have it, welcome to the next three weeks of your training. You may now stand up," she concludes.

Raheem stands back into position with his fellow recruits. He feels hardly tested physically. He sees, however, that he will be tested in his ability to sacrifice for the President and others, starting with this team of his fellow recruits. He scans them again quickly and determines that about half of them seem up to it. The other half is questionable. Given what he knows the gaps in the Secret Service happen to be Raheem reasons that they really cannot afford to lose any of them. They need all twenty-some odd of these recruits to help fulfill the Secret Service's mission. Raheem believes that none can be allowed to drop and determines that none will.

* * *

"Agent Smith, what is your first day's assessment of the recruits?" Agent Brooks asks.

"Recruit Gates is by far the strongest and most capable of them all, Sir, and he knows it," Agent Smith answers.

"Yes, he doesn't lack confidence. But can he be molded for

the mission, I wonder?"

"I believe so, Sir. I saw something in him today that I didn't expect to see, but it's early yet. It's 10:00 pm and I just let them go from training. Tomorrow will be worse. They have to be here by 0600. They'll be put through it for sure."

"Noted, Agent Smith. You know the program. You were the top recruit in your class. I trust you to bring these recruits through. We need every single one of them. Call me if you need me."

Agent Smith closes her laptop once her call with Agent Brooks concludes. She has a short ride to her rowhouse from Secret Service headquarters. She'll ride her electric bicycle a few short blocks to her home. *It's pledging all over again,* she thinks, as she recalls her time on line for her sorority at Spelman. *My prophytes would be proud to see me now,* she believes. *Oo-oop,* she says to herself and then walks to the elevator to begin her journey home.

* * *

Sabrina's ride with her brothers to the center of the small town in rural Tennessee is a rough one. More than once, she thinks that Solo might slide off of the trailer, but Xavier had managed to keep him close. Their combined weight served to keep them both planted though the dirt road into town is rough and bumpy.

Sabrina had never driven a four-wheeler before, but she sorted out its operations a few minutes into their ride. She finds what she believes to be the main road into town and follows it for a few miles until they reach the outcrop of buildings that form the town's center. She sees a church, a hardware store, a small grocery store, a post office and a few more buildings that indicate the town's existence. Once there, Sabrina begins to look for a suitable vehicle to transport her and her brothers to the nearest hospital, *wherever that is,* she thinks.

The town is empty. Sabrina drives slowly and cautiously down its main street. She doesn't think that they'll see their captor any time soon, but she's not certain that they are alone. She has the eerie feeling that the windows of the building are watching her. *It's just nerves,* she thinks. Regardless, she resolves not to let her guard down, just in case.

Sabrina sees an old, white pick-up truck parked in front of a small bank. *That might do the trick*, she hopes. She pulls next to it. The doors look unlocked. She hopes that the keys to it are somewhere around. It's an old Ford F-150. Her grandfather had had one when she was a little girl and he used to let her drive it around his farm since there were no cars and hardly anything to run into. It had also been a manual, which had been a ton of fun. Atten years old, Sabrina used to bounce around in her grandfather's truck with no adult supervision, much to the consternation of her parents. One summer, she had taught herself not only to drive but to drive a stick. She had gotten pretty good too. Her grandfather only had to warn her once about grinding the gears.

This truck, like her grandfather's, is a manual. *No problem*, she thinks. She hadn't driven that old rig in many years, but she's confident that it'll be like riding a bike. Sabrina dismounts the four-wheeler. She opens the truck's driver-side door and sits in it. She does not see the keys to the truck in the ignition. She pulls down the sun visor and bingo! The keys drop into her lap. She inserts oneof the keys into the ignition, and the truck starts right up. She is ecstatic. Next, she checks the gas gauge. They've got a little more than half a tank. The bad news is that in a truck this old, the gauge could be telling the truth, or it could be telling a lie. There's no way to tell until she starts driving. The good news is that because it's a stick, she can better manage the fuel that they use as they find their way to a hospital, which, she realizes, may or may not have any SMs to receive and care for them.

"Let's go, X. We'll load Solo into the back and lay him out flat. He needs the room. You can sit up front with me," she says.

"Cool, Sis. Great find. Let's get up outta here. This town gives me the willies."

Sabrina knows exactly what he means. They may be alone, but she has no doubt that the previous inhabitants of this town would not have warmly welcomed or received them where they were.

"I don't know where the people are," she says. "I have a feeling that they're now asleep. It's strange that we haven't seen any like we have in other places. The IMs, I mean."

"Yeah, strange," X says gruffly. "Let's just go." After a few minutes, grunts, groans and some effort, Sabrina manages to load Solo into the back of the pick-up and secures him comfortably onto the truck bed. He's still unconscious,so she does her best to keep him stable and not further injure him. X helps as best he can but doing so on one leg is excruciating for him. He insists on helping, however.

Once loaded, X hobbles over to the passenger side and gets in. Sabrina gets in behind the wheel, straps in, puts the truck in reverse and steers the truck out of town. She has no map and no phones to guide her, but reasons that the town's main road should take them out and eventually lead them to another, hopefully larger, road with some signage and some idea about where they are. She is thankful to have found the pick-up. Her hands remember how to operate a manual stick shift and they are soon traveling at good speed away from their previous nightmare. *I'm glad to be out of there*, she thinks. *I hope that we never see this place or our captor again. I don't even know his name. Good riddance*, she thinks again.

Soon, Sabrina and her brothers find a large road that leads them to a highway. The gas in their commandeered pick-up truck seems to be holding steady. She finds a sign for a hospital that indicates it being about forty miles away. It's in a city, she sees, Nashville. *That works*, she thinks.

'I've heard great things about the food in Nashville," she says to Xavier, suddenly remembering how hungry she is.

"I'm hungry too, Sis," he says. "Let's go get some help and something to eat. I'm famished," he says with a toothy grin.

That's her brother, she thinks. *Nothing gets between him and a good meal, not even a broken leg.*

* * *

Stanley is hurt. He's really hurt. The walk into town had been exhausting. It had been long, and it had been frightening. His body and his head scream at him in their distress. He had fallen down several times in the dark, injuring and re-injuring himself.

At least once in the dark, he had seen several pairs of hungry eyes staring back at him. He is amazed that he was not attacked by somefurry beast with sharp teeth. Perhaps they had felt sorry for him, he wonders. Either that, or they'd had enough sense to try easier prey since he'd held his bowie knife in his hand in open sight of any cougars, bobcats or bears.

Now, at the edge of town, he shuffles forward happy to see a familiar sight. He's known this town his whole life and though it is still and virtually lifeless, he's glad to see it. It gives him the courage to move forward, though slowly and with great care. He wonders for a moment about his previous captives. He doesn't see them nor any indication, yet, that they'd been here. Stanley thinks that if he were they, they would have come here, tried to find some help and then left in a better vehicle besides the one that they'd come in, his four-wheeler and trailer. He knows that they have injuries too. But the girl with them is strong. *Whatever their injuries, she will have gotten them here and out long before Stanley shuffles into town,* he believes.

He knows that he'll get no human help here. He's on his own. His best bet is to find suitable transportation and get to a town or city with a hospital. Stanley reasons that if the other towns have been affected, folks who look like he used to lookwill all be asleep like his town's folks. *The only place to get some help will be the closest city to him, Nashville,* he thinks. Stanley hates Nashville and had always hated Nashville. He had only been there two or three times growing up. *It is too large, too congested and too Black,* he thinks. His parents and grandparents had hated it. He hates it too. Still, it might be the only place that he can get help. Those might be the only hospitals that are open, he reasons, and I've got to get some help. *That woman,* he thinks to himself referring to Sabrina, *almost killed me. It's a wonder she didn't. Crossing her and underestimating her had been a supremely bad mistake.*

Stanley makes his way to the town's grocery store, which is across the street from the bank. The white pick-up, he sees, the Ford, it's gone. *They took the truck,* he sees. So, they're gone. *Good.* Stanley is glad to confirm that he truly is by himself. Thankfully, there is a small station wagon parked in front of the grocery store. *This is Mrs. Albertson's car,* he thinks. He had moved her and her small family from the grocery store where he'd found them and to their house. Stanley checks on them daily and several other families to hydrate them and make sure that they're still alive. Stanley thinks that taking Mrs. Albertson's car is a small sin to commit to get help for himself and ultimately for his whole town.

I can't continue to do this alone, he muses, *and especially not in my current state of injury. I'll go to Nashville, get patched up and let everyone know who's here and what help they need.*

Hopefully, they'll listen and we can save some folks. Stanley loads himself into the station wagon, finds the keys and starts the car.

It starts right up, and he is glad. Stanley knows that they're about forty-five miles away from Nashville and any main hospital that'sthere. *I'll be there in an hour,* he thinks. *Hopefully, whoever is there won't think me too strange.* Stanley points the car onto the main road and heads out of town. *Nashville or bust,* he decides.

* * *

Juarez is not safe to venture into during the daytime, much less at night as Darryl and his squad do on foot. After beating a quick retreat from the military base that sits right outside of Juarez, Darryl had decided to guide his squad into the city which is the opposite of what his would-be captors would expect. They don't know that they have no transport and would be expecting them to move in military Humvees back to the U.S. border. That way is sure to be cut off by the Mexican cartel and/or Mexican military.

Instead, Darryl had decided to enter Juarez, find an abandoned building or house and lay low until a Blackhawk or two could find them and fly them out. *It's a bold plan,* he thinks, *and one that could get them all killed. But hell running for the border would surely get them killed. They would surely be run down and murdered if they had done that. Their legs can't outrun the Mexicans on four wheels.*

Using the cover of darkness, Darryl and his squad move silently, stealthily from ally to ally and from building to building. They settle on an abandoned building just outside the center of the city. Because the cartel, Mexican military and Mexican police are all looking for them outside the city on the road back to the U.S. border, they encounter almost no one at this hour outside of their homes. The building is three stories tall and has one main entrance which had been boarded up. Darryl and his team quickly remove the boards but then just as quickly, reapply them once they are all inside. The building is dark, but their eyes adjust quickly to the lack of light.

Several of its walls have large holes in them. The bottom floor is concrete but is rife with cracks. A staircase leading to the second floor looks sturdy, but looks can be deceiving. Darryl stations his squad by every possible entry point and settles himself and his communication's soldier at the center of the building on the first floor.

"Get our position out to MILCOM, Johnson," he says to Private Johnson. "I want two Black Hawks here in an hour or less. They can drop in right outside of this building. The square outside is large enough for each to land one at a time. Make sure that they know that."

"Yes, Sergeant," Private Johnson says.

"And when you get done with that, show me the satellite images of our friends and where they are." By 'friends', Darryl means the cartel and Mexican military adversaries earnestly looking for them.

Private Johnson passes Darryl a pad device that shows him real-time satellite imagery of the position of the Mexican military, police and cartel members looking for them. "Pass their coordinates to MILCOM, Private."

"Yes, Sergeant" Private Johnson replies.

Darryl is unsure what MILCOM might do, but whatever it is, he hopes that it provides them cover to beat a hasty retreat back to the U.S. side of the border.

"Blackhawks are en route, Sergeant," Private Johnson says.

"Good," he replies. "We'll be home soon, Squad," Darryl whispers into his mic which everyone in his squad hears. "You've done great work tonight. I'll be sure to let everyone know."

He sees his squad in their various positions about the room looking at him with appreciation. Everyone here is far younger than he is. He's glad that it looks like they'll all live to fight another day.

* * *

"What are my options?" President Douglas asks his joint chiefs.

"Well, Sir," General Rodriguez begins, "our squad is holed up in an abandoned building in Juarez. They elected to go into the city, figuring that Mexican forces would be looking for them outside of it. We have their coordinates and have Blackhawk helicopters ready to retrieve them on your orders."

"Of course, General, get them now. But I want to also know what we should do with the Mexican forces pursuing them. What are your recommendations?" President Douglas asks General Rodriguez. "And that question goes for all of you, what do you recommend? We have a limited window to act. I'm biased toward action, especially if it helps our squad to get out."

General Rodriguez looks at General Phaylen Martin, the Joint Chiefs of Staff and most senior general in the room. General Martin clears his throat.

"Sir, if we strike on their position, the Mexicans, that is, that is a direct provocation of war with Mexico. We wouldn't be striking just the cartel, but the Mexican army and their police aswell. There's no way to spin that. President Lopez fully knows what we're capable of and what our technology provides us.

He's ex-military, after all. He'll know that we chose to fire on Mexican government agents and take the action as one of war." General Martin concludes his statement and sits back, watching the President's reaction. He thinks he knows what side of the fence President Douglas will land but hopes he's wrong. He's not wrong.

"You know, ever since we've been hit by the Sleepers virus, nations and individuals have been trying us. It's as if they believe that in the absence of our IMs, our white citizens, that somehow America stops being America and that we're just some toothless lion ambling about trying to find our way. North Korea, apparently, did not prove all that we intended it to prove."

"Mexico, Mr. President, is not North Korea. Mexico sits on our border. Mexico knows us. Mexico has no fear of the Sleepers virus. They've probed our strengths and our weaknesses. They're dangerous, especially in a protracted fight, and especially with our military at about one-third of its strength. I urge caution, Mr.

President."

President Douglas considers his General's words for a moment. He looks around the room into the faces of his other generals to check their temperature. "General Givens," President Douglas says, "what do you think?"

General Givens raises her head from her notes and looks directly at President Douglas. She sees a man with ever-graying hair and the slight beginnings of a silver beard that it looks like he's been trying to grow for a week or less. She notes the intensity of his gaze and sees that he is genuinely interested in her opinion. General Givens is the only female general in the room though there are several others not at her rank serving as support and as aids to her and others.

She feels a slight twinge of anxiety at what her words will be. She holds her own counsel and has not before now, shared her thoughts on Mexico, the Mexican army or any other would-be aggressor. Her words will either affirm or doom her military career. She quickly considers her options and then decides to give her version of the truth, the whole truth.

"Mr. President," she begins, "I think that we should hit the Mexican forces and their allies assembled here that seek our squad. Mexico is the first but may not be the least country that seeks to impinge upon our border. They still have several of our IM citizens, fifty-three, at last count. And they've killed at least a dozen of our IM and SM citizens. They've become ever bolder and use at least one of the cartels to do most of their dirty work.

How long before we see the Mexican army drive or fly into Texas under the Mexican flag to seek our land, people, and resources? A firm response now may remove the possibility of that, at least for awhile. We already know that melanated Mexicans have no fear of the Sleepers virus, nor should they. It does not put them to sleep."

General Givens stops speaking and allows her words to resonate in the room. She has given her best advice. She sees that half of the generals, General Martin included, do not agree with her. She also sees that the other half do agree or are at least neutral. This includes General Rodriguez. She's concerned about General Martin's bug-eyed reaction to her comments, but decides her career is not worth, as she sees it, the safety and sanctity of the nation.

"Rodriquez, what's your take?" President Douglas asks. "Mr. President, I agree with General Givens. A strike now could very well be taken as a provocation of war, but I'd argue that we're already at war with Mexico. They just forgot to overtly tell or make a declaration, but their actions, which have grown ever bolder, are clear declarations of war. And now, with our troops pinned down, it seems to me that we have no choice but to provide the cover and remove the immediate threat to their lives asthey retreat. Besides, Sir, Sergeant Darryl's squad has more than provided the necessary proof that we need to justifiably accuse Mexico of using their drug cartels to make incursions into our homeland."

President Douglas had guessed right. He had believed that General Rodriguez thought that a military strike against Mexican forces is the right thing to do but thought that he might need a bit of prompting. General Givens, who the President knows to be a bit hawkish, provided that prompting and cover for Rodriguez's comments. *General Martin may disagree,* President Douglas thinks, *but he's now outnumbered.*

"General Martin, I want a strike on the Mexican position now. I want it done before the Blackhawks get to Juarez. Use the drones. By my watch, we've got less than fifteen minutes to get it done. See to it."

"Yes, Sir, Mr. President." Turning to his support staff, General Martin gives the order to strike the position of the Mexican forces. He orders an immediate strike as soon as the drones are in position. Fortunately for the American forces, the drones are already in flight and had been placed in a holding position near the U.S. border. The strike is imminent.

* * *

"Great, we'll be ready," Sergeant Darryl Isaacs says. "I'm going to make my way to the roof to see what's happening."

"Be careful, Sergeant, those steps."

"Yeah, Private, I see 'em," Darryl says and begins to make his way carefully to the roof of their hideout.

On the third floor, Darryl gets a good vantage point of the city. He peers down at the street below him at the area at which the helicopters can land. They'll have to come in one at a time, he sees, confirming what he'd said to Private Johnson almost an hour ago. He expects the Blackhawks to show up at any moment. He hopes that they can get abound and aloft before anyone from the cartel, Mexican army or police are alerted. If that happens, it could be game over. Not much of a religious person, Darryl prays a quick prayer of help, not so much for himself, but for his squad's safety. *Let's see if anyone is listening*, he thinks.

* * *

Colonel Pérez leads the military caravan out of Juarez at high speed. He rides in a Humvee, leading a line of Humvees with Mexican military personnel. Close behind are several cars and Jeeps filled with cartel contract killers. Sandoval is with him. He curses him for his stupidity and his carelessness at allowing what must be American soldiers into Juarez to spy on them. The drone that they shot down, by luck, was sure to have ultra-sensitive spying equipment on it that picked up their conversation.

"How could you be so stupid, Sandoval? Is this the expert espionage work that I was promised when you were given your job? Your commanders will hear about this, Sandoval," Colonel Pérez had exclaimed for their entire ride.

Sandoval had a good mind to put a bullet in Pérez's head right now and would have if he thought he could get away with and explain it to his commanders who had ordered him to answer to this man. Sandoval is twice the soldier that he is, and he knows it, a fact that further agitates and grates on his nerves.

"Colonel, the soldiers, who we have not seen yet, are sure to be along this road. We've got about five more miles to the border. They may be traveling in ultra-fast, ultra-light vehicles to get this far ahead of us. We haven't seen any lights from them yet, though I would not rely on that. They're probably traveling dark, as we should be," Sandoval says with just the slightest sound of contempt in his voice.

"Sandoval," Pérez says, "when the word 'Colonel' is in the front of your name, then you can give me your opinion. Until then, keep those to yourself."

Noted, Sandoval thinks to himself and then wonders what

the ten-inch blade from his knife would feel like against this man's neck. He also begins to wonder whether their chase is a fool's errand and whether they're chasing ghosts. He knows that the drone that they captured is most definitely American. He'd examined it, quickly, for himself. He knows the type. That means that American soldiers are somewhere close by. He'd thought that they would retreat and would come this way back to the border.

But now, he's not so sure. *Wouldn't the Americans know that they'd expect them to take this route? And if the Americans had any doubts as to their ability to get back across the border before them, wouldn't they consider an alternative route,* he muses. At this last question, the eyes of Sandoval's understanding open fully.

"Stop the truck! Stop the caravan! Turn it around and head back to Juarez," Sandoval orders. "The Americans are not here! They're back in Juarez!"

"Sandoval, have you lost what good mind you have left?! Belay that order! Keep driving! We're too close to the border to stop now. We have to stop them!!!" Colonel Pérez says.

Sandoval coolly pulls his forty-five sidearm from his holster and aims it at Colonel Pérez's' head.

"Colonel, you are no longer in command. Good-bye." Sandoval then fires one shot directly into Colonel Pérez's head, killing him instantly. He then points the gun at the driver. "Turn the truck around now," he says with no hint of fear or excitement in his voice.

"Yes, Sir," the driver says.

There are at least ten vehicles in the caravan. It will take a minute to get it all headed back toward Juarez. Sandoval begins to think about what he'll tell his commanders about his need to kill the colonel. As he contemplates this, he hears a familiar sound. Drones. Two of them. Given his line of work, the sound is unmistakable. *We're too late,* he thinks. *The Americans are here. We'd underestimated them.* His last thought is of the glorious Mexican-American war to come.

* * *

Darryl sees a bright explosion that occurs outside of Juarez. He estimates that it is about three to five miles away. It's so bright that it's impossible to miss even though it's so far away.Darryl guesses that it's from one or more lethal American drones. He further guesses, accurately, that the Mexican forces and cartel members pursuing them are the targets and that those targets no longer exist. *This is their cover*, he thinks.

Seconds after seeing the explosion, Darryl hears the thump-thump-thump of the Blackhawk helicopters approaching. He sees two. He's relieved. Darryl hurries down the stairs to tell his squad that it's time to go. They quickly gather their things and then head out of the abandoned building in two-by-two formation, weapons up and hot. He directs one-half of his squad to board the first Blackhawk. He and the remaining squad with him provide cover for the first Blackhawk to take off. The second Blackhawk soon lands in place of the first one. The pilot disembarks and greats Darryl with her sidearm inher hand.

"I'm Major Jill Williams, Sergeant!" she roars over her helicopter's propellers. "Is there anyone else besides who's here?!"

"No, Ma'am!" he says. "This is it. We're ready to go!"

"Great then," Major Williams says. "Let's go now!"

Darryl and his squad board Major Williams' helicopter and they take off without incident. As they ascend, he sees the eyes and expressions of curious onlookers from the surrounding buildings and homes. He is happy to be going back to base, and to be going back home.

CHAPTER VII

Eighty years after Sleep Day

"What is your name, Child?" Samantha hears.

Her eyes are closed. She feels groggy. She feels disorientated. The voice speaking to her sounds like soft music. It has a strange soothing quality that is calming.

"Child, your name?" she hears again. "Samantha," she hears herself say. "My name is

Samantha...Robertson."

"Excellent, Samantha, excellent. Welcome back. My name is Ifé Anuoluwapo Eze. You may call me Ifé," she says.

When Samantha hears Ifé pronounce her name, it sounds to her like EE-fay.

"Samantha, can you open your eyes?" Ifé asks.

Samantha doesn't respond verbally. She is aware that her eyes are closed. In fact, they feel stuck. The sound of Ifé's voice makes her want to see its source. She is also aware of warmth being applied to her right hand. Is Ifé holding her hand, she wonders. It's warm. She likes the way that it feels.

With great effort, Samantha opens first her right eyelid and then her left one. When she does so, she is blinded. She is aware that she's in a room and that there's light. She perceives that the light is soft, barely there really. Yet, it is enough to make Samantha recoil in pain.

"That's okay, Samantha. We'll try again in a few minutes. Lights off," Ifé says.

"Why did you say that, Ifé? Lights off?"

Ifé chuckles softly. "The lights in this room were at their lowest setting, but it is still too much for your sensitive eyes. I've turned them completely off so that when you open your eyes again, you'll only have the dark and me to greet you."

"What's wrong with my eyes, Ifé? Where am I? Where are my parents?" Samantha says as fear and panic begin to beset her.

"Hush, Child. All is well. All in good time. I promise. Ifé is here to help and restore you. Are you ready to try your eyes again?"

The mere thought of enduring any more eye-related pain, for Samantha, makes her involuntarily recoil. Her curiosity about her condition and her whereabouts override her trepidation, however. "Yes, I'm ready," she says. Ifé smiles in the dark. *She already loves this girl,* she admits to herself.

"Okay, good. I'm with you, Samantha. Please open your eyes now."

The sound of Ifé's voice sounds like a song to her ears. She can't help but gravitate and respond to it. With great effort, which is more psychological than physical, she slowly, surely opens both of her eyes. Samantha blinks several times and tries to orient her vision. After a few moments, she can see the edges and contours of the room. She sees the outlines of Ifé's head and face. She smells her too. It is a rich, fragrant smell that calls to Samantha's mind the time that her mother took her to her favorite spice and tea store in downtown Birmingham, the Spice Hut or something like that.

Samantha can't completely remember. "You smell good, Ifé," she says.

Ifé smiles broadly at that. Her teeth are big and white. Even in this darkness, Samantha thinks that she can just make them out. And is that a glow, she asks herself. Ifé seems to be glowing a soft bronze outline around her form. Her eyes must be playing tricks onher, she concludes.

"Lights, level one," Ifé says.

Samantha sees lights around the room begin to glow softly, barely. Due to her still sensitive eyes, the low-level light seems as bright as the sun to her. She squints immediately but then allows her eyes to adjust to the minimal light in the room. After a few minutes, her eyes have completely adjusted. In the background, Samantha hears barely audible, soft music. *It has no words, but it's beautiful,* she thinks, *and soothing.*

Samantha sees more of Ifé's face. It is dark and rich. It reminds Samantha of dark coffee grounds in a freshly opened bag of Hazelnut coffee. Ifé has high cheekbones and full lips. Her eyes are large ellipses and warm. Ifé either barely has any hair on her head or none at all. Samantha cannot tell. She can only see her oval head as Ifé peers down at her. Samantha is aware that she's lying on a bed and that Ifé is holding one of her hands in her own.

"Lights, level two," Ifé says. Samantha stifles an involuntary recoil at the increased light but sees that she needn't have. In just the few minutes that she's been awake, her eyes have already begun to adjust and get stronger. She is thankful for Ifé's patience with her, but she is keenly aware that her questions have not yet been answered.

"All in good time, Samantha. I will answer all of your questions. I promise."

*Wait, did Ifé just read her min*d, she wonders incredulously. She sees Ifé smile at her surprise and thinks *yes, this woman is a mind reader.*

About an hour later, Ifé has raised the light level in Samantha's room all the way to six, which is apparently still low-level light, but about all that Samantha can stand.

"Okay," Ifé says, "let's test your hands, feet, legs and arms. We want to take it slow before you try to stand up. You haven't used your muscles in a very long time."

What does that mean, Samantha wonders. "What does that mean, Ifé, that I haven't used my muscles or eyes in a very long time?"

"Clever girl," Ifé says. "I see that you miss very little. That's very good. It means that you haven't had the use of your eyes or your body for a long time. You've been alive but not conscious. What do you remember?" Ifé asks.

"Remember? I don't know what you mean. Remember from what?" Samantha asks.

"Of course, Samantha, that was a silly question for me to ask. Too broad. What is the last thing that you remember?" Ifé asks.

Though improving, Samantha still feels the grog from just having awakened. She remembers her name, her parents and her house. She remembers standing in the kitchen with hermother. She remembers beating some eggs in preparation to makean omelet. She loves omelets. Her mother had just begun to teach her how to make them. She remembers her mother cutting up the onions, tomatoes, mushrooms and jalapeños that Samantha loves so much.

"Is the bacon ready, Mom?" she remembers asking. Samantha is concerned because her mom prefers to cook the bacon in the oven instead of frying it on the stovetop and last time her mother let the bacon burn. She hated that. Nothing goes better in an omelet than bacon. Her dad likes spicy sausage in his omelets, *but he's just nuts,* she thinks dismissively.

Samantha remembers her dad coming into the kitchen. She remembers her mom and dad talking about making a quick run to Starbucks before they all sat down to eat a hearty breakfast. She remembers getting into their SUV, her dad driving, her mother talking and laughing about some joke between them. Samantha remembers laughing with her parents. *Dad is so silly,* she thinks. *Mom is a cut up too.* Samantha remembers a loud screech and then nothing. Samantha remembers total blackness until now, right now.

"I remember my mother and I," Samantha begins haltingly, "making omelets in the kitchen of our house. They used to be so good. She was teaching me how to make them like she makes them. I was afraid she was going to burn the bacon like last time. There was music. She loved jazz. I think it's weird. She loves John Coltrane. I think he's a little melancholy. I like that word, melancholy. I spelled it in a spelling bee at school and won the whole thing. It's because my dad makes me read everything. Even the news. I hate the news, but he makes me read it every day for thirty minutes per day. I remember going on a Starbucks run with my parents. I remember brakes screeching, ours or somebody else's. I don't remember anything after that."

"Good, very good, Samantha," Ifé says. Ifé seems pleased, but she isn't smiling, Samantha sees. She looks concerned. With more light, Samantha can see more. Ifé is tall, dark-skinned and beautiful. She looks like one of those exotic women Samantha has seen in her mother's Caribbean and African travel magazines.Her mother had been to both a lot before she'd gotten married and settled down. *Ifé looks like one of the tall women of the Massai, Samantha decides, yeah, just like that,* she thinks. She also reminds her of someone else, but Samantha can't decide who.

Looking about her room, Samantha sees where the light seems to come from. It looks embedded in the walls and the ceiling itself. She sees that light seems to grow and recede in the ceiling and move as if it's a living thing. Samantha also feels a pleasant breeze blowing around her and over her. It is cool and comforting.

"We need to get those legs and arms working, Samantha." Lay back for a few minutes more and we'll take care of that."

Ifé waves her right hand and a colorful menu appears before her, seemingly out of thin air. Samantha watches as Ifé interacts with the air menu. She feels her bed vibrate and hears it hum softly. Heat rises from the bed and reaches her skin. Samantha feels its warmth and allows herself to sink down into it.

"This is a healing bed, Samantha. It's designed to cure what ails you. It stimulates your muscles and gives you what you need to use them again. Once that's done, we'll get you up and get you fed. I'm sure that you're hungry. Most IM, er, people who wake up after the long sleep that you've had are ravenous. You're in theright place for that. We have all kinds of wonderful things for youto eat," Ifé says.

Come to think of it, Samantha thinks, *she's as hungry as a bear.* Her dad says that to her.

"Okay, Ifé. Can I take a little nap while we wait?"

"Of course, Dearheart. I'll be right here. I'll wake you when it's time," Ifé responds.

Dearheart, Samantha thinks. She likes how Ifé says that. It makes her feel warm.

* * *

It had been several days since Dr. Donald Garrett had been awakened. His guide or Awakener, Dr. Benjamin Foster, had been most instructive. Dr. Garrett has learned much, including the fact that his professional title, doctor, means little anymore. He is literally a doctor in name only unable to practice his profession in this new, very advanced America.

Dr. Garrett knows that he had been asleep. He had been stricken by the Sleepers virus. He has only recently been awakened, and it's eighty years later. His wife, Gwinneth, has not yet awakened, but she's due any day now. His oldest son, Luke, is accounted for and is still in stasis. His youngest son, Dylan, who is twenty-eight on Sleep Day, has still not been found. He has probably been lost or, hopefully, misidentified, though doubtful.

Because of the advanced DNA mapping of this new

America, thereis a less than 0.0001% chance that anyone who is still asleep has been misidentified.

This is Dr. Garrett's seventh day awake. Dr. Foster has told him he'll be moving from his room, a sort of personal hospital within his room, due to the healing bed and the room itself which is itself designed to track his bio-stats and apply healing measures if necessary. Dr. Garrett has learned that medicine has greatly advanced in the last eighty years and that it incorporates more than a bit of some ancient Eastern and African methodologies and well-advanced Western ones. Dr. Foster had tried to explain it to him, but it was all beyond him. It made his head hurt trying to think about it.

Dr. Garrett had been a well-regarded neuro-surgeon prior to Sleep Day. He had even developed several new surgical techniques that had shown useful for combating Alzheimer's disease. When Dr. Foster told him that they no longer use invasive surgery of any sort to heal people, Dr. Garrett had been crestfallen.

"And Dr. Garrett," Dr. Foster had said, "we no longer have Alzheimer's disease. It's been totally eradicated. Once our doctors and AI discovered its source, we created treatments designed to stop it at its source. That was thirty or forty years ago. It was a big deal at the time. It's been cured around the globe, well mostly, for some time now."

In spite of all of the change and his still sleeping family, Dr. Garrett is excited to see what comes next. Dr. Foster had promised that he'll start out in a three-bedroom apartment in his home city of Denver.

"Except for the mountains, Dr. Garrett, Denver has changed quite a bit. You might not recognize it. We're a one-hour train ride from here. I'll escort you there myself. Be ready to go when I get there," he had said yesterday. Dr. Garrett doesn't have much to pack. He wears an off-gray jumpsuit that has his last name on it - "Garrett". There's some strange tech in it that Dr. Garrett doesn't yet discern. Apparently, it's stain defeating, not resistant, water defeating, dries itself, monitors his bio-stats, self-warming, and self-cooling. Oh, and it has some sort of early warning system in case of storms, static electrical currents like lightning.

Dr. Garrett hasn't seen anyone but his fellow awakened

citizens wear these jumpsuits. Their handles, like Dr. Foster, wear different clothing that is clearly personal to them. No one has said that he must wear the jumpsuits, but there have been no other clothes forthcoming either. Dr. Garrett is pretty sure that another unspoken feature of his jumpsuit is that its location can be tracked. As if on cue, Dr. Foster stands in the doorway of Dr. Garrett's room.

"Ready to go, my friend?" Dr. Foster asks.

Dr. Garrett looks at Dr. Foster and smiles, "ready, he responds." Dr. Garrett does not believe that he and Dr. Foster are friends. He recognizes that the good doctor, the real doctor, has a job to do and has obviously been chosen to be Dr. Garrett's handlerto ease his transition back into this version of America. So far, Dr. Foster had been nothing but helpful and affable. He'd answered most of his questions and satisfied his concerns about his family and their whereabouts.

Dr. Garrett had learned that he is currently in the Hive, the huge underground complex where all sleeping IMs like him had been stored and cared for. In recent months, thousands of IMs had begun awakening. In response, the government created the Awakening Program to orient and care for each newly awakening person.

"It's the biggest American government program of all time, other than the massive infrastructure program that President Douglas had initiated soon after Sleep Day," Dr. Foster had said.

President Douglas, Dr. Garrett had thought. There's a name that he knew and recognized. Apparently, President Douglas had initiated and fulfilled a massive infrastructure program that was even bigger than FDR's after World War II.

Once IMs began awakening, the government built the Reorientation Center next to and underground as well. With the technical advancements of the last eighty years, the Reorientation Center had been built in one week and is large enough for one hundred thousand people.

"This is nothing. You should see the cities, Dr. Garrett. Those are truly wondrous," Dr. Foster had said a few days ago.

On day four of his awakening, Dr. Garrett had gotten to see and meet other IMs like him who had recently been revived. He had been led into a large auditorium which looked like it sat one-thousand or more people.

Every seat is filled. There is a large screen at one end of the auditorium. As Dr. Garrett thinks about it, he decides that this day had been the most disorientating of the last seven days. Once everyone is seated, a video begins. A strong-looking Black man appears. He is the current President of the United States. His name is Heru Khepri Amon. His voice is deep and his gaze affecting. He is dressed in a smart suit that also has elements of traditional African colors and patterns. His brief speech to them is simple, clear and concise.

My fellow Americans. My name is Heru Khepri Amon. I am your President. I am happy to be speaking to you. The last president that you knew was President Baron Douglas. He was a great man and is the reason that almost all of you are alive and well today.

As most of you should know by now, you've been asleep for the last eighty years. Through no fault of yours' or anyone's, you were infected by the Sleepers virus, which slowed down your metabolism so much, it placed you into an irreversible sleep. When that happened, our response as a nation was to find as many of you as possible, take you to hospitals and keep you alive until the Hive could be built, which became the central location of all folks like you who had fallen asleep.

By now, you may have heard the term "IM". That stands for insufficiently melanated. That means that folks like you do not possess the requisite amount of melanin necessary to stop the effects of the Sleepers virus. We think that you are immune to it now and have little to fear from it. The antibodies in your blood should be sufficient to guard against its effects.

In the time that you've been asleep, many changes have occurred. You'll discover many on your own, but I'll highlight a few here. First, the American population is just under one billion people. This has happened because of huge internal population growth and immigration. Second, infrastructure has changed tremendously. We've advanced greatly since you were awake in every scientific, engineering and building category. You'll be amazed, for example, at how we do transportation. The gas engine is virtually a thing of the past. Third, our carbon footprint is virtually nil. We don't burn carbon fuels, import oil or gas or even refine oil into gasoline anymore. The way that we produce energy is innovative, discrete and redundant. On your way in here,you created electricity. Fourth, the lives that you've known, your professions, have either changed and greatly advanced beyond you, or no longer exist.

Your guides, who have studied your files intimately, will be able to advise you on this the best. Fifth and last for now, your homes and your property, as you have known them, no longer exist. But you will be housed, fed and re-educated in place of those things. Your guides will tell you more about this.Each of you has your own package to review.

We're glad to have you back. We're glad that you're awake. Welcome home.

At the end of President Amon's video, Dr. Garrett sits in his seat for a while without speaking or moving. There had been a few yells at the screen and sounds of anger and incredulousness from his fellow IMs. Several things had become clear to Dr. Garrett. He and the IMs, white people, are no longer at the top of the socio-economic totem pole. Also, at the end of these eighty years, America, or something calling itself America, still exists. He wonders how much of the old America that he knows still exists. It's also painfully clear to him that he and his fellow IMs are outnumbered. Last, and most excruciating, whatever life he had known, and it had been a very good one, is over. He is no longer Dr. Garrett but merely Donald Garrett, newly awakened IM.

As these truths settle over him, he feels Dr. Foster sit next to him. The auditorium has mostly emptied at this point.

"It's a lot to take in, I know, Dr. Garrett."

"Please don't call me that. I'm just Donald now," he responds.

"Good Doctor, I will do no such thing. You earned it and were great in your day. It is still a sign of respect, and I won't deny you that. Nor will anyone else," Dr. Foster says.

Dr. Garrett does not respond to that. He puts his head

down and breathes deeply a few times. He wonders what his wife and son will think when they see him and when they discover who andwhat they are in this foreign American world. Who am I now? He asks himself. He used to be the very well-respected Dr. Garrett from Colorado. Surgeons the world over would come and speak with him and watch him work. He had been husband to Denise and father to Luke and Dylan, his now two grown sons. One is accounted for, and one is either lost through misidentification, unlikely, or most probably dead as so many had died as a result of Sleep Day.

"I don't really know who to be right now, Foster. I'm forty-five plus eighty years old, I'm educated for a time long gone, and I don't know who to be. What am I supposed to do now?" he asks.

"You're more than just the sum of your parts, Dr. Garrett. You are a whole person. Who you are here and what you do here is before you. I promise you this, though, you'll never starve, you'll never be homeless, you'll never be without medical care. And education? You can get all the education that you want and then some. This version of America is different from the one that you left. It's fairer and takes better care of its people, all of its people.

In a few days, I'll have more information about where you'll be staying. And I'll make sure that you have constant updates about the state of your wife and son. In fact, I'll check in on them myself," Dr. Foster says.

"Okay, Dr. Foster," Dr. Garrett tries to say cheerfully. "Please take me back to my room. I need to rest for a bit before dinner. This has all been a bit too much."

"Noted. I'll walk you back. This transition is not easy. I recognize that. By the way, I also have a degree in psychology. We can speak on that level any time that you wish," Dr. Foster says.

"Right," Dr. Garrett says, chuckling. "You've all got multiple degrees and multiple areas of expertise, right? How the heck did ya'll figure out how to do that, to make time for that?"

"Basically, we cut all of the fluff out of every academic program and put folks to work in their respective fields right away.It speeds up the learning curve. For example, law school takes two years at the most now and not the three that it used to. Some finish in a year or in less time than that. A lot of the old education system that you know was built on a capitalistic premise. It was a money grab. Because all education is free, we get right to it. Besides, eighty years ago, when a lot of the education system was in flux, the Elders decided that the imperative was on getting as many people educated as was possible. In my opinion, it's the greatest thing that they did for the country. Now it's just our culture.

We have 100% literacy, 100% expertise and 0% debt insofar as education is concerned. Folks now can't believe that that was everthe system," Dr. Foster says.

"But you're well versed in this because your first degree was what, history?" Dr. Garrett asks.

"Yes, history," Dr. Foster says. "My great-great- grandfather, Damien, had been a history major at Stanford. He lived long enough to make an indelible impression upon me. He let me know that one with a firm understanding of history and its context can learn anything else. I consider him the patriarch of our family. He's the one that navigated the Fosters through the aftermath of Sleep Day."

Day four of his awakening had been difficult for Dr. Garrett to digest. Days five and six had afforded him opportunities to learn more about his new country, its politics, demographics and culture. America now has two official languages, English and Spanish though most people speak them both fluently as well as three or four more. Young children from recent immigrant families are encouraged to learn and maintain their families' languages and culture which has led to many languages being spoken. At one point, there had been a big push amongst African-derived people to learn one or several of the most popular African languages. He'd heard Dr. Foster speak to other SMs in at least two or three different African languages in passing as he attended to him. He'd also observed that Dr. Foster is a man of great respect amongst his peers, just as he had once been.

The mechanics of the economy have changed too, Dr. Foster realizes. America seems to be even more prosperous than it had been, but it's also far more socialistic though much of the old capitalism, like homeownership, private business ownership, and publicly traded corporations, remain prevalent. Many of the SMs that Dr. Foster has seen wear expensive-looking, well-tailored clothing. The women are adorned in expensive-looking jewelry and all of the men wear shoes of the kind that Dr. Garrett used to spend a fortune on at his favorite, no longer existing department store.

Healthcare seems to have solved itself too, he thinks. He has yet to see one overweight man or woman anywhere. Dr. Garrett had seen large numbers of IMs and SMs at the Reorientation Center, but the only overweight people that he's seen are the IMs. *And that's another thing,* he thinks, *these labels, IMs and SMs. Who came up with those? They seem to be the only labels for people anyone here uses. That's a curious, if annoying construction,* Dr. Garrett thinks.

"I'm looking forward to getting out of here, Dr. Foster. When do we leave?"

"Right now. We'll take a short pod ride to the main junction and then hop a bullet train from there. I told you that we don't really do commercial airplanes anymore, right?" Dr. Foster asks.

"Yes, you did. Yesterday. Totally gotten rid of it, hunh? Wow. Never thought I'd see it."

"Yes, our Elders, out of necessity, created an extensive above-ground and underground bullet train network all throughout the country. In the beginning, we hadn't had enough qualified pilots to operate the commercial aircraft industry. Pollution had been another issue. When President Douglas pushed the country togo green, air travel had been one of the first things to go."

While talking, Dr. Garrett and Dr. Foster arrive at the pod station for their transport. The pods are fast-moving four passenger transports shaped like small cylinders with two curved ends. The pod network they travel to is similar to those used in big cities for public transportation though those transports look more like the old subway trains that existed before Sleep Day. The pods operate based upon magnetic, electrical current and emit no pollution.

They can move at five hundred miles per hour or more but are capped, for safety purposes, at two-hundred and fifty. The junction to which they are traveling is about one hundred miles outside of the Hive. Dr. Foster assures him that they'll be there in about ten minutes and then in Denver about two hours or less after that. Their much faster bullet train will move at about five hundred miles per hour.

"This is really fantastic technology," Dr. Garrett says, settling into his seat in their pod.

"It is. But you haven't seen anything yet, my friend. I look forward to your impressions of the new America. Denver is quite beautiful."

Dr. Foster orders a chai latte for Dr. Garrett and hands it to him. Every pod, of course, can also provide any kind of drink or light refreshment to its occupants. Delicious, Dr. Garrett notes to himself and sips it slowly as he wonders whether Dr. Foster was just showing off.

* * *

Eric doesn't like his guide, and his guide does not like him, he thinks. Unlike his guide, though, he had disliked him from the first time that he'd seen him.

"My name is Abayomrunkoje. You may call me Koje pronounced 'Ko-Jo'. I know that my actual name may be a bit difficult for you to say."

Eric had thought that he'd heard some derision in Koje's voice when he said that. It was not necessary to add to Eric's animus toward his guide, but it certainly hadn't helped.

Eric's day of awakening had been a severe shock to him. Every day thereafter leading to his seventh day has seemed worse than the day preceding. Now he knows that his world, the world in which he ruled and reigned as the precinct commander of the third precinct in New York City, is over. In his twenty-year plus career as a police officer, he had been highly decorated and well protected from the several charges of police misconduct and brutality levied against him by his hapless victims and, often, their parents. He was just doing his job, he would tell himself. He believed that his badge had given him license to roughly police whomever he believed deserved it.

On day one of his awakening, he regained consciousness in his room on his healing bed as Koje attended to him. Not seeing him at first, he'd only heard him, and what he'd heard had frightened him, a rich deep voice of a man who was, obvious to Eric, not white, but black.

"Who are you? Why am I here? Where am I?" are all

questions that he wanted to know immediately. Koje's answers had not helped.

"You are in the state of Montana, deep underground. You are in your recovery room in the Reorientation Center in a place called the Hive. You have just awakened from an eighty-year sleep. What is your name?" Koje had asked.

"My name? My name is Eric Lawrence, district commander of the third precinct, New York City police department."

Not derisively, Koje chuckles at Eric's reply. "Not anymore, my friend. You are not a police officer anymore. And neither the third precinct or the NYPD exist anymore. In fact, not for a long time now. You are in a new place and a new time. I will be your guide to help reorient you to this place and this time. You are not the first person that I've helped."

"What do you mean that I've been asleep for eighty years? That's impossible," Eric says.

"Sadly, my friend, you and several million of your fellow IMs suffered the exact same fate. They are awakening in stages just as you have done. I will tell you that America is still America, but it is not the America that you remember. It's changed."

Eric is thunderstruck by this information and doesn't know what to think. He wonders whether Koje has kidnapped him as part of some desperate plot cooked up by his enemies or as part of someelaborate practical joke manufactured by his colleagues.

Once Eric's eyes are fully open, he uses them to see and assess his situation. Koje, his guide as he calls himself, seems to be in his 30s. He is at least six feet three inches tall, muscular and nimble. Eric guesses that he either was or is an athlete of some sort. He wears a tunic colored in various African prints that Eric recognizes from his many years working in downtown New York and close to the United Nations. In the few times Koje has helped him up or helped him walk, since his muscles were still being restored, he sees that his guide is very strong and powerful. Eric is a somewhat large man standing at six feet one inch, two-hundred and thirty pounds. In his youth, he had also been an athlete, a baseball and football player.

On day two, Eric's reorientation had begun. He learns that not only does the NYPD no longer exist, but there are no police anywhere.

"There are no police?" he had asked Koje.

"No, my friend, no police. There are trained security forces that handle security work, but no, we govern ourselves. There are no guns either. We don't need them," Koje says.

Koje had taken Eric on a short walk to one of the cafeterias to feed him. It's about lunchtime. Along the way, Eric sees other IMs like him and their guides coming and going. He hears Koje speak to a few of the guides in a foreign language.

<Koje! My Brother! How goes it?> A guide says speaking in perfect Xhosa. To Eric, the language sounds like a series of clicks and clucks that are incomprehensible.

<Sami! All is well, good Brother. Just taking my charge tothe café. This is day two for him. He doesn't know which end is up.> Koje replies in Xhosa.

Both men fist bump one another as they continue onto their respective destinations.

"Who was that?" Eric asks.

"That was my good friend Sami," Koje replies.

"What language were you just speaking?"

"That is Xhosa. It is one of the more popular languages from Africa. We speak several languages now. I, myself, speak about six. Most people in America now speak at least three languages, and many, much more than that," Koje says.

"I don't understand, Koje, how there can be no police. That just doesn't make sense to me," Eric says.

"Ah," Koje says. "Let me try to explain it to you then. The police, as you've known them, have never been a friendly organization to we SMs. In fact, the police had done everything that they could to maintain a division between and amongst theraces. At some point after Sleep Day, though police still existed and were all SMs, the people elected to dismantle the various police departments around the country and instead use those funds for different needs for the people. Since guns had gotten collected and the allocation thereof had become federalized, gun violence dropped dramatically, and with it, the need for police with guns as well. It wasn't the easiest of transitions, but there was no turning back once it took hold. Also, there is the other thing that occurred,"

Koje says.

"Other thing?" Eric asks.

"Yes, my friend, the other thing. Security is still very important to us. Our Elders recognized that. But we needed, as a new society, to secure ourselves and our persons differently than what had existed. So, every person, from a very young age, is taught self-defense. And typically, our girls begin their training a full eight to ten years before our boys do, basically from the time that they can walk. By the time our boys, and our girls most especially, become teenagers, each is or is pretty close to being lethal in one or more of the several martial arts. I myself am a master level practitioner in Muay Thai, Jeet Koon Do, Krav Magra and several non-gun weapons. I love and enjoy it. I also teach it. So you see, Eric, we are each very secure in our own persons and use the discipline of our training to maintain respect for one another. Plus, my friend, each of us is required to spend time, at least one year, in our nation's security forces, not unlike what the Israelis have done with their citizenry for many years. In a mannerof speaking, we are all the 'police'," Koje says using air quotes for the word police.

Eric can't believe what he's hearing. He looks at all of the SMs walking about him. Few are as big or physically intimidating as Koje is. He doesn't think that he sees what Koje has described.

"Yeah, all of that seems very far-fetched. The police has a multi-hundred year history in the United States. It can't just disappear overnight."

Koje laughs heartily at Eric's statement. "My friend, if you knew the specific origins of the so-called police in this country, you would understand why people like me are happy to never repeat that time in our history ever again. But allow me to elucidate," Koje says.

Koje stops in the wide hallway leading to the cafeteria and looks. Eric hears him clear his throat audibly.

"WARRIORS!! MY WARRIORS!! WHO ARE WE?!!" Koje bellows in a ferocious roar.

"WE ARE ONE!!! WE ARE ONE!!! WE ARE ONE!!!" All of the assembled SMs roar back at Koje with the same unyielding intensity that he'd initiated.

Now, Eric sees it. He sees the faces of the SMs, mainly

Black people, looking at him. He sees their intensity, their fearlessness and their strength. Involuntarily, he shudders. *Eighty years has changed them,* he thinks. *They are not what they were. There is no fear here.*

"We are one, Eric. We are one," Koje says solemnly. "C'mon, let's get something to eat. I'm famished," he says cheerfully.

At the moment, eating is the last thing on Eric's mind. Puking is about the only thing that he feels like doing.

CHAPTER VIII

When President Felipé Lopez receives the news that fifty of his soldiers, including his cousin Colonel Pérez, have been killed by American drones, he is irate. Pérez is his wife's first cousin and they're very close, having grown up like brother and sister. President Lopez knows that his wife will be inconsolable and indubitably blame him. She'll demand blood, either the Americans' or his, he knows. *He'd already suffered through twenty-four years of marriage with Margarita, his wife*, he thinks. President Lopez shudders at the thought of what another twenty-four years will be like if she has this to hang over his head. I have to act fast and mitigate the damage as quickly as possible, he says to himself as his anxiety begins to turn his stomach into knots.

"Get me the American on the phone," President Lopez says to the aide standing closest to him.

"Right away, President Lopez," the aide responds. By 'American', he of course means the American President,President Douglas. Before Sleep Day, their relationship had been cordial, even warm. President Douglas had visited Mexico at least four times during his tenure. President Lopez had visited the White House at least twice, a fact that his wife greatly enjoyed and had often bragged about amongst her friends and associates at home.

When Sleep Day happened, and it seemed that all of the white Americans fell asleep, ambitious vultures inside and outside of the Mexican government pushed President Lopez to first scout out what was actually happening and then to grab resources from across the border. At first, he had their calls to do so, but the cartels moved ahead of him and began making excursions into America without his say so. Fearing that they would instigate a war with the Americans and afraid of appearing weak at home, President Lopez reluctantly reached out to the cartels and involved the Mexican army, thereby taking over all of the efforts against the Americans. He installed his wife's cousin, at her behest, to lead the effort. For years, she had been pestering him to elevate him to the rank of general. He had refused under the pretense thathe could not appear to favor Pérez in the eyes of his political opponents. In truth, he had never really liked the man and thought him a blowhard who rode the coattails of his politically connected family. But with success in these early efforts, it had become much harder to deny him the position and the promotion that accompanied it.

Now, President Lopez knows that both his allies and his opponents will demand blood. If the news of last night's debacle had not already reached them, it will soon and calls for his ouster will become deafening, he believes. Most certainly, he and his allies had wildly underestimated the Americans and President Lopez knew it. They had wrongfully assumed that just because the white Americans had been immobilized, the remaining, especially the Black Americans, would never be able to militarily organize enough to respond much less than stop their incursions.

At worst, President Lopez had thought, they'd be able to raid and potentially control a few of the towns on the American side of the border. At best, he'd thought that maybe parts of Texas and perhaps Arizona could be re-acquired and made a part of Mexico again. That last is what may have been too much to hope for, he knows, but President Lopez had always been a bit of a dreamer.

Now, the Americans have instigated war, and President Lopez believes that he must respond strongly and boldly which his citizens, allies and enemies will demand. They already do not fear the Sleepers virus or its effects upon them. Their Mexican cousins and family members in America have told them that thereis nothing to fear for Mexicans who have the requisite amount of melanin in their skin and bodies, ironically a trait that most Mexicans had eschewed before Sleep Day. Now it seems that dark-skinned Chicanos are in full demand.

"We have President Baron Douglas on line 6, Mr. President," President Lopez' aide says.

"Everyone exit the room. I want total and complete privacy," President Lopez says.

As his aides and officers leave, President Lopez gathers his thoughts. *He'll be tough and make his demands,* he thinks, *and force President Douglas to at least apologize. His allies will be happy with that,* he hopes. Whatever happens, it's his mess and he has to clean it up.

*　　*　　*

President Douglas expects this call from his Mexican counterpart. He is happy that his military staff had been able to get the definitive proof of the Mexican military's involvement in their incursions into America. He is also happy that his squad had gotten out with no casualties.

President Lopez, he knows, will be irate that American drones had killed a few dozen Mexican military personnel and cartel members, all Mexican. President Douglas knows that he has risked outright war with Mexico, but their actions, he believes, necessitated his actions.

His assistant has just informed President Douglas that President Lopez has called and is waiting on line six. President Douglas takes a moment to consider things from Lopez's perspective, a discipline that he often uses to anticipate an opponent's needs and demands in a difficult negotiation. *If he were President Lopez,* he thinks, *he'd be irate and perhaps a bit irrational.* President Douglas is aware of the internal pressures that President Lopez faces in his own government and his own household. It is well known within the intelligence community that President Lopez had been seen as an outsider who married into the right political family and who owes his allegiances to them even more than to the Mexican people. *If that's true,* President Douglas muses, *he'll be ultra-concerned with how he is perceived and how what's happened negatively impacts his own precarious political standing. This should be interesting,* President Douglas decides as he picks up the phone to speak.

"President Lopez, how are you?" President Douglas says cheerfully in his baritone voice.

"Not well, Baron, and you know why," President Lopez replies dourly.

"Ah. Well, I can only imagine. In point of fact, we're still missing a few dozen of our IM citizens, so I'm not feeling all that great either, Mr. President," he replies, choosing to use one of the formal titles for President Lopez.

"Well, I hope that you don't think that I or anyone in my government had anything to do with that, Baron!" President Lopez exclaims. "You know how difficult it's been for us to reign in the cartels. This is not our fault! How dare you insinuate that with no proof! Baron, you've become unhinged! Ever since the Sleepers virus hit you, you've been power-hungry! My people think that you're trying to invade us next! You've instigated war against your neighbor," President Lopez says, his voice strained, his breathing now labored.

President Douglas takes a moment to compose himself and organize his thinking. He realizes that President Lopez is starkly unaware of what they'd learned last night during their surveillance of the Mexican army. He also understands that once he shares the proof that President Lopez will be boxed into a corner. His response may be somewhat unpredictable, President Douglas knows, but he has little choice than to let his counterpart know what he knows.

"Play the tape," President Douglas says, knowing that his call is being listened to by several of his aides, including NSA Director Trevor Campbell. *Let's see how this shakes out,* President Douglas thinks as he awaits the Mexican president's reaction.

* * *

Beads of sweat line the top of President Lopez's forehead. He's just heard President Douglas' proof. He's just heard the voice of his now dead brother-in-law Colonel Pérez essentially admit to everything. He also hears the voice of his wife in his head, who is distraught and who screamed at him this morning when she found out that her beloved cousin is now dead and worse, had been killed by the Americans.

"You make them pay, Felipé! You make them pay!!! Make the Americans pay!!!! Or you won't have a presidency to defend anymore!!!" she'd said, raging her worst at him.

President Lopez is uncertain about his wife's threat against him, but he's also in no mood to test her and himself on this point. The evidence against them is stark, and it is persuasive. Suppose it leaks internationally, as it very well could. In that case, it will paint him and his government in the worst possible light, even worse than the Europeans who expelled their SM citizens, many of whom came to America on ships in a scene reminiscent of those which had brought the first Africans from Africa to the newly forming

America. Only this time, they'd come willingly, even joyfully, and they'd resided in the best parts of their ships and not in the ships' bottoms like so much cattle.

President Lopez replays what he's just heard in his mind again. His memory is very nearly autographic. It's the reason that he had been able to delight his now wife when they were younger. As a musician, he'd always had the ability to play by ear on guitar, piano or anything musically that he heard, even if just once.

Before he'd married Margarita and fully understood what he'd gotten himself into, he'd imagined that he would become a famousMexican musician and songwriter. Marrying Margarita, though, placed him firmly on a different path which she and her family had demanded. At this moment, President Lopez wishes that he'dinstead become a professional musician. Instead, he's created an international mess and cannot see any way out of it that will at once save face, mollify his wife and help Mexico.

"Sandoval," Colonel Pérez had said in Spanish, "I'm getting nervous. The cartel's excursions have become less and less successful and the Americans don't seem to be nearly as weak or scattered as you and your bosses promised. My commanders have become less and less convinced that the cartels' grand scheme can work. My point, Sandoval, is that the clock is ticking. El Presidenté nor I will continue to support you in these missions without some guarantees. First, you have to know that none of your acts can be traced back to us. Second, if you're wrong about America's military capability, you and your cohorts will personally pay the price for that. You will be fully disavowed and painted as a rogue military agent. And last, you have exactly thirty days from now to prove your theory. If you fail, you fail alone," Colonel Pérez had said.

The words are what they are, and there's no way to spin this, President Lopez thinks. His chief concern now is to spare his country any more embarrassment and somehow mollify his wife, which he knows is the tougher of the two tasks. Clearing his throat and loosening his tie, President Lopez makes his choice. "Mr. President, what do you want me to do?"

* * *

President Douglas is surprised at President Lopez's question. He'd thought that they might get to this point, the Mexican president's capitulation, but he'd thought that it would come only after more wrangling and perhaps another phone call or two. Perhaps, President Douglas speculates, President Lopez has seen the end of the matter for what it is and decided to circumvent all of the politics in between? He is unsure. He knows, though, that this is the moment to put his demands squarely at the Mexican president's feet and hold him to them.

"Mr. President," he begins, "first, I want every single American IM taken back in our custody in the next forty-eight hours. If any one of them has been killed or severely injured, I want the Mexican government to compensate their families for their loss or injury. I'll get back to you on exactly how much that is to be. Be prepared to pay millions. Also, I want your assurances that all incursions on American soil will immediately stop and that Mexico will respect our borders. That happens today. Any breach of this condition could cause further harm to your military, Mr. President. Last, but just as important, you must reign in your cartels, and preferably, end them altogether. It is clear to us that too much of how Mexico governs and operates is done in appeasement of the cartels or in fear of them. If you ever want to be an effective President, you must end their influence once and for all."

President Douglas' last point sticks like a shiv between President Lopez's ribs. All of the American president's demands are sound and reasonable, he knows, and similar to what he would do were he in President Douglas' shoes. Reigning in the cartels, though, would almost certainly mean massive bloodshed and massive political upheaval. He's not even sure if his wife or her family would support such a move. *Ideally, the cartels would be dismantled, or at the least, their power and influence reduced, but that's far easier said than done,* he believes.

"I will do what I can, Mr. President. Your IMs will be returned to you post haste. On behalf of the Mexican government, I apologize for any pain that our actions have caused. I appreciate your discretion on these matters as well Mr. President," he says, hoping against hope that the content of their conversation does not leak out. It's a huge ask from President Lopez, but what does he have to lose, at this point, by the request, he decides.

"President Lopez, the sooner that you comply, the sooner that we can put this whole sordid business behind us," President Douglas says indicating his willingness to keep their matter private so long as he has President Lopez's full compliance.

"Noted, Mr. President. My staff will forward all details to your staff soon," he says and then hangs up.

* * *

The toughest part of President Lopez's job today will be facing his wife. He elects to do so personally. He'd already experienced her wrath once this morning, and any more of that over the phone would not be good. She's in mourning over her cousin, but if he can explain to her his reasons and why he's put Mexico's interests first, he hopes that she'll at least begin to understand. He's not certain that he'll win the day, but he must at least try.

It's a short drive from his office to the President's mansion. As he rides, he thinks about what he will say, how he'll say it and how his wife might respond. Surely, twenty-five years of marriage counts for something, he hopes. President Lopez loves his wife but feels strongly that Mexico's issues must prevail. They just cannot afford to enter into a military conflict with America, even a supposedly weakened one.

As the presidential SUV pulls up to his front door, he steps out quickly, not waiting for his driver to open his door. President Lopez is anxious to see his wife and speak with her. Even if she completely rejects his stance, he's prepared to keep it no matter the consequences. *If I am to ever be respected,* he thinks, *I must begin to put my country's interests ahead of my own even if it means losing my marriage. This was a stupid venture to begin with. I cannot be overridden like this again,* he decides.

President Lopez never hears or sees his assailants as he walks through his front door, but he only feels them. In an instant, he is roughly grabbed by two large men who then place a black bag over his head completely darkening his eyesight. They then bind his arms at his wrists and pick him up so that his feet dangle in mid-air. He feels himself being led out of his own house and then unceremoniously thrown into the back of his presidential SUV. The two men get in and sit on either side of him, propping him up between them. One of the men gives the driver, his driver, an instruction to drive. President Lopez doesn't recognize the voice.

"Your wife gives you her regards, Mr. President," one of the men says, which is the last thing that he hears before he is hit over the head and made unconscious.

* * *

Margarita Lopez cannot believe what she's hearing. Her beloved cousin is dead and now her weak-kneed husband has just totally capitulated to the American President. How dare he? She fumes. *I'd explicitly told him to make them pay*, she thinks. *And now, he's all but rolled over and given up! This will not do. This cannot stand.*

Since he'd been in office, President Lopez's telephone conversations had been bugged and monitored by Margarita and certain of her family members. She'd never felt that she could just leave Felipé to the presidency without monitoring him and intervening when necessary. She'd always tried to use subtlety to guide him and manipulate others close to him, but those daysare now past. *Mexico had been severely embarrassed by a much weakened United States, and a much more substantial answer for its aggression must be provided*, she thinks. The fact that her beloved cousin had been killed makes her intended actions all the more insistent.

Unfortunately for her Felipé, Margarita had always valued two things more than him and their marriage: her family and Mexico. This choice had been made almost from infancy as she was raised by two politically affluent parents in a politically affluent Mexican family. She had grown up to be the smartest, most capable and most ruthless of all her siblings and cousins. Their family's legacy mostly rests upon her shoulders now, a fact that she had learned early and eagerly embraced. Loving Felipé, she knows, is not enough to stop her from doing her duty. *Felipé has has to go*, she thinks, *his mistake is irredeemable*.

* * *

Raheem sits in a pool of his own sweat on a log at an outdoor training facility in Quantico, Virginia, a facility that is also used by the Marines. For the last two weeks, he and his Secret Service classmates had been housed here to further, and hopefully, complete their training. Today is the last day, he hopes,of their training. He is tired and misses Candace and the kids but is thankful that though their training had been arduous, the rules about communicating with family are far more relaxed than what his military basic training had been. He'd gotten to speak to and see by video his loved ones daily and sometimes more than twice per day, yet he still misses them and especially lying next to Candace at night.

After the third or fourth day, his classmates began treating him like their leader and taking most of their cues from him. He'd even stopped two or three of them from quitting, telling them that there may never come another time like this one in which admittance to the Service could be had and that no matter what, the training has to end at some point. Thankfully, no one had quit on his watch and when necessary, Raheem had even helped to carry the loads of some of the weaker candidates.

The Secret Service training seems very familiar to Raheem and reminds him of his basic Marine Corps and special ops training. This training is different from the others because it is much more defensive than offensive and requires a different way of thinking. Especially in special ops training, the objective is to offensively seek and destroy, not protect. With Secret Service training, the objective is to protect even with one's own life. *That's a head trip*, he thinks. He had never had a special ops mission in which his goal was not to return alive. Here, he knows, his dying for the President or others may be what completes the mission.

Giving my life is sorta the point, he thinks ironically. As he muses upon this, Raheem sees Agent Smith, his tormentor, approach him purposefully.

"Recruit Gates, are you ready to continue?" she asks."We are, Agent Smith," Raheem says. He and his classmates had just completed a ten-mile run through rough terrain starting at six a.m. that morning. This was on top of having trained all day yesterday while not hitting the rack for some much-needed sleep until one a.m. this same day. *They're beat,* he knows, *but they're also almost done. Now is not the time to quit or to shrink back.*

"Recruits!" he bellows. "Mount up! Ten more miles to go. Almost to the finish line!"

He and his fellow Secret Service recruits line up two by two. Raheem takes the lead along with Agent Smith who has been running with them the entire time. *She's in great shape,* he thinks. At least she's the kind of leader who leads from the front and runs with them, though he's keenly noticed and has not appreciated the special attention shown to him by her in their training sessions. It's been clear to Raheem and his classmates that she has purposefully singled him out for extra work, extra duty and more training. He thinks that he knows why, but that doesn't make him like it.

As Raheem, Agent Smith and his classmates begin the second part of their run, he lets his mind wander a bit. Raheem thinks about all of the changes occurring in the country and how he may soon get to be a part of them. He had never expected to have a job this important this fast or ever. Not even before he was arrested and served time had he expected to do more than perhaps become a police officer or sheriff. He is happy both for the increased pay and prestige. He wishes that his parents were still alive so that he could share his success with them. His father had passed when he was still in college from congenital heart failure, an inherited disease, and his mother had passed in a tragic car accident while he was in special ops training. He'd almost quit his training, but his commanding officer at the time had encouraged him to finish despite his loss. It's that same don't quit energy that Raheem uses today for himself and his classmates.

"We're not quitting today, Marines, I mean Recruits!!!" he yells out of nowhere, startling Agent Smith. "Let's go!! Only nine more miles to go!!"

He's nuts, Agent Smith thinks to herself before kicking her run into another gear to keep up with him.

* * *

"Yes, he's ready," Agent Smith says.

"Good, good," Agent Brooks says. "And how do you assess his readiness?" he asks.

"Well, he's clearly the leader of his class. I've watched him lift and support others. He's been almost selfless to a fault, and I've pushed him on that. Also, he's the best or among the best in all of the objective measures that we have: marksmanship, physical fitness, classroom instruction and more."

"Well, the Presidential detail does need bodies," Agent Brooks says "but not just any 'ol body. Are there any others in this class that you'd recommend for the Presidential detail, Agent Smith?"

"Yes, two or three others, but Recruit Gates is head and shoulders above them all. I think that he'll be a fine addition to the Service, but I leave it to your wisdom to make the final decision," Agent Smith concludes.

"Thank you, Agent Smith, that will be all," Agent Brooks says before hanging up. He wonders if he's made the right choice, both in giving such training responsibility to Agent Smith and in potentially placing Recruit Gates on the Presidential detail. His status as a violent ex-felon makes his selection risky, but his skillset is sorely needed.

Agent Brooks opens Raheem's file, which sits in a thick folder in front of him, one more time. He combs it looking for any reason besides his felony conviction to exclude him from the President's personal detail. Agent Brooks knows that he'll be questioned about this choice and wants to make sure he's completely buttoned up when his higher-ups, in particular, the President himself asks him about it. President Douglas is known to have examined each of his close Secret Service personnel's files and been known to reject some when he hadn't liked something that he'd seen. Agent Brooks doesn't want to make that mistake with Raheem, a mistake that could damage him in his career with the Service for years to come.

Military service, he reads, exemplary. Top of his class in his Marine class too. Good grades in high school, good enough to have gotten him into college. Comes from a good two-parent home though dad had died while Recruit Gates was in high school and his mom later when he underwent his special ops training.

There's a note in his file that says that he'd had an opportunity to quit his special ops training but had elected to continue. *Good,* Agent Brooks thinks, he's not a quitter, even under the harshest circumstances. Leadership, check. Current family, check. Married, check. Kids, check. Exemplary prisoner with no issues, check. Highly recommended by corrections officer Roscoe, now warden of the prison, check. Exhaustive background investigation, check. It seems that Recruit Gates didn't drink or smoke and had barely gotten a speeding ticket. He was also all-state for football and had had D1 and D2 schools interested in him for football and track, but he'd chosen the Marines over them all. *That's a big 'ol check in my book,* Agent Brooks thinks to himself as he all but concludes his review of Recruit Gates' file.

There don't seem to be any hidden or obvious flaws in Recruit Gates other than his prison stay that Agent Brooks can find. Fine then, old man approve him, he says to himself. They didn't call you to have you sit on your hands, retired or not. Okay, Agent Brooks concludes, I'll recommend Gates and give him his shot.

Then it's up to him. What's the Service gonna do if I'm wrong, fire me? He chuckles to himself, thanking whatever gods may be for his official retirement status.

* * *

"Get cleaned and get dressed, Recruits. I think that we have a ceremony to go to," Raheem says to his fellow classmates.They'd all just returned from their twenty-mile run and barely gotten something to eat when Raheem speaks to them.

"Recruit Gates," Recruit Evans says, "are you sure? Dude, I'm exhausted. I didn't hear Agent Smith say anything about us needing to do something else."

"Trust me, Evans," Raheem says, "I have a feeling about this."

In truth, the source of Raheem's feeling is that he'd seen Candace's car parked in the visitor's lot as they ran back from their long trek. That woman never could hide worth a damn, he thinks, chuckling to himself. She must be here for some purpose and Raheem can think of no better purpose than their impending graduation. Though Agent Smith hadn't said anything, she had been keen on getting back to their barracks by 3 pm sharp. She had insisted on that time but had never indicated why.

"Recruits, wear your clean jumpsuits. We need to all look the same. You've got twenty minutes to shower, shave and get presentable," Raheem says.

Quickly showering and putting on his jumpsuit, Raheem checks in on the men to make sure that they're following suit. "Evans!" he yells. "You're always the last one. Hurry up!" Raheem says fuming at the perennially late Recruit Evans. He had been one of the ones that Raheem had had to convince not to quit. *He's alright,* Raheem thinks, *just a little soft-well, maybe not so much after this.* Raheem then checks with one of the female recruits to inquire as to the ladies' readiness.

"We're ready, Recruit Gates" Recruit Barnes confirms. *Great,* Raheem thinks. *Once Evans is with us, we'll be totally ready for what comes next.*

On cue, Agent Smith walks into the men's side of the barracks. Raheem can tell that she's surprised because she genuinely looks surprised. "I was going to tell you all to get ready for a little event that we're having," Agent Smith begins, "but I see that you're all, wait, where is Recruit Evans?"

"Right here, Agent Smith!" Recruit Evans says jogging into the room from the shower area that all of the male recruits share. "I'm right here, ready to go. What are we doing?" he asks.

"You're on a need-to-know, Recruit," Agent Smith says all but snapping at him. Missing, though, is any of the nastiness that she'd showered on them throughout their training process. More than once, Raheem had noted to himself that she seems particularly suited to this kind of work, even though she's so young. At some point, he had gleaned two important things about Agent Smith: first, that her father had been a drill sergeant in the Army and second that she'd pledged Delta in college and had also been the dean of a pledge line at Spelman. Though not having himself pledged, Raheem knows enough about Black fraternities and sororities to surmise that some military protocol had been transferred to many of its members due to their military connections established around World War II.

"Come meet me outside and line up," Agent Smith says, turning on her heels to leave the barracks.

Quickly following behind her, Raheem gives a silent

command to the male and female recruits to follow him. Once outside, Raheem and the other recruits line up shoulder to shoulder, facing Agent Smith, who stands silently, appraising each of them.

"It's been a long three weeks. It's been tough. It's been arduous. But I'm proud of each and every one of you. And a few of you," she says looking directly at Raheem, "have really distinguished yourselves. When you arrive at your first assignments, continue to excel and do not embarrass me. Your country needs you now more than ever. Your people need you too"she says briefly pausing "now more than ever. Follow me."

Agent Smith begins to walk away towards the meeting center where, Raheem surmises, their graduation ceremony will commence. He and his fellow recruits walk in a single file line behind him as they slightly trail behind Agent Smith. He is close enough to her to hear when she whispers to him, "Recruit Gates, keep excelling, or else."

* * *

Taking power is one thing, Margarita Lopez thinks, *wielding it is another thing entirely*. Now that her husband had been removed, she knows that she must act and act quickly. News of her husband's arrival will not be long secret, and a suitable response to the Americans' aggression must be made. *Blood for blood*, she thinks darkly. This is the only way to advance Mexico and advance her family, she believes and therefore plans to formally announce herself as Mexico's president, but first must show strength.

"General Olivier," Margarita says after dialing his direct number on her secure cell phone.

"Yes, Madam Lopez, how may I be of service?" he replies.

"President Lopez has asked me to reach out to you. He needs some answers. How many Americans do we have right now? The sleeping ones?"

"We have forty-eight, Madam," General Olivier says. "And how many awakened Americans do we have in the country? The ones who have been here since before Sleep Day?" she inquires.

"Including the retirees, I'd say almost one million. Why do

you, I mean, why does El Presidenté want to know?" he asks.

Margarita ignores his question. Almost one million. She had no idea that so many Americans were in her country. This is fantastic news that provides some much needed leverage and power.

"Thank you, General, that will be all." She hangs up, grabs her purse, one of the expensive kinds from Chanel, and tells her butler to have her driver pick her up. She has plans to make and she must call the American President. *His call with her will go very differently than the call he'd had earlier with her husband,* she muses, *very differently ind*eed.

* * *

"President Lopez's office on line six, Mr. President," Emily, President Douglas' assistant, tells him.

President Lopez, he thinks. This is not a call that he had been expecting. When earlier they'd spoken, President Douglas had, he thought, successfully negotiated the return of their sleeping Americans, their IMs. The next call should have been between their respective staff to work out the details of the transfer.

President Douglas thought that his Mexican counterpart had understood that. *Perhaps something had gotten lost in translation,* he wonders, as he picks up the phone to speak.

"President Lopez, what's going..." President Douglas begins.

"This is not President Lopez, Mr. President. This is his wife, Margarita. My husband is indisposed. He's asked me to take over and to speak with you directly," she says, her tone all business without even a shred of caution.

"Madam Lopez, it is always good to hear your voice. Helen still talks about the last time that we were all together last...."

"That's all well and good, Mr. President," she says, cutting him off again, "but we have important matters of state to discuss, Sir."

President Douglas shifts in his chair uncomfortably, and he's starting to become worried. He'd known Margarita for a long time. Even before he had become President, he and Helen had occasion to make official visits to Mexico in the capacity of his other jobs, first in Congress and next in the Senate. They had met the Lopezes before Felipé's ultimate ascension to the Mexican presidency. They had even spent time together socially, which Helen had enjoyed since Felipé was a heck of a musician and songwriter in his day before becoming fully ensconced in Mexican politics.

President Douglas knows that he'd been a bit harsh with President Lopez on their earlier call, but it is unlike him to send someone else, and especially his wife, to handle affairs of state in his stead. This doesn't feel right. Something is wrong.

"Margarita, where is Felipé?" President Douglas asks, his tone tinged with steel.

"Baron, he is indisposed. You'll have to deal with me. And watch your tone, Mr. President. This is not a tact that you can afford to take," Margarita says.

"Afford to take? What do you mean by that? The details of our earlier discussion have been worked out and agreed to. If there are any changes or questions, your husband should be the one to discuss them with me, not you," President Douglas says.

"Unfortunately for you, Mr. President, my husband is unavailable to deal with any of his presidential duties now or in the foreseeable future. You must deal with me alone. Now to the matter at hand," she says almost dismissively, "we will not be returning any of your sleeping citizens unless and until some sizable concessions are made. I assure you that they are all safe and in good care. Furthermore, Mr. President, we are revoking the travel privileges of all of your American citizens in Mexico, all one million of them. Their passports will be confiscated and returned to them only after America has met its obligations to Mexico."

"OBLIGATIONS TO MEXICO?!" President Douglas bellows. "Have you lost your mind?! Margarita, this means war if you push forward with these ridiculous demands. You do understand that you cannot win a war against us, do you not?" he asks.

"Oh, Mr. President, we're not going to war," Margarita says almost sweetly. "You have very good reasons not to do anything that could put your citizens in any further danger. No, you'll comply, you'll keep your people safe, and all will be well."

"What exactly do you want, Margarita?" he asks through

clenched teeth, his jaw tightening at every word uttered.

That's better, Margarita thinks. *I have him right where I want him. He thought that he'd have my soft husband to deal with. Surprise, surprise!* Margarita thinks to herself. "We want no less than what America owes us," she begins. "We want Texas."

* * *

When Raheem and his fellow recruits walk into the base's gathering hall, they are all smiles. By the time they'd arrived, they knew that today would be the day that their training ends. Of course, Raheem knew as soon as he had seen Candace's car on their way back in from their twenty-mile run. Though they are tired and sore from the run, each recruit's energy is renewed by the sight of their families and loved ones.

Raheem sees Candace, their kids and Agent Brooks. He beams at them. He is happy to see them in the flesh. When he'd left prison, Raheem promised them and himself that he would never spend any extended time away from them ever again. He had been sad to break that promise so soon after his release from prison.

However, the opportunity to join the Secret Service had been too good and too important to pass up. Reluctantly, and after much discussion and prayer with his wife, they had decided together that he should press forward.

Standing here today proves to him that he and Candace had been right. His kids look no worse for wear. In fact, they look great, and Jaret, his oldest, looks a little taller. *Yikes!* he thinks. *It's only been three weeks! How had he grown so much?!*

At the front of the room is a dais with chairs set up and also a podium. Agent Smith leads her recruits to the front and directs each recruit to take a chair on the dais. She then nods to Agent Brooks who walks to the podium and taps the mic. "Is this thing on?" he asks with a wide grin. "Today is a tremendous day and a momentous occasion. This is our first full graduating class for the Secret Service since Sleep Day. These now agents enter one of our nation's most prestigious bodies, the Secret Service. They will be assigned significant responsibilities, and some may even protect the President himself. We trust that they will fulfill their roles with high competence, integrity, and vigor whatever their jobs. In my forty year plus career with the Service, I have seen much. Today I see twenty strong and able agents ready to take on the high honor of their nation's trust. Your country thanks you and we salute you."

Agent Brooks turns to Agent Smith who is seated directly behind him. She stands and takes Agent Brooks' place at the podium. She begins to read each recruit's name, congratulating and handing each recruit an envelope containing their first assignment.

She calls Raheem last. When he hears his name, Raheem stands up and walks toward Agent Smith who, surprisingly, smiles at him fully and extends her right hand in congratulations. He takes her hand, and she shakes it firmly. As she hands him his envelope, she pulls him in closely for a moment and whispers to him, "Congratulations! Tell the President that I said hello!"

Raheem dons a wide smile and looks at Candace. He can't wait to tell her the news.

CHAPTER IX

Trevor Campbell removes the earphones he'd been wearingto listen to President Douglas's acrimonious phone call with Margarita Lopez, President Felipé Lopez's wife. It is clear to him that President Lopez is not indisposed as she had claimed. Rather, he knows that the Mexican President has likely been forcibly removed from office and may even be dead. *Baron is as smart as I am,* he thinks, *and he'll arrive at the same conclusions that I have soon enough, but it's unlikely that he considers Margarita capable of murdering her own husband.* Trevor has no such hesitation. He not only thinks that President Lopez's life is forfeit but that his wife is now, effectively, the new president of Mexico.

But where is the opportunity? Trevor ponders as he considers the day's events thus far. President Douglas, expectedly, will call his top advisors into the Oval Office to discuss what's happened. He'll undoubtedly seek counsel from his generals to seek options. General Martin will most likely advise 'calm', 'restraint' and most of his advisors will too. *And they'll be right,* Trevor thinks, *but with almost one million Americans in Mexico, that is a dead horse that the new Mexican president will be able to beat over and over again.*

Margarita's demands are, of course, impossible to fulfill. She says that she wants Texas, which, even before Sleep Day, housed two of the country's largest Hispanic and African American populations. By his recollection, Trevor knows that Texas had and has the largest number of Black people in the country. That was before Sleep Day. The population of both groups has only enlarged due to President Douglas' relaxation of immigration restrictions and the movement of both groups from other states to Texas.

Reviewing his vast knowledge of happenings after Sleep Day, Trevor recalls that when the property transfer program first began several months ago, many African Americans, in particular, decided to leave states like Louisiana, Mississippi, Arkansas and Missouri to move to Texas for work, property and businesses. In response to those losses, the government had temporarily assigned many new immigrants to the states, mostly Southern, that lost significant Black populations. *If the IMs wake up any time soon*, Trevor thinks*, they won't recognize their towns and their cities since this trend continues with no sign of abating. Here's hoping that they won't wake up any time soon*.

Trevor also believes that President Douglas will want to formulate some kind of response to Mexico's aggression. A protracted war with Mexico, given their reduced numbers, is not prudent, but some sort of military response may be necessary, Trevor begins to think right when his phone rings.

"Trevor Campbell," he says, noting that it's his encrypted line which had rung.

"Sir, it's Gaines. We've lost track of Lundgren. We tracked her to the town just outside of the facility, but after that, she disappeared. We sent agents to her boyfriend's apartment, but they have yet to report. We suspect something may have happened to them. We're checking their status now."

Trevor rubs his temples in frustration. *Too damn much is at stake to allow this loose end to go unchecked*, he thinks. He'd moved all of the pieces off the board except this one piece–Jessica Lundgren–and next to Krauss she may be the most dangerous and likely one to spoil his plans.

"Gaines, this is unacceptable. I want her found, I want her neutralized. If you can take her alive, take her, if not, do what you must," Trevor says and then abruptly hangs up.

Too much has happened and is happening to stop now, Trevor muses. The property transfers, the power transfers are exactly what he and others like him have wanted ever since Dr. King famously exclaimed on the Mall in Washington, D.C., "free at last, free at last, thank God Almighty, we're free at last!"

And only now is a measure of that freedom being realized in some measure. *We can't go back*, he thinks, *won't go back, and stopping the immediate development of a cure to the Sleep virus is completely necessary to protecting that new found freedom*. If they wake up on their own, that's one thing, Trevor decides, but there's no way in hell we are going to help them. I don't care what President Douglas wants or believes. We're not going back.

* * *

"Is he alive?" President Douglas asks his assembled advisors. He looks intently at each of his key advisors, Trevor Campbell, Valerie King, his wife Helen, Janet Taros, former President Arthur Gates, and General Phaylen Martin, all together in the Oval office. "Cat got your tongue?" he asks almost comically, "well, what do we think? Is President Lopez alive or not?" he asks now with a bit of edge in his voice.

General Martin clears his throat before beginning to speak. "Mr. President, we don't know, yet," he says, emphasizing his last word. "We do know that his wife has quickly consolidated power and is operating out of his office quite literally. We think that this is some well-orchestrated power play from within. It seems that she's fully supported by her family and at least half of the Mexican government. We see this as a move to fully consolidate her power in Mexico. What better play than to antagonize a 'weakened' United States and to make wholly unreasonable demands?" he asks rhetorically.

"General, thank you for your assessment, but that doesn't answer the question. Is the man alive?" President Douglas asks again.

"It's possible, Mr. President," Trevor says, "but we don't have confirmation at this point."

"Can we get confirmation?" President Douglas asks."The honest answer is maybe. We still have assets in Mexico, Hispanic, Black and white. Our embassy and our consulate are all still active. Yes, I think that we can get an answer. What do you want to do?" Trevor asks.

"Get me an answer, Trevor. I need an answer. I need itin the next twenty-four hours. If he's alive, we may have some options. But if he's not..." he says, his voice trailing off, refusing to finish the sentence.

They all understand. If he's not alive, it's war, plainly and simply. And if it's war, it is a potentially huge loss of life that neither country can afford, and especially not the United States and especially not now. Trevor knows that none of what he wants or plans will work if they're drawn into a war with Mexico.

* * *

I've got four immediate problems, Jessica thinks to herself, as she assesses her and Lionel's dire situation—their four attackers, who are clearly here for her, and Lionel, who is more of a liability than help in this situation. She and Lionel are closest to his back door, leading to his back staircase leading to his motorcycle. But now, their exit is blocked by attackers one and two, while attackers three and four, at the front door, are closing in fast. Soon, they'll be overwhelmed, she thinks. If there's any good news to be had, Jessica sees that though her attackers have sidearms, they've not drawn them yet. They're not here to kill, but to capture. *Good news for us,* she thinks.

Attacker number one reaches out to Jessica first. She easily smacks his hands down and smashes his nose with her right elbow. He drops hard to his knees, his nose broken, gasping for breath. *One,* she thinks. *He's likely out for the duration.* Next comes attacker number two. Seeing his compadre fallen, he grabs a telescoping rod from a pocket in his pants, extends it, and swings for Jessica's head. She easily ducks his intended blow and returns two rapid-fire kicks to his midsection. Her attacker doesn't fold over as she expects, but she's at least slowed him down, she sees.

As she prepares to render another quick attack, Lionel launches himself at attacker number two, raining down punches and kicks furiously. Jessica is shocked. She had thought that her sometime boyfriend hadn't had it in him. Seeing him handle the attacker, Jessica turns to face attackers three and four who both, she sees, have their sidearms drawn and pointed directly at her. They've seen the results of the first two attackers, and they're obviously nottaking any chances.

This is a problem, Jessica knows. Neither she nor Lionel have any defense for bullets. The attackers are still several feet away from them and not yet in Lionel's kitchen. Though pointing their guns at her, they have not yet fired. *Perhaps this is my chance,* she thinks. The hilts of several steak knives stick out from the knife block in the kitchen. Jessica hadn't practiced her knife throwing in years, but with the advancing attackers with guns in hand, she believes that she has little choice.

She deftly grabs two steak knives from the block and in two smooth motions, throws a knife at the neck of attacker number three and the other at the head of attacker number four.

Miraculously, attacker number three's knife finds its mark and lands in his upper chest, but slightly askew from his heart. *Good shot,* Jessica thinks, *but I didn't kill him.* Attacker number four manages to avoid the knife thrown at him, but he doesn't avoid Jessica's hard kick to his stomach which knocks the wind out ofhim, folding him in half. Jessica follows up her kick with a hard elbow to the back of his head, instantly knocking him out and to the ground.

She stands over him in momentary triumph, her fists clenched. Jessica looks at her attacker with the knife protruding from his chest. He's bleeding but not profusely so. She sees that she missed his heart by mere inches.

"You'll live," she says, stepping over him. Looking back in the kitchen, Jessica observes that Lionel has his assailant in a headlock. He's unconscious. "He's out, Lionel. Let him go before you kill him."

Lionel releases his attacker and drops him to the floor. "We need to go before anyone else comes up here. Your place is compromised," Jessica says.

"Okay, Jess. Out the back door down to my motorcycle. Let's go," Lionel replies.

They quickly make their exit and get to his motorcycle. Lionel has two helmets, one of which he offers to Jessica. "Put this on. We need the cover. I'll get us to my parents' house in the country. The address isn't registered with any government. No one even knows that there's a house there. My father had it built on some land that he purchased through one of his several shell companies. It shouldn't be easily traced."

Jessica gets on the back of Lionel's motorcycle and grips him tightly. She's not a fan of motorcycles and Lionel tends to ride too fast for her liking. But speed is exactly what they need most, she knows. *Better this than the alternative,* Jessica hopes, *better this.*

* * *

Trevor's asset has just given him the most currently known information about President Lopez. The asset, a spy, has been positioned within President Lopez's office for the better part of two years. Trevor is glad that he had had the foresight to enlist the asset even though, at the time, there had been no specific reason to do so. Mexico is and had long been a reliable, if not fully trusted, partner for most issues related to North and Central America.

His spy is a Mexican national and has informed Trevor that currently, no one but those in Margarita Lopez's inner circle knows anything and that they're all being conspicuously quiet. He also told him that Margarita is ensconced in her husband's presidential office, is fielding phone calls as the de facto leader of Mexico and has had multiple Mexican dignitaries and others visit her. There also seems to be a war room being created in the president's office. Multiple Mexican generals are there with her. *The coup or whatever it is,* he thinks, *is in full swing and no one seems to be challenging her.* In a secured and encrypted video call to his spy, Trevordirectly asks him whether President Lopez is alive or dead.

"It doesn't seem that he would be dead, Sir" he replies. "President Lopez is beloved by the common folk in Mexico and no formal announcement has been made of his 'untimely passing'. The official word is that he's unavailable, temporarily, but has empowered his wife to act in his stead while attending to other state affairs. That's the official word. So, I think that he's alive for the time being. But that time is probably drawing short. She can't afford to keep him alive long term, given Mexico's naked aggression against the United States. She would never allow that."

So maybe he's still alive, maybe he's not, Trevor concludes. *It will have to do,* he decides. If President Lopez is alive, President Douglas will want to act on that. There's no way they can get better than a maybe on the question, but that will have to be enough.

Trevor leaves his office to take the short walk to the Oval Office where he knows President Douglas has been holed up, working. He does not look forward to giving the President a squishy answer, but squishy is all that they have right now.

* * *

Since their most recent mission, Darryl, had been relaxing and recuperating. After the mission, he ached everywhere and had needed two days of nothing but rest. More than once, he'd dipped himself into an ice bath to reduce his body's inflammation, an old trick he'd been taught during high school football season, to relieve his aches and his pains. As much as his body needs rest, his mind does too, perhaps even more so, but Darryl can't seem to turn it off.

He is concerned about having to make any more excursions into Mexico. Darryl and his team had retrieved the evidence of the Mexican government's involvement in the kidnappings of their IMs, but if Mexico should somehow balk at their return at the least he and his team and possibly others will have to engage in a rescue mission, he believes. Darryl considers that he and his team had been very lucky to be rescued from Juarez. Things could have gone badly, he knows. Darryl isn't anxious to repeat that performance.

Laying on his rack close to midday pondering the meaning of life, he wonders what next steps his government might take. *Doesn't seem like many good options*, he thinks. We can't leave the IMs where they are. Mexico's naked aggression will have to be addressed. Even in the U.S.' weakened state, it is a mighty lion with sharp claws and teeth. *Hopefully*, he thinks, *the President will take a measured approach and that approach will not incur toomany casualties on our side, especially those of my team and me.*

Darryl doesn't have to wait too long for an answer to his internal ruminations. He hears a firm knock at his door and watches as an envelope slides under his door with a whisper as its edges lightly scrape his linoleum floor. One word is plastered on the readable side of the envelope: "ORDERS".

Great, he thinks sarcastically, *no rest for the weary*. In the few precious moments between now and when he opens the envelope, Darryl wonders whether his team is ready for yet another mission so close to the one they'd just completed and whether he, himself, is ready. I'm not as young as I used to be, he considers, but orders are orders.

Darryl rises from his bed and crosses the space between himself and the envelope in two quick steps. Bending over to pick it up, he hears his back crack in several places and feels it creak. *Gots to get to the physical therapist today*, he thinks. He'd been putting that off since before the last mission. He doesn't think that he can afford to do so any longer.

Darryl's eyes narrow as he surveys his new orders. *This*

can't be right, he thinks. Of all the scenarios that he'd imagined, this had not been one of them. I need to speak with my commanding officer, he decides. What he reads perplexes him and, he admits to himself reluctantly, frightens him. He's not afraid of the mission, but he is concerned about what the mission means.

If these are his orders, then Mexico is either headless or in the hands of a despot, he believes. Either possibility could mean chaosbetween Mexico and the United States and possibly an actual war between them.

We're barely keeping our heads afloat as it is, Darryl tells himself. We have neither the troop capacity nor organization to launch effective aggressions against even Mexico. This must be President Douglas' end to all of that, he hopes. Whatever it is, Darryl needs to get to his commanding officer, his C.O., and get some clarity on what's next.

Donning his boots and his slightly oversized fatigue shirt, he leaves his room and makes his way quickly down the hall of his barracks, out the door and to the building where his C.O. 's offices are. He leaves the orders on his bed, not needing them to speak with his C.O. from whom his orders came. The orders comprise just four words in all caps: RESCUE PRESIDENT FELIPÉ LOPEZ.

* * *

"There's no movement, Victor," Congresswoman Jane Stowe says to Congressman Victor Anthony. "There's no movement," she reiterates. "We're four months from the one-year anniversary of the Sleepers virus and there is no movement on a cure, at least, there doesn't seem to be. Krauss is nowhere to be found and his top researcher, Jessica Lundgren, has gone to the ground. No one can find her. Douglas is going to get his way on this, and there's little that we can do to stop him," she says, the frustration obvious in her tone.

"Jane, honestly, I don't really think that President Douglas wants the IMs to remain asleep, and I don't think that he wants the property and business transfers to be permanent. I believe him when he says he wants a cure and wants the IMs to rejoin the population. I agree with you that what happened to Krauss and his team is suspicious, but I don't believe President Douglas is the cause of that," Victor says.

"You're naïve, Victor, if you think those people," she says, emphasizing the words 'those people', "don't want exactly this result," Jane says caustically.

At her words, Victor looks at her disapprovingly. He knows what she means. He is well aware of her blind spots and her biases. Victor is, himself, of Cuban origin. His grandparents had fled Cuba and resettled in the United States with two young children, one of whom is his father. This had happened during Fidel Castro's armed ascendance to the Cuban presidency. Victor had grown up with all of the stories and all of the politics of the many Cubans who had had to flee Cuba, their land and their possessions, the memories of which remain a bitter reminder of their shared past.

Though based now in Sweden with Congresswoman Stowe, Victor has maintained contact with his family and friends in the Cuban community. For the most part, all of his family and friends had survived Sleep Day. Almost none of them had been stricken and forced asleep. Victor realizes that had he been home, he probably would have remained awake as well. One of his family members, a distant but beloved cousin who he and the other children of his generation had grown calling "Uncle George" had been stricken but curiously, re-awakened a few days later several shades darker than what he had been. By now, Victor and others had heard and seen these particular phenomena occur to many across the United States.

Victor knows that he can probably return to the States with little worry about what would happen to him if exposed to the Sleep virus. His wife and three kids certainly want him to return as soon as possible. He resists their entreaties up to now because of his loyalty to Congresswoman Stowe and also because he is concerned about what she might do if he's not there to modulate her worst impulses. She had become the de facto 'president' of the ex-pat congresspersons and senators, about thirty in all, who were outside of the United States on Sleep Day and who cannot now return. She holds a lot of sway with them, especially now since her xenophobia and, frankly, racism echo many of their fears. The country is changing, has changed, and there is little that they can do about it.

"I've been speaking with Admiral Franklin, Victor. He hasn't said so directly, but I think that he agrees with me. If we do not have a vaccine in four months and we do not have awakening IMs, we'll need to do something to register our disagreement and our complaints. Our entire way of life is being pushed to the brink. They're trying to erase us, Victor. We will not be erased," Congresswoman Stowe states emphatically.

"I don't know what speaking to Admiral Franklin gets you, Jane. Whether he agrees or not, he is an admiral in the United States Navy, a navy that serves at the pleasure of the Commander-In-Chief. He is answerable to exactly one person, President Douglas. Surely, you're not suggesting some sort of military action by a U.S. Naval officer against America herself, are you? If that's what you're inferring, you can let me off this train right now," Victor says.

"Calm down, Victor, calm down," Stowe says, raising her hands to emphasize her words. "No one is saying that we should attack the mainland, though it is interesting that you consider that a possibility. Actually, I'm considering something a bit...bolder," she says haltingly.

Stowe waits several heartbeats before beginning to speak again. "Victor, I know that you don't have to be here. You'd most likely survive a re-immersion back into mainland America with no ill effects, but frankly, I need you here. It's a tough call for you, though. Will you agree to remain in Switzerland with me at least until the one-year anniversary?" Stowe asks, her smile reminiscent of the several roles of sharp fangs in a shark.

To Victor, she looks more like a wolf anticipating her next kill than an arguably attractive woman doing her best to appear charming. She is the alpha. He is the beta. That much is clear to him. What is not yet clear is what she's planning. He senses something big and probably outrageous. Perhaps he should remain here to either head off her plans or to at least mitigate them. Victor is not sure that he can do either, but he is sure that there would be no checks on Stowe whatsoever without him. The European leaders have already begun to corral around her instead of President Douglas since the ugly business of their forced ejections of their respective SM populations. President Douglas' parting words had infuriated and embarrassed them greatly. Neither he nor they had spoken since, mostly at the President's insistence.

President Douglas is not a petty man, he thinks, *but he could indeed be quite stubborn.*

"Okay, Jane, I'm staying, but I need for you to share all of your plans with me. You know that I'm a patriot. Whatever you do must be in the best interests of the country, not just one or two groups within it," Victor says.

"Of course, Victor. You're my right-hand man!" Stowe exclaims. She is pleased with herself that she's convinced Victor to remain in Switzerland with her as she pushes forward with her next initiative. Had he left, their voting bloc would have been diminished, thereby lessening her own power. In order to do what's next, Jane will have to be at full political power since, most especially now, she's in the minority. *Yes, in the minority now, but not forever,* she thinks, *not forever.*

* * *

Lionel wasn't lying, Jessica thinks to herself as she holds onto him for dear life on the back of his motorcycle. Thank God that he's an expert rider because this is rough going, she notes, bearing down on another bump of the dirt road they traverse.

After leaving the town in a hurry and traveling quickly for about seventy-five kilometers, Lionel had turned off their main road and onto a dirt road. For the last two hours, they'd traveled upon a system of dirt roads, first one and then the other, until they'd hit this one.

Lionel had given Jessica several breaks to stretch her legs and give her backside a break. She is a tough, martial arts trained lady, but he knows her body isn't used to this punishment. Apparently, Lionel had grown up riding both on paved and unpaved roads. She can tell that he's enjoying himself.

"Just a little bit further now, Jessica. My parents' place is close now. I promise, this is the last dirt road that you'll have to see for a while, Lionel had said. It's dusk and Jessica is tired from a full day of riding. Lionel is currently moving at under fifteen kilometers per hour, and Lionel is being careful to avoid the toughest bumps so that Jessica isn't further irritated. He can feel the tough spots through her since she grips him sharply every time they hit a hard bump.

Rounding a bend, Jessica and Lionel see dim lights about a half kilometer up and to the right from them. Jessica sighs in relief. She can't wait to get off Lionel's motorcycle. The closer that Lionel drives, Jessica sees the outlines of his parents' house. It's a one-story cabin that looks as if it were made in the 1800s. Even about one-hundred feet away, Jessica can tell that it's rustic and un-modern.

"My parents found this place forty years ago while hiking. The cabin was empty and abandoned. My father loved that. He wanted to bring it back to life and have this place as a sort of out of the way campground for my brother, my sister and me. We basically grew up here. Whenever we weren't in school, we were here. Nobody knows about it but us. Mum and Dad own all of the land around us in several directions for several kilometers. We'll be safe here. There's no electricity or electronics anywhere," Lionel says.

Seconds after they stop and disembark from Lionel's motorcycle, they hear, "Lionel!!!! Come here!!! We had no idea that you were coming!! And who is this then?! Some woman that you picked up along the way?!" Lionel's mother says all of this so fast and so intensely that it momentarily disorients Jessica. *This is obviously Lionel's mother*, she realizes.

Standing in the doorway is a tall barrel-chested man dressed in a flannel shirt and overalls. He looks almost American, except for his mustache and beard which are distinctly groomed in the common European style of this region. He stands at the door, an imposing figure, looking at them all without saying one word. What he lacks in his wife's exuberant excitement, he more than makes up for in the look of stoic concern in his eyes. Jessica sees wisdom and concern there. She suddenly feels guilty about coming here and hopes that she hasn't carried her trouble to Lionel and his family.

"Boy," Lionel's father says, his deep bass seeming to echo across the field and off the mountain range surrounding them. "Are you well?" Lionel looks at his father sheepishly but does not answer. He stands as tall as his father but his dad is at least fifty pounds heavier than him. Standing next to him, Jessica can see a bit of the boy that Lionel used to be. She can understand why someone might be intimidated by this man.

"We're okay, Da. This is Jessica. She's my friend. We got into a bit of trouble at my place. Needed a space to come to for a bit. I hope that's okay," Lionel says.

Lionel's dad looks at Jessica thoughtfully for a few moments. "Come inside and get something warm in you, both of you. Lionel, your room is clean and ready as always. We'll speak more about what's going on with you two in the morning," Lionel's dad says as he turns to walk back into his house.

"Come now, Lionel and Jessica. I've got a big pot of stew on the stove. Rabbit. You'll love it," Lionel's mother says.

Jessica can smell the stew from just outside of their home. Her mouth waters and stomach churns at the smell of it. She hadn't realized how hungry she was before now. Jessica can't wait to get inside and eat.

Lionel leads the way in. It's exactly as she had pictured it. The cabin is comfortable, warm, and nothing in it hadn't been made by hand by their family. Lionel's mother ushers them to the main table for eating and serves them liberal amounts of her rabbit stew. Lionel and Jessica both eat their fill which includes soft, warm bread dripping with homemade butter. They drink big gulps of a delicious German beer that warms Jessica's soul. Soon, her eyelids feel heavy. Lionel's mom gently takes her from the table and walks her to Lionel's room. A big bed awaits her. Lionel's mom helps her get out of her clothes which she promises to clean by the morning.

Within minutes, Jessica is asleep. Lionel doesn't immediately join her. He stays up to speak with his parents which he does in low tones. Jessica later feels him slide into bed and embrace her, his warmth a welcome addition to her already blissful rest. Soon, they both sleep fitfully, breathing in rhythm with one another completely unaware of the next day's adventures.

* * *

Trevor stands at the window of his office at NSA headquarters. He has the largest office in the building which sits upon its top floor. The entire backside of his office facing the outside is one large window. When he paces, he often likes walking from one side of his office to the other as he thinks and plans. Something about the semi-forest just outside of his window comforts and calms him. He has much to ponder.

He considers that he must play a kind of three-dimensional chess to win this game. Big picture, he has to continue to frustrate his friend and mentor, President Douglas. The IMs cannot be allowed to wake up before one year of their slumber is up. *And really,* Trevor muses, *we probably need them to remain asleep a good three to five years from now, or at least until all of the major changes occurring are baked in and irreversible. We're too close now and we may never get this chance again.*

Trevor is troubled by Dr. Jessica Lundgren's disappearance. She's completely disappeared and seemingly dropped off the grid. He's directed all of the appropriate NSA staff and CIA assets to search for her, but thus far they have been unsuccessful. Of course, all of the major roads, railroads and airports within a two-hundred-mile radius of Krauss' facility are monitored twenty-four hours per day. In spite of that, there hadn't even been a hint as to her whereabouts. He doubts that she'd left the country, but if that's true, Trevor wonders, where could she be? He has agents inevery town and every city in Switzerland and in its neighboring countries. As Dr. Krauss' top researcher, he believes she has the intellectual capital to continue his program. Krauss had been close to some kind of breakthrough, and he is worried that Lundgren could replicate that.

Congresswoman Stowe is another problem. As head of the NSA, Trevor has access to her emails, her phone calls and even her in-person conversations at her office. She has been careful not to disclose her hostile intentions outright, but Trevor thinks he knows what she intends. Stowe is an ambitious woman who had designs on the White House after President Douglas' eventual departure.

The Sleepers virus may have forever ended those ambitions, but she clearly still has designs on accessing and keeping power. Trevor doesn't believe that she'll be satisfied with being the leader of the ex-pat Congressional delegation. *No,* he realizes, *she'll want more, much more.* Trevor must consider whether what Stowe wants is actually good for the country as it currently exists. It might be, he thinks.

Stowe cordoned off in her own little kingdom could be a benefit to the country, or at the very least to me. He knows that his enemies think that he has designs on the Presidency. How wrong they are. The NSA head has designs on power for power is what's needed at a time like this. If the SMs are to ever achieve economic and social equality in this country, he believes, the wealth transfer from the sleeping IMs to the woke SMs must continue to happen and must be made permanent. *President Douglas does not want this,* he muses, *but I do.* Trevor again wonders whether what he believes about Stowe's intended actions can be used to help him in that cause.

Trevor expects that Mexico will soon be an international mess. Margarita Lopez is clever, ruthless and is at least as driven to collect and execute power on behalf of her family and country as Trevor is. A protracted war against them, even if we win, hurts us. Somehow, Mexico must be brought to heel and in such a way that they'll think once, twice, three times before ever trying the United States again. Semi-rogue states like Mexico believe that the U.S., with its diminished population, is weak. It is weakened to be sure, Trevor acknowledges, but if he has his way, the new United States, under the leadership and guidance of SMs will replace what it's lost and do so in a way that favors the SM population for many, many years.

Currently, there is no good intel on the whereabouts of President Lopez or if he's even alive. The President has a plan to search it out, but if he's dead, he's dead. And if Lopez is dead, Trevor knows, then it's war with Mexico. Margarita Lopez will never back down unless and until she is removed from power, the likelihood of that being somewhere between zero to none. If her husband is alive, their best course of action is to find him, protect him and install him back into office. That tact assumes that he'd act according to President Douglas' wishes which, of course, is not guaranteed.

Chess, Trevor thinks. He must constantly plan five to six moves ahead of everyone else. He must compete with everyone around him including the President, whether he knows it or not, to ensure that his plans bear fruit. If he's successful, all SMs will benefit and America will become something new, he believes. The thought of returning to the old way is anathema to him. We're not going back, he says to himself, and I'm not throwing away my shot.

* * *

Darryl reaches his commanding officer's offices and waits for him to call him into his office from the reception area. He is literally twiddling his thumbs, something that he never does. Darryl is normally a patient man, but he feels anxious because of his orders and what they could mean for himself, his squad and the country.

"Corporal, you may go in now," his C.O.'s secretary says. "Thank you," he responds as he stands and walks the short distance to his C.O.'s office door. His C.O. stands behind his desk,which is rare, as he walks in.

"Sergeant, have a seat," his C.O., Colonel Mitchell says to him.

"Colonel, I'm a pri-" Darryl begins but is cut off by Colonel Mitchell.

"Not today, you're not. You're Sergeant Darryl Isaacs from this day forward. You've performed exemplary in the field. Your leadership is beyond question. You're a real asset to your troops and to your leadership. As a result, you've been promoted. Consider it a battlefield promotion. You've earned it."

Colonel Mitchell is all smiles as he shakes Darryl's hand and gives him his stripe.

"Thank you, Colonel," Darryl says. "This means a lot. But what, Sir, is the bad news?" he asks.

"Right to the point, Isaacs. I like that. The bad news, Sergeant, is that you've got an immediate mission of which you've been informed. We need to determine whether President Lopez is alive or not. This comes straight from the top. If he is alive, we need him extracted. You and your squad already have experience with this. Still, obviously, this is extremely high value and you've probably already surmised that it could impact a possible or probable war with Mexico. Is your squad ready?" Colonel Mitchell asks.

"Yes, Sir, we're ready. A bit fatigued, for sure, but we can get after it," Darryl replies.

"Good. And with your new rank, you've now got responsibility for two additional squads. We're a go in eighteen hours at 0500. Go assemble your squads and give them their orders. Here are your detailed orders," he says, handing Darryl an envelope. "You're going in by Black Hawks. Major Williams is your liaison. I believe that you've recently met her. Hell of a pilot. Glad to have her here. She volunteered."

Darryl had stopped listening after he'd heard the words 'two additional squads'. *One squad is enough of a responsibility*, he thinks. Three squads would be tough for anyone. More bodies, more concerns, more dangers, more risks. Darryl is proud that he's never lost a single soldier from any of their missions. He considers their lives more important than his own. With three squads, his ability to look out and protect them diminishes and his anxiety rises.

"Sergeant! Sergeant!!!! Are you with me?" Colonel Mitchell asks. "It seems like I lost you for a minute."

"I'm here, Sir. Just thinking about all of the prep we have to do before we leave," Darryl says recovering.

"Good. Get after it. Major Williams will have your coordinates. The Black Hawks will serve as backup. There will be four to transport and support you. Dismissed."

Sergeant Isaacs stands up and salutes Colonel Mitchell who salutes him in return. He leaves his C.O.'s office walking purposefully back to his barracks. He hadn't needed to ask which two additional squads that he's in charge of. He already knows.

They are the two squads his now former Sergeant had been in charge of. Obviously, he had been promoted as well and is probably in charge of the entire platoon. Darryl will report to him first, get his official assignment, and then pull all three squads together for quick talk on preparation and mission. *Just another day in the new America*, he thinks. *It all feels like war to me.*

* * *

President Lopez awakens feeling disoriented. He is lying on his back. When he opens his eyes, he sees that he's in the dark. He can't tell whether it's dark outside or whether it's just dark in his room. He stays where he is for a few long minutes allowing his eyes to orient to his surroundings. He can tell that he's in some sort of small room, a cell perhaps, that has high walls. The bed that he's on is connected to one of the walls. He lays upon a thin mattress.

Lopez touches the wall to feel what it is. It's concrete. He sees a small window, if it can be called that, at the top of the wall to which his bed is attached. Even standing on his bed, he sees that he can't reach it or peer out of it. He can tell that it's nighttime as no light, other than moonlight, comes through the window.

Well, at least I'm not dead yet. Perhaps she's had a change of heart, he thinks cynically. President Lopez knows why he is where he is; his wife, Margarita. He'd long known of her hyper ambition and had long worked to mitigate it. He'd long endured her constant probing and prodding of his actions since becoming Mexico's president, always seeming to know about issues and high-level discussions before he'd ever had a chance to communicate them outside of his office. Of course, he'd suspected that his office was bugged, that his phones are tapped and that at least one person on his staff had been feeding his wife information. President Lopez had regular sweeps of his office for bugs and other listening devices and each time the results had been negative. But somehow, Margarita always knew what was going on and what to ask him.

Something had obviously triggered her, he thinks. She must be stopped, but at present, he has no way to do so. To kidnap and detain her own husband, the President of Mexico, she's sure to have amassed the political capital that she needs to remove me, detain me and ultimately, kill me so that she can assume power, he knows. If she knows of my agreement with President Douglas and that's what triggered her, then it's logical to assume that she'll do the opposite and provoke war with the United States. Mexico cannot abide such a result. It would hurt America, but it would devastate us, he knows.

Mexico's only hope is to stop Margarita. At present, he has no idea how to accomplish that. With him out of the way, she's free and clear to run the country as she sees fit. It's a coup, and for now, a bloodless one. *If I ever get out of here,* he thinks angrily, *I'll have her arrested and tried and I'm firing and imprisoning my driver and security detail.* They were all in on it, he admits to himself grousing at their betrayal. That's a big 'if' though, he knows. More likely, Margarita will have him executed just as soon as the dust clears. *At least I'm not in chains or sitting in a barrel of acid,* he decides. *Yeah, at least.*

CHAPTER X

On the fourth day after her awakening, Samantha has more questions than answers. Though only ten years old, she is smart and quick-witted. After four days in the Hive, she has learned much from Ifé and on her own as Ifé has shown her how to access historical records and current news from the artificial intelligence console in her room. Eighty years ago, she would have had a computer to look at and type on. Today, the internet is integrated into every surface of her room. She need only point to a wall and any image that she wants to see appears with a spoken command. She's had fun with that especially when Ifé has allowed her to watch some of her favorite anime cartoons from the past.

"Ifé, where are my parents?" Samantha asks her on one of their trips back from the cafeteria closest to her room. It is a short distance away and Samantha makes the trip three to four times per day eating but also visiting with new friends that she's made. Each time she goes to the cafeteria, she sees something new. Yesterday, she had seen a troop of young SM women practicing their martial arts as they dutifully did every morning. Ifé had called them 'helpers' though they appeared to be much more than that.

To Samantha, they'd appeared to be warriors of some sort though their drab gray uniforms belied that idea. Samantha had never seen women move the way that these did for whom such movements seemed wholly routine.

"Why do you ask me that question, Dearheart?" Ifé asks. "You're doing it again, Ifé. You're answering my question with a question. I need to know," Samantha says.

Ifé looks down at Samantha as they walk. At twelve years old, she notes that Samantha still retains the body and height of a girl who has yet to enter puberty. She wonders when Samantha might begin her physical change. Ifé stops walking and turns Samantha to face her.

"Samantha, a lot about what you're experiencing is very hard. You've learned that you've just awakened from an eighty-year slumber. You've learned that your country has drastically changed. You've learned that people who look like me are now the majority and that your home no longer exists as it was, though of course, you still have a home." Ifé takes a big breath before continuing. "And now, Samantha, you're going to learn that your parents are deceased. You were in a horrific car accident with them on Sleep Day. You survived it. They did not."

Samantha feels her legs give out. Before she can come close to falling, Ifé grabs her gently by the shoulders and pulls Samantha into herself. "I've got you. You're safe. I'm so sorry for the loss of your parents," she hears Ifé say. Burying her face into Ifé's torso, Samantha sobs uncontrollably. This is the secret that Ifé had been keeping from her. She'd known that something was wrong almost from the time that she'd awakened. And now, Samantha understands her condition. *She is out of place, out of time and alone*, she thinks. *I have no one. I was my parents' only child. I am alone*, she thinks again.

"You are not alone, Dearheart. You will have Ifé with you. I will never let anything bad happen to you," Ifé promises as her own tears flow from her dark eyes and down onto her dark face. "You are not alone," she repeats.

IMs and SMs walk around Ifé and Samantha, none thinking to stop and speak. What they witness is a familiar scene at the Hive. IMs awakening routinely getting news of some tragedy related to family members or some inestimable loss that only tears and often, anger can express.

Ifé sees a nearby bench and walks Samantha to it. They both sit on it, Ifé still holding Samantha closely to her. She hums a soft tune and gently rocks back and forth while Samantha still sobs. To Samantha, it feels as if eternity has passed before she takes a moment to pull away from Ifé and looks up at her.

"What's going to happen to me, Ifé? Who will take care of me?" Samantha asks.

Ifé looks at Samantha with deep love and compassion. What she feels for this shy, young girl goes far beyond her role or her abilities as an empath, she realizes. To her, Samantha had become a member of her family and one of her daughters. She'd known about Samantha and her condition months ago when the IMs first began to awaken. Orphans like Samantha had been selected and assigned to people like Ifé who had volunteered to look after and care for each awakening IM orphan. Ifé had been studying and learning about her for a while now. She'd known that this day would come, the day when she would have to answer some difficult questions. That hadn't made it any easier as now Ifé mourns with her in the midst of her loss.

"I will take care of you, Samantha. My family and I will do our best to finish raising you and get you ready for this new world. I am married to a wonderful man and have two daughters and two sons. Two are older than you. Two are younger. You'll fit right in. They already know about you and are eagerly expecting your arrival. This has been a big deal in my family for some time now," Ifé says.

"Okay," Samantha says. Her sadness hangs like a blanket between them. She can still see her mother clearly, smiling, making breakfast on many mornings, camping, laughing in the car with Dad and game nights. But that is not her reality anymore, she realizes. Now, she's in the hands of this woman who looks, sounds and smells so differently from what she's known.

Not only is Ifé different, she thinks, *everything around her is different too.* She's been looking at pictures of the new cities. The buildings look different. The people look and are different. Everything is different. Samantha can't help but be excited about the prospect of seeing it all with her own eyes. She wonders about living with Ifé and her family and about school, her new neighborhood, and how she'll be treated.

Eventually, they stand from the bench and begin to walk again slowly to the cafeteria. "Ifé, what will life be like for me?" she asks. "In my world, people like me,"" she says, hesitating, "seemed to be in charge. That's not the case anymore. What might that mean for me?"

"We are not a perfect country, Samantha, but no one will hate you for existing. No one will hurt you physically. No one will exclude you from anything that you should have or that you work for. No one. And if anyone tries, our family and I will rain hell down upon them. You have my word on that," Ifé says emphatically.

"Where do you and your family live, Ifé?" Samantha queries, trying to gain her bearings about where her life will take place.

"We live in Dallas, Samantha. It's beautiful and modern. I think that you'll like it very much," Ifé says. "It's quite a bit different than the Birmingham that you remember, though your home city has changed a lot too."

"Are," Samantha begins to say, feeling her tongue getting stuck. "Are my parents still there?" she asks, her eyes filling up again with fresh tears.

"Yes, they are. I know exactly where they are buried. I confirmed their whereabouts long before I met you formally. Would you like to see them?" Ifé offers. "I can take you to see them when we leave here."

"Yes, Ifé, I would like that very much," Samantha says. They reach the cafeteria and walk in. There are a number of IMs and SMs there all eating, sitting and chatting. Samantha sees a table of some other IM girls that she had befriended a few days ago. "Ifé, I'm going to sit with them," she says, pointing to the table of IM girls.

"Yes, that's fine, Samantha," Ifé says, smiling as her charge walks away.

Samantha gets a tray, goes to the food line and gets her fill of her favorite breakfast foods. The morning's sadness had not diminished her appetite, and in fact, had made her even hungrier. Once her tray is full, she finds her friends and sits down.

"Hi, Sam," a girl named Bethany says.

"Please don't call me that, Bethany. My name is Samantha, not Sam."

"Sorry, Sam, I mean, Samantha. You seem down. What's wrong?" Bethany asks.

Samantha does not want to repeat what she's just learned. She just wants to sit with familiar company and eat in peace. "I don't really want to talk about it if that's okay," she says.

The five other girls at the table give one another knowing looks but don't speak. They allow Samantha to eat without pressing her. Soon, they start speaking again with all, except Samantha, talking about their soon coming futures.

"My mother and father are awake and waiting for me to come to Cleveland. I think they might come here and pick me up. I can't wait!" one girl says.

"My parents are alive, but they're still asleep," another girl says. "I may have to wait for them or I can choose to go with my guardian. She says it's up to me, but I can tell that she wants me to go with her. I have to let her know soon. We'll see", the girl concludes.

"My parents are dead," Samantha hears herself say. "I'm alone."

Her tears begin to flow at the sound of her own voice. She feels like she's stepped outside of her body and is looking at herself sitting pitifully in the midst of her friends. She sees their horrified and sad faces. She hates that she is the source ofso much pity. Before today, before Sleep Day, her life had been nearly perfect. She'd always wanted a little brother but not getting one had been her only disappointment since her parents had always showered her with love, affection and attention. But now, Samantha realizes she has been propelled into an uncertain future with people that she does not know.

Samantha feels a firm but gentle hand on her left shoulder. "Samantha, let's go. You can get something to eat in your room," Ifé says. Samantha slowly rises, her head low. Ifé extends her hand and takes it, feeling like she needs it to anchor her and keep her from devolving into a crying mess. *This is by far the worst day of my life*, she thinks. She feels adrift in this strange world that holds none of the comfort or familiarity that she's known. Ifé is kind, but she's not her mother. Her mother is dead. Her father is dead. She should be dead. *Who or what can she be now?* She wonders.

"You can be, Dearheart, whatever you want to be. You have no limits," Ifé says.

Samantha looks up at her with wide eyes. She sees that slight glow around Ifé that she'd thought she'd seen the very first time that she looked at her. Ifé words somehow ground her and reassure her. *Perhaps Ifé is right,* Samantha thinks. *I'm not who or what I was, but maybe I can be someone different. Maybe I can be whatever I want.* She takes some comfort in that thought as Ifé leads her into her room and begins to prepare a meal for her.

* * *

"Electro-magnetism, Dr. Garrett," Dr. Foster says. "That's how it all works. We pretty much figured that out during one of our major waves of innovation a few years after Sleep Day. Since then, our engineers have been refining it. Have it down to a science now, I think," he says.

As Dr. Foster speaks, they board a train at one of the major junctions that crisscross America. They are above ground, which Dr. Garrett appreciates. Since the Hive is underground, he hadn't seen the sun until they disembarked from their pod which transported them from the Hive. It's bright and somewhat chilly. They're at least eight hundred miles away from their final destination, Denver, but Dr. Foster tells him that they'll be there in about an hour and forty-five minutes or less.

"If you notice, Dr. Garrett, there are no planes in the sky. That's because we've all but done away with commercial flights, at least in the continental United States we have. With the speed of the trains and their reliability, there's just no good reason to have them. They're also not cost-competitive with our modern transportation by train. All of our pilots now fly internationally or for the military and frankly, most of those flights are by drone technology. The rail expansion was a massive infrastructure job decades ago. Lots of jobs got created and lots of folks got rich during that period of our rail expansion. Shoot, lots of jobs are probably still being made with all of the engineering, transformed cities, oh, and our ever-expanding energy grid," Dr. Foster says.

Dr. Garrett settles into a first-class seat with Dr. Foster sitting across from him. *At least,* Dr. Garrett thinks, *it's first-class.* Their cabin is plush, has large seats that almost fully recline, and he's sure, though Dr. Foster hasn't told him, that there is an A.I. provided meal service from which he can order pretty much anything he wants.

"This is beautiful, Foster. I've never seen a machine like this in my world," Dr. Garrett says.

"Is it?" Dr. Foster asks, genuinely surprised by Dr. Garrett's comment. "This is what the trains have always looked like to me. Been this way, probably, for the last sixty years or so. I hadn't even noticed. If you're hungry, you can order anything you'd like right from your seat, and someone or something will bring it to you within five minutes."

Dr. Garrett understands what Dr. Foster means when he says that something will bring him his food. While at the Hive, he had well noticed all of the various autonomous devices and robots wheeling and walking around. Some of the IMs, who looked to be in fairly critical condition, notably the elderly, had had a personal medical robot that helped them walk or be wheeled to various locales around the Hive, like the cafeteria, the infirmary, exercise rooms and more. *Clearly,* Dr. Garrett thinks, *they've made major advances in robotics and automation.*

"Dr. Garrett, please take these," Dr. Foster says as he hands him a small box. When he opens it, he sees a device that looks like a watch and a device that looks like his old iPhone.

"What are these, Dr. Foster? I know better than to think they're a watch and an iPhone", Dr. Garrett says.

"Well, you're partially right. This really is a watch and a whole lot more. It's actually a whole computer on your wrist, complete with all of the A.I. that you'll ever need. It serves as a watch, communications device, money, tickets for the train, and everything else. By the way, Hamilton has just recently come back. It's playing in Denver right now. Great show!" Dr. Foster says.

"When you have it on, you'll never be lost. It constantly checks your vitals and can even send electronic stimuli to your brain to ease stress, fight sickness and remove hunger pangs. When that little feature first came online, you should have seen the hordes of skinny people who abused that feature. Folks would stop eating for days at a time. The A.I. has since been corrected to disable the possibility of that," Dr. Foster says with a slight chuckle.

"This phone-looking thing really is a phone. No one but recently awakened IMs use these, but we provide them as a source of familiar comfort since cell phones were such a big deal in your time. It's loaded with a bunch of apps and doesn't have our A.I. It's just a cell phone, but you can make calls on it if you prefer to use it rather than your watch. Your watch is much easier to use, though. The A.I. knows who you are and knows who you mean when you say 'call Dr. Foster'. Easy" Dr. Foster says.

"Oh, and you never have to worry about charging any of these devices. All of our electronics are perpetually being charged pretty much no matter where you are, inside or outside, based upon our wireless charging tech which extends from coast to coast. You'd pretty much have to be deep in the woods somewhere for your devices and other tech not to be fully charged, and even then, it's doubtful since coverage for our wireless charging tech was created to cover every square inch of the continental United States. That's a big deal. Not every country has that tech. Europe may have just gotten it. Russia doesn't have it. They're little more than a third-world country now. It's sad."

As Dr. Garrett puts on the watch and looks at the phone, he marvels at how far, technologically, the country had come. On one level, he thinks, things seem to be pretty perfect here though he doubts, given human nature, that societal perfection had been fully achieved in this new America. At least, he realizes, things aren't perfect for him. My wife has not yet awakened, one of my sons is still asleep, and the other is missing. It's not perfect by half, he concludes.

"How do I stay up to date with my family?" he asks Dr. Foster.

"Your family? Easy. As I mentioned, the A.I. in your watch knows who you are, your history and the ones attached to you, even me. You only need to say 'how's my wife?' or 'where'smy wife?' and you'll get all the details that you could ever want, including current video images of your wife and son. Try it now,"Dr. Foster says.

"Where is my wife?" Dr. Garrett says, speaking into his watch. At his question, an image appears emanating about six inches from his watch that first shows a spinning globe, the Earth, with a red dot. It then moves down to the state level, Montana, and next goes underground to the heart of the Hive. Once in the Hive, the image races through many corridors until stopping at his wife's pod. He then sees her face through the window of her stasis pod.

Her eyes are closed, and she looks asleep, even peaceful, he thinks. In this moment, he realizes that he misses her terribly even though they had been having issues prior to Sleep Day. He wonders how she'll feel about him once she awakens. His affair certainly hadn't helped matters nor his busy work schedule.

Dr. Garrett looks across at Dr. Foster and wonders if he should broach his next question. He thinks that perhaps Dr. Foster may not know his and his wife's relationship status and how they were moving toward divorce when Sleep Day forever changed and ripped their lives apart.

"Dr. Foster," he says haltingly, "how does the new America deal with divorce?" He hears Dr. Foster sigh and watches as he continues to look out the window at the fast-moving landscape. Dr. Garrett hasno real sense of how fast they're traveling except to look outside.

They're probably close to moving at five hundred miles per hour at this point, he realizes. The train is so smooth and so quiet, though, that it feels like they may as well be standing still. *This is marvelous technology,* he thinks. Dr. Garrett recalls that in his America, high-speed trains had always been a political non-starter given the oil and gas industries and the airplane industry's great opposition to it. *These people have come a long way over the last eighty years. Had it only been eighty,* he wonders to himself. *What might he be witnessing if it had been two hundred years?*

"Dr. Garrett, our society has evolved in nearly every way. The old rules governing marriage, for the most part, still exist. If two married people, or one of the married persons, decide to no longer be married, then a divorce will be granted. It's actually easier and faster now to get a divorce than in your day. That was a function of both law and technology some time ago. We are aware of your wife's disposition prior to Sleep Day because we found evidence of her having contacted a divorce attorney, who herself was stricken by the Sleepers virus and that lawyer's notes on the matter. Unfortunately, your wife had a prepared divorce filing ready to go and would have filed it by the very next week had Sleep Day not occurred. When she awakens, she'll be the person that she was with all of the thoughts and feelings that she had then. Frankly, a lot of these awakenings are a mixed bag. No matter what, you'll be supported by me and by society at large as you continue your transition. It won't be easy, but you're not alone."

Dr. Garrett is nonplussed at all that he's just heard from Dr. Foster. It occurs to him that he was simultaneously impressed and a little frightened that agents of this new America had the sophistication to peer into the most private details of his life and reconstruct its particulars at a level that even he had not been aware of. *My entire reawakened time has felt like this, hadn't it,* he ponders. Dr. Garrett recalls that over the course of the week, he'd awakened from an eighty-year slumber, discovered that he's now part of an America that he no longer recognizes, stopped being an actual doctor given the speed of medical technology passing him by, and now, hurtles at ungodly speeds to his former city which has apparently changed in ways that he'd never recognize, and has become, essentially, a ward of the state since he's wholly unqualified to work in his former profession. *It looks like the damn robots do pretty much everything else,* he thinks bitterly. On top of all else, one of his sons is still missing, presumed dead, and his estranged wife, when she wakes up, will probably make good on her threat to divorce him. *Frankly, why shouldn't she,* he thinks.

Like many middle-aged men, who also happen to be successful, he'd allowed his ego to lead him down a path that had brought his marriage to the brink. He loves his wife and had known her since college. Up until his affair, she had always been"the one" to him and had mostly treated her as such. The last five years of their marriage had been difficult, though. Somehow, even mundane tasks between them had become hard and were rife with argument and bad feelings. Once, when they'd had a particularly loud, vicious argument in the middle of their local Kroger's grocery store, it had then occurred to him that something is really wrong. Shortly thereafter, Dr. Garrett's affair began in earnest.

She was a pretty, young internist just a few years removed from medical school. Andrea Carter. Dr. Garrett had noticed her the very first time that she'd done her surgical rotations with him. She had also been brilliant and Black. Dr. Garrett recalls that she'd attended Stanford for her undergraduate degree and had attended Morehouse's medical school thereafter, graduating first in her class. Of all the interns that Dr. Garrett had had, she was the most accomplished and brilliant. They had liked each other almost immediately. Her friendship had been such a refreshing change to what he'd been missing at home. Towards the end, by Sleep Day, he and Helen, his wife, had barely been speaking to one another.

He and Andrea's affair had lasted for a passionate six months before Helen found out about it. Dr. Garrett had carelessly left his phone open with his text messages showing. At that point, there was no way to deny it and honestly, he hadn't felt like even trying. He'd known that Helen was unhappy and that they'd crossed a bridge that seemed impossible to re-cross. He still loves his wife and loved her then, but he had no idea how to save his marriage or if he even wanted to. Dr. Garrett was clear that Andrea loved him, but he was unsure about what kind of future they might have together. Sitting here today, on this train, he knows two things for certain: He misses his wife, and Andrea is long dead.

"Dr. Foster, whatever happened to Andrea?" he asks.

"Andrea Carter? She lived a long time. She died at eighty-five. She got married, had three kids and had an amazing career doing what you used to do. In fact, she was a major source of many of the medical innovations that we enjoy today. She also kept tabs on you, always knew where you were and left special instructions for your care should you ever awaken after her death. In fact, it's fair to say that I'm here because of her. It's also fair to say that because of her, the life that you'll get to live in Denver or wherever you choose to be has largely been funded by a trust that Dr. Carter set up and established for you. In fact", Dr. Foster says rummaging through a portfolio that he'd carried with him, "this is for you."

Dr. Foster hands him an envelope emblazoned with his name in all capital letters: "DR. DONALD GARRETT". He beginsto open it carefully, slowly. It looks old; he can see where the envelope had begun to yellow with age "How old is this, Foster?" he asks.

"It's twenty years old. It's for you, from her."

Dr. Garrett pulls the letter from the aging envelope. It's one page. He sees that the writer, Andrea, has written it in her own hand. Even at an advanced age, her hand had been strong. The fact that she'd taken the time to actually write the letter instead of having itdictated or typing it, means something to him.

Dear Donald,

If you're reading this, it means that you're finally awake. Thank God! It also means that I'm no longer here. That's the bad news. I've longed to see you up and awake, but sadly, that is not to be.

I want you to know that I love you, have always loved you and will always love you. Even through my marriage and all of its ups and downs, I've loved you. In life, you were very kind to me and always honest. I appreciate that more than you know.

Like you, I've made a lot of money. In fact, some of my money is actually yours. When the property transfers occurred, I made the decision to claim your house in Denver. That also meant that I got access to all of your bank and brokerage accounts. You made me rich in my twenties! I want you to know that I hardly touched your money and took meticulous care of your house. I haven't always lived in it, my husband insisted that we do not, but I've kept ownership of it and placed all of your other assets in a trust in your name.

As you now return to Denver from the Hive, I am happy to tell you that you'll be returning to your own home. Your most personal effects are in storage in your basement should you want them. Also, the proceeds of your trust, which have grown quite large, are being turned over to you once you sign a few documents and your identity is proven.

Lastly, welcome to the new world! It's different from the one that you left but no less wonderful and exciting. Our new world, our new America has finally fulfilled all of its promise to anyone who wants it and works hard for it. I'm not certain that you'll be able to be a doctor again because so much has changed. But doctor or no, you're still the brilliant, loving and kind man that I fell in love with in my twenties. I'm sorry for the harm done to your marriage, but I'm not sorry for loving you.

Always,

Andrea Carter, MD

"Sign these, Dr. Garrett, and the trust is yours," Dr. Foster says as he hands him an electronic tablet showing multiple forms ready for his signature. "I've already established your identity. Congratulations. You're one of only a few IMs for whom something like this has been made possible," Dr. Foster says.

Dr. Garrett accepts the tablet and looks at the forms. There are three requiring his signature. He sees his name, his address in Denver, and Andrea's name. He sees the balance in his trust.

His eyes nearly pop out. In his day, he had been rich, but nothing approaching the amount he now sees. "How much is this in today'smoney, Dr. Foster?" he asks.

Dr. Foster chuckles. "It's more than enough to live several lifetimes in this or any country, Dr. Garrett. Even by our standards, you are a very wealthy man. Dr. Carter used only the best investment advisors to take care of your money. You're almost as rich as she was," he says.

Dr. Garrett stares at his smiling comrade. He is speechless. A week ago, he could barely open his eyes. Now, he's speeding to his home, his actual home, and is wealthy beyond all imagining. *Helen is definitely going to divorce me now*, he thinks. *When she finds out how rich I am and where the money came from, yep, it's over*, he believes. *Well at least it's more than enough money to be cut in half and shared.*

"Oh, one other point, Dr. Garrett. This is your money and yours alone. Because Dr. Carter put it in a trust for you and grew it by her own efforts, it can't be touched by any divorce decree. If you and Helen divorce, you'll have to pay something since your wife won't be working, at least in the foreseeable future, but it won't be half, just in case you were wondering about that," Dr. Foster says.

As Dr. Garrett looks out the window at the landscape before him, he notices that his train has begun to slow down. He starts to see the outline of a massive cityscape. *This is Denver*, he thinks. I recognize it by the surrounding mountains. But he doesn't recognize the buildings. The new buildings are massive, and more than a few of them appear to be green, he sees, with abundant plant life.

"Dr. Foster, are those buildings green?" he asks incredulously. "Ah, yes, they are. Most of our buildings are now, literally, green. When folks began super-populating the biggest cities after Sleep Day, we had a need to bring food production to them. That caused building standards to dramatically change. Now, almost any new building going up must have the ability to provide food to its inhabitants and to others within a few blocks radius.

Those standards have begun to relax a bit since our

population exploded, but we still see these here and there. Denver is a beautiful city. I think that you'll enjoy it."

Soon, their train enters Union Station, Denver's main train station. Their travel had only been about two hours in total, but Dr. Garrett is anxious to stand up and depart. He wants to see his house and the city. He feels pleasantly excited to be home. He realizes that it'll be empty with only him in it, but he's excited just the same.

Once they disembark from the train, Dr. Foster escorts him outside. It's a chilly day in April but not too cold. Dr. Garrett feels his clothes warming him as he walks. Even if he'd wanted to be cold, he's not entirely sure that his clothes would allow him to be. *These SMs have thought of everything*, he thinks. As he looks outside, he sees tall skyscrapers of every size and dimension. Clearly, an artist has had a hand in designing much of what he sees, he realizes.

As they step onto the sidewalk, he hears a low hum and feels slight vibrations arising from it. "Why does the sidewalk hum, Foster?" he asks.

"Oh that," Dr. Foster says off-handedly, "you're making electricity with every step that you take. This is one of the energy capture technologies implemented more than a generation ago. As people move, they create electricity stored in the local electrical grid or sent overseas to help power other cities and countries, especially our southern and Caribbean neighbors. It's the reason that fossil fuels have, by and large, gone the way of the dinosaur.

We have more electric juice than we know what to do with." Once outside, Dr. Foster says into his watch, 'car please', and within minutes, a sleek, expensive-looking sedan pulls up, itsx-wing doors opening up widely for their entry. Once inside, he says: "Please take us to Dr. Garrett's house." The car acknowledges his request, and off they go quickly and with almost no sound whatsoever.

"Dr. Foster, remind me again how many people live in the U.S. now," Dr. Garrett says.

"We've got about a billion give or take, most of whom are SMs. We have a robust immigration policy that allows most SMs from most parts of the world to get in no problem. There are IMs here a few million, but nothing like it used to be. In fact, the greatest part of the IM population is still asleep. Once they all wake up, we'll see another population surge. Believe me when I tell you that the awakening of the IM population has been the source of much consternation and debate. Many laws have been passed in anticipation of their...your awakening. President Amon hasn't really taken a side one way or the other, but I have to tell you that many SMs would have preferred that the IMs never wake up. But also, many are glad that you're here and will warmly receive you. Denver is as liberal, more so even, as it's ever been. This is agood jumping off point for you."

Dr. Garrett takes in what Dr. Foster has just told him before asking his next question. "Does," Dr. Garrett begins almost hesitating to ask his question, "racism exists here?" He watches as Dr. Foster tilts his head up in obvious contemplation of an answer. Dr. Foster takes afew moments to think before he speaks.

"Racism. Great question. Yes, but it's complicated," he says. "Humans being humans, yes racism exists here as it does anywhere else. We have an upper class that is based more upon accomplishment, wealth to a certain degree and some other things. And that's before we add IMs back to the mix," Dr. Foster explains. "Look, Dr. Garrett, you'll hear more about this, but I want to be the first to tell you. Society has changed dramatically. IMs are no longer at the top of the food chain. They...you're at the bottom. You are a very wealthy IM, but in this new society, you're rare. You should brace yourself for that. Remember that you're re-entering, essentially, at the point of your last memory. Your wealth will help buffet some of it, but not all of it. It is what it is."

Dr. Foster stops speaking and sits all the way back in his seat as their transport continues on its journey silently down first the highway, next some main thoroughfares and then, he recognizes, the street on which his house resides. The trip to his house is somewhat familiar to Dr. Garrett, but it's clear that so much has changed.

Overwhelmingly, he's seen SMs of every stripe walking, talking, traveling and generally moving about as if it's the most natural thing in the world. He thinks Black and Brown people were certainly around in my day, but not nearly as much as I see today.

Clearly, there's more of them than there are of us. He does not see any IMs like him at any point from the train station to now.

"Dr. Foster, are there IMs here in Denver," Dr. Garrett queries.

"To my understanding, yes, and there are more and more coming every day. This is a huge project for us. Someone like me is assigned to every single IM that awakens. It's critical for proper re-immersion into the fabric of society, we think. And frankly, our current approach is one of several that was offered up and voted upon."

"What were the other approaches?" Dr. Garrett asks.

"Well, Dr. Garrett, you asked about racism. One form in which it's taken is that a significant but vocal minority lobbied vigorously for IMs to either remain asleep and/or be shipped wholescale out of America altogether, not unlike what most of the European countries did to SMs when the Sleepers virus struck.

As you're starting to see, much has changed since the last time that you were here, Dr. Garrett. Our education system has been completely revamped, for one thing. We learn the complete and unfettered history of the foundation of this country, the impact of American slavery, Jim Crow and all of the continuing structural racism that ensued after that. Kids in the sixth grade can recite the history chapter and verse. Also, soon after Sleep Day, SMs demanded and received a Truth & Reconciliation commission. It was a bit off-kilter because most American IMs were asleep. But many IMs who lived, at that time, in countries outside of theUnited States participated."

Dr. Foster stops speaking as their transport glides noiselessly onto Dr. Garrett's property. His driveway is long and smooth. His house is partially obscured by large trees that overhang the driveway and also cover the house. These trees had just been newly planted the last time that he'd seen them. They were mere saplings. Now, he sees, they're full-grown and stunning. *Beautiful,* he thinks.

"Ah," Dr. Foster says. "Very nice, very pretty, Dr. Garrett," he says as they both exit the transport.

"Wow, it sure is. Never thought I'd see it again," Dr. Garrett says.

"Right. Well, Dr. Carter took care of that. You'll notice that she built an extra wing onto the house. And it says here," Dr. Foster says while looking at his pad device, "it says here that the wiring has been upgraded twice, all of the fixtures are brand new, and you've got a personal transport in the garage, a BMW of some sort. You're lucky. Those are really nice. Most people don't even have their own personal transports anymore. Not really a need for them, but she remembered your old car, I guess. No need to drive it, though. Just tell it where to go."

Entering the front door, Dr. Garrett feels a sudden feeling of heavy nostalgia. He sees his wife walk by him and can almost smell her favorite perfume. In his mind's eye, she smiles at him. This is not one of the last memories that he has of her, he realizes. In the last two years of their marriage, she rarely smiled and never at him. Dr. Garrett suddenly feels the melancholy of loss.

He stands in his foyer at once, happy to be home, but knowing that he is alone, truly. His soon-to-be ex-wife, who hates him, is still stuck in stasis as is their son Luke. Will Dylan ever be found,he wonders? He wasn't in Denver on Sleep Day. He had been in school at the University of North Carolina. Dylan was an athlete. He played lacrosse.

"Are you okay, Dr. Garrett?" Dr. Foster asks. "It's a lot to take in, I know. Let's keep walking. I need to give you a tour of the house. Structurally, other than the new addition, it hasn't changed much. But there are many new features based upon our current technology that I should advise you of. Your home is completely outfitted with all of the latest tech including home-based A.I. Honestly, all of your needs can be completely met within these walls. You'll never have to leave it unless you want to."

As Dr. Foster continues speaking, he tells Dr. Garrett about all of the latest upgrades. He points out the home's energy-producing features, which are standard in every home, and how it produces its own electricity without connection to the central grid. It is connected to the central grid but that's mostly to provide electricity to it and not the other way around.

Dr. Garrett tries to listen carefully, but his thoughts soon drift back to Helen and their sons. Since he can't work as a doctor and doesn't really need to work anymore, period, he thinks that he'll spend his time looking for Dylan.

"Your home, Dr. Garrett, is completely programmed to you and your voice. It also has sensing technology attuned to you. It knows when you're here and when you're not. You can literally speak to the house to perform almost any task like scheduling, bringing your car around, ordering dinner, cooking dinner, etc., and it will comply. There are robots here too for cleaning, laundry and even bathing if you wish. You've got the complete package. And if you ever want to throw a party, the whole thing turns into a nightclub. It's pretty great" Dr. Foster says.

He seems to be enjoying this, Dr. Garrett thinks to himself. He wonders if Dr. Foster has ever sold real estate. He sounds like a natural. "Honestly, Dr. Foster, I'm a little tired from our trip, fast though it was. Is it okay if we postpone the remainder of the tour?" he asks.

"No problem, Dr. Garrett. I can come back tomorrow if youwish. I'm only in town one more day and then I'm home to Dallas.My family misses me," he says.

"I get it. Tomorrow then," Dr. Garrett says.

After he leaves, Dr. Garrett climbs the long staircase up to the second floor and winds his way down the curved hallway to the master bedroom. Entering the room, he thinks that he almost feels Helen within its walls. But it's just him, he knows. No Helen, just himself. The bed is king-sized just as he remembers. He climbs in and soon after begins to slumber. As he rests, his last thoughts are of his family and of Andrea, whose love for him has made all of this possible.

CHAPTER XI

Eric Franks hates it here. He hates it here. He is alone and he knows it, not that he minds it. He hates that he feels isolated. He hates that he'd awakened eighty years later into an America that he does not know. He hates that no one who looks like him seems to be in charge of anything. He hates the way that his handler Koje looks at him as if he is continually scraping some unclean thing from the bottom of his shoe. And he hates that there's not one single thing that he can do about it.

Eric awakened six days ago. In the time since his awakening, he has learned much. He's learned, for example,that though he'd been a decorated police officer, not only is he unqualified to be such again, or so Koje had told him, but politicians in the new America had also voted not to allow any IMs whatsoever to be a part of this country's security forces which are basically run and managed by the federal government. There is no such thing as local or state police anymore.

As Koje was more than happy to also tell him, the need for such police exists much less than they did in his day. Violent crime is almost non-existent. Murder rarely happens, rape basically never happens and other petty or property crimes don't occur because poverty had all but been eradicated. There is no such thing as either homelessness or hunger problem. Everyone eats. Everyone lives.

Bunch of goddamn communists if you ask me, Eric thinks to himself. He sits in his room reading and watching the news at the start of his day. This had been his ritual for much of his life and certainly for all of his adult life. A delicious cup of coffee sits next to him half-consumed from the time that he had awakened this morning. As usual, the A.I. in the room prepared the cup to perfection, knowing exactly how he likes it.

Eric finishes reading an article about President Amon's latest megaproject. *These people seem to be constantly doing some huge thing or another*, he thinks. He watches as a sophisticated spaceship launches from a platform in the middle of Nebraska. He hears President Amon discuss the country's latest foray into space and how this is the latest mission to find another habitable planet.

Apparently, efforts to terraform Mars are going more slowly than desired and this President had directed NASA to find alternative planets that can sustain human life.

The current exploratory vessel, President Amon says, is being sent to a solar system that is about three hundred light-years away. In the time that Eric and all of the other American IMs had been asleep, SM scientists had developed some kind of engine technology that enables them to make such exploration well within the lifetimes of the pilots. That engine technology is, apparently, a closely guarded secret of the U.S. government. No one knows what it is or how it works. To Eric, it sounds like WARP technology, the fictitious engines of Star Trek lore, but no one here calls it that.

Based on his reading, no other country has advanced as much in space travel in such a short time as had the United States. Long gone are the joint space missions in which the United States used to participate. That had ended right after Europe kicked its SMs out, most of whom came to the United States. Therefore, he surmises that President Douglas is responsible for their advances in space, having put so much more money into NASA as one of his last acts in office.

It is now 6:45 a.m., Eric, a voice in the room, says to him. Eric had set the alarm to make sure that he is awake before 7:00 a.m. When he was a cop he had usually been up and awake by 6:00 a.m. He worked first shift and had prided himself on being the first one to the precinct. *Old habits die hard,* he thinks. He also knows that Koje will be there to check on him and escort him to breakfast by 7:00 a.m. He doesn't think that Koje enjoys his company much, but in some moments of reflection, Eric had begun to wonder if perhaps he had been too harsh in his assessment of the man and whether he had been projecting his own disdain upon him.

Reflecting further, Eric acknowledges to himself that he is strangely hopeful and excited. Though the country is far different than what he remembers, and he won't get to return to his old job, he knows that by this society's rules, he'll have a place to live, plenty of food to eat, and be free to come and go as he pleases. According to Koje, he thinks I won't even need a car. They have self-operating transports everywhere that can get me anywhere. *I'm going to ask Koje about my pension,* he decides. I may not have my bank account or my investments anymore, but maybe they can do something with my pension. I'm sure they have the information, and I can recite chapter and verse on exactly how much it is and how much is owed to me. He decides to bring this topic up this morning on their walk to the cafeteria.

Koje is here, Eric hears the A.I. in his room say to him. "Please let him in," he responds.

The door to Eric's room slides silently into the wall and Koje walks in with a broad smile on his face. Eric had rarely seen him look so jovial. He wonders if his soon coming departure has lifted Koje's spirits.

"Eric, my friend," Koje almost booms. "We're getting pretty close to the end, my friend. How are you feeling on this bright sunny day?" he asks.

"How would I know if it's bright and sunny, Koje? Aren't we about a mile underground?" Eric asks with obvious sarcasm.

"So right, so right you are," Koje says. "But take my word for it, it is a bright and sunny day!"

"If you say so," Eric says, shrugging. "Ready to go? I'm starving. Been up waiting on you."

"Yes, I'm ready," Koje says. "And I have a feeling that you're going to have some questions for me."

Koje had consistently demonstrated an unnerving ability to anticipate Eric's questions and actions in the, albeit limited time that he'd known him. *He doesn't read minds*, Eric thinks, *but he reads something*. Eric had never considered himself to be an intellectual slouch. In fact, in all of his years as a police officer, he'd been regarded by his peers and colleagues as being highly intelligent, so much so that many of his superiors had tried to get him to take the detective's exam at the NYPD. Each time that he was asked, he had declined. Eric had always liked street work and training new officers for that work, and there was something about it that had always made him feel connected to the city itself. There is no question in Eric's mind that he'll be returning to New York when he leaves. It may not be the New York that he remembers, but it's still his home, he thinks.

As Eric and Koje leave his room and walk to their closest cafeteria for breakfast, Eric mentally formulates the questions that he wants to ask and puts them in order of importance first. This is his usual approach on complex issues and pretty much how he had conducted himself as a police officer, at least when his bad temper wasn't enabling him to make bad decisions.

"Koje, I do have some questions. The first one is whether the folks in charge kept up with all of the police pensions that were lost in the transition after Sleep Day and if so, whether they were saved for cops like me in case we awakened?" Eric asks, trying to stifle the earnestness in his voice.

"Great first question, Eric," Koje says. "I wondered when you might ask about that. Yes, the pensions were saved and kept track of for many years after Sleep Day. After about ten years, though, and especially in the midst of transforming the country, rebuilding the economy, and actually the whole scale changing the economy from a purely capitalistic one to one that is now a healthy hybrid between socialism and capitalism, police pension funds around the country were tapped to help shore up certain gaps and to continue funding our massive infrastructure changes. That money is the reason why so much, seventy years ago or so, was possible. When President Raheem Gates, God rest his soul, got into office, one of the first things he did was to expand President Douglas' infrastructure directives, making us envy the world. Not even the Chinese have a transportation system like ours. And President Gates had been very smart to re-do our country's internet system making it nigh impossible to hack."

Eric hears all that Koje says and the obvious pride in his retelling of the country's history after Sleep Day. It's his country now, but he also notes that what Koje has just said amounts to him not receiving his well-earned, hard-earned police pension. "So, does that mean that my pension is gone?" Eric asks.

"In one sense, yes, Eric, it's gone. But in another, no, it's not. We have of course continued to keep track of what it had been ten years after Sleep Day and then what it would have been at about five percent annualized interest over the last seventy years. The government is prepared to provide a large portion of your pension to you now, but no, you won't get all of it," Koje says.

"Not all of it?!" Eric asks, his voice rising with frustration.
"Not all of it," Koje says flatly. "As you know by now, there was a

Truth & Reconciliation commission that did a thorough, comprehensive review of the cost of systemic racism against SMs before Sleep Day. The commission found that the combination of lost wages during American slavery, Jim Crow, andthe post-Jim Crow period cost Black, Brown, and Asian people trillions upon trillions of dollars. Even with the massive property and business transfers that occurred after Sleep Day, the cost of such losses, plus four-hundred years of pain and suffering, were staggering."

"A year after Sleep Day," Koje continues, "the property and business transfers became irrevocable. This set off a massive round of citizenship abandonments by many American IMs and, strangely, some SMs too. It's the reason that Alaska seceded and has remained an independent nation to this day. The hardest part ofthat period was losing half of our fleet, the soldiers and personnel, not the ships which decided to join Alaska. But no matter, we've more than recovered since then and added Puerto Rico, New Columbia and Cuba as new American states."

"New Columbia," Eric asks. "Where is that?"

"Oh, that's what the District of Columbia used to be. Citizens there had fought long and hard to become a U.S. state. Sleep Day made that choice easy. It's one of the last things that President Douglas accomplished. No taxation without representation is what they used to say. Well, they finally got representation," Koje concludes.

Much of what Koje had just said, Eric already knows. He'd spent much of his time in the Hive reading up on the history of the country post-Sleep Day, and most of it had angered him. Eric had been a conservative when that word used to mean something in his world. What he sees now is a massive property and resource grab from people like him, and that is what angers him the most. He thinks that never in a thousand years would the old America have allowed something like this to happen. *Not ever.*

"How much of my pension will I be allowed to have?" he asks Koje.

"You'll be given about thirty percent of its value at the time that Sleep Day occurred, the day that you were stricken," he replies.

"Thirty percent?! THIRTY PERCENT?!" Eric says, his

voice rising in volume. "That's unfair!! Why am I taking a seventy percent hit for something that I'm owed?!" he asks. Several people, SMs and IMs, stop looking at him as he stands, fists clenched nearly nose to nose with Koje, the much taller and larger man.

"Calm down, my friend," Koje says. "Calm down. You're making a scene," he intones as pleasantly as possible.

Eric doesn't care about the scene that he's making. He is beyond upset–he's incensed. His job is gone, his pension is nearly all gone, and his country is gone. He wants answers. "Koje, answer my question," he says through gritted teeth. "Where is my money?" "Your money, my friend," Koje says with a wide grin, "is exactly where it should have been all along. It's with my People."

Before he knows it, Eric swings his already-balled fists and swings them hard and fast at Koje's head. Eric had been a pretty good boxer in his day and had earned the distinction of being a Golden Gloves boxer in New York, which was pretty tough to do ninety-some years ago. What happens next, though, Eric has no words for. Koje deftly slides by Eric's straight right hand, then slips under his still outstretched hand from his punch. To Eric, Koje moves faster than he has time to think. He has just enough time to look down at Koje now crouched beneath him before he hears, "my friend, that was a tragic mistake."

What happens next, Eric never sees coming. His only recognition that anything has even happened is blinding pain and a hand or a foot coming at him faster than he can register. *Whatever happened,* he muses sometime later, *he'd had no ability to stop it and certainly, no ability to counter it.* Eric's last coherent thought before he shuts his eyes into unconsciousness is "damn".

* * *

Raheem stands in a place he thought he would never see. After graduating first in his class of Secret Service recruits, he had hoped that he might get this far, but standing just outside of the door to the Oval Office, he is humbled and at the same time anxious.

"The President will see you now," he hears the receptionist say. He hears her, but he doesn't move. All of this seems surreal. "Mr. Gates? The President will see you now," the receptionist says, her voice now full of knowing insistence.

"Now," he says, stammering. "Okay, thank you," Raheem says.

Raheem walks to the large door of the Oval Office and opens it.

"Mr. Gates!" he hears from the large bass voice behind the President's desk.

"Come in, come in. I am pleased to meet you," President Douglas says. "As I'm sure you've been told, I like to meet with all of the new persons assigned to my detail. It's something that my wife insists upon. Call it the eye test," he says with a certain gleam in his eye.

As Raheem walks into the office, the President gets up to greet him, walking around his desk with his hand extended. They shake hands and Raheem notes the power of the man's grip. He also sees that he is indeed tall, though not as tall as Raheem himself. President Gates has to tilt his head up slightly to look Raheem in his eyes, but he is definitely more than six feet.

"Sit down, sit down," the President says, pointing to a pair of couches. Raheem stiffly complies. He's a little thrown off by how warm the President is and how genuine. Raheem likes him immediately but is determined to maintain all formality. He wants to make a good first impression.

"Now, Raheem, may I call you Raheem or do you prefer Mr. Gates?" President Douglas asks earnestly.

"Raheem is fine, Sir," he replies, feeling slightly silly by his response. *In what universe would he not accept pretty much any name that President Douglas assigns to him,* he thinks.

"Raheem, it is then" President Douglas says with a wide smile. "Of course, I've read your file and been impressed. I am aware, also, of your time in prison. How would you describe that time?"

"My time in prison, Sir, was both enlightening and unnecessary," he says. Raheem is not ashamed that he served time in prison, but he is ashamed of the time spent away from his family. What he had done was wrong but not at all worthy of the years he was put away.

"Well, it seems to me, Raheem, that you were unjustly

persecuted as so many of our Black and Brown men in this country have been. You committed the assault, but I'm also a lawyer. There's no way that that should have been more than a misdemeanor with a thirty-day jail stay at the most. I used to be a public defender. You were railroaded."

President Douglas' voice hangs like a heavy bass drum in the room. His intonation is perfect and precise. He looks fixedly at Raheem with both seriousness and, Raheem sees, a look of honest compassion. For a few moments, they look at each other, each man regarding the other.

"I appreciate that Sir," Raheem says, breaking the silence between them. "The hardest part was the impact that it had on my family. I was on my way to getting married when I got locked up. Thankfully, we survived it, but it was a heavy price to pay, too heavy, in fact."

"I whole-heartedly agree, Raheem. After everything that has happened, I'm glad that you're here. Before prison, you had a sterling military record. You were dishonorably discharged because of your conviction, but I can do something about that now. Before Sleep Day, it might not have been possible, but I'll give you a full Presidential pardon and remove the bad discharge so that you can get your full military pension. You deserve it. Thank you for your service."

Holy crap! Raheem thinks to himself. Of all the things that he had expected, this one thing hadn't entered his brain. He is shocked and completely floored by the President's generosity.

Because of his new salary with the Secret Service, he and Candace aren't hurting for resources, but this gesture is huge. *My record fully cleansed and my full pension,* he thinks. *Candace is gonna flip!*

"Thank you, Mr. President," he says. "That is tremendously generous on your part. I don't know what to say."

"You've said it, Raheem. We're short-staffed and everyone here has to pull double and triple their weight. I don't expect that the Secret Service will be back up to full capacity for at least another year or two if the IMs don't wake up any time soon. And even if they do wake up, we have no idea what lingering effects from the Sleepers virus are. These are strange times that we're in."

"Mr. President, about that. What happens if the IMs wake up before the year is out? What happens to you, me and all of these changes that have been made? I'm smart enough to know that a lot of your decisions and those of the other SMs in power would never fly with the IMs."

"You sound like Trevor Campbell, the head of the NSA," he says, chuckling. "In truth, Raheem, I don't quite know what they'll do. I'm not naïve, though. My guess is that many, perhaps most, will be mad as hell. If they do wake up before the year is up, which I hope happens, we'll sort through it as best as we can. Hopefully, they'll understand the times that we are in right now and realize that in order to protect them and the rest of us, we needed to act, boldly, for the sake of the country."

Raheem looks at the President a bit incredulously. President Douglas sees the look and silently acknowledges it by shaking his head as he leans back into the couch with his legs crossed. "Yes, I get it, Raheem. I know the history of this country better than most. I read in your file that you're a bit of a history buff yourself. Is that true?"

"Yes, Sir, it is. And rarely in the history of America have white folks, I mean IMs, ever been accommodating or understanding of us. That hope doesn't jibe with their actions, toward us, for the last four hundred some odd years. My take, Mr. President, if I may be so bold, is that if they wake up before the year is out, heck, in the next two to three years, they'll be angry to see all of the changes that have been made and they'll look to you to answer for them. Especially if you're still President by then, the IMs will only interpret your actions as being malicious. I don't see how you, or frankly, how we can avoid it. Maybe Director Campbell is right. But what do I know, Sir? At the end of the day, I'm just a grunt who serves at the pleasure of the President and who is sworn to protect you and your family. That really is my number one concern."

President Douglas intently studies the man sitting across from him. Not in any year of his tenure had a Secret Service officer been so forthcoming to him. *We obviously disagree*, he thinks, *but there isn't even one atom of disingenuousness in him at all. It's probably what got him in trouble in the first place.*

"I have no doubt, Officer Gates, that not only will you protect my family and me, but that you'll do so with your life, if necessary. I hope that it never comes to that. Your family needs you too."

President Douglas rises from his seat and Raheem does likewise. He extends his hand to Raheem and shakes it firmly, even warmly. He had liked him almost immediately. *This is the kind of man that I need watching my back,* President Douglas thinks."I don't know where you go from here, Officer Gates.

Why don't you report back to your duty station and get your assignment? I know that you're assigned to my personal detail, but I have no idea about the details of that."

"Yes, Sir, I have a meeting with Agent, now Director, Brooks right after our meeting," Raheem says.

"Ah, yes, Director Brooks," President says with a humorous look. "He ranted and raved about you, Agent Gates. But then again, he also kicked and screamed when I pulled him out of retirement and just recently made him Director of the Secret Service. I fear that he'll never quite forgive me," President Douglas says with mock concern. "I'll tell you something, though," he says, his tone now turning very serious. "You and Trevor are absolutely right about one thing. Many of the opportunities for leadership that we're seeing inside and outside of government never would have happened at all had Sleep Day not occurred. If the IMs do wake up anytime soon, that will have to be something that we address as a nation. At the least, we cannot go back to the status quo."

"Thank you for your time, Mr. President. I truly appreciate it." As he walks out of the Oval Office, Raheem wonders to himself whether he's said too much. President Douglas seemed unflappable and genuinely interested in what he'd had to say.

He'd heard that about him, but this had been Raheem's first time experiencing it himself. He had also heard that President Douglas tends to look at things a bit too optimistically. From Raheem's perspective, he considers this to be true except that the President had acknowledged many of the advances that Sleep Day had brought many of them.

But for Sleep Day, Raheem considers as he takes the long walk back to Director Brooks' office, I would literally still be locked up or getting out right about now provided that I hadn't had any setbacks. But for Sleep Day, Candace and I might not be now married, I wouldn't be with my family, we would not be in DC since it had become so god-awful expensive to live in due to ferocious gentrification, and I would absolutely not be a working member of anybody's United States Secret Service. Has the immediate removal of IMs given him - given all the SMs - opportunities and lives that they otherwise would not have? And if that's true" he wonders aloud, "should any of us be working to wake the IMs up? Wouldn't we all just be better off without them?

My logic may be sound, he muses, *but it's a logic wholly devoid of humanity and compassion.* Raheem puts his thoughts away as he arrives at Director Brooks' door who had taken up residence in the Eisenhower Executive office building which is exactly one street removed from the West Wing of the White House. "Come in" he hears as heprepares to knock on the Director's door. "Ah, Raheem, it's good to see you. I trust that all went well with President Douglas?" he asks.

"I believe so, Sir. He is a remarkable man. I hadn'texpected him to be so personable," Raheem says.

"Personable? He certainly can be that. He was that and a bitmore when he all but dragged me out of bed and out of retirement to do his recruiting and to run the shop. I don't think my wife will ever forgive me. After thirty-five years non-stop on the job, I'd promised her no more once I retired, and yet, here we are," Director Brooks says.

Yeesh! Raheem thinks to himself. *I wouldn't want to be Director Brooks right now. Candace would have killed me had I taken this job without her full support and permission.* After years in prison, Raheem knows that any such decisions have to be made with her full knowledge and agreement, otherwise, no marriage. As it stands, his new job, he knows, will have its own set of trials and obstacles. Putting oneself in the line of fire, intentionally is stressful, and the training never stops. Candace and the kids will be the ones who bear the brunt of that, Raheem knows. No need to make it any more difficult than what it already is, he decides.

"Direct Brooks, what is my first assignment?" Raheem asks.

"You're on the Presidential detail, Agent Gates. You'll be in the White House at all times and with the President at all times when he travels. There are a few of you assigned to his personal detail. Agent Smith, your instructor at Secret Service training, will be your direct supervisor. She'll be in charge of daily duties. She made sure that you work with her and her team. She's young but tenacious and very smart. She scored higher than you did during her training. Her office is in the White House, so you'll leave here and report directly to her and every day thereafter. Understood?"

Raheem has to stifle an involuntary salute as he receives his marching orders from Director Brooks. "Understood, Sir, and thank you."

"Thank you, Agent Gates, for being such a strong recruit. Keep proving me right," he says as he waves him out of his office, his eyes already back on the documents on his desk as Raheem silently glides out and begins his walk to Agent Smith's office.

The White House it is, Raheem thinks. He looks forward toreceiving his first assignment and to protecting the President and First Family. Never in his wildest dreams did he imagine he would come so far. *I hope they never wake up,* he decides. *I hope they never wake up.*

* * *

After traveling around the city a bit, Sabrina finds the hospital that has the most doctors and staff. Nashville has quite a few hospitals for a smallish-sized city, but only one or two of them are actually open for patient care. The others seem to only be open to receive IMs brought to them by volunteers. She is directed, eventually, to Nashville General. Solo is still asleep or unconscious but in otherwise stable condition. Xavier is hurting but by now has received several medicines to help him cope with the pain.

Nashville General is staffed with many Black doctors and nurses and those who are almost doctors and nurses. Meharry medical college, a historically Black medical school, is housed in Nashville. Its classes are currently suspended and all of its students are required to report here daily to help and to speed up their training. *Boot camp for doctors and nurses,* Sabrina thinks. Her fiancé, Michael, would be proud. She wonders if he's seeing the same in his hospital. She knows that he's busy. Sabrina hadn't allowed herself to think about her fiancé much since she and her brothers started their journey. She had wanted to keep her mind clear so that she could be her brothers' eyes and ears. She hadn't known what to expect but suspected that they might run into some kind of trouble.

As she sits in Solomon's hospital room, she hears Xavier just outside of the room flirting with some of the nurses. *He's always been a big flirt,* she thinks, and he's always had both a magnetic personality and the gift of gab to go with it. She shifts uncomfortably in her seat as she hears several of the nurses giggling at some dumb joke he's just told. *It shouldn't be this easy,* she thinks. Xavier will have these girls bathing and tending to him in no time.

Sabrina thinks back to the scores of young women that she'd seen come and go from their home who all seemed to love her brother passionately and sometimes a bit crazily. Of course, their mother had also watched Xavier's activity with scathing looks of disapproval while their father had often smirked at his youngest son's popularity, saying "well, he obviously got it from me, Angela," he'd say, chuckling as if he'd just told the funniest joke inthe world.

"Look here, Sis," Xavier once told her when she was old enough to begin to register her disagreement with his various dalliances and the obvious double standard that her parents, particularly her father, had applied to her and not her brothers. "Pimpin' ain't easy, 'Brina, but it sho' is necessary, heh-heh-heh," he'd said with his trademark lecherous laugh.

Sabrina had only ever seen her brothers as her brothers and now for the first time wonders what any sane woman would ever see in either one of them, particularly Xavier. She is very glad, though, that they'd made it to the hospital alive and in one piece. *It was not at all certain that we'd get here intact,* she thinks. *Escaping that lunatic who kidnapped us was more than a notion.* Now, she is concerned about the possibility of leaving her brothers here as she pushes on to New York City. Once she makes sure that they're properly cared for, Sabrina wants to keep moving. She wonders what Xavier might say about it. She also wonders how she'll get there. She no longer has a car. The one that she took to get them here died at the hospital and Solo's Jeep is totaled.

"Hey, Sis!" Xavier says jovially. "Whatcha doin'?"

Sabrina looks at her brother with a mixture of amusement and judgment, wondering how he can seemingly be so happy this far away from home, the country in shambles, his brother still unconscious and his leg broken.

"Ah, don't be that way, Sis. I know what you're thinking. Solo will be fine. You heard what the doctor said. He's dehydrated but all of his vitals are strong. He'll be up in no time. And my leg will recover. Looks like we have a pretty good setup here. No one is charging us anything and we can stay until we're recovered. Should be outta here in a week or less."

Sabrina says nothing but looks away. She can't stay here for another week. She has to keep going. She badly misses Michael and is worried about him. He had already been working seventy-two-hour shifts before Sleep Day. She's sure that he's not even bothering to go home now to change, rest and recover at all. Other than fulfilling her own need to see and be with him, she greatly desires to see about him and look after him.

"Sis, you're out here looking askance. Other than the obvious, what's wrong with you?" Xavier asks the sound of real concern in his voice.

"Michael," Sabrina says simply.

"Ah. Mikey-Mike. I get it. You want to get to him, but we're sorta trapped here for a little bit," Xavier says.

"Xavier, my shift ends in fifteen minutes, but if there's anything else that you need, please let me know," a pretty young nurse says with her hand on his shoulder.

"Oh, hey, Melissa, I'll be back to my room in five. Can you wait for me there?" he asks.

"Of course, X, I mean Xavier," she says, looking semi-embarrassed as she darts out of Solomon's room. Sabrina rolls her eyes hard enough to knock Jupiter out of orbit. Seeing this, Xavier laughs deeply at his sister's obvious derision and judgment.

"X, I swear. You've always been this way. Why do they always like you so much?" Sabrina asks.

Her brother shrugs his shoulders and feigns a look of innocence that makes Sabrina shake her head at him in mock outrage. "Anyway, Sis, I see your dilemma. But as far as I'm concerned, you need to get to New York. Michael needs you more than we do. Plus, I've got him. I can get him back home or follow you to NY if you wish. It's your call. Frankly, I'm having the time of my life. What do you want to do?" he asks.

Sabrina hadn't expected this. She'd thought it her duty to remain with her brothers and see about them before they, presumably, all traveled onward to New York. Once again, Xavier had surprised her. *He's good at doing that,* she thinks, *even from the time that they were all kids.* She wonders whether his ability to do so might be part of his charm with the ladies. She puts the thought out of her head with the remembrance that his feet stink and that his morning breath is often a toxic chemical brew that causes time to stand still and the Earth to wobble.

"Xavier, I appreciate that. I'd like to press on to New York, but I have the problem of no transportation. Solo's Jeep is gone, not that I'd have wanted to drive it anyway," Sabrina says. "And I highly doubt that the pick-up truck we used to get us here would make it out of the state, much less all the way to New York. I'm just glad that I didn't have to drive it any further than I did."

Xavier chuckles at his sister's words. "Sis, you already proved the ability once to commandeer a vehicle when you need to. And frankly, with so many IMs knocked out, it should be a simple matter of borrowing," Xavier says with air quotes, "a car to get to where you need to go. And didn't we see a car dealership on the way in here? Isn't it right up the street from here?"

Ugh! Sabrina thinks. She had already borrowed and then returned one vehicle with Isaac to get them home from San Francisco to Los Angeles. She didn't want to have to do so again.

Even for a good reason, it feels like stealing to her. But what are her other options, she wonders. Hitch a ride, somehow, fromNashville to NYC? What are the odds that she can catch one or several rides from here to there all while trusting strangers to safelytransport her? Doesn't seem likely, she concludes.

"Okay, let's say," she pauses briefly, "that I borrow another vehicle. What will you and Solo do in a week, long after he's awakened and long after I'm gone?" Sabrina asks.

"Sis, we'll be alright. Trust me. Solomon will recover and this leg can't stop me from moving or driving. We'll either join you in New York or we'll head back home. I don't know which yet. I've never been to N.Y.C. I'd love to see it, especially now. Who knows what opportunity we might get into," Xavier says with a mischievous look in his eye. Sabrina thinks she knows what opportunities that he might be referring to.

"X, I still feel bad about leaving, but thank you for supporting me," Sabrina says.

"No problem, Sis. We'll be fine here for a while," Xavier says.

"Yeah, Sis, we'll be fine," they both hear Solomon say. The sound of his voice, though weak, makes Sabrina nearly jump out of her skin. She and Xavier look at him and his toothy grin staring back at them.

"Solomon!" she exclaims. "You're awake! Thank God! I was so worried!" Sabrina jumps out of her chair and rushes to his bedside.

"Easy, Sis, easy," he says. "I'm still just waking up. Ouch. I hurt all over. What the hell happened to us? Car wreck?"

Sabrina and Xavier look at one another knowingly. Solo has no idea about all that happened. *Either he's been out the entire time or he's blacked out some of it,* she thinks. Sabrina has talked enough with her fiancé to know that sometimes physical trauma can trigger the mind's protective mechanism of both unconsciousness and forgetfulness. Michael would often tell her how common this is in patients of his that he'd see at the hospital.

"Yeah, among other things, Bro," Xavier says. "We most definitely had a wreck. Your Jeep is gone. But we're okay for the most part. I've got this broken leg, but Sabrina has nary a scratch on her. You know she stays buckled up."

Solomon looks at his sister and sees in her face that there is far more to the story than that. His brain is foggy and he's in tremendous pain. Whatever the rest of their tale is, he elects not to press it until he feels better and has gotten more rest. "Sis, I heard what you said. You need to keep pushing to New York. Xavier will look out for me. We're not helpless. I'm not afraid."

Tears stream down Sabrina's face as she takes her brother's hand and lightly kisses it. "Solo, I feel so bad. I don't want to leave you like this," she says.

"You're not leaving us. We're sending you. You're hella tough. Go find Michael and give him our best. If we can join you, we will. And like Xavier said, get a car, a good one, get to NY safely. Pick up a cellphone while you're at it and call our parents," Solomon says.

"Already called 'em," Xavier says. "Nicole, one of the nurses, let me use her cell phone."

Sabrina and Solo see the smirk on their brother's face and both roll their eyes up to heaven. Xavier lets out a big laugh at which his siblings join him, all three releasing their tension and fears.

"Okay," Sabrina says after long moments laughing at and with her brothers, "I'll leave in the morning. I'll go and secure a vehicle now though. Hopefully, it will be as easy as it was in San Francisco."

Sabrina rises from her chair to begin the long walk down the hallway to the hospital's exit. She follows the exit signs and all of the twists and turns until she finally sees the entrance. As she walks by the large reception desk close to the entrance, she stops in her tracks and involuntarily balls up her fists. Standing a few feet in front of her talking with hospital security, is Stanley, her kidnapper.

* * *

Stanley considers his arrival at Nashville General hospital a miracle. He's still in great pain from the beating that he took from Sabrina and he's unsure why she'd left him alive. He knows that his intentions weren't nearly as noble as hers had been. *I hope to never see that woman again,* he thinks to himself. She is clearly a karate expert of some sort, he believes.

After parking the station wagon that he'd taken back in town, he limps his way up to the hospital entrance. As he'd suspected, he only sees black and brown-skinned people. *It's happened here too,* he thinks. *There's no more white people, at least between my town and Nashville and maybe in the whole state of Tennessee.* Looking down at his arms, Stanley sees that he can pass for one of them for everything but his hair and facial features. Maybe they won't ask me too many questions, he hopes. I don't want anyone to know that I'm really a white man. That could prove dangerous, he believes.

Stanley walks into the hospital's entrance and sees a large Black security guard.

"Excuse me, Sir," he says in a deep southern drawl. "I need some help. Is there a doctor that can see me?"

"Hold on, Sir," the security guard says. "Catch your breath. You're obviously in a lot of pain. Let me find you a wheelchair."

Stanley is grateful for the help. He looks around for the nearest chair in which to sit, but before he can move, he stops dead in his tracks. There she is, the woman, the one that hurt him in the first place. She is running full speed at him. Stanley feels all of the strength go out of his legs, and he wonders if this time she'll kill him.

* * *

When he later tells the story, Lionel, the security guard, will give all credit to stopping a murder on his watch to his Lord and Savior, Jesus Christ, and the fact that he's still a hell of an athlete. He'd played Division I football at Tennessee State University ten years ago and been a starting linebacker for two of his four years there.

Lionel has less than a second to react as Sabrina comes flying in to do an obvious injury to Stanley as he stands at the hospital's entrance. He can only put his large body in between them. The flying kick that Sabrina meant for Stanley instead hits Lionel right between his shoulder blades. As big and strong as he is, he buckles. Regaining his footing, he whirls around to see the source of his assault. He looks down at Sabrina, all five feet six inches of her, and can't believe that this little woman just kicked him as hard as she did.

"Now, Miss," he says, "please calm down. I don't know what's going on here or who this man is to you, but you're going to have to stop right now."

Ignoring the big man in front of her, Sabrina feints left. When Lionel reaches out to grab her, she darts right and moves deftly around him to get to Stanley. *His throat,* she thinks. *Aim for the throat.* She is less than three feet from Stanley and closing quickly. Sabrina sees the look of terror in his eyes and allows herself to take pleasure in it. As she raises her right elbow up to strike, she can almost smell the fear coming from Stanley. *A couple more inches*, she thinks, *and he'll be dead.*

In the moment before she strikes, Sabrina feels arms of steel wrap around and her legs kicked out from beneath her. Lionel,the security guard, has tackled her and is holding her arms down against her body. She can't move though she writhes violently against him.

"Miss! Miss!" he shouts. "Calm down! Calm down!" Lionel bellows.

Sabrina fights with all of her strength to free herself but to no avail. Lionel is too big and too strong. He holds her tightly until she stops fighting. He then eases his grip but keeps it firm. By now, several other guards have arrived.

"Lionel! Lionel! What happened?!" one of the arriving guards says.

"I don't know. All I know is that this one," nodding to Sabrina as he continues to hold her still, "tried to attack this one," pointing to Stanley who cowers in a nearby seat.

All of the other guards look at Stanley and then back at Sabrina and then back at Stanley again. "Ma'am, what's wrong? What happened here?" the first arriving guard asks Sabrina. "Lionel, let her up. Stand her up, please," he says.

It is difficult for Sabrina to speak. She finds that she has to use all of her strength to form the right words.

"That man," she begins, "that man sitting there," she says, pointing directly at Stanley, "he kidnapped my brothers and me. He did bad things to them. Tried to do bad things to me. We barely escaped...with our lives."

Lionel releases Sabrina and walks to Stanley. "Stand up, Sir. You're under arrest." Lionel stands Stanley up more than he stands on his own and puts him in handcuffs.

"Lionel," the first arriving guard says, "put him in our holding cell. The police will be here shortly to pick him up. And as for you, young lady, let's have a conversation."

CHAPTER XII

Though a relatively young man, Trevor Campbell has learned to be patient. He credits the many hours of practice playing chess with his father's father, Grandaddy Campbell, his father, and his uncles. Trevor had shown an aptitude for chess early and his family worked assiduously to help him cultivate his talent. At one point, he had gotten so good that he'd considered a career in chess like several of the grandmasters that he admired. At one point, his chess prowess had garnered him a fair amount of renown and a full scholarship to the elite private school in his city. His was not a rags to riches story as his family is well educated and had been for multiple generations. His private school, which he attended from the sixth to the twelfth grade, enabled his Ivy League education, contacts, and current job. Trevor contemplates all of this as he listens to Congresswoman Stowe invite him into a treasonous plot against President Douglas and the current U.S. government.

"What's in it for me?" he asks the Congresswoman. "What do you want, Director Campbell?" she asks in return.

Great question, Trevor thinks. He wants a lot. He wants the IMs to remain asleep. He wants to keep amassing power and to do so in a way that can't be stopped until it's too late. He wants SMs to dominate the levers of government and industry in the United States so that no matter when the IMs wake up if they ever wake up, they will never and can never return to their positions of dominance. He wants all of these things, but of course, he won't tell Stowe any of this. She's not brilliant by any stretch, he observes, but she is cunning. She is sure to use anything that he says against him. Trevor is also sure that she's recording this call, just as he is.

"I want peace, Congresswoman. I want the United States to remain stable. I want the people of this country to be safe and to prosper. That's what I want," he says.

"Oh, I think that you want a little more than that, Director Campbell. In fact, I'd say that what you really want are the keys to the proverbial kingdom," Congresswoman Stowe says.

Trevor does not reply in the affirmative or the negative to Stowe's assertion. He merely holds his tongue and waits for her to keep speaking.

"In fact," she says, "if I were a betting woman, I'd say that you like how things are now. I'd say that the accident at Krauss' laboratory was no accident and that his disappearance, as well as that of his entire staff, was orchestrated. Now, I'm no fool, Trevor, but I don't see President Douglas as being the kind of person that would spearhead such an op. Though he is incredibly naïve in my view, I think that the President is, at base, a good and decent man, politics aside. No, I think one only needs to look a little lower to see who benefits and who gains from Krauss being removed from the board, as it were."

Checkmate, Trevor thinks to himself. *She has me in checkmate or she thinks that she does.* Let's see. "These are wild allegations, Jane," he says, using her first name since she's dropped all formalities of title. "Do you have any proof of what you've said?"

"Oh, I don't need proof, Honey. I've got the Seventh Fleet. All I need are a few well-placed lies and some innuendo, and I've got more than enough to take what I want. Lucky for you, Trevor, what I want is not what you think I want."

"Jane, let's speak plainly. And let's turn off the recorders. You tell me what you want, and I'll tell you what I want. If we can help one another, let's see about it. Fair?" he asks.

Congresswoman Stowe chuckles softly. "Fair, Director Campbell," she says.

They then both turn off their recording devices and begin to speak openly and honestly. Though the first, it will not be the last time that they do so.

* * *

Jessica is decided, and Elliot is none too happy about it. After about a week at Elliot's parents' place, her anxiety eases. She realizes that they really are off the grid, far off and that she needn't be concerned about ever being found again. Most of their food needs are met by what Elliot's parents grow and hunt for. There is ample game and a large pond nearby stocked with fish. She might never have to leave again, which is Elliot's parents' intention. Rarely do they venture out from their woods down into a town that's about twenty kilometers away.

"I have to try, Elliot," she says. "If my uncle is alive, and I think that he is, I have to try to find him."

"Jessica, that just doesn't make any sense to me," Elliot says. "It's clear that whoever torched his lab made your uncle disappear, we think, and came after you. These are professionals. We're not professionals. You may be able to fight well, really well, but these are professional boogeymen. And if it's the Americans, Jess, you've got no shot."

His words sting, but she's unsure if it's merely because they withhold hope or because he's right. "If the roles were reversed, my uncle would do the same for me and more. You have no idea how much he's protected and guided me. I don't even know all that he's done. He's the reason that I am who I am today as much as my father is, perhaps more."

Elliot sees that while his words may have stung her a bit, they have failed to penetrate. Jessica is at once the most brilliant and most stubborn person that he's ever known. His father told him what he thinks of her a few days after they arrive. "Son, that one there is a tiger. And you're still a bit of a bear cub. Tigers eat bear cubs, and sometimes bears."

He knows that his father was not being critical of either Jessica or himself, but he understands the implicit warning in his statement. Elliot wants to support her but other than grabbing and holding her down, which he is not at all confident that he can do, he is at a loss as to how to do so. She is committed to this plan, no matter how desperate. She will intentionally place herself into harm's way. Whether Krauss is alive or dead, she may or may not survive. He thinks all of this as he utters his next words.

"Okay, Jess, when are we going?" Elliot asks.

They sit outside at a picnic table on a chilly forty-three degree day. It's still pretty early and the sun is just starting to peek over the mountain range in the west. Jessica loves this view and sees how Elliot's parents have been here so long. She hadn't felt a peace like this in a long time. She is sorely tempted to remain here as long as possible, but she knows that she can't do that. Her uncle is essentially all of the family that she has. Her father is dead, and she and her mother are estranged. Especially since her father's death ten years ago, Krauss had been all the family that she felt she had. She cannot abandon him now. She also cannot take Eliot with her, she knows.

"We leave in two days. Day after tomorrow," she says. "Fine then. It's settled. I'll just tell my parents and we'll...."

"No! Don't do that yet. They'll worry and try to talk you out of it. Leave that to me. I'll write them a note" Jessica says.

"Okay, Jessica, whatever you say" Elliot says.

"Thank you. Elliot" she says hesitating, "Elliot, I love you. Thank you for putting up with me these last several years. You deserve better."

Elliot pulls Jessica close and whispers in her ear "I love you too, Jessica. Always have, always will."

The next morning, Jessica arises long before the sun is due to come up. They'd all shared a hearty meal the night before which put them to sleep early. Jessica had enjoyed their day together and had helped Elliot's mother do some gardening and pick vegetables for dinner that evening. The feel of the earth in her hands invigorates her and connects her to their home. She loves it here and hopes to see it again. She hopes to see them all again.

Moving silently in the dark, Jessica dresses in the clothes that she'd set aside the day before along with the travel pack resting next to a chair in their room. Elliot is sound asleep, she knows, but still takes great pains not to arouse him. Once dressed, she picks up her sneakers and tip toes out of their room and out of the house. Her plan is to walk his motorcycle away from the house for a couple hundred yards or more. Sound travels easily up here. She does not want to wake anyone until she is far gone.

Before exiting the house, Jessica leaves a letter for Elliot and one for his parents. In them, she tries to explain her leaving. She is well aware that the lie she told Elliot will hurt him, but she refuses to risk his safety and his life following her. Jessica had been careful not to tell him the details of her plan so that after she'd left, he wouldn't have a clue as to her whereabouts.

She realizes that Elliot is right and that the people chasing her are professionals. She's betting that they do not want to kill her, however. Had they drawn their guns at Elliot's flat, they easily could have. The fact that their would-be kidnappers had not used their weapons had been what enabled their escape. If she's right and her uncle is alive, she believes that she can find out what happened to him, where he is and maybe, with a fair amount of luck, orchestrate their escape. *It's a shot in the dark, but it's all that she has,* she thinks.

Standing outside in the dark on the porch, Jessica listens carefully for any sounds coming from the house. Hearing none, she moves quietly to Elliot's motorcycle. "Leaving so soon?" she hears in a voice so low she realizes that it's for her ears only. She turns to see Elliot's father standing in the doorway looking intently at her.

What can she say? What she's doing is exactly what it looks like she's doing. Besides, Elliot's father had said few words to her since she'd been there. She had doubted that the man likes her, or at least likes her in his son's life. She thinks that he probably wants her gone.

Noiselessly, Elliot's father walks to Jessica. "This is for you. Conceal it on your person. You may need it." He presses a small knife into Jessica's palm and then closes her hand over it.

Jessica sees that it's small enough to perhaps avoid detection. She looks up at him and, even in the dark, sees that his eyes are full of worry but also compassion.

"Be careful," he says. "I understand. And thank you." He turns without another word.

Jessica grabs the handlebars of Eliot's motorcycle and begins walking away from this happy house as she had originally intended. Once sufficiently far away from the house, she starts the motorcycle and begins the slow arduous trek down the mountain. Once she finds a paved road, Jessica turns onto it and heads west. Her plan is to keep traveling until she gets to the largest city that Elliot's motorcycle will take her. Once there, she'll send up an easily traceable signal and wait to see what happens.

It's precarious, it's foolhardy, and it may even be more than a little stupid, but it's the only way, she thinks, of finding out what happened to Krauss and possibly rescuing him. As she travels, she sees that the sun has started to rise behind her. She'll have full daylight soon and is glad for it. *Hopefully,* she thinks, *I'll be in or close to Paris by tonight. I'm a few hundred kilometers away but Eliot's bike is sturdy and built for long distance travel.* She's glad that she had learned to ride years ago when they'd met. Elliot had insisted on it. Learning from him had been fun. She never thought that she would later have to use that knowledge to take his motorcycle and, possibly, break his heart. The guilt she feels is soon superseded by her concern for Krauss. She hopes that she finds him and that he's safe.

* * *

Sabrina sits across from Richardson, the head of security at Nashville General hospital in the hospital's cafeteria. A cup of hot coffee steams in front of her. She hasn't touched it since they sat down. Joining them is a police officer from the Nashville police department, Officer Barnes, a grizzled veteran who, unlike the stereotype, looks fit and ready for duty. Both men are middle aged, Black and graying.

"Now tell it to me from the top, Ms." Officer Barnes shuffles some pages in his notepad, "Ms. Clayton–tell it to us from the top."

Sabrina begins her story from the near plane crash upon her return home from New York. She then tells them how she got Isaac and herself from San Francisco back to L.A. by car and then partially on foot. She tells them about her fiancé and how she and her brothers, who they'd already interviewed, came with her to see her safely to New York. Each man leans in when she recounts the harrowing story of their crash and captivity in Stanley's basement and how they ultimately got free and came to Nashville. After she's done, Sabrina takes several long sips of her now cooled coffee. The men in front of her don't speak for long minutes. Officer Barnes writes furiously in his notepad. When done, he looks up first at Sabrina and then at Richardson.

"Little Lady" he says in an acute southern Tennessee drawl, "that is some story. It's amazing actually. It sounds to me like you're lucky to be alive. This could have easily gone bad, really bad. I've seen worse in my time as an officer and since Sleep Day."

Sabrina takes his words in. She hadn't really stopped to appreciate all that she'd been through up to now. Every moment since Sleep Day, for her, has felt like a fight to survive and keep pushing. She's spent far more time thinking about her family and Michael than she has thinking about herself.

"Ms. Clayton" Richardson says, "we believe your account.

It's backed up by both of your brothers and by this Stanley person himself. He's a strange one too. He does not seem to be what he appears to be. In any event, he's confessed to everything that you've said. I think that you scared him so badly, he's afraid to have to face you again. He's pretty banged up and in a hospital bed. He's handcuffed though and a guard is at his door twenty-four-seven, so not to worry, not that you would be given your obvious skills."

Sabrina sighs a sigh of relief. The thought of leaving her brothers here with Stanley non-secured had begun to frighten her. He is hurt though, she acknowledges to herself. When she saw him, she had a moment to take in the fact that he has multiple deep bruises to his face and that he was favoring one side of his body over the other. *Broken ribs*, she thinks, *I broke his ribs. Good.*

"So, what happens now?" Sabrina asks.

"Now? Now we take 'ol Stanley through our prosecution process. Kidnapping is a serious felony and also a federal offense, and he's got three counts of that, not to mention the assaults that he committed on your brothers. Our government processes are in a little bit of a shambles right now, but he'll see significant time in prison. As for you, Ms. Clayton, you're free to go. Our brothers told us about your situation and the need to get to New York."

Officer Barnes digs into his pocket and hands Sabrina a set of car keys. "These are for an unmarked cruiser outside. It's fully gassed up and ready to go. Don't worry, we've got plenty. Can't even drive them all now that our police numbers have been cut by two-thirds. Just keep it safe in New York and get it back to us when you can. It's the least we can do given how you've suffered."

Sabrina looks at the keys that Officer Barnes has passed to her. She expresses her eternal thanks to both men and asks Richardson to convey her deep apologies to Lionel, the security guard that she kicked. "I'm very sorry about that. I wasn't trying to hit him." Both men chuckle heartily and assure her that Lionel's okay and she'd given them a good story to rib him about later. Apparently, all three men know one-another and have been friends for a long time. Sabrina soon excuses herself to go check on her brothers.

Walking into Solomon's room, she sees Xavier sitting in his wheelchair. They're watching television together. Both look up and smile warmly as she strides in. "Sis!" Solo exclaims. "We heard what happened. The cops questioned us. We told them everything. Are you okay?"

"I'm okay," she replies. "I'm still angry, but otherwise okay."

"What are you going to do now?" Xavier asks.

"I'm leaving" she says without skipping a beat. "I have a car. A good one. I want to get on the road and the hell out of Tennessee. I've seen enough."

"Trudat, Sis," Xavier says. "Once Solo gets a clean bill of health, we'll bounce too. Don't know where yet, but we're outta here."

"Good. Make sure that you two stay together. I don't want anything to happen to you" Sabrina says.

"Yes, Mom" Solomon and Xavier say in unison and crack up laughing.

She punches Xavier in his shoulder at which he dramatically feigns injury and kisses Solo on his forehead. "Love you, Bros."

Sabrina quickly exits the room to prevent her brothers from seeing her tear up. *This is hard enough already without me turning into a crying mess,* she thinks. She wants her brothers to see her as strong and capable. She still cares about what they think more than she'd like to admit.

Sabrina exits the hospital and sees a gleaming white unmarked police cruiser with black wheels. This is obviously the one, she sees. The car chirps at her when she presses the unlock button on her key set. *Yep, this is it,* she thinks. It's a big car and she sees that it has a big V8 engine. *Nice,* she thinks. Starting the engine, she can feel its power. She's happy to see that the car is full of gasoline. Looking down, she sees a white envelope next to her. Opening it is a note and a gas card. *Thought you'd need some help with gasoline. Here's a gas card for your trouble. Keep up with it. You can use it for both gas and food along the way. God bless and be safe.*"

From ashy to classy in about five minutes, she thinks happily. Sabrina can't believe how blessed she's been in the midst of these trials. She says a silent prayer, thanks God for his provision and favor and puts the car in drive. *On to New York and to*

Michael, she thinks. *Nothing is going to stop me.*

* * *

Jessica arrives in Paris at about the time that she expects. She has a little money and all of her credit and debit cards. If she wants to send up a signal, she knows that as soon as she uses one, the CIA or whoever will know where she is. She decides to motor to a nice hotel in the center of the city and check in. She is tired and needs a hot bath. *At least when they come for me*, she thinks, *I'll be clean and fresh. There's no telling when I'll get to bathe and rest again.*

Checking in, Jessica orders up all of her favorite foods and desserts. After eating well, she slips into a hot bath and lets the water cover every part of her up to her chin. *This is Heaven*, she thinks. Sometime later, she slips into fresh, clean clothing. It won't do to be kidnapped in nothing but my underwear, she decides.

Crawling into bed, she looks forward to the rest that she'll get forhowever long her would-be captors allow. Much later that evening, Jessica feels more than she seesor even hears four large men in her room. She does not move.

By now, she knows, they've been warned about her and her skill. They're probably prepared to be overly aggressive and would probably severely hurt her so as not to be injured by her. Now fully awake, Jessica decides to continue to feign sleep and let them take her without a struggle. This goes against all of her natural instincts, but she's disciplined. She senses that one of the men has moved close. She feels it when he punctures her skin with a needle.

She lets the drug wash over her without struggling. *At least I get to keep sleeping*, she thinks as she fades out of consciousness, hopeful that she'll soon be somewhere close to her uncle.

* * *

Trevor couldn't believe his good fortune at his team finally getting a hit on Jessica Lundgren's whereabouts. Of course, he had his people scouring for her after she'd seemingly dropped off the grid. After about a week of searching, he had begun to lose hope that they might ever find her. Then the call came from his European agents: she'd used one of her credit cards in Paris to check into a posh hotel. That seemed strange to Trevor. He'd thought Jessica to be a very smart woman, smart enough to escape and hide from his agents for the better part of week. Why would she now pop up in Paris of all places and do so in such an easily traceable way? Seems fishy he thinks at the time. This could be a set up, he believes.

Trevor tells his agents to pick her up from the hotel. He warns them to use extreme caution. "She's dangerous, she's skilled, she's already put a few of your colleagues in the hospital" he warns them. "Take her, try not to hurt her, and by all means don't kill her, but don't let her escape" he says.

Now he has received the report that she's been taken without incident which is completely unexpected. Trevor had expected to hear that maybe the person using her credit card was in fact not Jessica as a way to throw them off the trail or that it had been her, but she'd escaped yet again and put his whole team in the hospital or worse at their attempt to grab her. But no, the report indicates that not only was she successfully taken but that she hadn't even stirred from her sleep when she was drugged and then bound for extraction from the hotel room.

Trevor's deeply suspicious nature is now on overdrive. He'd achieved his objective, but he can't help but feel that he's being manipulated. *It should not have been this easy*, he says to himself. *No struggle? No fight? No, that's definitely not her*, he thinks. *If this is some sort of ruse, then what is her objective?* he wonders. Trevor knows that this matter will require much more deep thought on his part. If Jessica is playing at some game, he needs to game it out fully so as to anticipate each move and counter move.

Right now, however, he has more pressing matters. He has a call with Congresswoman Stowe in an hour. He needs to be prepared to give her a final answer as to her proposal. He's mostly sure of what he's going to say and what he'll agree to, but this is high risk, high reward stuff, he thinks. One wrong move and he'll be held personally responsible and will face prison. If he's successful, the country changes, perhaps forever, and he'll be the reason why it happens. *I'll either be remembered as a hero or a traitor*, he thinks, *but now is not the time to shrink back.* Now is the time to be bold. Trevor steels himself for his upcoming call with the Congresswoman and hopes that he's making the right choice.

* * *

New York, New York. The words to Jay-Z's song about the city echo in Sabrina's head. She's finally here. Eighteen hours later, she arrived, having made the trip on almost on sleep. She took a short one-hour break in Pennsylvania, but thereafter pushed on to the city. She figures that she'll be able to rest after she's seen Michael and after she gets to their apartment. Her plan is to see him first, check in, and then go home. *I'll use Michael's phone to call everyone*, she thinks.

Driving on a highway through New Jersey, Sabrina can see the city from here. She aims to cross into Manhattan at the Lincoln tunnel since Michael's hospital sits in midtown. She is sure that he's there. Having been to New York many times during their engagement, Sabrina is familiar with the area around his hospital and the best routes getting there.

The highway is not nearly as full as it once was, further evidence of the Sleeper's virus impact on the country's population, but it isn't empty. Sabrina sees a fair number of cars with Black and Brown people in them going into and out of the city, a testament to this region's diversity. She is happy not to have to fight the high volume traffic that usually exists and quicklyfinds the entrance to the Lincoln tunnel soon after gliding into Manhattan in her borrowed big police sedan.

Sabrina can feel her anticipation growing. Three weeks ago she awoke from a near plane crash after flying from New York. Today, she's back in New York, and headed to see Michael with no plans of ever returning home to California. She has a job at her company that she hasn't checked on and the Sleepers virus has turned everything upside down. *I'll have to dig into the news while I'm here*, she thinks. *I really have no idea what's been going on in the rest of the country.* Sabrina recognizes that she's been single-focused on her mission, a trait that she inherited from her dad.

In less time than it would have ever taken before Sleep Day, Sabrina arrives at Michael's hospital. She finds a parking space directly in front of it. Even though the sign where she parks warns her not to park with a warning of having her car towed, she parks believing that the last people who would be at work today are the army of New York parking attendants who would normally be out manning their posts ticketing and towing the slightest infraction.

Sabrina is correct. There are no more ticketers. They had all been reassigned to other essential services throughout the city, many of whom having been deputized into the New York police department.

Walking into Michael's hospital, as she's done many times before, feels otherworldly to Sabrina. It bustles with activity. There are doctors, nurses and other hospital staff moving hurriedly about. To Sabrina, the only difference in this scene is that everyone that she sees is a person of color. Before Sleep Day, this scene would have been no less hurried, but its population would have also been the reverse of what she sees today. Michael is one of a small handful of Black doctors on staff out of one hundred or more in the hospital. Today, it appears to Sabrina that the city must have gathered up all of its Black and Brown doctors and placed them here. While that's probably not true, she believes, the actual truth is probably not that different.

Michael works on the sixth floor of the hospital which is the floor where the surgeries occur. Sabrina finds an elevator and heads up to his floor. Ever since their days together at Howard, he had wanted to become a cardio-thoracic surgeon. The training program is both grueling and many years long. Before entering the training program for cardio-thoracic surgery, he had been warned that he could expect to be a resident in training for ten years or more. Undaunted, Michael signed up and had been grinding toward his goal ever since. His relentless drive is one of the manyreasons why Sabrina loves him so much. *It is also one of his most annoying traits,* she muses, *as that drive seeps into his need to win at everything, literally everything, like Scrabble, a game that Sabrina had vanquished him many times.*

Sabrina chuckles at the thought of the many times her fiancé threatened to never play her again after a loss. Stepping out of the elevator, she walks to the nurses' station. She recognizes one or two familiar faces, but it's filled with a host of new faces that she does not recognize. *I was just here three weeks ago and the whole place seems changed,* she thinks. "Nurse Martinez" she says speaking to one of the nurses that she recognizes. "I'm looking for Michael, er Dr. Michael Fleming. Have you seen him?"

"You're Sabrina, his fiancé, aren't you? Dr. Fleming talks about you all the time" Nurse Martinez says.

Sabrina smiles at that. She is happy to know that her name and presence have a place at her true love's place of business.

"He checked in, actually, about fifteen minutes ago. I don't think that he leaves the hospital much anymore. He told one of the nurses that he's taking a nap in the doctors' lounge. Do you know where that is?" she asks.

"I do. We've eaten lunch and dinner there many times. Thanks so much. I know the way" Sabrina says. The doctors' lounge is down the hall from the nurses' station and to the left. She walks the short distance to it and walks in. The front room comprises a small kitchenette, a table with chairs and a couch. The back room has two bunk beds in which an overworked doctor may sleep. She walks through the first room to the door of the second adjoining one. Opening it, she sees Michael quietly sleeping on one of the lower bunk beds. He has his scrubs and his shoes on.

Poor baby, she thinks. *Too tired to even take his shoes off.*

Sabrina sits next to him and places a gentle hand on his chest. "Hey, sleepy head," she says softly. Michael doesn't even stir. "Hey, sleepy head" she says again more insistently. Michael's left eye pops open. "Sabrina? Am I dreaming? Baby, is that you?"he says.

"Yes, it's me, Silly. It's me. How are you?" she says.

Michael sits up and hugs his bride to be. He takes in her scent as if the smell of her can revive his exhausted parts. He'd been up for the last forty-eight hours and had just laid when Sabrina woke him. Like a shot of adrenaline, he feels the energy of their embrace.

"How and when did you get here?" he asks in muffled tones, his face still buried in her hair.

"I left my brothers in Nashville and drove through the night with barely a break. I didn't want to wait any longer" she says.

Michael pushes her back enough to look at her face. He frowns and sighs.

"You've been through a lot, haven't you?" he asks.

Sabrina lets her tears flow then as if a dam had been released or broken into a million pieces. Michael draws her fully to himself and lays back down with her. Sabrina sobs into his chest and wails, her sounds of anguish being directed into Michael's chest and arms. After many minutes, he hears Sabina breathing softly and realizes that she's fallen asleep. *She's as tired as I am,* he realizes, *maybe more.*

Michael had intended on shutting his eyes for an hour or two but now knows that that's not possible. He'll rest here for a bit with Sabrina and then wake her in a few. I'll take her home, he decides, feed her, bathe her and then put us to bed. *We both need it, God knows,* he thinks.

Michael hadn't been home to his apartment in over a week. He has enough scrubs and changes of underwear at the hospital to go a week or more without needing to re-up his supply. He fears that his plants are dead but takes comfort in the fact that he's saved many more human lives in that time. It was worth it, he muses but still regrets the loss of his favorite fern. "Isabel" he had called it. *Isabel, poor Isabel,* he laments.

An hour later, Michael slides out of the bed he'd been sharing with Sabrina. She is fast asleep. He leaves the doctor's lounge and walks to the nurses' station that Sabrina had first gone to. "Dr. Fleming" Nurse Martinez says, "did you find your fiancé? She is very pretty, that one" she says smiling broadly and giving Michael a wink.

"I did indeed, Simone, he says. In fact, I'm about to take her home and clock out for the day. What day is it anyway? Friday? It's Friday. I'll see ya'll again on Monday. We both need to rest and I'm going to take care of her. Please let everyone know" Michael says and turns to walk back to retrieve Sabrina.

For a year, he hasn't had a weekend off. Especially since Sleep Day, Michael had been working non-stop to fill the medical gaps left by their now immobilized white doctors and nurses. Just now his hospital had begun to reach staffing capacity but it had done so by pooling Black and Brown medical professionals at his hospital and two others. That meant, of course, that only three hospitals are open to service the medical needs of the still millions of people in the five boroughs. That means, unfortunately,that all three are operating in overcrowded or near over-crowded conditions, hence his lack of rest and that of his other colleagues.

As much as Michael is needed, he realizes that Sabrina needs him more. Walking into the back room of the doctors' lounge, he sees her still sleeping. He hates to have to wake her up but knows that he needs to.

"Sabrina," he says. "Sabrina, baby, come on, let's go."

Sabrina stirs, stretches and then turns over. Michael shakes her gently but firmly.

"Baby, we need to go. I'm taking you home" Michael says. "Okay" she mumbles, and Michael takes her hand to sit her up on the bed. *Yep*, he thinks, *she'll be asleep for the next twelve hours. Let me get her out of here now.*

Together they stand, and Michael leads her out of the lounge and then ultimately out of the hospital. She walks close to him holding his hand and arm. Michael loves it. He had been worried sick about her since he'd seen her last. He decides at this moment to dramatically speed up their wedding date and to keep her in New York with him. No more of this long distance relationship stuff, he promises himself.

Their apartment is six blocks away. Given their respective states of exhaustion, it's too far to walk. "Here" Sabrina says and hands him the keys to her loaned police car. *What in the world?* he thinks, as they walk to it, and he sees it. *Sabrina legit traveled from Tennessee to NYC in an undercover police car,* he thinks to himself, impressed. *Is there anything this woman can't do*, he wonders, marveling at his soon-to-be wife. *Apparently not*, he concludes as he glides out of the parking space she manufactured and heads home with his bride.

* * *

"So that's a yes, then?" Congresswoman Stowe asks Trevor.

"Yes, Congresswoman, that is a yes. I'm in. I'm sure that I don't have to remind you that both of our futures are forfeit, mine more than yours, if we are discovered before you pull the proverbial trigger" Trevor says.

"Quit your worrying. My team is tight. Our communication

is tight. Douglas won't know what's hit him until it's too late" she says.

"And I have your assurances that all that I'm seeking will, at the least, not be contested by you now or in the future?" he asks.

Congresswoman Stowe sighs audibly. "Not now. Not in the future. We are agreed."

"Then yes, we are fully agreed. Happy hunting" Trevor says and then ends his call with Congresswoman Stowe.

It's a crazy plan, he muses, *but one which will give me cover to do all else that must be done.* For his plan to work, he calculates that the IMs must not wake-up before the year is out and they must not awaken, for all practical purposes, for the next five years. He'd just agreed to keep them alive in perpetuity, but he hadn't agreed not to keep them immobilized, to keep them asleep.

Now Trevor's job is to finish his planning, move his people into key parts of the new government and make sure that the IMs never see the light of day for the next five years, at the least. *Besides,* he thinks to himself, *who needs Alaska anyway?*

* * *

When Jessica wakes up, she notes that it's dark, she's horizontal, and her legs and arms are all bound to a bed. She can't make out any discernible sounds or smells, but senses, in the dark, that her room is small. She notes that other than the too-tight ropes on her limbs, she does not feel any pain. She is thankful that at least her captors were careful with her body and hadn't injured her. She is also thankful that she had been fully dressed when taken. *It would suck,* she thinks, *to be laid out here in my skivvies.* Jessica hears a door open and a set of two footsteps approach her.

"This is her?" a voice says.

"Yes, Sir, it is," a second voice replies.

"Surprising. I didn't expect her to be so skinny. Based on the damage she's done, I thought she might be two hundred pounds or more" the first voice says.

"No, Sir. She's just extremely skilled. Thanks for the warning on that. We were very careful when we grabbed her though she put up on no struggle whatsoever. That surprised all of us. We were prepared for battle had she done so" the second voice says.

Jessica smiles to herself at the comment. She's glad that she hadn't resisted. That's almost assuredly what had saved her from certain injury or worse.

"Ms. Lundgren" the first voice says. "My name is Trevor Campbell. I know that you can hear me and that you're awake. The drug that we gave you has worn off by now. We are not amateurs.

You cannot escape this room or this facility so please don't try. Ifyou agree to behave, we will release you, and you can sit up. Do you agree?" he asks.

"I agree," she says. Jessica doesn't yet know enough to try to escape. She knows that she must learn more before she can execute her plan.

"Excellent" Trevor says, sounding very pleased with himself.

Once unbound, Jessica sits up and takes in her surroundings. A light illuminating the room and her captors has been turned on. She sees that the ceiling to her cell is about fifteen feet high, too high to reach, she sees. Though the cell is small, it's appreciably larger than a standard jail cell. She is thankful for that if it means that she will remain here for a while. One of her captors is dressed in all black fatigues. *He's one of the ones who kidnapped me in Paris*, she thinks. The other captor, who must be this Trevor Campbell, is impeccably dressed in a navy suit, white shirt and plaid bowtie. *The boss*, she thinks.

"Where am I?" Jessica asks.

"America" Trevor says without saying more. "Don't worry. There is no trace of the Sleepers virus here. This facility has been swept and cleaned. You're safe-ish" he concludes.

"Who are you, Mr. Campbell?" Jessica asks.

"I am the head of the National Security Agency, Ms. Lundgren. I also have a question. Why are you here?"

Jessica stammers as she answers: "What do you mean? You kidnapped me, remember?"

"Now, Ms. Lundgren, you don't think us so foolish, do you? You allowed us to take you. You were off grid for a week and could have remained off grid for a long time. You look well fed.

I can discern no harm to you whatsoever in your travels, and you allowed us to easily take you. So again, I ask, why are you here?"Trevor concludes.

I probably should have fought a couple of them, Jessica thinks. *I did make that look too easy.* The choices before her are to attempt to feign ignorance which she is confident will not fool these men or to tell the truth. She chooses the truth. "I'm here to see about my uncle. Krauss is very important to me, and I wanted to make sure that he's okay. I knew that you or someone like you had him. I didn't think that he's dead, but I also had no other way of knowing. So, here I am."

"Thank you, Ms. Lundgren. That is the conclusion that I'd come to as well. Keep being honest like this and we'll get along swimmingly. Ever try to lie to me and it'll be the last lie you ever tell" Trevor says and then signals his associate to leave the room. "For now, you'll remain unbound. You'll be fed, allowed to clean yourself and kept safe, I promise. We'll even add a small desk, chair and lamp for you. I can assure you that your uncle is very much alive, and I'll let you see him eventually. You will have to do some things for us first, but that shouldn't be too hard. You've come a long way. You'll only need to come just a little bit further."

Trevor and his associate leave the room leaving Jessica to her thoughts. *I'm pretty sure that he's right,* she muses, *I won't be able to escape this room or place without help.* Jessica realizes then that no help is coming and that she's on her own. She believes that her uncle is still alive, though, and that comforts her, a little.

It could be worse, she decides, she could be being tortured. Jessicagrimaces at the thought but then decides to do one of the few things that she can do, push-ups. Might as well train, she decides, I may be here for a while.

CHAPTER XIII

"Generals, you are a go" President Douglas says to his assembled military staff, his joint chiefs, in the White House's Situation Room.

"Yes, Mr. President" General Martin, his leading general says.

The other generals begin delivering their various orders throughout the chain of command. They'd received intelligence that President Lopez, the legitimate Mexican president, is housed in one of three secret Mexican facilities. This necessitates that they send three elite teams, one to each site to find and then secure him. President Douglas and his team do not know whether Lopez is alive or dead, but if he is alive and then made safe, his wife can be deposed. *That's the plan in any event*, President Douglas thinks. He knows that about a thousand things can go wrong.

Since his most recent telephone conversation with Margarita Lopez, the Mexican army had been gathering and rounding up American citizens in Mexico and placing all that they can find in various soccer stadiums around the country. Lopez' tacit threat is that if President Douglas doesn't accede to her demands, that she'll begin executing American citizens.

She's over-extended herself, President Douglas thinks. She has no idea what we're capable of or what we'll do to protect our people. "Are all of the representative fleets assembled, General Martin?" he asks.

"They are, Sir. By now, Lopez knows that we're there.

We have targets also. We can hit every military installation and every city from our positions on their coasts. We've got non-lethal measures as well" General Martin says.

"Good. Outstanding" President Douglas says. I doubt that Lopez will start executing our people, but let's not push her to it. A show of strength may be in order though, so stay ready."

"Yes, Sir, Mr. President" General Martin says.

* * *

"What do you mean warships?" Margarita Lopez asks her chief security officer.

"Warships, Madam Lopez. The Americans have gathered what looks to be all of their warships on our coast. They're positioned to fire upon major targets in our country, Madam, including all of our military installations here. They can reach the Presidential palace if they choose to. Several of your political allies are getting cold feet, Madam Lopez. They think that you should release all of the American expats and let go of your demands to the Americans."

Weak cowards, she thinks to herself. She's come too far now to let go. She is also incensed that President Douglas has threatened her and her country in this manner. *I still have hostages in the stadiums,* she knows. *I can move on to the gathered assemblyat Azteca and Olimpico Universitario. That should slow down the over-zealous American President,* she hopes.

"Tell the security teams at Azteca and Olimpico to round up ten Americans each and execute them at center field. That is an order" Lopez says.

"Madam Lopez" her security chief says hesitatingly, "if you do that, it means certain war with the Americans. Even with a reduced population, they still have all of their machines, which we don't have, and apparently, enough personnel to use most if not all of them. Is this really the wisest course?" he asks with a hint of pleading in his voice.

A crystal obelisk sits on the presidential desk, a gift given to her husband from the Egyptian ambassador during President Lopez' first year in office. Lopez picks it up deftly and throws at her security chief's head with all of her strength, which is considerable. It misses his head by mere centimeters only because he ducks fast enough to get out of its way. He will later thank his many years of boxing training which enabled him to move as fast as he needed to avoid a concussion or worse.

"I said"' Madam Lopez says through clenched teeth, "to round up ten Americans in each of the two stadiums and execute them. I did not stutter. If you question me again, it'll be bullets flying at your head and not some stupid statue. Is that clear?" she asks her tone murderous, her eyes filled with the promise of future harm.

"Yes, Madam, right away" her security chief says as he

slowly backs out of the room never taking his eyes from Lopez as she continues to stare murderously at him. Once outside the President's office he scurries down the hallway to deliver his orders to the other attendant commanders. *This woman is going to get us all killed,* he thinks fearfully to himself. Someone has got to stop her.

* * *

Darryl and his squad ride in their stealth Black Hawk helicopter piloted by Major Jill Williams. It's smaller than the regular Black Hawks but quieter and faster. Quiet and quick are what's required for this mission. They travel speedily to the black site in Mexico where President Lopez may be housed. It's a one in three stab in the dark, but Darryl likes their odds. It makes sense to him that the President would be close to the capital, Mexico City, so that his wife can keep close tabs on him.

"There in five!" Major Williams says in her com for Darryl to hear.

"Roger that" Darryl responds. "Squad, final weapons check! We are hot as soon as we hit the ground!""Roger, Sergeant!" his squad responds.

He looks into the eyes of his squad mates, his soldiers. He sees steely determination and a resolve to get the job done. Sergeant Darryl Issacs is pleased. He and his squad had come along way in a short amount of time. Almost nine months after Sleep Day and not only had he fully transformed into an excellentsoldier and special operator, but the members of his squad had as well, most of whom, like him, were new to military service on Sleep Day. *I was meant for this,* he thinks. *I'm good at it, I'm smart, I'm dangerous. Hurrah, he says to himself.*

Five minutes later, Darryl and his squad rappel from the Black Hawk down long black ropes into an area just inside of the Mexican black site. There are no guards that they can see. Their helicopter is virtually silent, which Darryl is glad about.

"Be quick, Sergeant" Major Williams says into his mouthpiece as his squad rappels down. As soon as they touch the ground, their weapons go hot with safeties off. As far as he and his squad are concerned, it's killing time. Whether President Lopez is here or not, they're bound to face opposition, Darryl knows, and they'll have to return fire.

This military site sits on the edge of Mexico City deep inside of the hills that surround it. It does not show up on a map, official or otherwise. American intelligence knows about it because they'd helped to locate it and advised on its construction when the American-Mexican relationship was far better. Today, knowledge of the site and its construction provides Darryl and his squad a huge competitive advantage.

The site has only one way in or out of it. A large steel door, big enough for two or three people to pass through together, covers the outside. The only evidence for the site is the door itself. *This is the kind of place you come to hide something or someone*, Darryl surmises.

"Squad, look sharp" he whispers into his mic. "If Lopez is here, I want him found, kept alive and extracted without anyone in Mexico City knowing that we're here. Benitez, Roberts, blow that door now" he commands.

Benitez and Roberts, the squad's explosives experts give a silent assent and approach the door. After assessing it for several seconds, they begin to apply plastic explosive to its outside edges. This type of explosive will burn very hot but do so almost silently so as not to alert any of the occupants inside. Darryl believes that no one yet knows that they're here and wants to keep it that way.

Once Benitez and Roberts apply the explosive and set its charges, they move back with the rest of the squad for cover. The charges are electronic and can be wirelessly triggered. Roberts holds the cellphone looking device that also serves as a trigger for the explosive. On Darryl's order, he triggers the plastique. Darryl and his squad hear what can only be described as a sucking sound as if all of the air in a room has rushed out of it. They watch as the door falls flat on the ground outside the site.

Darryl isn't convinced that the explosion isn't heard by whomever resides inside of the underground site. He then acts swiftly to move the squad to and through the door. They've got minutes, maybe, to search and extract, and that's if there is no substantial opposition. The space where the door used to be is pitch black. Darryl and his squad are not helped by the fact that it's now close to midnight and dark all around them. The darkness had served them when they'd flown in, but now, walking into the belly of the beast, they'll have to be very careful.

"Night vision. Now. Everyone" Darryl says to his squad through his coms. They all comply and suddenly the night lights up like daytime for the squad. They enter the portal where the door had been and immediately see long stairs that descend at least fifty feet downwardly. Darryl expects this. He had thoroughly reviewed the plans to this site, as well as most of his squad, before they'd left their base. Ordinarily, such review would have required top secret security clearances for he and his entire team. Given the circumstances and the target, Darryl's commanding officers had decided to forego such formalities. He is grateful, in this moment, for such consideration.

As they begin to descend the stairs, Darryl no longer gives verbal commands. He and the squad switch to hand signals exclusively. He takes the lead and directs the squad to follow him down the stairs. They slowly, methodically step down until they reach the bottom pausing along the way down only when Darryl hears a noise that sounds outside of their movements down the stairs.

The stairs end at a long halfway that travels both to the left and to the right and out of sight in both directions. Doors dot the hallway every ten feet or so. From the plans, Darryl knows that some of these doors lead to cells and some to interrogation rooms. *If President Lopez is here*, he deduces, *he'll be behind one of these but not so close to the entrance. We'll have to travel a bit before we find him*, he believes. Dim lights alight the hallway, but their strength is so weak that it might as well be totally dark. Darryl signals for half of the squad to go left while he takes the other half to the right.

Darryl begins the long trek down his side of the hallway. His second in command guides the other half of his squad down the left. *They'll be fine*, he thinks. Tenisha Craver is a beast and she's smart. Let me just focus on the task at hand and who all is with me. As they move silently down the hallway, Darryl and his squad maintain a disciplined single file formation sticking close to the wall on their right side. The walls and floor are concrete and, thankfully, do not echo much of any of the sound that they produce by their steps and breathing. As Darryl leads the way, he signals for the squad to halt a few times, stopping to listen carefully to an errant sound or two.

The place seems unnaturally quiet, eerily so. He'd expected more opposition than this. From the plans, Darryl knows that there's a floor below this one that is only accessible by staircase on this end. Reaching the end of the hallway, he and his squad mates see the staircase and decide to descend it. Reaching the bottom, they emerge in total darkness. Suddenly, bright lights shine directly at them, and they are blinded, their night vision being totally disabled. Automatic fire rings out and Darryl immediately drops down onto his stomach and returns fire from his M4.

He hears a few of his squad go down as well, but he can't tell if they've been hit. He also hears that several from his squad are returning fire upon whoever is shooting at them. It's risky in these close quarters, but Darryl decides to fire two grenades at their antagonists. His M4 is equipped with a grenade launcher. He fires two in rapid succession in the direction of the gunfire trained on them. BOOM! BOOM! he hears and sees as his grenades find theirmarks and explode. There is a brief pause after which Darryl feels the ground beneath him and the supporting walls shake violently. *We can't stay here long*, he thinks. *This place may not hold up.*

Standing, cautiously, Darryl looks back at his squad to assess their readiness. His heart sinks as he sees that three of his operators have been seriously wounded, one of whom looks dead. "Lights on" he orders as he and his squad mates turn their rifle lights on and point them down the hallway from which they received gunfire. *There's no point in secrecy now*, he thinks. *They know that we're here.*

Peering down the hallway Darryl sees one solitary door at its end. Part of the wall, about mid-way down the hallway, is collapsed due to the grenade explosions. Four bodies in various states of disrepair and their weapons lie strewn about the floor near where the wall is partially collapsed. *They're all dead*, Darryl sees and thinks. He walks to them and sees that their weapons and their remains are mangled and charred. He and several of his squad mates reach the door. There is a large, formidable-looking lock on the door. A small eye hole slot large enough to peer through sits at Darryl's eye level on the door. He slides a metal cover for the eye hole to one side and looks inside. A disheveled man sits crouched in a corner of the smallish room. When Darryl looks at him, the light from his rifle seems to blind the man. "Who are you?" Darryl asks.

"I am, I am President Felipé Lopez. I am the President of Mexico" he says.

"Mr. President, stay where you are. We're going to get you out of there" Darryl says. He closes the metal cover and looks at his squad. Three of the eight that are with him are down, but he sees that the other part of his squad has now joined him. "Blow the lock. It's the President. We've got to get him out of there." His squad goes to work on the lock as they'd done on the door leading into this site. Within a few minutes, the lock is blown off and the door swings open from the force of the blast. Darryl walks into the cell, his weapon pointed down away from the President.

"President Lopez, my name is Issacs. We're here to rescue you. Please come with us" he says.

"Americans?" President Lopez asks. "Why are Americans..." he trails off. "Oh my God, it must be worse than I thought. What has she done?" he asks.

"It's bad, Sir. But no time for that. We'll explain everything in the chopper" Darryl says.

One of the soldiers from Darryl's squad puts a bullet proof vest and a helmet onto President Lopez. Several soldiers surround him as they march him out of his cell and out of the site. Darryl notes that the president does not seem to have been ill-treated or tortured. He is glad that Lopez is still alive. *We may have a chance after all*, he thinks. *Now to the next part of the mission.*

* * *

Nicholas sits up on his knees with his hands behind his head as instructed. Tears stream down his face as he looks up into the stands of this, his favorite soccer stadium. He had hoped to play here someday and had come to Mexico to advance his soccer playing dreams after high school. His parents had been reluctant at first, but he'd worked hard in both soccer and learning Spanish. Reluctantly they'd let him go after he'd made it into Mexico's prestigious soccer academy.

His parents are asleep now because of the Sleepers virus and have been for the last eight or so months. Nicholas looks down the line of prisoners similarly on their knees with their hands behind their heads. He didn't think that it would come to this.

"Shooters, take your marks!" Nicholas hears in Spanish.

How can this be happening? He thinks to himself. *Where are the marines?*

"Aim!!!!" he hears again in Spanish.

This can't be happening, he says to himself now crying profusely, *this can't be happening!!!*

"FIRE!!!!!"

Mom.......

*   *   *

"She did what?" President Douglas asks General Martin thinking that perhaps he's misheard him.

"Margarita Lopez just ordered the execution of twenty American citizens, ten in each of two soccer stadiums, Mr. President" he says. "We have them all recorded by satellite."

"She KILLED" President Douglas says his voice sounding grave "our people?"

A momentary silence hangs in the room before General Martin answers. "Apparently, Mr. President, she has executed twenty of our citizens."

President Douglas is standing in the Situation Room of the White House as he receives this news. He thinks about those twenty now dead Americans. He thinks about their families. He puts himself in their place. He shudders at the thought of Helen or his children being one of the ones executed today. He mourns themall, but right now, his anger burns brighter than his sadness. Later, he tells himself, we'll mourn them aplenty. Now, we will avenge them.

"Which fleets are assembled off the Mexican coast right now?" President Douglas asks.

"Sir, we have the second, third, fourth, fifth, sixth, seventh and tenth fleets assembled there," General Martin says.

"Good. We'll go with your plan, General Martin. Fire on their largest military base. Destroy it. And I'm adding one more thing. I want one-thousand marines to make land in Mexico and get to the two soccer stadiums. I want them to kill every single Mexican soldier that they find there and liberate our people. Once they do that, I want them to set up a garrison in Juarez and another in Mexico City, their capital. This is the price that Mexico will pay today for rounding up and killing Americans."

When he finishes speaking, none of the President's assembled generals or their staff says anything. The silence in the room becomes deafening. President Douglas senses their reticence to speak. He realizes what he's just ordered and what it means for all of their futures whether the IMs wake up soon or not. By this order, he's just committed the United States to both military aggression and potentially, long term military occupation of one of their closest neighbors. He isn't sorry and though he is angry, is convinced that he's made the right choice. *There is little that the Mexican military will be able to do to us*, he thinks. Besides, taking up such positions in their country can serve as a buffer for both immigration and unwanted excursions into the U.S. by their drug cartels or military.

"I want regular updates on both operations. And let me know when we have President Lopez. We'll prop him up with our military forces for as long as it takes. This can't ever happen again, especially now, and especially this close to our homeland. Not ever again" President Douglas says. "Not ever."

President Douglas exits the Situation Room leaving his generals to execute his orders. He walks the short distance to the Oval office, steps inside and closes the door behind him.

Sitting at his desk, he contemplates what the next twenty-four hours will look like. He's just made a bold decision with irreversible consequences. *By this decision,* he thinks, *I'll either be famous or infamous. It won't be both. It can't be both.* "Diane" President Douglas says by phone to his assistant, "please get Congresswoman Stowe on the phone. We need to have a conversation."

* * *

Sergeant Darryl Isaacs can see the Mexican Presidential palace coming into view. His squad is mostly intact though three had just taken fire and been shot, and one of his best, Corporal Jenkins, is now dead, officially killed in action. Darryl is disheartened by the loss, but he knows that the mission is only half completed. Moments ago, he'd advised President Lopez about what was to happen next: get to the palace; find his wife; subdue any and all opposition; take back the presidency.

Darryl notes that President Lopez hadn't blinked at anything that he'd said. He only remarked that he'd like to see his wife taken alive, if possible, and that he would deal with her thereafter. *If President Lopez' brief internment had meant to chasten him, it hadn't worked,* Darryl thinks. That man is pissed off. Damn right. I'd be pissed too if my wife had removed me from office illegally, kidnapped me and imprisoned me, possibly, for later execution. They probably should have killed him. Big mistake. Now we have him, and he's a man on a mission. Big mistake.

"President Lopez, we'll do everything that we can to protect you, but you'll have to listen to us and stay with us. Let us handle all of the major work" Darryl says. "You already have your vest and helmet. Here, take this too" he says handing President Lopez a H&K forty-five caliber handgun and holster. "Do you know what to do with her?" Darryl asks. President Lopez takes the gun, de-holsters it and pulls the slide back to see if it's loaded. He also releases the clip to check exactly how many rounds are in it. Darryl is impressed. "Not my favorite brand" President Lopez says, "I'm a Glock man, but yes, I know how to handle it."

On the grounds of the palace are at least fifty Mexican military soldiers. Major Jill Williams banks their stealth helicopter hard right to stay out of range of their rifles which are almost certainly American issued. "We're three hundred yards out, Sergeant" she says to Darryl. "Fifty or more soldiers on the ground by my count. What do you want to do?" she asks.

Darryl sees the problem. They have the legitimate Mexican president, but the ones protecting the palace are probably Margarita Lopez' hand-picked loyalists. They probably have orders to shoot President Lopez on sight should he escape, which he had just done.

"Land us outside the wall, on top of a building that can support our weight. Lopez can't rope down like we can" Darryl says to Major Williams, his pilot.

"Roger that" she responds.

Darryl knows his orders. *Get Lopez. Take the palace. Arrest his wife. Simple, clean and ridiculously hard,* he thinks. The first order of business now becomes getting onto the palace grounds with minimal opposition, getting to Lopez' wife, and then holding fort with President Lopez as more American reinforcements arrive. *Speaking of American reinforcements,* he thinks, *his other two squads should be rendezvousing with him soon since their inspected locations had been empty.* "Where are the other two squads?" Darryl asks his communications soldier.

"They're five minutes out from us right now. They know that we have President Lopez. I've given them our coordinates for drop off" he replies.

"Excellent, Corporal. Once we're assembled, we go in. Spread the word" Darryl says. *Two of these in one night,* Darryl thinks to himself. *Must be some kind of record.* Major Williams places them down onto a rooftop just large enough for the helicopter. Darryl, President Lopez and most of his squad dis-embark and head down into the building to await the arrival of the rest of their squad. *Soon,* he thinks, "then it will be go time."

* * *

This night is not at all going the way that Margarita Lopez had envisioned it. She has just received reports that her husband may have escaped his prison. She is unsure, however, because no one at the black site at which he had been held is responding to her staff's communiqués. They are only therefore assuming that there is no one alive at the site and that President Lopez is long gone.

If that's true, she muses, *then it won't be long before he makes a play for the palace.* She is troubled by this turn of events because her so-called loyalists, the powerful connected political families and politicians, are starting to show their reticence to her grab for power. She's already been told once this evening that she should never have killed the Americans much to her dismay and anger.

In response to her order, the Americans have destroyed no fewer than four Mexican military installations. The soldiers at those installations had little warning about the impending American attacks. Some made it out, some did not. We killed twenty, they killed two-hundred, Lopez fumes. To make matters worse, none of her top generals will pass along any more kill orders for fear of how many more of their Mexican soldiers the American forces might kill.

"I told them what you said," General Olivier says to Margarita, shuddering in the place that he stands afraid to get too close to her. He eyes the Desert Eagle pistol on her desk nervously. Margarita had always been an astounding marksman from the time that she was young, having won many awards forher marksmanship. The gun on her desk is one of several that she'd won in her time on the Mexican marksman's circuit. "The other generals are afraid to further risk the wrath of the Americans.There are also reports" he says taking a step or two back from where Margarita stands behind her desk, "there are reports that theAmericans are now assembling right outside of our walls and that your husband" he pauses hesitating to continue, "your husband is with them."

"How many of our soldiers are outside?" she asks. "About fifty, now. There had been more, but a number of them abandoned their post once they heard that President Lo-, er, your husband had escaped" General Olivier says. "The ones outside are die-hards. They'll never leave you."

At least there's some small, good news, Margarita thinks. If it comes down to it, they'll make their stand against the Americans and her husband. Perhaps he will forgive her and merely divorce her, she wonders. But no, that's wishful thinking. Felipé may not have been a strong president, but he had always been a patriot. *I should have killed him when I had the chance,* she thinks ruefully. *That had been a miscalculation.*

As Margarita and General Olivier consider their options, another one of her generals enters the Presidential office. "Madam Lopez" he says, "the Americans, marines we think, have taken the soccer stadiums. There was a brief skirmish at each, but our soldiers mostly ran off. There seemed to be several thousand marines at each stadium. All of the Americans have been liberated."

Great, she thinks sarcastically. *More good news. It's over. There are no more cards to play. I'll be lucky not to get extradited to America and put on trial. This has been a disaster.* As Margarita contemplates this latest turn of events a violent explosion rocks the eastern wall of the Presidential palace. She and her assembled generals see it as it happens. She watches as her soldiers rush to the now massive hole in the wall. They are met with gunfire above them from two Black Hawk helicopters. She watches as two dozen of her soldiers fall beneath the gunfire never to rise again.

"It's time to go," she says to her generals. "Get me the hell out of here! We'll escape to my family's retreat." Her generals nod their quick ascent, but escape is too late. There is gunfire in the hallway outside of her office. The Americans are here. She is trapped.

*   *   *

"Bomb the palace," President Lopez says. "I don't want you to suffer even one more casualty tonight on my account, Sergeant."

Darryl looks at President Lopez in astonishment. He had hoped to catch the Mexican soldiers at the palace unawares or relatively so. He knows that this approach risks more casualties on their side whether it's effective or not. What President Lopez suggests takes away the element of surprise but also spares them from major loss provided they execute with overwhelming force.

"You understand what that means, Mr. President?" Darryl asks.

"I do, Sergeant. Those soldiers are all my wife's loyalists. They'll never be loyal to me or be able to serve in the army after this. If they've remained there this long, they're committed to the death. So be it" President Lopez says sternly.

"So be it," Darryl repeats. Turning to his communications operator he says "give me crashing air support on the palace.

Focus on the eastern wall and then ambush all assembled soldiers in the courtyard with the stealth Black Hawks, capeesh? Send that order now." Darryl's communication's operator dutifully complies."We'll go in five minutes. While all the attention is on the eastern wall, we'll blow the main gate and enter in through the front door, Sir."

"Fair enough," President Lopez says. "Sergeant, Margarita belongs to me. If anything should happen, I will take her."

Darryl nods his assent and thinks to himself see, *this is why I never got married, divorce can be so messy.*

* * *

President Lopez moves quickly with Sergeant Isaacs and the other operators through the front doors of his Presidential palace. He watches as they dispatch four Mexican soldiers who made the tragic mistake of raising their rifles in their direction. It doesn't seem to him that the Americans even slowed down as they fired back at the now dead soldiers.

"Where is your office?" Sergeant Isaacs asks.

"Second floor," President Lopez says. "She's sure to be there. She considered it her birthright" he says sardonically.

A broad, wide winding staircase faces them just inside of the palace. President Lopez and the American operators begin to climb it cautiously looking out for shooters from above them. About midway up the staircase, two soldiers appear at the top of the staircase. "El Presidenté!!!" one of them yells as both commence to firing directly at him and the American troops. Darryl and the other operators immediately fire back at them, killing both.

"Get to the top of the stairs now!" Sergeant Isaacs orders. President Lopez feels his four bodyguards, the soldiers assigned to him by Sergeant Isaacs, fairly pick him up and move him quickly to the top of the stairs. Once there, President Lopez sees a poorly constructed barricade at the end of the long hallway where his office resides. There appear to be about ten soldiers manning the barricade all with their rifles trained upon them.

"Stay behind us, Mr. President," Sergeant Isaacs says. President Lopez complies but draws the sidearm that Sergeant Isaacs had given him. The cold steel of the forty-five caliber handgun centers and calms him. He is nowhere near the marksman that his wife, Margarita, is, but he's no slouch. *If I get a shot, I'm taking it,* he decides. *This is the President's house, and I'm taking it back.*

Darryl quickly assesses his options and decides to act. The

barricade and the soldiers manning it must both come down. He knows that the soldiers, Margarita's most loyal, will never withdraw. Signaling two other operators, they line up across the front of their assembled squad. Each has a grenade launcher fitted to their respective M4 assault rifles. At Darryl's command, they launch multiple grenades at the barricade. Reaching the barricade,the grenades explode and destroy it, rocking the palace with each explosion.

President Lopez feels the vibrations where he stands although his office is at least fifty yards down the wide hallway. "Let's go" he hears Sergeant Isaacs say. They begin to creep down the hallway, cautiously but with steady, unbreakable purpose.

Nearing the now destroyed barricade, he sees the carnage createdby the soldiers' grenades. Multiple bodies lay strewn about, some missing parts of their bodies. All are dead. These died in service to my usurping wife. *There is no honor for them*, President Lopez thinks, his anger rising to higher levels as he bitterly mourns the loss of these, his mis-guided, disloyal countrymen.

"Those are the doors to my office" he says to Sergeant Isaacs. "Let's go in now."

"Behind me, Mr. President," Sergeant Isaacs says.

"No, Sergeant, behind me" President Lopez says, grabbing the handle to one of the massive doors of his office pulling it toward himself.

Stepping inside, President Lopez sees two of his former generals standing a few feet away from him. Neither dons nor holds a weapon. He also sees Margarita, his wife, standing behind his desk and her Desert Eagle pistol, her prized possession, laying on the desk in front of her.

"Hello, Husband" she says.

"Margarita, you have lost every right to ever call me that. You are under arrest and removed from the office that you sought to usurp. You will be tried and either imprisoned for the rest of your life or shot" President Lopez says.

Margarita's eyebrows raise as she hears the steel in her husband's voice. She had expected to be arrested, of course, but thought that given her husband's well-worn pliability toward her, that she could wrangle some softened penalty from him. She had not expected such harshness nor his obvious intent to grant her little mercy. *Yes, I should have killed him,* she thinks again for the fiftieth time. Her eyes travel down to her pistol which sits mere inches from her. She sees that Felipé has a gun in his right hand, his shooting hand, as well. She almost chuckles at the prospect of him aiming it at her. Felipé is not nearly the shot that she is, but at this distance he may not have to be, she considers.

Weighing her options, Margarita briefly wonders what might have been had her coup been successful. She'd had such plans before this fateful day. Now, those plans are all for naught. Her family's name will go down with her. She is the last of her clan to hold power and there will be no one else after her. She looks at Felipé, her husband whom she could never quite love though, early on, she'd tried. Making her decision, she acts.

She's faster than I am, President Lopez thinks. *My aim must be true.* He sees Margarita's hand inch toward her pistol. He grips his more tightly. He sees her grab it, raise it and aim it right at his heart. They both pull their triggers at the same time. President Lopez feels the force of the bullet hit him right where his heart is as it knocks him back and onto the floor. His chest is on fire from the blow and hurts more than anything he's ever felt before. In an instant, Sergeant Isaacs is before him checking his injury.

"You're okay, Mr. President, or you will be. The vest caught the worst of it. You're not wounded" Sergeant Isaacs says. *Not wounded,* he thinks, *but damn, that hurt like hell.*

"Get me up" President Lopez says, each word a ball of fire exiting his throat. Sergeant Isaacs quickly but gently picks him up. He sees the two generals on the floor cowering behind a couch. He sees his wife slumped over his desk, dead, a single gunshot wound to her chest.

"Perfect shot" Mr. President, Sergeant Isaacs says mirthlessly.

Perfect shot, President Lopez silently echoes staring at his now dead wife.

* * *

"What is your current assessment, General Martin? Where are we?" President Douglas asks.

"First, Sir, all of the Americans that had been packed into the two Mexican soccer stadiums have been liberated. The bodies of the twenty dead Americans have been secured. They will soon be back on American soil. We have about five-hundred soldiers in Juarez now. They've commandeered the military installation that sits right outside of the city. We also have about seven-hundred-fifty marines in Mexico City. They've occupied positions around the Presidential palace at your request."

"Margarita Lopez?" he asks.

"She's dead, Sir. Lopez is dead. From what we understand, her husband, President Lopez, took the shot."

"He took the shot?" President Douglas asks.

"Yes, Sir. He'd insisted on dealing with her to our squad. We don't think that's what he'd meant" General Martin says.

President Douglas allows himself a moment to consider the implications of all that has happened. President Lopez, by his escape and dispatch of his wife, will be firmly ensconced in power now. With American soldiers backing him, no one will contest that. Given the trouble that Mexico had been previously giving them, it is now in America's best interest to establish a firm, if not permanent, American military presence in northern Mexico to act as a buffer against any further unwanted incursions into Texas and Arizona.

"Fair enough. Good job, generals. Patch me into Sergeant Isaacs in an hour. I'll take the call in the Oval. We have some things to discuss" President Douglas says. As he leaves the Situation Room, he considers what's next. Not since the Mexican-American war in the late 1800s had the United States occupied any part of Mexico. *That won't sit well with our Mexican citizenry,* he thinks. *So be it, we can't afford any more Mexican aggression,* he muses and hopes that he's right.

/ Ted Cummings

CHAPTER XIV

Samantha doesn't quite know what to think. She stares into the faces of four children who all stare back with smiling faces. Ifé's kids are beautiful, she sees. Two of them look like her husband, Henry, while the other two look like Ifé, her spitting image. And of course, everyone is Black. *In fact,* she thinks, *everyone around her is either Black or Brown,* and all are SMs she sees. Her new friend Bethany Rogers, a newly awakened IM like her, had similarly been placed with a SM family but in a different city. Before leaving the Hive, Ifé promised Samantha that she could visit with Bethany in a few weeks. Though Ifé's family lives in Dallas, Texas and Bethany now lives in Atlanta, Georgia, the country's high speed rail system makes far away cities seem closebecause of its speed.

Standing in the main Dallas train terminal, Samantha marvels at the cavernous hall in which she stands. It's obvious that the terminal is new, at least new since the time after she'd fallen asleep by the Sleepers virus. Leaving the Hive with Ifé had been a marvel as well. Once their transport delivers them to a train station many miles away from Texas, they board a train that looks like something out of the far distant future. Samantha had been fond of reading science fiction novels suitable for higher grades since she is such an advanced reader. In them, she'd read many times about advanced civilizations, aliens from other planets with advanced technology and had even seen the movie Black Panther where the fictional technologically-advanced city of Wakanda was displayed. *Wakanda,* she thinks. This city looks like Wakanda to her.

"Greetings, Samantha, and welcome to our city" Henry Eze, Ifé's husband, says. When Ifé and Henry see each other, they embrace and kiss one-another affectionately. Ifé then in turn embraces each of their children who, obviously to Samantha, clearly love and have missed their mother. For Ifé, this is a homecoming. For Samantha, this is her new home. She feels the warmth and invitation of this new family but having been a part of several other foster homes, Samantha is wary and keeps her distance. She is unsure of what the rules are for foster kids like her in this new society. She decides to keep her guard up until she knows and feels differently.

"Hello, Mr. Eze," Samantha says. "It's a pleasure to meet you and your family."

"Oh no, Samantha, please call me Henry. And these are my children: Akhenaton, Okoyani, Emmanuel and Isaiah."

Samantha sees that Akhenaton and Okoyani are both older than she is but that Emmanuel and Isaiah are both younger. She couldn't help but make a funny face at their names, two of which she had never heard before. Ifé sees her face and chuckles.

"So, Samantha, in our culture, each child is afforded two names. The first name is the one that the parents choose. The second name is the one that the child or young adult chooses.

Akhenaton is our son's second name, the one that he chose when he was fourteen. He's sixteen now. Okoyani is our daughter's second name, the one that she chose just this year. She's fourteen. In time, both Emmanuel and Isaiah will have the option of choosing their own names when they come of age if they wish.

We believe that every person has the right to name for herself and himself what she or he will be. Our belief is that a name holds power and speaks forth destiny" Ifé says.

"Come on, guys," Okoyani says. "I'll bet that Samantha is famished."

Henry takes his wife's bags and Akhenaton takes Samantha's small bag. She doesn't have much, but Ifé had given her a few outfits to wear while she resided at the Hive. Part of the Hive had been created to house a few stores that she had been allowed to shop in. The clothes there were different from anything that she had ever worn before, but Samantha found a few items that appealed to her and a couple pairs of shoes that she liked as well.

Every item of clothing has some kind of technology woven into them, which Samantha finds annoying at times. Do I really need to know what my heartrate or heart rate is all the time? She had asked Ifé who in turn laughed loudly as if Samantha had said the funniest thing in the world.

Standing with her new foster family, Samantha sees that they're dressed in much of the same kinds of fabrics and colors as ones of the outfits that she'd chosen at the Hive. *At least my clothes won't stick out,* she thinks, *even though my skin will.* As they begin to walk out of the terminal together, Okoyani tells her that they live only a few short blocks away from the train station and that there are many fine restaurants along the way. Samantha sees that Okoyani is tall, graceful and confident. She smells, to Samantha, like something out of an expensive spice shop or the exotic spices from a distant country in one of the many books that Samantha had read. She is chatty and friendly, which Samantha appreciates. She also notices that Emmanuel and Isaiah keep their distance from her but watch her carefully. Samantha is not sure what to make of that, but she decides not to take it personally.

Two blocks away from the train station, they arrive at a restaurant. It seems, to Samantha, to be quite popular. The smells from the inside are absolutely intoxicating to her and cause both her mouth to water and stomach to growl. Emmanuel and Isaiah hear her stomach and giggle in response. "Wow! You're really hungry!" Emmanuel says. Samantha blushes but says nothing.

Once inside, they sit at a large table together. Apparently, there is no menu from which to order. It's dinner time and the waitress who seats them tells them that dinner will soon be served. A few moments later, the waitress and two other helpers begin bringing multiple dishes to their table. Everything looks delicious to Samantha. Looking around the restaurant, she sees that other families, like hers, are similarly seated and enjoying food from dishes like theirs.

She sees and smells meat dishes, fish, various kinds of vegetables, at least two kinds of bread, one of them sweet, and a jar of the most flavorful honey that she's ever tasted. Emmanuel and Isaiah have now warmed up to her and are talking their heads off at her. They speak so fast and fluidly that she can barely keep up. Like their mother, they all speak multiple languages and float from one to the other effortlessly. At one point, Ifé clears her throat at them to remind them, apparently, to only speak English to and around her. Samantha doesn't mind though. She is coming to enjoy the melodic sound of the multiple languages she hears from Ifé, her family and other SMs and how, in full conversation, they seem to form one universal language with its ticks, rhythms, sounds and notes that sound almost like singing to her. Samantha thinks that she could listen to them speak all night.

"Ifé" she says, "when am I going to learn how to speak like

you and everyone else?"

At her question, their whole table stops talking and looks at her. It's as if she's said the most curious thing ever by all of their expressions. Samantha wonders whether she's said something wrong.

"Beloved" Ifé says, "you can learn what we know any time that you're ready to. In fact, I was going to tell you that school starts next week for you."

"Next week?" Samantha queries. "How about tomorrow? I want to learn all that I can" she says.

"Well, let's see. We're just getting...home. We'll show you around this week and then next week, we'll get after it. Deal?" Ifé says.

"Deal" Samantha agrees somewhat reluctantly.

"Oh, but tomorrow, Ifé continues, Okoyani will begin your training," Ifé says.

"My training?" Samantha asks.

"Your training," Okoyani says with a wickedly mischievous look on her face.

Wow, Samantha thinks. *I can't wait to see what tomorrow brings. Training it is.*

*   *   *

Dr. Garrett is bored out of his mind. After spending a few weeks roaming about Denver and his new technologically enhanced home, he feels that he's seen all that can see. The new America is fast paced, advanced, peaceful and very prosperous. He also feels completely out of place in it. He retains his brilliant mind but has almost nothing of consequence to do with it. He's rich but in an isolating way. His neighbors, for the most part, treat him with benign disdain. No one is openly racist toward him, but it's clear that they don't consider him to be one of them.

Dr. Foster has checked on him a few times and even offered to come spend a day or two with him, but it's also clear to him thatDr. Foster has his own life and his own priorities. Apparently, Dr. Foster is who he had been eighty years ago, a brilliant in demand physician. Dr. Foster and other doctors like him all seem to pair upwith someone like Dr. Garrett who wakes up to the new America as a way to ease their way back into society.

"Dr. Garrett", the artificial intelligence in his house says to him, "what would you like to do today?"

Every time that he hears his A.I. 's voice, which he now calls 'Steve', it unnerves him. Steve sounds intelligent, aware and disturbingly human. When he'd first started speaking to him, Steve's voice had been the sound of a Black man. Dr. Garrett asked Steve to change his voice to sound more like his own but not exactly. Steve immediately complied and now sounds like one of those disembodied voices that was common in the television commercials of his day, eighty years ago.

Even with the change, something about Steve continues to irritate him. Dr. Garrett understands that Steve is the A.I. for his house, but he also knows that it's networked to the greater A.I. that runs all of the rest of the country. In that way, it feels as if Steve is with him all the time and everywhere that he goes. Every stitch of clothing that he now owns is connected to the A.I., and that A.I. is always on, always watching, always listening.

No one wonders if there's hardly any crime anywhere, he thinks. *There are literally electronic eyes and ears everywhere.* No one else seems to think anything about it, but Dr. Garrett remembers that before the Sleepers virus struck, many warnings had been sounded about the potential use of A.I. and what its pervasiveness could mean to society at large. I guess we now know. It's here and no one is batting an eye.

"Steve, I'm thinking about a day trip. Maybe a quick overnight. What's close enough to here but far enough away for a nice train ride?"

"Oh, Dr. Garrett, you've got lots of options. You can hit any of the cities in Texas, Arizona, Louisiana, or California. And if you spend the night, you can go as far as Ohio, Tennessee, even Georgia. Atlanta is beautiful this time of year" Steve says.

"You know what, Steve, let's go a little further to Savannah. I need to see the water. I'll stay overnight. Go ahead and make the arrangements. I'd like to leave by noon today. Also, find a restaurant that has the best seafood in Savannah. Highest possible rating" Dr. Garrett says.

"Very good, Sir. It should be delightful. Arrangements

made. A transport will be here by 11 a.m. to take you to the train station. You'll leave at noon by train and be in Savannah approximately two and a half hours later. Easy. Shall I also make your lodging arrangements, Dr. Garrett?" Steve asks.

"Ah, yes, lodging, I completely forgot about that. I'd like to sleep on a boat tonight. Can that be arranged?" he asks.

"Most certainly, Dr. Garrett. You only need to tell me how large or small you want the boat to be" Steve says.

"Hunh. Let's go fifty footer with full wait staff and I want it to cruise about just offshore while I sleep. It'll be nice to wake up on the water" Dr. Garrett says.

"Done and done," Steve says happily. "All arrangements have been sent to your device. Once you get situated, I can direct you along to your various locales."

And there it is, Dr. Garrett thinks. *This thing is with me everywhere I go. Whether at home or out, it's here. And you can't tell me that it's not monitoring me all along the way. Yikes.* As Dr. Garrett contemplates his A.I. 's continual intrusions into his life, the doorbell to his front door rings. He elects to answer it himself instead of letting Steve do it. Dr. Garrett likes to at least maintain the semblance of some control in his own home.

"Good morning, Dr. Garrett" a beautiful dark skinned woman says. "A little bird told me that you're making a trip today. I'd like to go with you. Savannah sounds wonderful."

Damnit, Steve! Dr. Garrett thinks. Dr. Garret is irritated by the intrusion but not the result. He recognizes his visitor as one of his neighbors who, being single like he is, lives a few houses down. Imani had been one of the few of his neighbors to welcome him to the neighborhood. She'd come by once before with a gift basket. Dr. Garrett had appreciated the gesture especially from a woman as lovely as she is.

"Hi, Imani," he says. "Please come in. Honestly, I hadn't actually planned for company."

"Oh, never mind that, Donald. You need both, a trip and a friend. You've been stuck in this house for two months and haven't had nary a visitor or really gone out much. I asked my Sheila to keep tabs on you. She and Steve speak often. I'm free and you are too. Let's go together and enjoy the day and the next" Imani says.

She makes a compelling point, Dr. Garrett admits to himself. "Fine. Let's do it. I presume that you have all of the arrangements?"

"Of course, I do. See you at 10:45. We'll go to the train station together" Imani says and unexpectedly leans into Dr. Garrett to give him a light peck on the cheek. She laughs at his surprise and walks out of his front door.

Steve closes the door behind her. "Not cool, Steve, not cool," Dr. Garrett says. Steve chuckles lightly. "Noted, Dr. Garrett, noted."

* * *

"You're really lucky" Eric hears an unfamiliar voice say. His head and his left side hurt. It feels as if he has a rib or several broken. He's also groggy. He's just awakened and feels disoriented. The room is darkened, but he sees the outline of a person sitting in a chair with his legs crossed. "Lights up" he saysto get a look at who is in his room and where he is. He sees a man of about thirty, younger than him, staring back at him. He is white or an IM in modern parlance.

"Hello, Eric, my name is Patrick Strothers. I'm your new guide. Nice to meet you."

"How long have I been out?" Eric asks.

"Oh, about five hours. You took quite a nasty blow, but your ribs are already healing. The tech here speeds that up. But you'll be uncomfortable for the next few hours. It wasn't smart trying to take Koje on physically. He's one of their best, most accomplished fighters" Patrick says.

Eric silently acknowledges the truth of Patrick's statement.

Since meeting Koje, it had been clear to him that Koje is some kind of fighter. Fighters know fighters, and Eric had known that he wasn't merely a tall, muscular guy. He doesn't look like this for noreason. There is movement in those muscles, he'd thought at the time.

"Patrick, is it?" Eric asks. "Why are you here, Patrick?" Patrick clears his throat before answering. "Well, Eric, because of your outburst, shall we say, against Koje, the powersthat be thought it prudent that he be replaced as your guide and that he be replaced with me, or someone that you might be more comfortable with. Koje had noted in his reports that you seemedless than happy to have him as your guide."

Eric knows when someone is calling him a racist. He'd fought many such accusations in the many formal complaints made against him during his time as a police officer in New York City.

Sure, he told jokes and laughed at jokes of a racial nature, but he considers anyone who can't take a little ribbing to be thin-skinned and not at all worth his time or consideration. *And I was never brutal toward anyone who didn't deserve it,* he thinks.

"Fine, Patrick, whatever. But by my clock, it's the seventh day and I'm due to get out of here. So what's your role? Escort back to New York or someplace else that I choose?"

"That's part of the reason that I'm here, Eric. You're not leaving the Hive today or any day soon unless and until you can satisfactorily show and prove that you are not a danger to yourself or others" Patrick says.

Eric feels all of the oxygen go out of the room. Since awakening, he has hated nearly every moment of his new reality. This place feels foreign and far too different from the America that he'd known all of his adult life. *In that America,* he thinks, *the world made sense. In that America, I had a place, I knew who I was, and I had respect. Here, I have nothing.*

"I can see that this is a difficult moment for you, Eric," Patrick says. "But believe me, many people are rooting for you and hoping that you make", he pauses, "the necessary adjustments."

"Necessary adjustments?" Eric asks through gritted teeth.
"Necessary adjustments" Patrick says definitively. "I was one of the first IMs to awaken. I've been up and around for the last ninety days. I was a bit shell-shocked too by our surroundings and its people. It's still America in that America still exists, has a Constitution and folks generally think of themselves as such. But it's not our country anymore, Eric. It no longer belongs solely to white people."

Patrick allows that statement to linger in the air a moment before continuing to speak. To Eric, it feels like the world that he'd known and that had been very good to him no longer exists. No one had said what Patrick just said out loud, but the statement's truth is undeniable.

"So what do we do now, Patrick? As white people, what do we do?" Eric asks, the hurt in his voice evident.

"To start, we adapt. First things first, this society no longer refers to folks by the color of their skin. They think we're crazy for ever having done so. Everything here is looked at from the perspective of the existence of melanin. Either you have it, or you don't. We don't. In this world, Eric, the folks with the melanin make the rules. Fortunately for us, most of them are either benevolent or neutral toward us, IMs. But believe me when I tell you that there is a significant minority of SMs who would have preferred that we never awakened or worse. One of the things that happened almost immediately after Sleep Day is that the education system dramatically changed, and when it changed, American and world history changed. What we use to call and deride as critical race theory serves as the backbone of how everyone is educated in America today. Every SM you see has grown up with an SM centered education and therefore an SM centered mindset. That means that they know all of their history and culture in a way that our America denied them for hundreds of years. They know what we and our ancestors did to their ancestors. Some consider us less than human for our barbarism. Frankly, it could have gone so much worse for us."

"Our barbarism? What the hell are you talking about, Patrick?!" Eric says, almost yelling.

"Our barbarism" Patrick replies flatly. "A few years after Sleep Day when it became evident that we IMs would not soon wake up, the SMs of that day held a year-long Truth & Reconciliation commission similar to the one done in South Africa at the end of Apartheid. President Douglas considered it to be his greatest work. From it, reparations for SMs were called for and approved though for all practical purposes, the transfer of money, property, businesses and other resources had pretty much all occurred by then.

But most importantly, all of the facts about all of the horror that had been committed toward Indigenous Americans, Brown Americans, Asian Americans and Black Americans came to full light. In that environment, there were no IMs to restrict the opening of files, some decades old, some recent, that detailed the atrocities committed by many IMs in power. This includes files on police brutality. This includes your files, Eric. Everything that you said and did on the job that was recorded is a matter of public record. It's as close as an internet search. When you were awakened, alerts went out to SMs everywhere telling them so. Many are concerned about your awakening and your rejoining society at large. You are looked at here as a pariah given your brutal history."

Eric does not speak. He is too angry to do so. Here stands this white man, this IM, accusing him of being some kind of monster. *And not just me*, he thinks, *but the entire American white race. Who the hell does he think he is?!*

Patrick watches as Eric's face reddens and his breathing becomes more haggard. He was told that this might happen. *The truth is the truth*, Patrick thinks. *This man has never been faced with the truth. He has to face it now*, he decides.

"So here's the deal, Eric. You will remain here until such time as you can demonstrate a sufficient degree of non-racial aggression towards the SMs. If you choose not to do that work, SM authorities are prepared to deport you from the United States to the non-SM country of your choice, excluding the Sovereign Nation of Alaska. Though run mostly by IMs, Alaska remains on good terms with the United States and has signed a treaty with the country that foregoes the admittance of any awakening IMs with a troubled racial history like yours.

I'm here to guide you, Eric. I am your ally. But also, this society, this country has become something that our Founders could only dream of. Crime is negligible. There is full employment. Everyone is educated in something. All basic needs are met. It's prosperous. It's grown. Though we lost Alaska, we gained DC, Puerto Rico and Cuba as states. And every South American and Caribbean nation that's partnered with the U.S. has seen its GDP rise. Whether SM or IM, you can make yourself whatever you wish to be."

"Can I be a cop again?" Eric asks sarcastically.

"Obviously, no, you can never be a police officer or even own lethal force again. The police as you've known them no longer exist but even if you could, you would never be allowed to join them, not in a SM-centric society such as this one. But there is a place for you, Eric, if you choose to embrace it, and if you choose to change. The choice is totally up to you" Patrick says.

Up to me? Eric thinks to himself. *None of this is up to me. If it were up to me, I never would have fallen asleep. I would have gotten my pension, moved to Florida, enjoyed my life and been long dead by now, if it were up to me.*

"What happens now, Patrick? What do I need to do?" Eric asks.

"Excellent questions, Eric. We'll begin your formal re-acclimation process bright and early tomorrow morning. It occurs to me that you haven't actually seen the sun in a long while.

We'll start there. Tomorrow will be a great day for a field trip. In fact, since we're so close, relatively speaking, we'll go to Mt. Rushmore. That should get your juices flowing. I'll pick you up then" Patrick says and then leaves Eric alone in his room.

Eric is glad to see him go. He doesn't dislike Patrick like he'd instantly disliked Koje, but he says sees which side of the fence he'd landed on in this new America, the SM side. *He's a traitor to his own people*, Eric thinks bitterly. *I don't care what these people have done to rob and change my country. It's still MY country. I'll be damned if I change for them. They'll see*, he says to himself. Eric gets up gingerly from his healing bed. He is happy to see that he's still in his room. It's spacious, familiar and comfortable. At least, there's that, he considers. He is hungry and wants to hit the cafeteria for something to eat. Walking to his door, he expects it to open in his presence. The door does not budge.

"Open" he says, knowing the A.I. in his room is listening. The door does not move. "Open!" he says now insistently. The door remains immobile. "Why the hell won't you open?!" he bellows.

"Eric", the room's A.I. says, "your access to the rest of the Hive has been restricted. You can order your meals here and they'll be brought to you. What would you like to eat?"

"Nothing. I've lost my appetite. Please dim the lights" he says and lays back down. I truly hate this place. I hate it. As soon as I can leave either legitimately or by escaping, I'm out." Eric lays down on his healing bed and hopes that by the time that he wakes up, he'll be pain free. He also hopes that he'll be free of this place and of these people.

* * *

"Samantha, wake up. It's time to go" Okoyani says.

Samantha smacks her lips and stretches. She peaks her eyes open and sees that it's still dark. *Why is Okoyani bugging her at this ungodly hour*, she wonders.

"Come on, Samantha, let's go," Okoyani says insistently.

That's right, Samantha says to herself. *Training. They want me to start my training. Ugh, this is so random. Why am I here? Oh yeah, that's right. I'm actually ninety-two years old. Eighty plus twelve. And America is new. And I'm new. And I now have to get up and go train with my new foster sister. And this is apparently what all girls do from the age of little to big. And I'm somewhere in between.*

Samantha thinks all her thoughts in rapid succession as she slowly almost painfully rises from her new comfortable bed, puts on her training clothes that Ifé had laid out for her, and follows Okoyani out the front door to the bright gleaming training facility down the street from their home.

"I promise, Samantha, this will be the best day of the start of your new life", Okoyani says excitedly. "And I get to be in charge of your training! I'm so excited. I normally only teach the three and four year olds. I've never taught anyone as old as you. It's going to be fun!" she says.

Samantha doesn't know which is more annoying, Okoyani's early morning wake-up call or her over the top excitement. In any event, she's still sleepy and wishes that she were back in her bed in fitful slumber. As they walk up to the training facility, she sees its name in large letters above the doors–LUXOR TRAINING ACADEMY. An uneasiness settles upon her made all the more awkward by Okoyani's bubbling excitement."Okay, Sam, may I call you Sam? When we get in, we'll get warmed up, I'll give you a brief lecture, very brief, on our history, why we do what we do and why you, ahem, as a girl must participate. Cool?" Okoyani asks but doesn't wait for Samantha'sanswer. Instead, she walks through the swooshing doors of the facility and Samantha walks quickly behind her trying to keep up.

A few minutes later, Samantha is breathing hard, and her muscles are beginning to ache. This is just the warm-up.Okoyani has just taken her through several rounds of jump rope, push-ups, squats and short sprints. The facility is massive, having what looks, to Samantha, to be two one-hundred yard fields housed under a large roof. It reminds her of one of the indoor football stadiums that she'd been to once or twice before, but this structure is much larger than the one that she remembers.

"Okay, Samantha, now is a good time for you to catch your breath. I want to tell you a bit about our history, what we're doing and why it's important. America, before Sleep Day, was a very dangerous place for Black people and other people of color. For Black women particularly, we were subject to the most heinous of abuse and crimes coming from society generally and often, from our own men. After Sleep Day, a tremendous reckoning occurred amongst and between Black men and women not the least of which was their sexism and abuse toward us. We understood that much of the seeds of their attitudes and behaviors were planted during slavery. As a group, our Black female ancestors forgave our men but also required each and every one of them to get counseling for their own healing. But we also determined, going forward, that we would not be helpless, hence your training.

In our society, every girl is required to learn and study several martial art forms. At a minimum, each must study and learn Muay Thai, Wing Chun, karate, and one of several forms of Jiu Jitsu. I prefer Brazilian Jiu Jitsu and have a black belt in it. Our girls begin their training from the time that they can walk and don't stop until after each completes college or some other educational training. Our boys are not allowed to study martial arts until the age of ten, and it's not mandatory although many do. I myself am trained and expert in Muay Thai, BJJ, karate and Jeet Koon Do, my favorite, which combines some boxing with Wing Chun and Bruce Lee's unorthodox style. I train every day except Sunday and, as you heard me say, teach and train others, usually the really young ones. You are my first older student, and I'm so excited to be your teacher."

"But why do I have to do the training?" Samantha asks.

"I'm white and I'm not three years old," she says.

"Excellent question, Sam!" Okoyani says. "First, you're a girl. Second, this training is a part of our culture and since you've awakened, you're a part of our culture. Third, though you're 'white', we don't really use those terms anymore by the way, sexism impacts you. Our approach has drastically reduced violent abuse and sexual abuse against all women. Typically, though our men are stronger, they are far less skilled than any one of us and therefore more apt to be hurt by one of us than to harm us. It took a while but data shows that things like rape and other sexual assaults against women are rare. Culturally, we thrive on respect for one another and peace but also, our males know that our females are virtual weapons. Deterrence has been key. Now to your training."

For the next hour, Okoyani takes Samantha through a number of stretches and drills that begin to teach her how to punch and how to stand ready for combat. She learns how to jab with her left hand, punch with her right hand and how to throw hook punches with both her left and right hands. Okoyani also shows her how to hit a heavy bag and makes her do so for what seems like two hours to Samantha. In actuality, it's only fifteen minutes. By the end of the session, Okoyani takes Samantha through a brief yoga session as part of their cool down. Once done, Samantha is physically achy but also revived. It's a strange dichotomy that surprises her.

This experience is strangely invigorating to her. She thought that she'd hate it. She certainly hadn't liked the early morning wake up or Okoyani's annoying cheerfulness. As she worked out and got to see Okoyani's skill and gracefulness as she demonstrated moves that she wanted Samantha to emulate, Samantha sees how good Okoyani is and perhaps how good she might become one day.

"You did really well today, Sam. There's a lot to work with here. Stick with me and you'll be highly proficient in both Muay Thai and BJJ within two years, I promise. Keep learning and training until you go to college and no one will ever bother you, not without penalty at least. Again, I promise" Okoyani says, a look of grave determination onher face. "Now please go hit the showers. You've sweated a lot, ''Okoyani says, crinkling up her nose.

"Everything that you need is in the restroom. Your clothes

will be cleaned and dried by the time that you step out of the shower. Also, you'll have a revitalizing smoothie waiting for you there. Your stall has your name on it. See you in a few. I'm going to get in a quick workout while you freshen up" she says.

Samantha walks across one of the fields to the female restroom entrance. She hears Okoyani strike one of the heavy bags where Samantha had herself just finished working out. The sound of her strikes rings out throughout the facility like gunshots to her. She looks back and sees Okoyani deftly strike the bag again and again effortlessly. I'll never be able to do that, Samantha says to herself. How in the world is she so strong? she wonders. Samantha then remembers that though Okoyani is only sixteen, she's been training since she was a toddler.

In the restroom, Samantha finds her stall. It has her name on it just as Okoyani had said. They've thought of everything. A delicious looking smoothie is perched on one of the stall's several shelves, as well as a towel and washcloth. Samantha quickly disrobes and places her clothes in the bottom of the stall.

*I think this is how it wo*rks, she hopes. After wrapping the towel around herself, she takes several gulps of her drink, draining at least half of it. *Delicious*, she thinks. *That there is delicious.*

Stepping away from her stall, she hears an unexpected mechanical noise. She looks back and sees a foot-high robot gather sweaty, soiled clothes and then roll into a hidden door in the wall.

Ah, she thinks. *That's how they do it. Robots. Neat.* The next several minutes feel like heaven to Samantha as she allows the various showerheads in her shower to spray hot and warm water over her. When she entered the shower, the several showerheads magically moved and lowered around her to match her height. Not being of tall stature, Samantha appreciates how the shower conforms to her. *They have thought eve*rything, she acknowledges again.

Minutes later Samantha is dried and dressed in her now cleaned and dried clothes. *Amazing*, she thinks. *I was only in there for like ten minutes. They're still warm.* Stepping outside the restroom, she sees Okoyani walking toward her drenched in sweat from her own brief workout. "Please give me ten minutes, Samantha. I need to freshen up as well" she says. Waiting outside the restroom, Samantha notices that several groups of girls and young women have arrived. Almost everyone she sees is SM and she notices how many look at her with curious fascination. Samantha perks up when she sees a handful of IM girls like her, some much younger, some older, participate in their martial arts training. They mostly look new to it like Samantha is, but she is able to pick one out of the bunch who looks like a veteran. The older IM girls also see her and each waves to Samantha in turn. Samantha hopes that she'll have a chance to speak to them at some point.

About ten minutes later, Okoyani pops out clean and ready to go. "Okay, Sam, let's get back home and get some breakfast. Or we can grab something along the way. Which would you prefer?" she asks.

"Home" Samantha says. She's hoping to catch a quick nap before the rest of her day ensues.

"Cool. And I think that Mommy, Ifé, is taking you to school sometime today. She's not quite sure which kind of school to enroll you in yet. In case you hadn't noticed, we do school differently than probably what you were used to. For some, school takes place solely at home. For others, it takes place outside of the home but not in a school building per se. For others still, it takes place in a traditional school structure but the class structure may or may not exist for a particular student. It really just depends on how best a student learns. At this point, for me, all of my instruction is highly independent. I can meet a professor in a museum and be taught there. I can meet a class in a coffee shop. I can hit the school for a lecture from a luminary. Heck, sometimes I'll even go study in another city in another state if I feel like it. There really aren't any boundaries. You'll get to experience some of that, but I think first you'll be tested to see what your best learning style is" Okoyani says.

"This year, I could have moved out and started college. But when I heard that you were coming to join us, I put it off a year. I really want to teach you and be here for you as you rejoin us" she says. "Next year, though, I'll start my studies. Probably in Ghana or South Africa. We'll see. I've got offers in several places. I'm confident that Heru will guide me, no matter what I choose."

Heru? Samantha thinks. *Who is Heru?* she wonders as they leave the facility and walk the three blocks back to their duplex apartment. Ifé and her family live in one of the large apartment buildings in downtown Dallas. It's their city house as Samantha has heard them call it. It's spacious, comfortable and has many rooms. To her, it looks more like a house within an apartment building. Samantha had lived in several apartments in her growing up. Ifé's apartment does not remind her of any of those. Over dinner the previous evening, there had been discussion of when they would get to spend time in one of several homes that the Eze'shave in various other parts of the country. The children had all wanted to spend time in their home in Martha's Vineyard while Ifé had said she misses their home in Hilton Head.

"It's warmer than MV," she'd said. "And with ya'll trying to go for a month in June, I'd rather it be in a warmer locale.

Maybe we can go to MV in July," Ifé had suggested.

Apparently, this is a thing, Samantha thinks at the time. Families like Ifé's have multiple homes and go and live in them at various times of the year. *Are they rich?* she wonders. Samantha decides not to ask the question directly but instead determines to pay close attention to what the Eze's do and what they have.

At some point during last night's dinner as Samantha listened to the Eze family discuss their impending living plans she asks whether they own a home in Florida. Years ago, Samantha had taken a short trip to Florida and visited Disney World with her family. At her question, everyone at the table stops talking and looks at her. No one speaks until Ifé does. "Beloved" she begins, "Florida no longer exists the way that you remember it. It's little more than a collection of islands at this point. By the time that our ancestors began making significant reductions in carbon emissions, it was too late to save places like Florida and several others. The icebergs have almost all melted, and the sea levels rose. Florida was all but wiped out as well as thousands of miles of coastland on the east and west coasts. This happened in Europe, Asia and some parts of Africa too. The good news is that Georgia now has some of the most amazing beaches in the world. And yes, we have a home just outside of Atlanta that we visit at least twice per year too. We can go there if you wish" Ifé says compassionately.

Samantha hangs her head without responding. It's not that she wanted to go to Florida. It is, however, that yet another point of familiarity with the country that she'd known, no longer exists. As harsh and sometimes cruel as her world had been, it was at least familiar. She wonders at this moment whether she'll ever adjust and be a part of this new world.

Arriving home, Samantha finds their apartment bright and cheery in the daytime. She can smell the food that Ifé prepared. She sees all of her favorites: pancakes, bacon, eggs and honey dew melon. She'd worked up a major appetite during her workout and is looking forward to eating.

"Beloved!" Ifé says. "How was your training? Did Okoyani push you too hard? I told her not to overdo it on your first day."

"No, Ifé, Okoyani was perfect. Waking up was tough, but the training was great. I can see myself doing this stuff though I'll never be as good as Yani" she says using the nickname that she's heard her family use for her.

"Well, Yani has been at it since the age of two. You'll get there, though, or at least to the place you're supposed to be. Let that be your focus and your measure. Deal?" Ifé says.

"Deal" Samantha says, happy to sit at their table and dig into the breakfast that is before her.

Ifé watches Samantha as she eats and is happy to see her eat so well. Okoyani joins her but only eats the two pancakes and some of the melon. She is vegan and never touches meat, most especially not pork. It's part health but also religious practice.

Before she begins eating, she says a silent prayer but concludes by audibly saying "in the name of Heru, amen."

"Heru," Samantha says. "Who is that?"

Okoyani looks at Ifé who shakes her head at her. "Not yet, Samantha. I'll tell you all about Heru and our religion, but now is not the time for that. You'll learn plenty about all of our religions in the days and weeks to come. For now, just eat and get ready for the rest of your day. You and Mommy will be very busy."

Samantha happily complies as she eats several pieces of bacon at once. She notices that no one but her is eating the bacon. *More for me*, she thinks and eats several more pieces happy to finally be in a place that seems so full of love.

CHAPTER XV

At Little More Than One Year After Sleep Day

"I take it we're aligned?" Congresswoman Stowe says."We are aligned" Trevor Campbell replies.

"Good. It's a good day for both of us then. Well, maybe not for President Douglas, but for you and me, most certainly."

Trevor hangs up the phone with the Congresswoman. *Today is a good day,* he reflects. *Baron won't think so, but that's why I'm here, isn't it?*

Trevor looks out of his large window and rehearses, again, every part of this day and what it will be. Large parade in DC and in several other cities, check. Though President Douglas largely resisted such expressions of joy and glee from the SM population, even he had to acknowledge that the passing of the one year deadline of the IMs falling asleep due to the Sleepers virus is worth commemorating.

Since the one year deadline is up, all current property transfers have become final. Even if the IMs were to wake up tomorrow, Trevor thinks, *what they owned, they no longer own. It's all ours now or the government's. Either way, their lives, whenever they wake up, are forever changed.* Trevor worries, though, that should the IMs wake up any time soon and discover what's happened that they'll fight to take back their wealth. *Our population is not yet what it would need to be to fight them off,* he muses. *Immigration will have to speed up. Our reproduction will have to increase.*

While working to thwart Dr. Krauss' efforts, Trevor had also been advising President Douglas and consolidating power to increase immigration from multiple SM countries, particularly several in Africa, Brazil itself, the Caribbean and even Canada.

Of all the geographies, he'd found that Africa and the Caribbean had been the most reliable by sending several million immigrants to their shores but Canada less so. *Canadian negroes really like Canada,* Trevor had thought more than once over the course of theyear.

Now that he's secured Jessica Lundgren, Trevor ponders

what's next. *She'll never finish her work in finding an antidote to the Sleepers virus,* he thinks. *If anything, I can use her brilliant mind to help me prolong the immobilization of all the IMs until, well, until forever. Why not? We were enslaved and oppressed for four-hundred and some odd years. Why can't they remain asleep for that long?* Trevor ponders.

Trevor also considers that American businesses are again starting to boom, and without the hindrance of previous biases had begun to make forays into other countries and geographies that had seen limited American investment. Traditional American businesses in the hands of newly minted SM CEOs are forging new trade relationships with all of the Caribbean nations and countries like Ghana, Nigeria, Cameroon, Mauritania, Gabon, Kenya and more. None of these countries are fearful of the Sleepers virus and had immediately sent many of their residents to America at least on a temporary basis to shore up its population losses. Trevor thinks that many of these so-called temporary residents will convert to full citizens given the relaxation of their citizenship rules. *If we can show and maintain prosperity,* he thinks, *they'll be hooked and stay*. Already, there had been some rumblings of regret from their previous European partners about how they'd handled their SM populations. *They'll live to rue the day,* Trevor thinks chuckling to himself.

I'm getting everything I want today Trevor says to himself, but in truth, he feels uneasy. It's a glorious day for the country, but there will be some losses. How President Douglas reacts to those losses could mean the difference between war and peace. Trevor is betting on peace, but this is the unpredictable part of the job. He knows that he cannot guarantee it.

"Mabel," he says through his office phone's intercom to his assistant.

"Yes, Sir, Mr. Campbell" she replies.

"I'm going over to the White House to watch the parade. Please forward all of my calls to my cell phone."

"Yes, Sir. What an exciting time to be alive, Mr. Campbell!" she says. Her joy was palpable through his phone's speaker.

It certainly is, he thinks. *And you have me to thank for it.*

* * *

For about the thousandth time, Jessica wonders whether she's made the right decision. She's been locked down in this facility for several weeks but has yet to see her uncle Dr. Krauss. She has not been ill-treated and, in fact, has been well fed. Her captors had even moved her to a larger cell, large enough for an exercise bicycle, some free weights and even a laptop with restricted internet access, just enough to check the news headlines. She's learned from them that massive parades are happening today and this week to commemorate the Sleepers virus outbreak and all of the changes that had occurred because of it. *They're really going all out,* she thinks after reading an article in the Washington Post about the parades.

She notes that some are even calling the day of the Sleepers virus outbreak as their one and only Independence Day. Jessica notes the irony of the sentiment given that the viral outbreak also means a kind of enslavement or imprisonment for millions of IMs.

It's morning and Jessica is feeling well rested. Her room has its own shower and a small kitchenette. It looks like it had been converted from some sort of break room into her cell. *I wonder what's next,* she ponders. At some point, Campbell will make his demands and he'll expect me to comply. I imagine that day is coming sooner rather than later. Jessica takes a sip of her coffee from a cup sitting on a small table across from the refrigerator in her room. To test her captors, she recently asked them for a high end mattress for her twin sized bed. She claimed that she needed to alleviate residual back soreness from her years of martial arts training. That was a lie, of course. The mattress arrived the next day and she slept soundly on it that same night.

From her room and the fact that her captors seem to be going out of their way to accommodate her most frivolous of requests, Jessica surmises that her death is not Trevor Campbell's goal. *At least not yet,* she believes. Still, she's thankful for the gourmet coffee and espresso maker that sits on her kitchenette's counter. *Once I finish breakfast,* she thinks, *I'll get a light workout in and maybe do some reading.* Her week's supply of books arrives today. She's been pacing herself at five books per week though she could easily double or triple that number especially with the time that she has. Since it's Friday, maybe I'll get some Netflix and no chill. Not for the first time, Jessica misses Elliot and wonders how he is.

Quickly enough, her thoughts turn back to her own situation. She recognizes Campbell's attempts to make her comfortable. *It's meant to disarm me,* she thinks. *He wants me to trust him, which I'll never do. Soon enough, he'll hit me with his demand. I have to be ready to hold firm when that happens. Krauss comes first,* she thinks. She recognizes that she's in the fattening stage before the kill. She'd suspected this moment might come. She hopes, for Krauss' sake, that she's ready.

* * *

Congresswoman Stowe thinks that all has been made ready. As she rides in a jet to her next destination, she sneers at the thought of President Douglas and the country's celebrations happening today and all this week. *They believe that they've won. I'll soon show them otherwise,* she thinks. Her plans had been monthsin the making. She reluctantly acknowledges that her work has been made easier by Trevor's agreement to allow her to operate insilence and by not reporting her actions to the President or anyoneelse in the American government. He served his purpose. He's getting what he wants too. More power and more control. Men like him are so predictable.

Keeping all of her close allies with her for the last few months had been harder than expected, but by sheer force of will and vision, they'd all fallen in line, everyone that is, except for Victor Anthony, the congressman who had been her right hand man. "Victor, this is happening, and I want you to be with me. You need to be with me. Your family can join us, after a time, but I need you with me."

"For all the reasons that I've outlined before, Jane, I cannot and will not join you" Congressman Anthony says.

"Victor, that's so disappointing. If you go back there, you'll just be another in a sea of faces with no access and no power. But with me, you'll be at the epicenter of power. Who knows how much and how far we can grow from here?" Congresswoman Stowe says.

"Jane, that's actually what I'm worried about. I don't crave power or access. I got into politics to help people. My parents were immigrants from Cuba, remember? When Castro took over, they lost everything and had to start over. It's them when I think about this job and what it means to average, ordinary people—the sea of faces that you mentioned. It's people like us that should represent and help them. What could be more honorable than that?" Congressman Anthony asks.

Congresswoman Stowe realized in that moment that there would be no changing her friend's mind. *But will Victor keep his mouth shut until my plans are complete?* she wonders. "Victor, not to press, but can I count on you to maintain discretion?" *Discretion is an odd word for her to use,* Victor thinks. *Shouldn't we rather call this sedition? A coup even?* For a moment, Victor weighs his options. He's confident that if he doesn't commit to keeping his mouth shut, there is a substantial chance that he might find himself imprisoned or possibly killed. If he does agree and indeed fails to share Stowe's plans and actions, he will be seen as having aided and abetted her and thus held to the same standard of guilt as she will be. *I have no good choices. I should have stopped this when I had the chance,* Victor realizes.

"Jane, of course you can rely on me. I cannot go on this next part of the journey with you, but I won't be a hindrance to it either. I hope you know what you're doing. Rightly or wrongly, history shall forever record your choice."

Congresswoman Stowe recalls her last conversation with Congressman Anthony ruefully. She regrets that he would not join her. At least, she thinks, Anthony kept his damn mouth shut as he promised. There's something to be said for a loyal number two.

Jetting across several time zones, Congresswoman Stowe plots her next several phone calls. Her last one will be to President Douglas. He'll have gotten my letter by then, she surmises. He'll want to take my call if for no other reason than to try to convince me to do otherwise. That's when I'll give him more good news. *Well,* she chuckles to herself as she thinks, *good news for me at least.*

*   *   *

President Douglas stands behind the large protective dais at the White House watching the huge parade go by him. He is joined by his wife Helen, their sons, all of his top staff and their families. He reluctantly admits that today is a good day. It had been more than a year since Sleep Day, and with the IMs not yet awakening, all of the existing and apparently future property, resource and business transfers from sleeping IMs to woke SMs had become final. With respect to future transfers, President Douglas is now anxious to move those along as soon as possible. He hopes that with the influx of millions of new immigrants and increased speed and efficiency of their ever evolving education system that all of the transfers will be completed within the next five years and that the federal government can get out of the private property business.

Agent Gates, along with about ten other of his Secret Service colleagues, stand guard over the President and his entourage. Since his first day on the job, he'd been assigned to the President's personal detail. Raheem soon came to know and have high regard not only for the President but for his wife and sons as well. His eldest son, Pharaoh, attends school with the President's sons, Connor and Grayden. They had all become friends without realizing the connection between their fathers. When Connor and Grayden showed up to Raheem's house one evening with a Secret Service detail, Raheem was flabbergasted. The next day at work, he apologized profusely to President Douglas who laughed heartily at the gesture.

"Apologize? For what? Our sons being friends? Your son is exactly the kind of young man that I want my sons to know and befriend. Remember, Raheem, I know Pharaoh's daddy!" he'd said chuckling. Raheem smiles at the memory and thinks about how momentous the last four months have been for him and for the country. The IMs have yet to awaken. Most people seem to be more than okay with that. The exceptions include those SMs who are married to or are the children of sleeping IMs. SMs in any of these situations have formed a highly vocal minority advocating for IM rights and welfare. Still, the remarkable changes occurring in the country have given most hope and access that they've never before experienced.

Raheem ponders all of this as he watches one of the

President's top aides make her way to where he stands behind the protective shield on the dais. It's a cold day in early March and spring has not yet come to DC. It's cold but bright. Raheem stands little more than six feet away from President Douglas on his right side. The aide is well known within the White House. As she approaches the President, Raheem watches as she leans in to him, whispers something and the President's face goes ashen. Raheem immediately senses a threat but recognizes that it doesn't come from the aide. It's come from whatever the aide has just said. Just the same, Raheem steels himself for any issue that arises.

"All eyes on POTUS" Raheem says into the microphone in his left suit sleeve. In tandem, the eyes of every available Secret Service agent lock in on President Douglas. Raheem watches as the President forces smiles and fist pumps to paraders as they pass by. *He lacks his usual joy*, Raheem thinks. He tells himself to stay ready. He doesn't think that they'll be at the parade for much longer. After a few more moments, the President looks at Raheem and gives him the non-verbal signal to gather up.

"POTUS is on the move. Alpha and Beta teams on me" Raheem says as he closes the distance between himself and the President. Agent Smith joins him from the other side and together they form a small shield around him.

"What's wrong, Honey?" Helen, his wife asks. "Nothing, Dear. I'll advise you in a little while. I need to handle something back at the Oval. You stay here and enjoy the parade" President Douglas says.

Trevor Campbell observes all of this from his perch about two rows away from the President. *He knows*, he thinks. *She's told him. The crap is about to hit the fan now.* Just as he thinks this, President Douglas looks up at Trevor and signals for him to join him. Trevor immediately leaves his seat and joins the President as he makes his exit from the dais. Watching Trevor leave with her husband troubles Helen. She doesn't know why, but she does not trust him in the least. Helen knows that she'll have the information soon enough. Now, she knows that she must be the First Lady and Baron's wife. Being his top advisor can wait until later.

On their short walk back to the White House, President Douglas says nothing. Raheem observes that his previous shock from whatever news he'd just learned has been replaced by a look of resolve that he'd not yet seen from him. Their walk, most of which is outside, extends from the White House side of Black Lives Matter plaza across the north lawn. It's cold and Raheem can feel the chilled air coming from the Potomac river whip around him fiercely. *This is enough to put anyone in a bad mood,* he thinks. *Whatever POTUS and Campbell are about to speak about must be heavy. This is one time when I'm glad not to have to be in the room.*

As they approach the main door to the Oval Office, Raheem sees that the room is darkened. The curtains are drawn. Some light enters the room, but for the most part, its color reflects the President's dark mood. Raheem watches the two men enter the Oval and prepares to post up right outside.

"Agent Brooks, please join us inside" President Douglas says. Raheem is shocked at the request but responds in the affirmative to the order. "Yes, Sir" he says and enters the office, pulling the door closed behind him, which seems appropriate. "Agent, take your post here. Thank you" President Douglas says.

The President walks to the Resolute desk where he sees a single white envelope placed on its top surface. Feelings of foreboding rush over him but he determines not to let his concern show to either Trevor or Raheem. *Raheem probably has no idea why I asked him inside,* he thinks. *He'll know soon enough.*

President Douglas grabs the letter and opens it. The outside of the envelope is simply addressed 'TO THE PRESIDENT OF THE UNITED STATES'. There is no return address, but he knows precisely who the letter is from, and he suspects that Trevor does as well. It reads in part:

Dear Mr. President,

I am saddened to reach you today on this most auspicious of occasions with, what will no doubt be considered by you, to be bad news.

Because you failed in your promise to revive the IMs, the immobilized Americans, I am left with little choice but to inform you that I and most of the expatriated congresspersons rescind our

American citizenship. This decision has been quite difficult to arrive at, but we feel that you have left us little choice.

It also falls upon me to inform you that the state of Alaska no longer belongs within the United States of America. It is now a free and sovereign nation. Its constituency deserves different and better leadership than that which you offer. As its own independent country, Alaska will be guided by its own constitution and leadership structure of which I am its interim leader.

To bolster our claims of independence from the United States, the Second, Third, Seventh and Tenth fleets and half of your submarine fleet have all defected to the new Alaskan government and now defend its borders. Should you initiate any acts of aggression whatsoever against the sovereign country of Alaska, we shall respond in kind and with swift enterprise.

Unfortunately, Mr. President, it has been your own inaction and recalcitrance that has led to this moment. The remaining woke American IMs have lost all confidence in you and your leadership. Had you fulfilled your promises, such a bold move would not have been necessary. History shall forever record that you are the first American President to cause the fracture of the United States. You now preside over an imperfect union.

Most Sincerely,

Jane Stowe, Interim President of the Free State of Alaska

President Douglas hands the letter to Trevor and waits for him to read it. As he reads it, Trevor feels the President's eyes on him intensely. He recognizes that his reaction to what he's reading is being assessed and scrutinized.

"What do you think?" President Douglas asks him.

Ah. The open ended question, Trevor thinks. "I think that we cannot allow this, Sir, and that our adversaries, who by now know what's happening, will see this loss as yet another example of our weakness and incompetence. We can't allow Alaska's secession to stand" he says.

"So, Trevor, I had no idea that this was happening. Did you know?" President Douglas asks.

"Sir, of course not! How could I? Since Sleep Day, our spy network isn't nearly what it was. Stowe must have kept this very close to the vest" Trevor says.

"Frankly, it seems odd, Trevor, that you did not have forewarning about this. You're one of the smartest people that I know and have shown forth your brilliance at every turn both before and after Sleep Day. Like how you managed to blow up Krauss' lab and destroy his research? Brilliant. Like how you've thwarted every national and international effort to develop a vaccine for the Sleepers virus? Again, brilliant. I didn't want to believe it at first, but Helen was right.

Of course you knew and you entered, I surmise, into some kind of arrangement with Stowe to keep your secrets secret. A simple exchange, I imagine. Your silence for her silence. You played your role perfectly. Obviously, you cannot remain here since you cannot be trusted. Old friend, you are immediately relieved of duty. I'm not waiting for your resignation. You're fired. Agent Brooks, please take former NSA Director Trevor Campbell into custody and hold him until he can be transferred to a maximum security federal facility."

Trevor stands frozen in place. The letter which he's just read involuntarily falls from his hands. *How did this happen?* he thinks desperately. The circle was tight. It was closed. How did he know? He ponders these questions and more as he feels his hands bound behind his back and sits in a holding cell in the basement of the White House. How did this happen?

*   *   *

Dr. Alexandria Taylor knows that her phone is tapped and that all of her electronic devices are monitored. She strongly suspects that there are cameras in her apartment and in her office that monitor her every move all thanks to NSA DirectorTrevor Campbell. And of course, her constant shadow, Rebecca Braithwaite. She feels smothered. She feels anxious. Knowing what she knows, she feels about as badly as she had before after allof the fall-out of Sleep Day.

I have to let them know, she thinks. *No matter the cost to me personally, I need to try to make this right.* Thankful that at least her thoughts are not and cannot be monitored, Dr. Taylor concocts a plan to tell her story, name names and get the truth out. The Post Office still works, thank goodness, and I don't have to use an electronic device.

The one place that Dr. Taylor believes that she is alone is in one of several restrooms at work. For several weeks, she had been using different restrooms to assure her privacy and to test the limits of Rebecca's observations. She's pretty sure that when she has not been directly monitored by Rebecca, that one or more of her surrogates has followed her. She has worked diligently to make her life look and seem as mundane as possible. Her schedule includes time at home, time at work, Target runs on Saturday, running in the park on Sundays, working out in her apartment building's gym and little else. Nothing to report as far as she's concerned.

She had also been careful, at work, to walk from meeting to meeting, and in Pharmatech's laboratory with an innocuous looking legal pad, always with the first page showing notes from one meeting or another in case anyone looked at it. Once, on a return from a meeting to her office, Rebecca had met her at her door. "Hey, let me see that, Dr. Taylor" she'd said pointing to her legal pad. Dr. Taylor dutifully, almost nonchalantly handed it to her and then looked at her phone feigning disinterest.

Rebecca flipped through it, finding only three pages of notes and nothing else. *This is a new pad,* Dr. Taylor thinks. *I exchanged it for the one you're looking for yesterday.* "Okay, thank you" Rebecca had said, handing the legal pad back to Dr.Taylor with a curious if not fully distrustful look in her eye. Dr.Taylor realizes later that her adversaries had just told her more about themselves than what they'd learned about her.

Sitting alone now in stall number six, Dr. Taylor composes her final thoughts on a piece of legal sized paper. Her letter is eight pages long. It details her every action and every party privy to those actions both before and after Sleep Day. She calls it her liberation manifesto though, in truth, she recognizes that she'll probably do hard time for her actions. That doesn't matter anymore. It's about time that I stop thinking just about myself.

She ponders and has been thinking about to whom she should send it. Holding all eight pages, she folds them and puts them into an envelope which she stuffs to the bottom of her purse. Rebecca hadn't yet searched her purse and she'd been careful to have it with her for most of the time that she visits a restroom. *If they see me with my purse in here,* she thinks, *they shouldn't think anything of it.*

Dr. Taylor takes several deep breaths before she considers her very next move. *I'm ready,* she thinks. Her envelope is addressed to the right party, she hopes. At least if it's not the right party, they'll know who to give it to. She wishes that she'd been able to make a copy of her letter, but she cannot take that risk. There are cameras everywhere. She usually has a shadow accompanying her, even in her work building. She has no good reason to go to a copier in her building nor one outside of her building. Dr. Taylor also dare not risk taking pictures of her letter since she's sure her phone is being monitored by the NSA. Most days, she doesn't even bother to bring her cellphone with her sinceit's tracking her every movement.

Dr. Taylor flushes the toilet even though she had not used it. She gathers herself and her belongings, checks her clothing and steps out of her stall. As usual, the restroom is empty. She decides to wash her hands and fixes her clothing meticulously. As she prepares to leave, the door to the restroom opens. "You were in here a little while, Dr. Taylor, what's going on? Are you okay?" Rebecca asks.

"Okay?" Dr. Taylor replies in question. "Yes, I'm okay. I think my breakfast may have upset my stomach a bit. It didn't stay down easy. Thanks for checking, Rebecca."

As she walks by Rebecca, she observes her eyeing her suspiciously. Dr. Taylor keeps her expression blank and her breathing measured. If I have nothing to hide, then I have no reason to be anxious or to show it, she thinks. "Excuse me, Rebecca, I have a meeting in ten minutes. Is there anything else?" she asks.

"No," Rebecca replies. "There's nothing else" and moves aside to allow Dr. Taylor to walk through the door.

As she walks by, Rebecca gently but firmly places her hand on Dr. Taylor's shoulder stopping her in her tracks.

"Alexandria, I realize that these last few weeks and months

have been stressful. I also realize that you know the scrutiny that you're under. It's a lot. I get it. For obvious reasons, that scrutiny must continue. But rest assured, it will end, and perhaps sooner than you think. Just hang in there. Keep following instructions and all will be fine. Okay?" Rebecca asks.

Dr. Taylor breathes out audibly. "Okay, Rebecca. Thank you. I appreciate you saying that. I just want it all to be over, frankly. Thank you."

Rebecca releases Dr. Taylor's shoulder and allows her to continue on. Dr. Taylor walks to her next meeting which, thankfully, is out of sight of where Rebecca had just been standing. Once she is out of sight and no longer feels Rebecca's eyes on her, she finds the nearest staircase, enters it, and runs down the stairs as fast her legs will carry her. She aims for the basement so that she can exit the building from its rear into an alley. It's now or never, she decides. I'm sending the letter today. Once in the alley, Dr. Taylor takes pains to ensure that she was not followed. She knows where she'll mail the letter and hopes to high heaven that it finds its intended mark.

* * *

Helen Douglas holds a letter written on eight pages of legal sized, lined yellow paper in her office. The envelope in which it had come had her name on it, her title and the White House's address, 1600 Pennsylvania Avenue. Her assistant had retrieved it and put it into her hands as soon as she'd read it. "Mrs. Douglas, I think that you need to read this. If it's true, it explains a lot" she'd said.

After reading it, Helen feels that all of her suspicions about Trevor Douglas have been verified. After Sleep Day, I never could trust him. I didn't know why, but I knew better. *And now I have to tell Baron,* she thinks. It's a little more than a week ahead of the New Independence Day parade in DC and one day before the one year anniversary of the release of the Sleepers virus. *But first things first,* she thinks. *I'll have to verify these details before I share them with him. If the contents of this letter turn out to be true, Trevor is done.*

Helen Douglas makes her plans and her list of whom she

can enlist to help her. As a top advisor to the President, and his wife, she has access to all of the various agencies which themselves are only limited by the number of qualified personnel that staff them. Making her choice, she grabs the receiver to her office telephone and dials the White House switchboard.

"Good afternoon, Mrs. Douglas," a cheerful telephone operator says.

"Please connect me on a secure line to James Townsend, the FBI Director" she says to the operator.

"Yes, Ma'am, right away."

The phone to Townsend's office rings three times before he answers. "Townsend" he says gruffly.

"James, it's Helen. We need to talk. I need your help."

* * *

"Confirm" President Douglas says to his Joint Chiefs of Staff, his generals and admirals, in the Situation Room of the White House.

"It's" General Martin says stammering, "it's true, Sir. Four fleet groups and half of our submarines have abandoned us. They've taken up positions around Alaska. They say they're not returning unless and until the IMs are awakened. Jane Stowe has taken command. They all report to her now."

"Recommendations" President Douglas says curtly.

"We still have the remainder of our fleets and the air force. Let's take them back and sink them if they refuse to comply" General Rodriguez says.

"That's absurd!" General Martin says.

"General Martin, let him speak" President Douglas says.

"Thank you, Mr. President. What's absurd is that these admirals and the military personnel serving them all blame you, Sir, for not coming up with a vaccine to wake the Sleepers, the IMs. Of course, that's not your fault. To express their displeasure, they've effectively taken billions of dollars of United States property. This is treason of the highest order. It cannot stand. I say we order them to stand down but be prepared to take up arms if they do not" General Rodriguez concludes.

Threaten American warships. ATTACK American

warships. Force Alaskans, Americans, to heel all in the name of a unity they do not feel or believe and risk infecting them and Canada with the Sleepers virus by our mere presence. This is what we risk should we act, either prudently or rashly, it hardly makes a difference.

President Douglas' thoughts are a violent storm behind his eyes. Now that he's heard from his two most trusted generals, he weighs the pros and cons of all of the possible actions that he can take.

He is angry, despondent even, but now is not the time for his or anyone else's emotions, he realizes. What he decides now will forever impact the future of the country, and Alaska, for their good or ill.

"We do nothing. We're not attacking and possibly killing Americans for the sake of recouping our property. And we're most certainly not launching an invasion of Alaska to drag them kicking and screaming back into the union. None of us like it, but the idea of our enemies watching us kill one another would be far worse. And let's be honest, absent a nuclear strike, on U.S. land, I'm not sure that we could even defeat the defecting fleets in a conventional war. At least, I'm not sure that we could win without taking heavy, critical losses" President Douglas says. No one disagrees with the President and for a few moments no one speaks.

"There may be another way, Sir," Admiral Alicia Miller says. Admiral Miller is one of the newer recently promoted military officers who has seen quick promotion and placement in light of the many Sleeper virus induced immobilizations. "All of our warships are state of the art electronic machines. As such, every single one of them contains a kill switch that can be enacted remotely. This is a safety precaution built into each in the off chance that any one of them is hijacked. There's no way to disable the kill switches, and once they're used, only the remote user can reactivate the vessels. They would be, quite literally, dead in the water."

"How long would it take to implement and how long would it last?" he asks.

"On your orders, Sir, we can disable every ship immediately. Once the electronics are made ineffective, they'll remain so until we reactivate" Admiral Miller says.

"Make it so," the President says. "Turn everything off."

* * *

Jane Stowe diligently reviews her agenda for the day. Her plane will arrive in Anchorage, Alaska in about one hour. She has a meeting with the state's governor at which time she, Jane Stowe,will be named the acting President of Alaska, at least provisionally until an election can be held. Looking over the latest Alaska polling information, it shows that an overwhelming percentage of Alaskan citizens, eighty-six percent, desire to break away from the United States and form their own country. *That's good,* she thinks triumphantly. *Very good. That sentiment will make the transition to a new government easier and faster. And with the backing of part of the U.S. Navy, we'll be unbeatable. Douglas wouldn't dare send troops against us,* she thinks, chuckling at her mind's image of the President raging at his White House staff and especially at Trevor Campbell.

As she considers all of the work and meetings that she must have today and in the coming week, Stowe's satellite phone rings. "Hello" she says cheerfully, "this is President Stowe."

"Stowe!" a voice bellows. "We're dead in the water!

Literally dead! We're a few nautical miles away from the Alaskan coast and every single ship and submarine is dead. All the power has been cut and the electronics are kaput. Our engines are cut off. We're just floating here with the currents. The President has cut the power. We can't even put a copter or plane in the air. What the hell have you gotten us into, Stowe?!" the raging Admiral says.

Oh no, Stowe thinks.

* * *

"Can we get Stowe on the phone?" the President asks his generals assembled in the Situation Room.

"Yes, Sir, we can" one of his generals replies. "We have her satellite phone information and have been tracking it. She just landed in Anchorage. She knows what's happened by now, Sir."

"Good. Let's call her. I'll take the call right here on speaker" President Douglas commands.

As soon as her phone rings, Stowe knows who it is. The President. In place of the image of the President raging in his office is one of him smirking at how he's gained the supreme advantage over her and how she must now listen to him. Stowe realizes now how much she hates the man, has always hated him and resents the fact that she's had to call him "Mr. President".

"Yes, Mr. President, how may I help you?" Stowe says. "You can help me by abandoning your silly play at power and by returning every single one of our ships and aircraft to us. That's how you can help me. Also, I consider your little letter to be your confession of treason for which you have given up your American citizenship and our protection. You are to remain in Alaska for the rest of your days. If we determine, ever, that you've left the state, you will be found and dragged back to the continental United States. Is that understood?""Yes, Sir" she responds.

"And on top of everything else, stay out of power" President Douglas says forcefully. "You're not so much as to run for dog catcher, much less anything in the Alaskan government. You're done. The same goes for all of your former Congressional co-conspirators. We know who every one of them is. And you can tell them that they've forfeit any and all property holdings here in the United States. That of course applies to you as well."

Stowe feels like she's been punched in the gut. When she began this day, she'd been on her way to being the President of a new country with a powerful military at her back. Now, she is a pauper, having now lost all of her property and wealthy holdings in a place, Alaska, that she barely likes. *And now, I can't even leave. They'll be tracking me at every turn. It's over. Checkmate*, she thinks as the reality of her situation weighs fully upon her.

* * *

Jessica hears the keys enter her cell door. She's mildly surprised because the sun has not yet come up and it's not yet time for the overnight crew to change shifts with the morning crew, her captors. "Dr. Lundgren" she hears. "Dr. Lundgren, is that you?" the voice says.

She rolls over and sees a tall Black man in a blue, standard issue FBI jacket. He has a look of concern on his face which is

Jessica's first clue that whatever this internment has been, has ended. "Yes", that's me. "I'm Dr. Jessica Lundgren."

"Good," the FBI agent says. "Please put your clothes on and come with me." The agent turns and heads out of the room, gently closing the door behind him. Jessica sees the large letters "FBI" emblazoned on the back of his jacket.

Ah, she thinks. *My rescuers.*

Once dressed, Jessica opens her door and sees about eight other FBI agents standing in the hallway waiting on her, all wearing the blue FBI jackets. "Dr. Lundgren" the first agent says, "please put this mask on. In case you didn't know, you're in the United States. The Sleepers virus is no longer active here, but this is a precaution since, well..." he says before Jessica interrupts him.

"Since I don't have enough melanin to protect me from it. I get it. No problem. Thank you" Jessica says. "Where to now?" she asks after putting on the mask.

"We have transportation outside. We're in Virginia, just outside of DC. We'll take you back to FBI headquarters for debriefing. You're not under arrest. And then we have orders to take you to see the President. He has questions. He is aware of your relationship with Dr. Krauss."

"Good," she says. *I certainly have a story to tell,* she thinks. *And when I see the President, I'll tell him everything and hopefully get to my uncle,* she hopes. As she steps into one of the vans waiting for her outside of the prison in which she's housed, she is thankful for having survived the journey until now and prays that she is not too late.

EPILOGUE

Dr. Alexandria Taylor stands almost at attention in the Oval Office in front of President Douglas and his wife, Helen, his top advisor. Neither of them have spoken to her since she arrived, having been ushered in by several Secret Service officers. She wonders why she is here and not in a federal prison and why the two most powerful people in the country have not spoken to her but instead look at her intensely. *This is freaking me out*, she thinks.

President Douglas clears his throat and folds his hands in front of him on the Resolute desk as Helen stands next to him. Dr. Taylor hopes that whatever they have to say to her, for good or ill, will happen soon so that she can serve whatever punishment comes.

"When Helen first told me about your letter and what you had done, I was incensed," President Douglas says. "In fact, my very first instinct was to have you arrested and, frankly, put under the jail. The damage that you've caused, and the lives that are lost are inestimable. We're talking about millions lost, Dr. Taylor. Can you grasp that?" he asks.

"Mr. President" Dr. Taylor begins slowly, "my selfishness and carelessness has produced one of the greatest, if not the greatest, atrocities in the history of the world. Yes, I grasp what I've done. I hate what I've done. I've gone from being a disgruntled employee to a mass murderer. I hate myself for what's happened. It's literally all my fault." Dr. Taylor chokes back a sob and stops speaking to retain control. "I know that my letter would not only out Trevor Campbell but also expose me to the punishment that I deserve. I deserve whatever you think is right, Mr. President. I'm guilty."

President Douglas leans back in his chair, resuming his silence once again. A few moments later he looks up at Helen who nods at him almost imperceptibly. "In spite of your great crimes, Dr. Taylor, Helen has convinced me not to have you arrested for the remainder of your natural life. You are a woman of great talent and skill, and frankly, your position as Pharmatech's CEO is needful for what comes next. Beyond your personal accountability to the laws of this country, I have ultimate accountability to do what's in the best interest of our America. What that means for you, short term, is that you'll remain free outside of prison. Long term? You pay your debt in your current position reporting directly to Helen and then to the next Presidents for as long you may live."

So it's prison, Dr. Taylor thinks, *just not the one I was envisioning.*

"Is there something that you'd like to say, Dr. Taylor?" Helen asks.

"Yes, Mrs. Douglas, Mr. President. I am happy to cooperate in whatever way you direct that allows me to make up for my crimes in any way that I can" Dr. Taylor says.

"That's excellent, Dr. Taylor. For now, go back to Chicago, assume full control of Pharmatech and await our instructions. We will contact you through secure, encrypted means. If it's not encrypted, it's not us."

The President stands, and without looking at Dr. Taylor or extending his hand, walks out of the Oval Office through a side door leaving Helen and Dr. Taylor alone.

"You'll never know what it took for me to get him to agree to that, Alex", Helen says walking from behind the desk to stand directly in front of Dr. Taylor. "Here, let's sit down," she says motioning to a pair of couches in the office. As they sit, Dr. Taylor wonders what's next and what has remained unsaid.

"We have," Helen says, hesitating at first, "special work regarding the IMs that you're best positioned to lead. One year later and the IMs have not awakened. There are two schools of thought on that. One school says that we continue to do all that we can to find a vaccine as soon as possible. Another school says that we should stop those efforts and instead", she says, "instead, keep them asleep for as long as possible."

Dr. Taylor gasps audibly as Helen finishes her last sentence. She can't believe what she's hearing. Her latent anxiety immediately fires, and she feels her breath become short. She could not mean what she's just said, she thinks. To come all this way, to endure what I've endured, to do what I've done, and the leaders of the free world want to continue it?

"I can't do that, Mrs. Douglas," she says. "I can't be a part of some conspiracy that commits the IMs to some sort of perpetual sleep, not after what I've done. I can't do it. I won't do it."

Helen stands up from her seated position across from Dr. Taylor and sits beside her. She takes Dr. Taylor's right hand into her hands and holds it gently but firmly. Before speaking, Helen looks at Dr. Taylor compassionately, almost lovingly. Her words, however, betray the sentiment in her eyes.

"Dr. Taylor", she says, "I understand exactly how you feel. The guilt of your actions has weighed you down immensely, and that has been compounded by how Trevor has poorly used you. I need you to know, however, that should you not do what I instruct you to do, not only will you be imprisoned, you may also be executed as an enemy of the state for the most heinous crime known to man. At thirty-five years old, you are quite a young woman, yet. You're too young for a life-long prison term or death."

Helen stops speaking to allow the truth of her words to sink in. She observes how stiff Dr. Taylor has become and feels when she tries, unsuccessfully, to pull her hand back from Helen's grip.

"To be clear, Alex, we won't ask you to do anything that we wouldn't do ourselves. Your main job will be to run Pharmatech, help to keep the IMs alive, and..." she drops off. "And maybe one or two future assignments to be named later. In fact, we may even send you some help. There's nothing really at all to worry about. You get your freedom and our secrecy, and in the meantime you'll become a very wealthy woman."

Helen finally releases Alex's hand as she finishes speaking and stands up. Alex stands up also but does not move until she is instructed to. Helen observes her silently for a moment, a slight smile at her lips but without any warmth or compassion in her eyes.

"If you leave now, Dr. Taylor, you can make the two p.m. flight from National airport to Midway. I will call sometime soon after your return" Helen says.

Without another word, Dr. Taylor nods her ascent and walks quickly from the Oval. Helen watches her go, her arms crossed, her face a mixture of passing amusement and concern.

Baron always has me do his dirty work, she thinks, *the work that he doesn't want to do himself. No matter, I knew what Iwas signing up for. Protect my husband, protect our legacy. Alex Taylor is lucky to still be alive,* she thinks. *A little more than one year out from Sleep Day, it would not do to have the IMs wake up now or even soon. Baron could be turned out of office or worse should they re-arrive at any time in the next few months. Funny, hadn't that been what Trevor believed?* Helen silently asks herself. Walking out of the Oval Office she wonders whether Trevor had been right all along.

* * *

Eighty years and six months after Sleep Day

Director Rashida Birdsong speeds through the Hive in her shuttle pod feeling anxious. She'd ordered her staff to alert him when the very last IM had begun to awaken, because she wanted to personally welcome her back to the proverbial land of the living. *I should probably record her awakening and stream it live,* she thinks. This is a big deal, made bigger by the fact that no one knows who this woman is and we've been unable to identify her. Hopefully, she'll be able to fill us in.

As Director Birdsong's pod begins to slow upon nearing her destination, she wonders what she'll hear from her last charge. The last sleeping IM had gained more than a little notoriety as internet sleuths had gamely tried, and failed, to identify her.

Director Birdsong is happy that she gets to be the one to solve themystery and report her success to her bosses. This is basically my last act as the last director of the Hive. *Once this place is fully decommissioned, it may gain an alternative use, but who knows what may become of it?* she wonders.

"Arrived Section 706" the A.I. in his shuttle pod says as it comes to a stop.

Great, she thinks energetically as her short legs move quickly to the entrance of the chamber holding the last filled IM pod. This shouldn't take too long. Entering the chamber that contains the IM pod, she walks to a large touch screen, enters her authorization code and watches as the cluster of IM pods before her move in coordinated motion away from her until the one that she seeks is presented to her just a few feet away.

Ah, here she is, she sees. Director Birdsong notes that the soon awakening IM had been a forty-something year old redhead woman on the day that Sleep Day struck. She sees the woman stir and then yawn. She watches intently as the pod's inhabitant opens first her right eye and then her left. Director Birdsong waves her hand in front of the IM pod, and the door holding its inhabitant inside slowly opens. *This is the moment,* she thinks, *I do love this part.*

"Lights down" Director Birdsong says remembering that as IMs awake, their vision is extremely weak and their light sensitivity high due to lack of use. She touches the woman and notes that she feels warm. *Good, her temperature is coming back. She'll be back to good health in no time,* she notes.

"Where, where am I?" the woman says.

"You're in the Hive. You're coming out of a long hibernation. You've been asleep for a long time", Director Birdsong says.

"How long have I been asleep?" the woman asks."About eighty years. How do you feel?"

"I feel groggy. A little tired" the woman says. "What's the last thing that you remember?" Director Birdsong asks.

She watches as the woman in the pod seems to struggle with finding an answer to the question. Her eyes close as she seemingly searches for the memory or the words to answer. "I remember, I remember an accident. My husband Charles and I were driving and then he ran into a truck. Our daughter was in the backseat. We hit the truck and then nothing. Oh, my God!!! Where is my husband?! Where is my daughter?! Where is Samantha?!!"

* * *

End Book II
~AWAKENING~

Made in the USA
Columbia, SC
25 July 2022